ON SHIFTING SAND

ALLISON PITTMAN

THORNDIKE PRESS
A part of Gale, Cengage Learning

GALE
CENGAGE Learning·

Farmington Hills, Mich • San Francisco • New York • Waterville, Maine
Meriden, Conn • Mason, Ohio • Chicago

GALE
CENGAGE Learning®

LIBRARY OF CONGRESS CATALOGING-IN-PUBLICATION DATA

Pittman, Allison.
  On shifting sand / by Allison Pittman. — Large print edition.
    pages cm. — (Thorndike Press large print clean reads)
    ISBN 978-1-4104-8093-4 (hardcover) — ISBN 1-4104-8093-3 (hardcover)
    1. Large type books. I. Title.
  PS3616.I885O5 2015b
  813'.6—dc23   2015010370

Published in 2015 by arrangement with Tyndale House Publishers, Inc.

Printed in Mexico
1 2 3 4 5 6 7 19 18 17 16 15

ACKNOWLEDGMENTS

Thank you, Tyndale, for seeing this story when it was little more than a thought; and thank you, Kathy Olson, for helping me find its soul.

Thank you, Mikey, my husband and truly best-ever friend, for knowing when to give me space, when to hold me close, and when to quietly slide Twizzlers under the door.

Thank you, ALL of my writing friends, who encourage me every day and make me so glad I obeyed the calling God put in my heart. I love to see your victories.

And above all, I thank God for the gift of salvation and the strength I have in Christ. I could not write about grace if I didn't live it every single day.

For from his fullness we have all received, grace upon grace. (JOHN 1:16)

■ ■ ■ ■

Part I

■ ■ ■ ■

Call now, if there be any that will answer
  thee. . . .
Although affliction cometh not forth of the
  dust,
neither doth trouble spring out of the
  ground;
Yet man is born unto trouble, as the sparks
  fly upward.
I would seek unto God, and unto God
  would I commit my cause:
Which doeth great things and
  unsearchable;
Marvellous things without number:
Who giveth rain upon the earth,

and sendeth waters upon the fields:
To set up on high those that be low;
that those which mourn may be exalted to
safety.

JOB 5:1, 6-11

CHAPTER 1

The bathwater was hot when I first got in. Hot enough to steam the mirror and turn my skin an angry red, with white finger-shaped dots where I poked it. Punishing hot, Ma would have said, and that first sting getting in felt a lot like the touch of Pa's belt against my legs when I was little. But soon enough the water cools itself to comfortable. I wring out the washcloth and hold it aloft, letting most of the heat evaporate before pressing it against my face. I let my hair go damp with steam, debating whether I should dunk under to wet it enough for a good shampoo. It's Wednesday night, though, and I'm going to Rosalie's to get a new set on Friday, so I give it a run-through with my fingers and settle back with my neck on the porcelain rim.

The faucet lets in one fresh drop after another, and I count them. *Just ten more, and I'll get out.* But I lose track, drift off into pressing thoughts somewhere around number seven, and have to start all over again. Although, on this night, there's nothing to lure me out of the water. Ariel, my little girl, four years old, is in her room, deep in sleep. My husband, Russ, and the oldest, Ronnie, are at the church. Wednesday night prayer meeting, which seems to be running later than usual. And I, given the rare opportunity of an empty house and unclaimed bathroom, let myself soak in the water, the only light streaming in from our bedroom across the hall. I'd tuned the radio away from the midweek gospel hour, and turned up the volume loud enough that I can hear strains of Louis Armstrong, but not so loud as to wake the child. I hum along, singing when I can, my lips skimming the top of the bathwater, making bubbles with the lyrics.

The end to my peace comes with the open and slam of the back kitchen door, and Russ calling my name as if I'd been in danger of being sucked behind the baseboards.

"In here," I holler, trying not to sound too disappointed at his arrival.

The bathroom door opens a few inches, and Russ peeks his head through, averting his eyes to ask if I'm decent. Or, he qualifies, as decent as a woman who skipped out on prayer meeting could be.

10

"Your daughter was sick," I say in mock defensiveness.

"She seems fine now," Russ says. "Sleeping well."

"I gave her an aspirin, and then she needed to rest."

He turns to look at me, his grin accepting my explanation. I sink down into the water, shooing him away while I finish washing up.

"Ronnie needs to go."

"He's a boy," I say, lathering up the washcloth. "He can go outside. Then put him to bed and tell him I'll be in to kiss him good night in a bit."

Russ leans against the doorjamb, then rises up on his toes to get a peek inside the tub. "You gonna have a kiss for me, too?"

I fold my arms, hiding myself against the tub's wall. "Put away the supper dishes and set out his school clothes, and I just might."

He considers it for a tick before grinning and backing away. Soon the radio is silenced, and instead I hear the clatter of dishes accompanied by Russ's rich tenor singing "Jesus Is All the World to Me." When he draws out the long notes, I hear Ronnie laugh, and I know they're cutting up in the kitchen, the way they do when they're alone. Both of them too much a man to let on they can be silly.

By now the water is this close to cold, and I stand up, surprised as always at the displacement. There seems so little left in the tub, not nearly enough to have covered me, and I wonder if I haven't soaked it all up, straight into my skin. The towel is scratchy from years of rough washing and wind-whipped sun, but it feels pleasantly warm wrapped around my body, and I tread carefully across the tile floor to the mirror above the sink, where I wipe the last of the steam away and lean in close for a look.

My hair is dark now, but when it dries, the color will be on the lighter side of brown, and will frame my face in limp, soft waves. They'd been such a surprise the first time I cut it short, right before my high school portrait. I remember telling Pa I didn't want to look like a Chickasaw princess in the Troubadour yearbook, not caring how such a remark might be taken for an insult to my mother and her own. But Ma was long dead by then, and the sharpness of my cheekbones keeps her heritage fiercely alive.

Hearing Russ and Ronnie still occupied in the kitchen, I step across the hall to our bedroom and go to the dressing table, where my modest array of cosmetics waits. Nothing much, as Russ wouldn't have me paint my face, but I do have a new set of Avon just delivered. Ariel, my favorite scent for as long as I can remember, so much a part of me that my daughter wears its name. I dab a drop of perfume at the base of my neck and behind each knee, like I read in a magazine to do. Then, my skin now dry, I dust the fat, powdered puff across my shoulders. Drop the towel and dust more before sliding a clean cotton gown over my shoulders in time to hear Russ's voice leading Ronnie into his room.

Leaning my ear against the wall, I listen to the muffled sound of my son's prayer, knowing in my heart he lifts up me and Russ, and his baby sister, and Paw-Paw's farm, and all the people needing work and money. I owe him a kiss and want to be there for the *Amen,* as I am every night, so I quickly move next door, stopping short at the sight of Russ kneeling at the bedside, his elbows on the well-worn quilt.

"And help our family be a good friend to Mr. Brace," Ronnie prays. "And heal his arm in heaven. Amen."

"Amen," Russ and I echo, though my agreement is more than tinged with curiosity. I cross the room and bend low over the boy's head, smoothing back the unruly curls that are so much like his father's. Even in the dim light, I can tell he's done a poor job of washing his face.

"Who's Mr. Brace?" Our town, Featherling, is small, and the church even smaller, so to hear an unfamiliar name is rare indeed.

"Papa's friend from before the war." He speaks this last word with a yawn so broad I know he hasn't cleaned his teeth, either.

I look over my shoulder at Russ.

"Just came to town," he says. "You don't know him."

"He's comin' for dinner soon, though," Ronnie says.

"Is he?" My words are meant for Ronnie, but I keep my eyes trained on Russ. "I guess we'll talk more about that later."

I kiss Ronnie's cheek, and when I straighten myself, Russ brushes his hand across my back and settles right in the small of it, turning me to the open door. The boy mutters a final good night, but I expect he is sleeping before we leave the room. At twelve years old, he so often seems to teeter on the edge of being a man that I treasure the times when the activity of the day catches up and turns him into my sleepy boy again.

Together we walk to Ariel's room, which is nothing more than a partitioned-off section of Ronnie's. It isn't much bigger than a closet and we can't both stand in it without touching. Our girl sleeps soundly, her red hair a sea around her, and I lay the back of my fingers against her pale cheek.

"No fever?" Russ asks, his voice shy of serious.

"I'm telling you, she felt warm at supper."

She takes a deep, startling breath right then, and we back away, hushing each other lest she wake.

Russ reaches for the switch to turn off the hallway light, and soon our entire home plunges into near darkness, saved only by the lamp burning on my dressing table. He walks me to our bedroom door and takes me in his arms, like we are coming back from a date, and don't have two children sleeping not much more than an arm's length away. His kiss is like that, too. One of those kisses that comes along every so often in a marriage, like scales have fallen away from our very lips, and we're seeing each other for the first time in new love.

I break away — "Russ —" wanting to say that he hasn't even taken his boots off. That we haven't checked to make sure the doors are locked, or that the milk bottles are out, or that —

"You feel beautiful —"

My bare feet touch the braided rug that

runs along the side of our bed, and soon the springs creak below our weight.

"Russ." I speak his name, stalling. Calculating as I always do. I brace my hands against his chest. "It's not a good night."

He nudges the strap of the nightgown off my shoulder. "Feels good enough to me."

"You know what I mean." I push him away. "Unless you've got it in your mind you want another baby."

He stops, sighs, and rolls away. Sitting up, he removes his boots, tossing them into the large wicker basket in the corner of the room.

"Honey, I'm sorry." I reach for him, but only manage to pinch my fingertips around the fabric of his sleeve as he stands, bringing the creaking once again. "A few more nights, maybe? It'll be safer."

He shrugs out of his suspenders, strips off his shirt, and lets it fall to the ground. I bite my lip to stop myself from telling him to pick it up and take it across the hall to the hamper.

"Funny." He sends a smile sure to devastate my resolve. "I don't remember you always being so careful."

"And it's a good thing, too. Else you might never have married me, Pa's shotgun or not."

"I never had a chance from the first I saw you. Not my fault you look every bit as lovely tonight."

I scuttle up against the pillows and indulge myself in watching him. Russ Merrill is tall — taller than me, which was a rarity among my suitors. His shoulders are broad, his body imposing. A gentle giant of a man, with a head full of close-cropped curls, a wide, handsome face, and a voice that resonates with the kindness of his person. As a pastor, he is beloved by men for his overt masculinity, and by women for the undeniable gentle spirit beneath. I, too, love him for both these qualities, knowing the pinnacle and depth of each.

"Guess I need to send you off to church alone more often, if this is the treatment I'll get when you come home. I'm thinking Ronnie might be coming down with a case of sniffles. Should be full-blown Sunday morning."

With a quick flash of a wicked grin, he scoops up his shirt and takes himself off across the hall. I hear the water running for his washup and use that time to get up from the bed and take another peek in the mirror above my dressing table. The soft light makes his words true enough, though it helps that I rub my Pond's in faithfully each

17

night. It is the best I can do against the Oklahoma wind and sun. Lately, too, the dust has been so bad, with great dark storms rising up from the earth, though we've had a spell of sweet, clear days. Maybe that's what has Russ in such a mood.

The water turns off, and I move quickly to the bed, easing in to keep it quiet, and bring the cover up around me. Turns out I didn't need to rush, as I hear his steps take him into the kitchen, the rattle of the milk bottles, the closing and locking of the back door.

"Checked the kids one last time," he says, walking into the room. "Sound asleep, both of them."

He wears blue striped pajama trousers and a clean undershirt, and I have a moment of doubt in my calculations. If I get up now, I might have enough time to run across the hall and come back, better prepared. But he climbs in beside me, the weight of him tipping me toward the center of the mattress, and folds his hands behind his head on the pillow. I'm held, even if he's not touching me at all.

"Peaceful end to a beautiful day," I say. And it has been, clear and cloudless, the perfect kind of warm, and not a bit of wind. More than that, not a bit of dust, which means the windows are open, letting the cool night air seep through the curtains. The room feels fresh and alive, and a glance down at Russ's face tells me he appreciates it too.

"Too peaceful, if you ask me."

"How can a home be too peaceful?"

"Too quiet. What would be the harm of bringing in a bit of noise?"

"And what kind of noise would that be?" Though I know what he's getting at.

"Maybe a little one, cooin' in the corner." He says it with an affected accent, as if that will speak to my rancher's daughter's heart.

"More like cryin'," I say, steeling my resolve. " 'Cause he's hungry. You taken a look at the ledger books lately? I don't know how I'm going to feed the four of us in the next months. Let alone five."

"We can leave those worries off for a time, don't you think?"

He runs his knuckle, the one on his first finger, up the length of my arm, catching my heartbeat up with its travel, and that's all it takes.

Later, after, while Russ rests in slack-jawed sleep, I climb out of bed, put on my night-gown, and creep to the bathroom for a washup before checking on the children.

They, too, sleep with the peace that comes from innocence. Satisfied to be every inch alone, I make my way through the dark of the kitchen to the door that leads downstairs to the feed and hardware store below. It is ours now. My brother, Greg, and I own the property, but it's been up to Russ and me to run it since Uncle Glen died ten years ago, and that's just about the last time it turned a profit big enough to live on. The little it brings in supplements Russ's church salary, and minding the store gives us all something to do during these long days of drought.

Streetlight streams through the big glass window, casting the letters *Merrill's Tools and Feed* in shadow across the floor. Around a sharp corner at the bottom of the steps is a small storeroom, dwindled to empty these days, as we can barely move the inventory we have on the shelves. The storeroom has a door that opens out to a platform where the trucks backed up to unload pallets of cattle feed in the days when local farmers had the wherewithal to buy such a thing. On a hook beside it is my ratty gray cardigan sweater, a gift from my mother to my father that did nothing but baffle him from the minute she finished the last stitch.

I dig into the pocket of the sweater and

find what I'm looking for — a half-crumpled pack of cigarettes and a book of matches. With deft fingers, I slip one out of the pack and another one into my pocket and strike a match against the darkness. I touch the flame to the tip of the cigarette and inhale until it glows red, then shake the match and drop it between the slats of the loading dock.

Peaceful, Russ had said. Not so peaceful, perhaps, if he finds me here, and I briefly wonder if I wouldn't have been safer staying inside the storeroom closet. But our bedroom window is on the side of the building, meaning we never have complete darkness for sleeping, but also assuring me that the smoke from my cigarette isn't going to drift in past the starched white curtains.

I take another drag, determined not to be wasteful and let the cigarette burn to nothing of its own accord. I only get one a day, and not even every day — only those nights when Russ falls asleep first. Otherwise, he is always *there.* Working in the store while I clean the house upstairs. Sitting beside me on the sofa, across from me at the table. Staring down at me from behind the pulpit while I sit with the children in the pew at church.

Another drag. I hear the burning of the

paper and tobacco. Half-gone already, and I touch the one in my pocket, counting. Calculating, again, just how many are left, wondering when I'll have another perfect night like this one.

Clear and cool and clean.

"Beautiful night, isn't it?"

The voice startles me so, I fumble the cigarette before stubbing it out on the railing and dropping the butt to the platform, using my toe to nudge it between the planks.

"Good heavens, Mrs. Brown. I didn't expect to see you out at this hour."

Merrilou Brown lives across the street and down the block from the store, having stubbornly refused to sell her property even as business after business built itself up on what the town council renamed Commerce Street in an effort to persuade her and her husband to move. She is a tiny woman, bespectacled and beloved. Each week, the children in Sunday school scramble to measure themselves back-to-back against her, and it is an anticipated rite of passage to be taller than Miss Merrilou. Most achieve that status before the age of twelve.

"Luther needed a walk. And at his age, who am I to say no?"

Luther is a once-white poodle, his coat a perfect match for the neat cap of curls on

Mrs. Brown's own head. The two are inseparable, more so since Mr. Brown, as massive in stature as Mrs. Brown is diminutive, has taken to passing his days listening to gospel radio and writing fiery letters to stations whose programs fail to line up with Scripture.

"It's late, is all," I say, tugging my sweater tightly against me. "You might feel safer walking on the lighted side of the street."

She makes a dismissive sound. "I've been out and about around here before there was a street. What kind of life would it be if a person can't take her buddy out of her own backyard? I noticed you weren't in prayer meeting tonight. Thought you might be ill."

"I'm fine. The baby, she was sick."

Before she can respond, Luther takes that moment to lift his leg and do his business against the side of our building. Thankfully, I have a mask of darkness to hide my irritation.

"That's it, then," she says, unmistakable triumph in her voice. "Here, let me give you this." She wears a battered sweater of her own, and fishes around in its pocket as she approaches. Even though the loading platform is less than three feet off the ground, I loom above her like a monster. The night crackles with the sound of cellophane, and I see she is holding something up to me in her tiny hand. "A peppermint. For when you go back inside. I never developed a taste for the things myself, but I had a grandma who was never without her corncob pipe. And let me tell you, her breath . . ."

She makes a high-pitched sound that sends Luther into a frenzy as he howls to match her tone.

"Thank you." I take it with sincere gratitude and hope the howling won't wake Russ.

"And maybe a spritz of perfume in your hair. It's the hair that really traps the smell."

"I'll keep that in mind."

"And don't worry. Your secret's safe with me. And with Luther here, so long as he doesn't learn to talk."

I indulge her joke with a shallow laugh. "Really, it's not so much of a secret." Russ knows, of course. He simply doesn't approve. And because he doesn't approve, I think it best he doesn't know.

"Still," she says, "I won't breathe a word."

"Well, I appreciate that." She feels more like an ally than a conspirator, and I make a grateful show of unwrapping the mint and popping it into my mouth while Luther prances an arthritic circle around her leg. "Thanks again," I speak around the candy.

Mrs. Brown scoops Luther up, wishes me

a good night, and sets off in a purposeful stride. The second cigarette lingers, forgotten, in my pocket while I suck on the candy, the taste of tobacco mixing in soothing concert with the mint, until it is dissolved to nothingness on my tongue.

Once I'm back upstairs, having stolen my way into the bathroom, I wash my hands, tap a drop of Ariel eau de toilette on my fingertips, and run them through my hair, ready to slip back into bed beside my slumbering husband, all evidence of my secret erased.

CHAPTER 2

Like a burden around my neck, I carry all my secrets from Russ. The smoking, for one, though he knows but allows me the satisfaction of indulging without judgment. And the fact that I spend time each morning mercilessly plucking gray hairs from my head. I once spent an entire year inflating our grocery bill by ten cents every week and stashing away the extra dime until I had enough to buy a radio for our bedroom. I surprised him with it on his birthday but kept the details of the scheme to myself. I'd been halfway to a down payment on a new settee when the price of wheat collapsed and the earth dried up and that extra dime made all the difference in the world.

Pa says I have enough Indian blood in me to make me a liar. Just not enough to make me a good one. Says there is nothing like a redskin mask to hide the truth. My mother proved that well enough, as she was a half-breed who claimed to love him. How any woman could claim to love such a man as my pa, I'll never understand. He was steel-tempered and cruel, lashing out with a switch or a belt if he had one at the ready, and with a slicing remark if he didn't. His marriage to my mother was more like a trap she couldn't escape, and I never witnessed a day of her life that didn't include some sort of taunting torture.

I remember standing next to her casket, envying her escape, and laying out the plans for my own. Even then, at ten years old, I knew my escape would be with a man. Not one like my father, though. My mind constructed someone the opposite of him in every way — somebody without sharp edges at the ends of his words. A man with strong arms and a soft heart who could fill a room, but still leave enough space for the rest of us to breathe. I felt a hand on my shoulder and turned to look up into the face of my brother.

"It's going to be all right, Denola. I'm here. I'll take care of you."

For a time I thought maybe Greg would be my escape. Pa always declared my brother to have itchin' feet and highfalutin dreams, and I prayed that he might take me along wherever his feet and dreams took him. When the war came and he signed up, I think I would have gladly stowed myself away in his duffel bag rather than face those coming cold years with my father. Greg fought our war in France, I fought my war at home, until the day Russ Merrill offered me a path of desertion, free and clear.

I have these moments when I wonder if I loved him. Ask him and he'll say not only did he love me first, he also loved me more. And that's true. He had the luxury of loving me, because he wasn't running away from anything. I wasn't a source of rescue, and that's all he was to me. I love him now, of course, but since he loved me first, I fear sometimes I'll never catch up. And now that there's nothing to run from, I wonder if he'll ever be enough.

The morning Russ says he wants to invite an old friend for dinner — the same man our son had prayed for earlier in the week — I agree with my practiced enthusiasm.

"You realize," I say, "it can't be anything too fancy. I'll need to keep our groceries the same and stretch the portions."

"I'm sure he'll be grateful to have the meal." We are sitting in our kitchen, lingering with the last of the morning's coffee and listening for the bell over the door to the store downstairs.

"And it can't be Sunday, when Pa comes. I can stretch for one more, but not for two, unless I make a stew. But I wouldn't want to make a stew for company."

"I told him tonight. Six o'clock, and we can listen to the Harvest Hour after."

"Think you could watch Ariel for a bit then, this afternoon? Rosalie couldn't take me yesterday because the baby was sick, and if I don't do something about this hair —"

He interrupts me with a kiss. "You're beautiful just as you are."

Before I protest about the kerchief on my head and the bits of breakfast on my apron, Ariel comes bounding into the room, her curls flying wild behind her. Without the slightest hesitation in her steps, she bolts straight into her father's arms, and he lifts her high off the ground, as if months rather than a single night's sleep have kept them apart.

"There she is, the princess of dreamland." He says the same thing every morning, and has since we first watched her slumber in the packing-box cradle next to our bed the night she was born.

She buries her face in his neck, and any reservations I have about leaving the two to each other's company disappears. I envy

Russ's ease with her, the affection that seems to come to him as easy as breathing. I don't have a single memory of running into my father's arms, or any embrace that wasn't fueled by hurt. Perhaps that's why, with both my children, I have to steel myself for each embrace, and sometimes feel painful relief when they pass me by. I tell myself it's more important, anyway, that a daughter feel the ease of her father's love. Might keep her from running so fast to find it someplace else.

"Good morning, sunshine," I offer, hoping I don't sound like the interloper I feel myself to be. "We have Cream of Wheat this morning. With brown sugar. Would you like that?"

She scrambles down from her father's embrace and climbs into her place at the table.

"Where's Ronnie?"

"He's already gone to school," I say. "You are a late sleepyhead this morning."

The bell rings above the store entrance downstairs, calling Russ away, and I go to the stove to set a small pot of water to boil. Ariel comes to my side, hugs my leg, and I touch her hair, thinking for a minute that I might take her with me when I go to my friend's house to get my hair done. She could play with Rosalie's new baby girl while we chat. But then she asks a question about how long it takes for the water to boil, and why the boiling bubbles don't float away the way soap bubbles do, and how come they call it Cream of Wheat when it's dry like dust with no cream in it, and if she could have three spoons of sugar instead of two, please please please . . . I answer each question, careful to make my voice soothing and kind — even giving her the extra spoonful of sugar, though none are heaping. With each answer, I picture a long stretch of silence while Rosalie shampoos my hair. Finally, as Ariel tucks into her bowl of warm, creamy cereal, I kiss the top of her head and say, "You are going to have so much fun helping your daddy in the store today."

By noon I have cleaned up the breakfast dishes, made the beds, and dragged our sweeper across the bit of carpet in the front room. The whole of our home could be cleaned in under an hour, something that pleases and vexes me in equal measure. When we first moved in, newly married and poor as possums, with a baby due most any time, we'd been thankful enough at Uncle Glen's generosity to give us the apartment, rent free, as long as I helped out in the store downstairs while Russ was still away at school. I can look back now and count it as my favorite time of life, the evenings of solitude eating the warmed-over dinners while the baby kicked within me. I loved the anticipation of Russ's coming home on the weekends, and even more the quiet that settled in after he drove away on Sunday evening. It had seemed, at the time, so very adequate. One room for us, one for the baby. I painted it all a bright yellow that a dissatisfied customer had returned to the store, and filled it with bits and pieces discarded in the street or pilfered right from under my father's nose.

And there, in the same way we now watch the skies in hope for rain, I'd waited to become truly, exuberantly happy.

Downstairs, the feed and hardware store is half the size it used to be. Meaning the space is the same, but the inventory has been reduced to the imperishable: small tools, gardening implements, household fixtures, and the like. The price of feed has risen higher than the thin white clouds that refuse to rain, so much of the stockroom sits empty.

After seeing Ariel softly to sleep for her afternoon nap and hollering down the stairs to the shop to tell Russ to check on her in an hour, I tie a scarf around my head and take fifty cents from the grocery jar. I am in the bathroom, dabbing on a bit of lipstick — the single cosmetic Russ can abide — when I catch the change in the air.

That's how it happens. An electric charge that flickers at the top of the throat, something between taste and touch. There will be no afternoon at Rosalie's today. I put the cap back on my lipstick, drop it into my purse, twist the clasp, and prepare for another day of darkness.

I hear Russ coming up the steps and meet him in the kitchen, where I'm filling the sink with water.

"I know," I say before he can get a word out.

"Looks to be a mile out."

"They'll be sending the kids home from school."

"I expect."

We take the basket of old linens out from under the sink and one by one soak the torn, stained sheets and towels and twist them into thick, wet ropes. The first I carry to our sitting-room window, which faces west. I see the mass of dirt in the distance, like a mountain uprooted, being bowled straight for us, leaving crumbling excess in

33

its wake.

I lay the soaked linen along the windowsill, knowing within a matter of hours it will be caked with mud the likes of which usually comes with rain. We've been living in a reversal of nature for a while — dirt from the air with water waiting to meet it. Behind me, Russ drapes a sheet over the furniture and tells me he's already done the same over our kitchen table and chairs. Ronnie bounds in, excited as always to be released from school for the day, and I put him to work, soaking rags and stuffing them around every window, along the bottoms of the doors. The storms have revealed every crack in our walls — most would be invisible if not for the tiny drifts of dust we find after they pass by. We mark them with black wax pencil, and Ronnie plugs them with the smallest scraps of cloth.

We work silently, so as not to wake Ariel. While the rest of us see the storms as a necessary burden, they strike pure fear in her tender heart.

Looking outside, I see my fellow townspeople scurrying through the street, bent low against the onslaught of wind, hoping to get home in time to create the same defenses we have just completed. The air howls, and evening light takes the afternoon by force. Not pure dark yet, but soon. I've sent Ronnie into Ariel's room with a flashlight and a box full of funny pages and am stripping the linens from the beds when the sound of the store's bell pierces through the increasing volume of the wind.

"You didn't lock up?" I call from our bedroom.

"I wasn't sure if Ronnie would come up through the store or not."

He stops to kiss me on his way downstairs and, as often happens during these times, an electric shock passes between us. It is sharp and leaves a burn on my lips that I don't try to rub away, since I put on fresh lipstick not even fifteen minutes before.

Russ laughs. "We still got that spark, don't we, Nola?"

I pucker from a safe distance and send him on his way. Everything is almost ready, save for putting the bread box in the cupboard and the honey and jam jars in the icebox. I'm about to light a kerosene lamp when a voice from behind startles me.

"Russ says to come on up."

I spin around to find a man I've never seen before standing in the doorway. He doesn't fill it the way Russ does, but leans against one side, as if purposefully leaving a means of escape should I decide to take

35

fright and run past him. A shock of thick black hair, elevated by the wind, creates something like a dark halo, and even with the dimness of the room, I know he is looking straight at me with unapologetic challenge.

"Well, of course," I say, glad to have some excuse for my flustered state, though I keep it to myself. No man could possibly understand the difficulty of having a dinner guest arrive five hours early. "We are expecting you."

I strike a match and touch it to the wick of the hurricane lamp and see him in greater detail. He wears a set of well-worn denim overalls and a blue plaid shirt underneath. Before I can stop myself, my eyes are drawn to the limp pinned-up sleeve, empty at the elbow.

Immediately I'm angry at Russ for not filling me in on this detail about his newly resurfaced friend, given that he never failed to prepare me for the shortcomings of others. He'd lean close and whisper, *"Mrs. Mandle's goiter is almost double in size. She's very self-conscious. Don't stare."* Or, *"Mr. Wilder lost another tooth, right in front. Try not to make him laugh."* Not that I was in any way known for making people laugh.

My stare couldn't have lasted for more

than a second or two — barely long enough to be classified as such — but as I am bathed in full light, it is long enough for our guest to take note, and he twitches what remains, making the empty sleeve flutter.

"Rest of it got blown off in the wind out there. Your husband's chasin' it down for me."

It takes a beat for me to realize he's telling a joke, and though his face is still very much in shadow, I hear a lilt in his voice that makes me feel more comfortable than I should with a stranger.

"Please come in," I say, ignoring the opportunity to respond to his humor. "I'm Nola."

"Jimmy Brace."

Jimmy. A boy's name. Russ has only called him Jim.

"I'm afraid I wasn't expecting you so early."

"Job I had lined up fell through." He takes only one step across the threshold, leaving the door open behind him. "Dropped by to tell Russ I'd most likely be movin' on, but then this blew in, so I guess I'll be stayin' put for a while at least."

"Well." I still don't feel comfortable. Not frightened, exactly, but decidedly ill at ease. "I'm afraid I won't have much to offer besides maybe a sandwich and cold beans. Russ has to turn off the gas when the storms come through, for fear of fire."

"It's all right." He steps closer, walking with a sort of caution, as if trying to catch me unaware, though he's clearly in plain sight. "I'm thankful for the shelter."

The match burns nearly down to my fingers, and I shake it out. "I should go downstairs and see if Russ needs —"

"I helped him seal the door and windows. He's on his way up."

This last bit fills me with inexplicable relief, and I drop the cool, spent match on the table, taking the first real, deep breath since hearing his voice.

"In that case," I say, calculating before holding out my left hand in a gesture of true welcome, "come in and have a seat. He'll never forgive my rudeness if he finds you standing in the doorway."

An old bedsheet has been draped over the table and surrounding chairs, but I reach under and pull one out for him. He comes right up behind me, repeating the action with another chair, and we brush against each other, sending an electrical shock I feel in my teeth. He feels it too, and we offer self-conscious apologies before sitting on opposite sides of the table, the lamp blocking any view I might have of his face. All the better. I keep my eyes trained on the door, body crackling, and wait for Russ to fill it with his presence.

There's never any knowing how long a storm will last. Sometimes it blows for not more than an hour, hardly enough to even count as a storm. With those, it seems right when a body gets the wash brought in and the windows sealed up, the skies turn blue and the breeze settles and there's just enough dirt brought in to make the morning's cleaning count for naught. Other times, the sun might set and rise and set again behind a curtain of soil-driven darkness. That's when miles' worth of drought piles up against the door, and a person can't say his name without the crunch and grit of dust between his teeth.

So we've learned to sit silent in the midst of that howling wind. Not talking — not hardly breathing — so as to keep the taste of dirt at bay. Our eyes sting in the darkness, and a second skin comes to cover any part of the body left bare. If there is a time to sleep, we soak a rag with clean tap water and put it over our nose and mouth and marvel at the solid mud that greets us when we wake.

It is an enemy, this dust, and we all believe

it will kill each one of us in turn.

"Give me a tornado!" the old-timers say, longing for God's wrath to be quick, ripping homes from their foundations and sending cattle through the air.

Our neighbor Merrilou Brown longs for the blizzards of North Dakota. Clean, cold drifts that bring a man to freezing death ten steps away from his house.

This evening, as the five of us — my family and the stranger — sit around the empty kitchen table, trying to ignore the particles floating in the lamplight, we defy the tradition of silence and entertain ourselves with stories of death more mercifully sweet than the suffocating thirst of the storms.

"Blown clean to bits," he says, this Jim. "One minute you're makin' plans, thinkin' about your best girl, and then — *boom!*"

I bend my cheek to touch the top of Ariel's head. We've given her a drop or two of paregoric to help her cope with the storm, and her sleep-heavy body reassures me that she needn't fear the stories, either.

"It's a terrible thing," I say. "War."

"It's a necessary evil," says our guest.

"Did it hurt when you lost your arm?" Ronnie takes a spoonful of cold beans from beneath the saucer-covered bowl and brings it quickly to his mouth. I don't know how he can stand to eat them as such, but it's the best I could put on the table, and he attacks the food with a zeal equal to that of our guest, who appears not to have eaten in days.

"We shouldn't pry, Son," Russ says, his supper left largely untouched.

"It's all right." He — Jim — has adopted an efficient method of sliding the overturned saucer halfway across the bowl with his thumb, digging his spoon beneath it, and nudging it back in one smooth motion while lifting his spoon to his mouth. "It's a good thing for a young man to know that there's life to be lived, no matter how much of yourself is left to live it." He turns his attention to Ronnie, speaking to him as if my son had grown to be a man by the sheer courage of his question.

"It hurt. Worst pain I've ever felt in my life, or hope to ever again. There's a burning that happens, and when it don't come clean off, your muscles pull with the weight of it. And every time you move, even a little —" he shifts in his chair, a twitch so subtle I might have missed it had I blinked — "like it's startin' all over again."

Russ shifts in his chair too, though more elaborately.

"When we went over there," he says,

capturing all of France with a cock of his head, "we went knowin' we might not come back. And you'd hear guys braggin' that they'd rather come back dead than without their legs. Cowards."

He says this last word with the power of an expletive, then immediately shoots an apologetic glance at Russ.

"But you know what the Good Book says, don't you, Reverend? Somethin' about the body being made up of many parts. So the way I see it, the good Lord gave each of us more'n we need."

It is an odd and exactly right thing to say, and I reach my hand across the table to where Russ's sits listlessly next to his untouched food.

"The Bible also says that God can move the mountains," Russ says, curling his fingers around mine. "And it seems like he's doing so right now, a little at a time."

Jim laughs, as I imagine it is his first time to hear the joke. Ronnie and I, on the other hand, knew it was coming from as far away as California, so we groan in protest.

"Well, I tell you what." Jim's tone is suddenly more serious than what is called for in the moment. "If I've learned nothin' else, it's not to question the moments God gives you. Guy next to me? When the bomb hit,

42

we'd just traded places so's he could get out of the wind to light his cigarette. Never had a chance. I have to believe I'm alive for a reason."

"We're all alive for a reason," Russ says.

Something at the base of my neck irritates me, more than the dirt starting to form its drift beneath my collar. He is using his preacher's voice again, right here in the darkness around the kitchen table, and that snips my fuse.

" 'Course we are," Jim says, unfazed. "But most of the time we can be like all that dirt out there, blowin' in one direction, side by side against each other, and it's not until we settle for a bit that we know where we're goin' next."

"Where'd you come here from?" Ronnie asks.

"Oklahoma City, originally." He nods toward Russ. "It's where I met your dad. In college."

"You a minister too?"

"No, kid. Never had the cash or the callin'."

"He worked in the dining hall," Russ says. "And if you want to know the truth, I probably would not have passed my literature class without him. Lots of late nights, reading Shakespeare —"

43

"You drinkin' coffee. Me pushin' a broom."

The first uncomfortable silence of the evening follows. Ronnie looks from one man to the other, but I succumb to an opposite effect. I draw my hand away from my husband's, and as I do, the flame in the lamp flickers. Perhaps because we are sitting in unnatural darkness, the shadows seem to layer upon themselves, and the light narrows to encompass Jim's face alone, leaving all the rest to disappear. If not for the weight of Ariel in my lap, I might have thought myself to be disembodied, broken into a million tiny flecks discretely floating all around. I feel the thickness of the air and wonder if it wouldn't be best if none of us talked. Indefinitely. Or at least not until the dust settles on our lips to make our words worthwhile.

"So, Ronnie," our guest says after a time. "Short for Ronald?"

Ronnie rolls his eyes at me. "I wish. That's a normal name, at least."

"His given name is Byron," I say, encountering the same distaste my son has always had for his name. Russ, too, for that matter. It was our first true disagreement, and the only one in which I permanently prevailed.

"Ah. Like the poet?"

I suppose it is rude of me to register my surprise, but he hardly looks like a man to be familiar with such things. He, at least, is gracious enough to overlook my shocked reaction, and continues his conversation with Ronnie.

"Your mother must be a romantic," he says, taking in Russ's discomfort. "Have you studied him?"

"No," Ronnie says, his expression begging us to bring the conversation back to war.

Jim shifts in his seat, reaches into his pocket, and produces a coin that glints silver in the lamplight. A liberty half-dollar, and he sets it in the middle of the table. "This is the prize to whichever of you can solve Byron's riddle."

Immediately Ronnie is intrigued. I don't know that he's seen that much money in one place since Christmas.

"Are you ready?"

I tuck Ariel closer to me, anticipating, and look to see Russ nodding his assent.

Jim sits back. " 'The beginning of eternity, the end of time and space. The beginning of every end, and the end of every place.' "

Ronnie seems startled when the lines come to an end, and makes Jim repeat them three times over. Russ looks to the ceiling, mouthing them to himself, while Ronnie

45

spouts off a litany of desperate answers.

"Midnight? The chimes on a clock? A map?"

Jim answers each one with patience and encouragement, but gives no hints. He tilts his head back to look at me. "You know, don't you?"

I do, but I won't say. "It would be wrong of me to take your money, Lord Byron, you being our guest and all."

"But isn't that the most ancient exchange of hospitality? The trade of stories and entertainment for a meal and a roof? With that out there —" he gestures behind him with his thumb — "I'm mighty grateful to have both."

"Is it history?" Ronnie sounds hopeful.

"No," I answer, and then repeat the riddle myself, giving emphasis to lead him to the answer.

"You're making it too easy," Jim chides.

I look at the puzzled faces of my son and husband, stirring Ariel with my laughter. "Obviously not."

Russ moves his finger, writing abstract patterns as is his way when he wants to figure something out, and after a time, the patterns aren't so abstract anymore, and he knows.

"The letter *e*," he says, more to himself

than to us.

"You got it, buddy." Jim attempts to slide the coin across the table, but Russ stops it halfway.

"I won't take your money."

"You won it fair and square."

"Wouldn't be right."

Once again Ronnie looks from one to the other, this time seeing a new incarnation of pride. Risking Ariel's wakefulness, I lean forward, cover the coin with my hand, and draw it toward me. After all, I knew the answer all along.

"I'll buy us something special for supper next time. We all win."

It seems an amenable solution for the moment, and before Russ can protest, I ball my fist to hold it tight and stand, my legs creaking and unsure beneath my daughter's weight.

"Do you want me to take her?" Russ half stands in offering.

"No. I need to stash this someplace safe anyway so our son doesn't squander it on matinees and Cracker Jack." I look to him. "Why don't you get out the checkers? See if our visiting Lord Byron is as clever with that game?"

I walk with Ariel back to her room, immediately feeling the difference in the air.

This room has no window and never suffers the full blows of the storms like the rest of the house. Truth be told, if not for our guest, our whole family might be huddled back in here, as we have been in times past, taking turns napping on her narrow bed. I pull down the top cover, knowing it could not have completely escaped the dust. Nothing ever does. But the sheets beneath it are cool and relatively clean, and I turn over the pillow before resting her head upon it.

From out in the kitchen, I hear the first sounds of boasting. Ronnie, of course, and I worry that he might be crossing some invisible line, being too familiar with this stranger, offering the type of affectionate familiarity that should be reserved for his family. For his father.

Because Ariel is asleep, I kneel by her bedside to say her prayers.

"Lord —" And I stop.

"Lord Byron."

My words come back to me, clearer than any radio broadcast. More than hear them, I feel them, how they fluttered in my throat, edged with flirtation. And *"next time."* Presuming such a time would come. My hands clasp around the coin from his pocket, taken from his warmth to mine.

"Mama?" Ariel stirs. "Is the storm still

blowing?"

I kiss the top of her head, the tendrils of her hair still damp from being held so close against me.

"It is, sweet girl."

And then I pray that it will pass.

CHAPTER 3

In the morning, he is gone. *Morning* meaning, of course, when the storm has passed. It's hard to tell, sometimes, when darkness tacks itself onto darkness. We forget to wind our watches and can't even see the clock faces for the film of dust that covers them. So, in those early moments of peace, when the air is still and the sun shines high, we push our doors against the drifts and take to the streets, confirming with our neighbors.

Do you have the time?

Ten fifteen.

And is it Sunday?

Yes.

In this we are like old Ebenezer Scrooge, startled and pleased to find ourselves alive to see another day, with little time lost to the void.

I do not know what has happened to our guest, only that, after an indeterminate amount of sleep, I was awakened by the smell of coffee and the sound of silence. I crept about the house, feeling the familiar grit beneath my bare feet, and found Ariel playing quietly with her paper dolls, Ronnie sound asleep on the sofa, and Russ at the kitchen table, staring past his open Bible.

All of us.

"Did he leave?" My mouth feels like I slept with a towel wrapped around my tongue.

Russ looks at me, blinking, as if he doesn't quite understand.

"Your friend. Jim. Is he gone?"

"Yes." He returns to his reading with no further explanation.

I go to the cupboard, take out a cup, and rinse it under the tap. After three big gulps of water, I fill it with the fresh, hot coffee. He's taken the sheet off the table, so when I prop my elbows on it, I know the dirt I feel comes from my own skin.

"Where did he go?"

Russ mumbles something and makes a mark in his Bible.

"Does he have a place to stay? Or is he — ?"

"Nola." He sounds frustrated. Indulgent, but frustrated.

"I'm sorry." I sip my coffee. It is strong

and good, and I tell him so. Quietly, though, so as not to distract him again. I am about to ask if he plans to hold a church service, but his intent study answers my question. The regular service time has well passed, but when the storms became a commonality in our lives, Russ — leader at once of both the church and the community — made a singular declaration. Three hours past the storm, no matter the day of the week, no matter if it's the dead of night, we gather. To count our people, to lift our praises, and to pray for God's continued mercy in the days to come.

Ariel climbs into my lap and nuzzles my neck. It takes all my strength not to push her grimy face away. She tells me she's hungry, and thirsty, and asks when she'll be old enough to drink coffee, and if we have any Ovaltine, and can she take a bath before church, and can she bring her paper dolls if she keeps them hidden in the pages of her *Children's Book of Virtue and Verse*?

And is Paw-Paw coming over for dinner?

I answer what I can, giving assurances about the paper dolls and promises for Ovaltine, but maybe not right now. She'd have a shower, not a bath, because there wasn't time to clean the tub. And as for Paw-Paw, well, that would depend on whether or not he came to church.

Russ seems not at all disturbed by our conversation, but I can tell he listens. He has a smile that lifts nothing more than the corner of his top lip. I call it his secret smile, both for when he's trying to keep one, and when he thinks no one is watching. He's ignored me long enough.

"What are you smiling at, Russ Merrill?"

"Just listening to my girls." His eyes never leave the Scriptures. Upon closer inspection I notice he has already cleaned up, dirt free but not shaven.

"Might should stay home," I say, "in case Pa does come over. Clean up a bit, try to cook up something, since you got the gas turned back on."

"I'd rather you didn't."

It's not a command. Russ knows I'll obey as much as my conscience ever allows without his needing to be forceful, but his statement doesn't leave much room for argument. Still it leaves a little.

"I know. But if Pa —"

"Your pa's lived through the same storm we have. He won't mind a bit of dust in the corners. I like you to be there with me, Nola. It helps."

He reaches across the table and lays a hand against Ariel's hair, then my cheek.

His touch is cool and clean, and I turn my face to kiss the center of his palm. The request is a memorial to our earliest days when, he says, the sight of me in the back pew with my father gave him the courage to get through his first-ever sermon. How I'd calmed his nerves, inspired him to impress the congregation so they'd want to bring him back and he could see me every week. I've watched him grow in confidence and authority behind the pulpit over the years, but still, he insists, my presence brings him peace.

"Do what you can here, then," I say, "while I get your girls pretty."

He promises, and I make his first task that of slicing a few potatoes and putting them on to boil after finding a snack for our daughter.

In the bathroom, I strip to my skin while the water turns warm. A glimpse in the mirror reveals a perfect line where my collar kept the dirt at bay. Standing in the tub, I pull the curtain around the basin and lift the lever to bring warm water showering from the spigot above. More dust washes from me, and I imagine my hair harboring traces of Oklahoma farmland mixed with long-overdue rain. After all the precautions — all the rags stuffed around windows and doors, in every nook and crack imaginable — still, brown rivulets pour off my body, wash down the drain, and swirl away.

Quickly, knowing well the preciousness of water, I rinse myself clean and step into a pair of slippers to protect my feet from the unswept floor. Dressed in something suitable for Sunday, I take my daughter through the same cleansing, plaiting her wet hair into a single red rope. I leave Ronnie to the last possible second, having learned that, at this age, it is more pleasant to have him well rested than well scrubbed. He sates his hunger with a few slices of buttered bread and a cup of cooled coffee with milk — an indulgence we allow as of late — and with all the trappings of any other family heading off for Sunday worship, we walk out of our apartment door and down the steps to where our fellow townspeople emerge, none the worse for wear.

It wasn't the worst storm we've ever had. The sidewalk's still discernible from the street, and the hedges Merrilou Brown planted along her front fence still stand. That alone gives me the hope of seeing all our people accounted for — those who attend the Featherling Christian Church, that is.

I have my daughter by the hand, my

husband at my side, and our son trailing half a step behind. Just like earlier in the morning, in our small home, all gathered and accounted for. All that matters, and still . . .

I lift a hand in greeting to my friend Rosalie, who carries her baby girl in her arms, and the remaining fat around her belly. Her husband, Ben, leads on, their son in between. Rosalie and I call out a friendly greeting to each other, along with a promise to get together in the coming days.

My eyes scan the streets as I tell myself I'm only looking out of a sense of charitable goodwill. A concern borne from the ancient laws of hospitality. I nod my head in greeting to one neighbor after another, craning my neck to look behind and beyond their weary faces.

Ariel sees a friend and, with my permission, runs off in squealing delight.

"I see you all made it through safe and sound?" Merrilou Brown's small presence sidles up beside me, forcing me to slow my pace to match hers. In no time, Russ and Ronnie have left me behind.

"We did."

"This one had a bark worse'n its bite, I'd say."

I mutter something.

"The wind, I mean. Maybe more of a howl than a bark. Though sometimes, it'll pick up a gust, and make a sound —" She breaks into a series of breathy, midpitched sounds like nothing I'd ever heard in nature or beyond, but there's nothing to do but acknowledge.

She asks if Russ plans to preach, and I tell her yes, and I feel her birdlike grip on my wrist.

"Good. We all need words of hope. Now more'n ever."

"Yes. More than ever."

I try not to wrest myself away too impatiently as I make an excuse about needing to catch up with my family. Even with quickened steps, my escape buys me a few moments alone to ease my curiosity. Once alongside Russ, I loop my arm through his and ask if he's seen any sign of our Mr. Brace.

"Hide nor hair," Russ says. "But I told him we'd be gathered here. And invited him for a meal after."

I feel a fillip of fear and convince myself it's nothing more than the annoyance of having not one but two possible dinner guests, with no assurances of either.

"I hope we'll have enough."

"We'll be fine."

"But if Pa —"

He stops right in front of the church house steps and kisses me softly, like I'm some sort of new bride. "We always have enough, Nola. By God's grace and mercy."

I sense the approving smiles as people divide themselves to stream around us. A far cry from the reception we received the first time we stood on these front steps together when I *was* a new bride. I'd felt fearful fillips then, too, but realized soon enough they were the first movements of the young man who now pounded his father on the shoulder, saying, "Break it up, Dad. People are watching."

Russ smiles and takes my hand, holding it all the way through the coatroom and into the sanctuary. After that, all business. One after another, men — farmers, ranchers, bankers — greet him with a handshake and a grimness that make me wonder if a little bit of their very souls didn't blow away with the storm. Haggard women collapse in his embrace, forcing me to share the comfort of his strength.

"He's a good man."

I don't even need to turn around; his voice is already that familiar to me, and it feels like I am exhaling for the first time since opening my eyes. And then, feeling so depleted, I dare not face him, so I keep my eyes fixed upon my husband. All of my intentions for hospitality disappear in his reappearance. It is the first I've been able to see him in full light, and I realize the lopsidedness of his grin was not merely a trick of shadows, but a truth about his face, giving him a perpetual expression of mischief.

"He is. We're lucky to have him."

Without another word, I sit. Second row, left-hand side. Reserved since forever for the preacher's wife.

Russ takes his place behind the pulpit. Only recently, since the onset of the drought and dust, does he finally find it to be a place of comfort. He was such a young man when he took on this church, and always more comfortable speaking to people over a cup of coffee than from a platform above them. His early sermons were clipped straight from his seminary notes, with things like "add funny story" scribbled in the margins. He was stiff and nervous, terrified of failure.

The first time Russ and I saw each other was from this vantage — me sitting in the back beside my father, and Russ clutching sweaty palms to the pulpit's edge, trying to gather his thoughts. This is our legend — the meeting of our minds and the melding of our hearts before we even had a chance to say a single word to one another. In the telling of it, our love sounds immediate and mutual. He claims to have seen me, and in that moment, all his jitters held still, like Jesus calming the sea so he could walk right back to me at the greeting time. I watched it happen, the smoothing of his brow, the stillness of his hands. It became clear soon enough that he had a heart for saving people, and while I already understood the saving grace of Jesus Christ, I knew Russ Merrill would be the one to save my very life. Neither of us remember a word of that first sermon, and between his early ineffectiveness as a preacher and his love affair with Lee Mitchum's daughter, we have always counted it a miracle that he was offered the job here upon his graduation from the university.

"Brothers and sisters," he opens, naming us both his family and his flock, "I understand your discouragement and your frustration. I know some of you feel abandoned by God during these times, when the storms blow through, leaving nothing but dirt to show for all their bluster."

At that point, he runs his finger across the top of the pulpit, showing a grimy residue that brings a weary chuckle, mostly from the women in the crowd.

"But you must remember that God spoke to Job from the midst of a whirlwind. And his voice cannot be silenced. Do not let your hearts or your hope get lost in the darkness of these times. Scripture tells us that our troubles may stay for the night, but our joy will come in the morning. How blessed are we to have multiple nights, that we might experience unscheduled joy?"

After the short sermon, we sing a hymn, but only one, as our throats are too dry to bring any melody to life. The drawn-out notes, punctuated by coughs, don't leave us the breath for even a second verse. All stand for the final prayer, and I close my eyes, thankful for the darkness — more so for the assurance that I'm hidden from all around me. I know that if I were to spy around, I would see nothing but one bowed head after another, all silently nodding to punctuate the prayer.

"Protect us, O God. Deliver us from this drought. Bring rain, dear Father. Yes, Lord. Bring new life."

A voice rings out in agreement somewhere behind me, and I'm tugged away from my imposed night. I open my eyes and hazard a glance over my shoulder and learn that I am not the only sinner in the room.

His head is bowed, but his eyes are raised to look at me, and I know somehow that they have been since the beginning of the prayer. He is waiting — has been waiting. And I have rewarded his patience with a glance.

My husband's voice fills the space between us, asking God to protect our families, and I turn my face to the floor between my feet.

I know what it is like to be caught in a storm, those first pellets of dust striking your skin like bird shot. Under cover of prayer, my skin comes alive with fire, burning through the cold sweat at the back of my neck.

"And as we go forth . . ."

I know the rhythm of my husband's prayer. There'll be little time now. Seconds, maybe, to regain my composure, to be ready to greet his eyes with my own, open and welcoming and — above all — faithful.

". . . under the watchful eye of your loving care . . ."

I breathe in deep, as much as my burdened lungs will allow, and lift my head. This is why I sit where I do, at the front, in the most obvious home for his gaze. At the amen, Russ opens his eyes to find me waiting.

CHAPTER 4

I have few memories of my mother that don't involve some bucket of water, or rag, or mop. She'd grown up the daughter of a domestic in a wealthy Oklahoma City home, and her determination to keep her humble farmhouse equally pristine nearly drove us all to madness. She'd mop the floors within minutes of Pa's leaving the room, whether to head out to the barns or into the parlor to read the evening paper. Without saying so outright, she taught me that a woman could have no greater accomplishment than the cleanliness of her home. Her love lived in the vinegar and flowed through the water.

It all fell to me when she died, and while I may not have inherited her zeal, I had the motivation of Pa's approval to drive my efforts. Not to mention the constant reminders of her standards.

"Yer ma never did leave a dish in the sink."

"Cain't let that warshin' pile up."

"Gettin' to look like an Injun teepee, so much dirt tracked on this floor."

I never did complain, though it seemed unfair that he should have a dozen men working our ranch but wouldn't bring in a single woman to help with the house. It was his way, I suppose, of keeping me from having any hope of leaving, telling me every day that my duties were at home, with him. First'n last. Before I hightailed it into town, I'd better low-tail it on the floor, makin' sure he had a man's dinner waiting in the oven and a clean set of dishes to eat it off 'n.

Which I did. Every day. Some nights sleeping at the kitchen table while I watched a stew overnight. Baking biscuits at four in the morning. Madly putting everything right in that precious hour between his leaving the house for his work and my leaving the house to go to school.

Every book I read, every paper I wrote, every test and pencil worn down to the nub — all of it, to get away. My older brother, Greg, had the Great War to bring him escape. His letters fueled my envy, even those that spoke of death and danger. I would have risked it all, my very life, to get away from this place. Until I met Russ, and I knew for certain if he couldn't get me out of Oklahoma, he could at least take me away from my pa, and that was enough at the time.

When we get home from the church service, I have a single, precious hour to put my house to rights. To run a damp mop over the walls, wipe the countertops and floor with vinegar and water. My dishcloths are caked with as much mud as they can hold, and I use my tea towels to wipe up the remnant. I send Ronnie into the bathroom with a bottle of Lysol to clean in there, not allowing myself to think of Pa's disapproval of a young man performing such a degrading chore, and put a broom in Ariel's hand to sweep the outside steps. A useless gesture, but the least harmful, as she alone will have any hope of breathing fresh air.

Tomorrow, the curtains will be taken down and the rugs beaten, but right now I implore Russ to run our electric sweeper over the floors and furniture, just this once, as I know what harm the Oklahoma soil will pose to the machine's inner workings. He complies, and in the aftermath of silence, I hear Pa's labored footfall on the steps outside. There is a mumbled bit of almost-jovial conversation — his approval of Ariel's industriousness, no doubt — and then a knock at the door.

All the years this has been our home, and still he knocks. Even with my daughter on the porch and the shadows of ourselves inside, I knew he would stand and wait for the door to be opened for him. And if not, he'd leave. I used to cajole, "Pa! You're family. Come on in." But he'd set his jaw and say this weren't no more his home than was the drugstore down the street. I know he wishes Russ and I had moved in with him when we married, despite his ugliness at the matter. Truth be told, when we have those days of tripping over ourselves in this little space, I think about that farmhouse with only one old man to rattle around within its bones, and wish the same. I picture little Ronnie growing up running at his Paw-Paw's heels to help with the livestock in the morning before school; Russ in the cozy parlor nook, preparing his sermon; and myself standing apart from it all, ready for those quiet moments for my own pursuit. Reading, maybe. Or taking up some kind of creative hobby, maybe writing out one of the stories that used to stir in my head.

One meal a week, however, is all it takes to cure me of that delusion.

I open the door to find the man has aged another year in the days since I've last seen him. His gauntness makes me worry that he doesn't eat enough. Truth is, I *know* he doesn't eat enough because he has nobody at the house to cook for him. His cheeks are sunken, with an odd crisscross of wrinkles — the scars of a lifetime of smoking hand-rolled cigarettes. His eyes are pale gray, and on the odd occasion of his smile, his teeth — all present and strong — bear much the same color as his hair, a faded yellow with streaks of brown. Thick, and still bearing the tracks of a wet comb, it is badly in need of a trim. After dinner, if I have a clean towel to spare, I'll wrap it around his neck and do the job myself.

The moment he walks across the threshold, my eyes go straight to the fine layer of dust on his shirt lined up along the seams. It most likely came from the drive — all that fresh, loose dirt kicked up on the road, if the road was there at all. I don't ask, though, lest it stir up a kind of shame.

"See you got the girl workin'." He rarely calls Ariel by her name.

"Always lots to do." I glance over my shoulder to see Russ putting the sweeper in the closet and hope it will be shut away before Pa notices.

Too late. Those gray eyes narrow in disapproval, as do his thin, dry lips, but I refuse to rise to the unspoken challenge. Instead, I open my arms wide in welcome and invite him to sit on our clean furniture before offering a cool drink of water.

"Is the glass clean?"

"Yes, Pa. Washed it a bit ago, along with all the other dishes."

He grunts an approval and accepts the glass. Dark rings of soil frame his fingernails; more is caked in the folds of his knuckles. Such has always been the case with his hands: evidence of hard labor — and the sole measure of a man's value. He always worried my brother's hands would sentence him to a life of weakness.

"You get hit hard at your place?" Russ asks, sitting in the chair next to him with his own drink.

"No more'n anyone." If his house had blown down he'd say the same. His place is long past suffering any new losses from the storms. It has been two years since a single head of cattle grazed his land. He had a head start on the loss that now consumes us all.

I remain silent, knowing anything I say will only result in an accusation of abandonment. I haven't been out to visit my father's house in months, citing the convenient excuse of not wanting to be on the road should another storm kick up. Not that the same fears have stopped me from driving to Boise City when the need arises.

"Need any help out there?" Russ asks the same question with every visit, only to be rebuffed. Pa would rather work himself to raw bones than take help from a stranger. And to him, Russ is still very much a stranger.

"Dinner will be up in a bit," I say, knowing my place. "Haven't had much time at the stove, so it's just a corned beef hash and potatoes. I meant to bake a pie, but . . ."

"No need," Pa says, close to reassuring.

Thankful for the escape, I return to the kitchen. I scrape my wooden spatula along the bottom and sides of the skillet, moving the hash to a pile in the center. The potatoes were parboiled earlier, so I slice them thin and layer them in a surrounding moat of melted butter. Salt, pepper, and let them sizzle to a golden hue while I look down and divide the food into portions. Pa, Russ, Ronnie — Ariel and I can share. Just enough, but in the spirit of hospitality, I call out, "Russ? Is your friend coming for dinner?" and steel myself for the answer.

"What friend is that?" Pa asks, always wary of inviting strangers into our lives.

"A guy I knew in college —" to which Pa

gives the snort he always does at the mention of the institution — "and, no."

"Are you sure?" I reportion, imagining enough. My own stomach feels too rebellious to want more than a bite. "There's plenty."

"Not if I'm invited." Ronnie peeks over my shoulder. He smells clean and I twist my head to kiss his cheek, an act confined to our home.

"Don't make me have to choose," I chide before ordering him to summon his little sister inside to wash up.

When we gather around the table, hands joined for the blessing, I escape into the darkness and imagine the light of that single lamp, illuminating the faces of all gathered here. Try as I might to hear my husband's prayer, though, my mind wanders until he mentions his name. *Jim.* Asking God to keep him safe and lead him to a meal this day.

After we all say, "Amen," I ladle the food onto each plate and ask Russ if he knows where Jim *is* eating this day.

Russ shrugs. "I'm not sure."

"But you did invite him here?"

"I told him he was welcome to join us."

"But what exactly did you *say*?"

"I said something along the lines of,

'You're welcome to join us for dinner.' "

"But that's not the same as 'Please join us for dinner.' You made it his decision."

Russ chuckles at this. "My darling Nola, heaven forbid a man make his own decision once you've set your mind to something. Shall I leave right now? Track him down in the streets and bring him here?"

"Woman's just tryin' to do a kindness," Pa says. He rarely uses my name, either. He keeps his eyes trained on his plate, shoving food onto his fork with a torn piece of bread, but when he chews, he looks at me with familiar suspicion, stripping my facade away.

"I have two tins of peaches in the pantry," I say, perhaps a little too quickly. "Might make for a nice dessert. I can send one home with you, Pa, if you like."

He says nothing, not given to comment one way or another on domestic decisions. Of my own accord, after dinner, I spoon peaches into shallow dishes and sprinkle them with sugar and cinnamon. With all served, I fetch Greg's letter.

Reading my brother's letter after Sunday dinner has been a ritual since he left home, even when it was just Pa and me out on the farm. It was a voice from the outside looking in, with knowledge and familiarity

71

bridging the distance. More than that, his letters offered hope — a glimpse into a world far from here, and footprints to follow to get there. From college, he wrote about the antics of academia, the rigor of the classes, and the energy of a generation poised to take on a new century.

You need to be here, Nola, he'd written. *Girls — women, everywhere, taking on subjects they wouldn't have dreamed of a generation ago. You're smart, smarter than me in a lot of ways. Doesn't seem right that I'm the only one to get an education just because I'm a boy, not that Pa even holds it the right thing for me. I suppose it is strange, going off to study agriculture as a way to get away from a life on a ranch. But it's all I know. You, though, Sis. You know more about things that matter on a deeper level. I can't name a single soul in that place who thinks the way you do. Be careful you don't get stuck.*

Later, when Russ joined us as an element of courtship, Greg wrote from France about the horrors of war, though he left some details out for reasons of both security and sensitivity. Always he writes his letters to me. *Dearest Nola,* or *My Darling Little Sister.* We've always been each other's shield from Pa's wrath, and I know if I'd asked him to, he would have stayed home, a sometimes-physical barrier. But I all but shoved him out the door, asking him to scout a path for both of us. He met Russ through my letters and gave approval with a telegram, but never offered more than *Give my regards to Russ,* in case there would come a time when he might have to defend me on that front, too. And always, at the end, *Please share this news as you will with Pa. Give him my love.*

Which I do, faithfully, though Pa considers Greg's position working for the Department of Agriculture in Washington to be a greater betrayal than leaving the farm to attend college in the first place.

"Shall we see what he has to say?"

I slip the folded papers from the envelope, enacting a poor ruse that I haven't pored over the contents like a spy, deciding what and how to read it to keep a moment's peace at my table.

"Nothin' we ain't heard before," Pa says.

As if to confirm, Ariel tugs at my sleeve, asking to go to her room and play. I excuse her and look to Ronnie, but he has no intentions of leaving. Sitting in on the postdinner conversation — especially in the light of Greg's letters — has proven to be a rite of passage, along with a cup of coffee and a man-size portion of the meal.

73

"I think it's a good thing to have someone from home up in Washington," Russ says.

"Ain't been his home goin' on twenty years."

"As long as we're here, it'll always be home," I say before launching into the contents of the letter.

It begins, as they all do, with a greeting addressed to me, but in the moment I amend it to *Dear family.* And then the usual lines, hoping that all is well, before launching into startling details.

It amazes me how, from hundreds of miles away, Greg seems to be better informed about our crisis than we ourselves are. We are the ones who are living in the midst of a drought, passing the days under one cloudless sky after another, praying for rain without any hope of an answer. I hear his voice like he is shouting from a mountaintop above us. Acres of eroded farmland, the plight of the livestock, and the number of people fleeing in hopes of a better life.

"He's worried about us." I paraphrase the next paragraph or so, in which my older brother, living in a single room in our nation's capital, seems to strip away hope like it's Oklahoma soil. "Thinks we should sell, cut our losses, and go."

At this, Ronnie's eyes light up with familiar possibility, which Pa snuffs right out.

"Ain't nobody buyin'."

"This is our home," Russ says with a more comforting air. "Times of drought are always followed by seasons of rain."

As always, Russ speaks with such confidence it seems a sin to doubt. I don't want the taint of Pa's bitterness, nor do I share my husband's assurance. It seems all I know is that it hasn't rained this day, nor the day before, nor likely the next. Moment by moment, dry as stone, and weighed down. Any hope I ever had of leaving disappeared the minute I laid eyes on Russ, though I didn't know that until I was too gone with his child, and each year we sink down deeper to each other, and deeper in this place.

"Finish up," Pa says.

I read Greg's final line: *"We're doing what we can here, to help."*

"How're they gon' help? Think them fools can make it rain?"

"We'll have to see," I say, folding the letter and putting it carefully back into its envelope. He'd written hints of programs to purchase land and cattle, just to put cash into the hands of the people, something Pa would surely call a handout and refuse.

With the ritual of the letter complete, I take a few minutes to trim Pa's hair while

Ronnie entertains us with the play-by-play of his school's most recent baseball game. After, I fill a paper sack with the other can of peaches, a few biscuits wrapped in wax paper, a small ball of butter, and the remains of today's dinner — one portion, too small to be of any good to our family. He makes a show of refusing it at first — as he does every week — and I turn my back to allow him to take it in privacy. The dish holding today's leftovers is a pale blue, with apple blossoms painted around the rim. Not one of mine. Part of the illusion that we don't send food home with Pa comes from the fact that he never returns my dishes from week to week. To compensate, I've taken to buying plates and bowls for pennies apiece at rummage sales hosted by neighbors who, with no one to tell them any better, sell their worldly goods to seek a better life out west. Or north. Or east.

Anywhere but here.

■ ■ ■ ■

PART II

■ ■ ■ ■

When I lie down,
I say,
When shall I arise, and the night be gone?
and I am full of tossings to and fro
unto the dawning of the day.
My flesh is clothed with worms and clods of
    dust;
my skin is broken, and become loathsome.
My days are swifter than a weaver's
    shuttle,
and are spent without hope.

JOB 7:4-6

CHAPTER 5

There is a deceptiveness about life in a time of drought. Clear blue skies stretch like satin but hold no beauty. Clouds, rolling and gray in the distance, mock us, turning into rainless scraps of vapor before our very eyes. We feel thirst everywhere — our parched throats, of course, and the corners of our mouths. It seems, sometimes, that we are drying up from within. Our lungs rasp with every breath, our bones threaten to snap themselves to powder. There is not enough water to drink, to wash, to bathe. We are never quenched. We are never clean.

Russ, in all his sermons, reminds us that Jesus is the Living Water. And that all who come to him shall never thirst again. We might weep at the thought of such a thing, the coolness of his compassion, the refreshment of his mercy. But our eyes cannot make tears, so we nod and utter a dry amen, keeping our parched lips open for the smallest drop of grace.

This last storm took its toll on our town. In the weeks that follow, two more families pack what they can carry and drive away. I don't see them, of course, but Merrilou Brown does, and she wastes no time bustling into the shop with the news.

"The Campbells?" She stretches on her toes, trying to bring herself closer to my ear, as if what she has to impart is some great secret. A meaningless gesture, as there isn't a single customer. Only Ariel, playing log cabin by stacking sacks of chicken feed. "*Poof.* Let the bank take their house. Didn't even lock the front door when they left."

"How do you know?" I run an oiled rag over the gleaming counter. Every bit of our merchandise — what there is of it — might be covered with the film left by the storms, but I keep the counter polished to a mirrored shine.

"I was out walking Luther when they drove off. Before dawn, it was."

"No, how do you know they didn't lock their front door? Did they tell you that?"

She sinks back to her flat feet and gives me a look that is both innocent and mischievous. "I told them I'd keep an eye on their place."

"Did you wait until sunrise?"

"They have some very nice things, you know. *She* came here from Chicago, so there's lots of fanciness there. A couple of those — what do you call them? That you can put on the buffet to keep the food hot?"

"Chafing dish?"

"That's it!" She snapped her twig-like fingers. "Silver plated. At least three of them. Thought they might do well for the next church supper. Only to borrow. Take 'em right back after."

"Of course."

"And the bank's going to take everything anyway. Scrap it, most likely, what they can't sell. And who are they going to sell it to? Mrs. Campbell would have sold it herself if she thought she could get a dime from any of us for it."

"She didn't even try." The casual listener might think — by the tone of my voice — that I am a full conspirator, when in fact I find the glint in the eye of this diminutive pirate amusing. "Any jewels? Furs? Gold bricks buried in the back of the closet?"

"Oh, you." She swats at my arm. "I just wanted you to know, in case there's anything you need. Their little one's about her age." She cocks her head toward Ariel. "There's a few nice toys. Might put them away for

81

Christmas."

"Thank you." As if I would consider such a thing. I try to strike a note of finality strong enough to urge her out the door, but she seems to be dug in, ready to wait for me to link arms and accompany her on a scavenging expedition. I am about to come out from behind the counter to bring a friendly nudge toward the door, when the bell above it rings, and Jim Brace walks into the shop.

He hasn't been here since the night of the storm, when he sat at my kitchen table with the rest of my family. Somebody once granted such a familiar privilege should not inspire the nervous fluttering I feel at his arrival. I grab the abandoned rag and begin rubbing the already too-clean counter. Merrilou catches my eye, looks at him, then back at me, questioningly. It's not good business form to ignore a customer, not in days when one is so rare, but I count nearly thirty seconds gone, and none of us have said a word.

Finally Jim clears his throat. "Good afternoon, Mrs. Merrill."

"Good afternoon."

He looks much the same as he did that night, though somewhat roughened by the days spent away. His hair, if not longer, is

82

less kempt. His skin, darker. And his clothes — the very same he'd worn to our dinner — crusted over with dirt.

"Is Russ around?"

He works just as hard to avoid my eyes as I do to avoid his, though neither of us can escape the crosshairs of Merrilou Brown.

She chirps, "Who is this?" looking at him, but talking to me.

His name sticks in my throat. I don't trust myself to say it. In the wake of my silence, however, Merrilou's brows rise up above the rims of her spectacles.

"This is —" I tap my finger to my temple, as if in the throes of recollection — "Mr. Brace. James Brace."

"Jim," he says, and I repeat it, proving it to have no hold on me.

She holds her hand out in welcome. "Merrilou Brown." She points to the empty sleeve. "Lost that in the war, did you?"

"Yes, ma'am."

When he smiles at her, warm and flirtatious, Merrilou giggles like a girl and compliments the strength of his grip.

"He's Papa's friend from college," Ariel says from behind her feed-sack wall.

"Is that right? Well, any friend of Pastor Russ is a friend to all." Merrilou, yet to take her hand away, gives me a quick glance for confirmation.

"Russ is visiting some folks," I say, my tongue looser as it draws his attention. "I expect he'll be back within the hour. You're welcome to wait here."

Ariel comes out from her structure complaining, "But, Mama, it's lunchtime. You said . . ."

And I had, moments before Merrilou came in, that we would run upstairs for a bite and a story and a nap — though she would only acknowledge the first two. Now she is behind the counter and wrapped around my leg. I pat her head, telling her not to be rude, and fight my instinct to shake her off.

"Go ahead," Jim says. "I can watch things down here, if you like." He's taken the opportunity of distraction to disengage from Merrilou's grip.

"Is he working for you?" she asks, and somehow I know she's planned out the rest of our conversation no matter what my reply.

"Not exactly." I look at him. "Nothing official, anyway."

"Just helping out when I can." He speaks with the confidence of a truth long understood by all parties involved.

"Well, then," Merrilou says, "I'll leave you

to it. Nice to meet you, Jim. And you, Nola — we'll talk later? I saw a lovely glass punch bowl."

Without waiting for a reply, she scuttles out of the shop. Jim looks at me, and Ariel tugs on my skirt.

"Go ahead."

He releases me, and Ariel tugs harder.

"Thank you, Jim. If you need anything . . ." I gesture around the store. "If somebody comes in —"

"Mama, lunch."

"It'll be fine, ma'am."

I hate how I bristle. *Ma'am.* The same as he called Merrilou, but for me the word has an intimate touch of irony. With final reassurances I take Ariel's hand and lead her upstairs to our apartment. Once the door closes behind me, I lean against it, my head pounding.

"What — ?" I clap my hand over my mouth. *What are you thinking?*

Ariel pulls a loaf out of the bread box. I follow behind, bumping her gently aside with my hip as I take a knife from the drawer and instruct her to get the cheese out of the icebox. I hold the loaf steady against the countertop, but the hand with the knife shakes so, I hardly trust myself to slice it. The serrated blade grates against the crust, sending flakes and crumbs to the countertop. There was a time I'd take a damp cloth to wipe them up before even getting the sandwiches on the plate, but this afternoon I leave them, along with tiny remnants of cheese. I set the butter knife right in the midst before pouring a small glass of cold milk for Ariel and taking it to where she waits patiently at the table.

"Aren't you gonna eat, Mama?"

I've left the second sandwich on the counter.

"No, baby." I tell her I'm not hungry, which is easier than trying to explain the odd fullness in my stomach.

"Is it for Papa? Is he home?"

"No." I answer her second question.

"Is that for Mr. Jim, then?"

"I suppose it could be. Now, no more talking 'til you've finished your lunch."

In general, I tend to encourage conversation at mealtimes, trying to school our children in its art should they ever have the opportunity to dine in a fine establishment. Once, when Ronnie was three years old, Russ and I went on a weekend away to a prayer gathering in Tulsa. We stayed in a fine hotel and had occasion to share the dinner table with other ministers and their wives, and I was appalled at some of the attendees' inability to carry on an entertaining dialogue. Nothing beyond parables and the country's moral decline.

Now, though, I need quiet, as my mind races with the ravings of a banshee. There is something new, yet familiar, about this tightening clot within me. Something equally detested and welcome, and I can only think of Lucifer in his finery, jeweled and beautiful and deadly.

Ariel hums as she eats, clearly in defiance of my instruction to be silent, because it isn't a tune, but unvoiced talk, with all the inflection and rhythm of banter. She pauses as if listening to a reply, raises her eyebrows in reaction, and nods, shoving another bite of sandwich into her mouth.

"Who are you talking to?"

She puts a finger to her lips and hums what I'm sure are the words *It's a secret.*

"You shouldn't keep secrets, girlie. It's impolite."

But I hardly get the words out, because I feel secrets sprinkling my thoughts, grabbing hold of my lips and tugging them into a half smile as I remember the evening spent around this very table, and how very schooled he was in the art of conversation. At ease with Ronnie, amiable with Russ, attentive to Ariel, and to me.

I remember every word of it. Everything he said, everything *I* said, though for myself I reshape my words, making them wittier. I knew the answer to the riddle before he even spoke it. The two of us shared a secret before we even met.

"The beginning of eternity, the end of time and space. The beginning of every end, and the end of every place."

I adopt Ariel's performance and hum the cadence of the phrases as I take her empty plate, give the crumbs a halfhearted swipe with the bottom of my apron, and put the dish back in the cupboard. She drinks the rest of her milk and runs her arm across her lips, a habit I allow of late since we so rarely have clean, dry napkins lying about. Besides, straight from the table, she'll go to the bathroom to tinkle and wash her face and hands before meeting me in her bedroom to read three selections from her *Children's Book of Virtue and Verse*.

"I don't wanna take a nap." She is pouting, as she does every afternoon.

I point to the big hand on the small, round clock by her bed. "Watch it fall, slowly, slowly. Until it's all tired out. When it touches this six on the bottom, come find me." It is our normal routine, just to see if she needs to sleep. Some days she might come running with her clock, thirty minutes to the dot after I've left her side. Other days, more often than not, I check in to find her lost to sleep. The only constant is the fact that she must not leave her room. Nor her bed, since the day I checked in to find her playing with her paper dolls and took them away for two whole days.

I shut her door — not all the way — behind me and set my mind for thirty minutes. I've always been selfish with this time, using it to sip a glass of lemonade and read a book, or listen to a radio program, or lie down on my own bed to see if I need to sleep myself. I might even indulge in some household chore more readily accomplished without Ariel's childlike "help," like running our finer glassware through a vinegar rinse, or dusting the tops of the picture frames. But there is little use in such frivolous pursuits these days, and I am still standing in the hallway smoothing my hair when I realize more than three minutes are gone.

My mind awash with the rules of hospitality, I go back into the kitchen to find the cheese sandwich right where I left it, though I can't imagine what other fate it could possibly have suffered. I take the knife and cut it into halves, and halves again, thinking that to do so will make the eating of it less ungainly. I spoon a few slices of pickled beets into a small dish, wondering if he likes them, irrationally *hoping* that he likes them, as I put them up myself, and fill a glass with the remainder of the milk in the icebox. All of this I assemble on a tray with a clean blue napkin resting underneath a fork, and make a halting journey to the shop downstairs.

"Lunch?" I say upon arrival. There is no one else in the store, and he stands behind the counter leaning over a battered, well-read book.

"You didn't have to do that." He doesn't call me *ma'am.* In fact, nothing about him matches his demeanor of an hour ago.

"It's just a cheese sandwich and some pickles." The milk sloshes in the glass, making me grateful there hadn't been enough to fill it to the top. "I still owe you a good, hot meal."

"I look forward to that."

He stands straight and closes the book, showing it to be a Rand McNally road atlas of the Western Plains. I tighten my grip on the tray handles and take a few steps closer, thankful to set it down at last.

"Are you planning a trip?"

He looks at me quizzically, then acknowledges the book and grins.

"Nothin' else much to read in here."

I try to ignore the relief I feel at his response and offer to find him something more suitable. "If you like cowboy stories and the like, Ronnie has quite a collection."

"What about Russ?" he says before taking the first bite of his sandwich.

"Oh, he has several books too. Not so much fiction, but several religious texts and philosophy."

"From college?"

"Some." The mention of the word makes us both uncomfortable, yet somehow allied, our resentment creating a common enemy — one I feel compelled to defend. "And since, too. From all of his years preaching here."

"I don't know that I'd be interested." He stabs a pickled beet, puts it in his mouth, and chews thoughtfully. "It's good. You put them up yourself?"

I nod, pleased. "Maybe you could get a library card? If you're going to stay here awhile, that is. And you could read whatever you want."

"This town has a library?" He sounds teasing.

"A small one, yes. So, if you're staying . . ."

He pushes the atlas away and takes another bite of sandwich.

"I could take you if you want. Or Ronnie — or Russ, if —" I am flustered, desperate to fill our silent, dusty shop with noise. He just eats, his jaw working slowly, as if he is terribly entertained at my discomfort. I blather on a bit more about our town's sparse book collection, mostly agricultural tomes and the complete collection of Mark Twain, until I run out of things to say. My final words dissolve into something akin to a giggle, and I twist my apron, wishing it had the ability to make me disappear.

"Well now, Mrs. Merrill, as attractive as all of that sounds, I don't know that I'm the type of fellow to have a library card."

His inflection leaves me no choice but to suggest an alternative — some other condition to make him stay in town, stay *here,* at least long enough for him to read a book. Or two. None of mine, of course. The thought of taking a book from the battered, three-tiered shelf next to my bed and handing it to him seems a gesture far too intimate to be appropriate. Our eyes scanning the same words. Licking his thumb to turn the page the same way I do, especially these days, when my skin refuses to be anything but dry.

I want him to stay and I want him to read.

I want us to have a reason for interacting — a shared reaction, perhaps, to a common story. Better yet, for him to read something I haven't, so he can introduce me to something new. Nothing in Featherling is ever new. Not the people, not the thoughts, not even the books in our pittance of a library. They're all donated, culled from estate sales, or rescued and catalogued from abandoned attics.

Which makes me think.

"There's a family," I say, even as the idea is forming. "The Campbells that just left. Packed up and gone. They're from Chicago — well, she was. Their house is empty, and I know she was a reader, so they might have left —"

"What are you suggestin', Mrs. Merrill?"

I blush, because there is more to that question than I care to admit to myself. "It's an understanding we have here. What's left behind is —"

"Fair game?"

Now he is outright flirting, and I flush clear down my neck. I can only plow through my thoughts, speaking too fast and too loud for him to wedge himself between my words.

"I thought you might go out to their place. We could take you — Russ could take you, if he wanted, or I'd write you the directions, though it might be better if you went with someone from town, in case anybody asked questions. Mrs. Brown, even, might escort you. She usually heads up these things. . . ." My mind wanders briefly to the image of the minuscule Merrilou Brown and Jim, picking their way through abandoned Campbell finery, and I immediately change tack. "The point is, you can go and look and see what they have before Mrs. Berry, our librarian, takes them all. Or before the bank comes for the auction. I myself might be heading out there to take a peek. For the kitchen . . ."

I haven't run out of things to say, but his growing amusement at my speech stifles me.

"So, you're sayin' I've stumbled into a town of sanctioned squatters and thieves?"

I don't laugh, really, not wanting to indulge his judgment. "Is that what it sounds like?"

"No," he says, his voice gentle now, and low. "Sounds like you're just people, hit hard and hurtin', like everybody is. Takin' care of each other best you can. Times like these, seems best to throw right and wrong out the window. This whole part of the country's livin' in a cloud."

"It seems that way." Which makes me

wonder why he would choose to show up in a place where the rest of us longed for escape? So I ask him, but before he can answer, the bell above the shop door rings, and Russ walks in. In that moment I have my answer. Jim Brace has blown in to test me, and my feet are too shaky to stand.

CHAPTER 6

We spend nearly every afternoon of the next nine days together. I've managed to pilfer a copy of Fitzgerald's *The Beautiful and Damned* from Mrs. Campbell's nightstand, along with a lovely cut-glass candy dish, should we ever again feel safe to have a dish of candy exposed to the open air. Every day, when Russ leaves to tend to his pastoral visits and Ariel waits for the minute hand to fall to the six (sometimes taking longer than thirty minutes, due to my surreptitious setting of the clock), I venture down to the shop with a tray of lunch for Jim, stationed behind the counter should a customer wander in. Few ever do, and those in need of a saw blade or a bag of nails find me busy feigning inventory while Jim, engaging in enough charming banter to encourage a return visit, completes the transaction with a notation in our book of pending payment. Then, alone again, the novel emerges, and we read.

I take my turn first, reading while he eats, a tacit acknowledgment of how difficult it might be to accomplish both tasks at once. Then, when he finishes, he asks politely if I'd like to take a break.

That first day, I am thankful for the refuge of text — something to keep me in his company while excusing me from small talk. By the second day it is an accepted habit, as he tells me he doesn't read a single word in the time between. I am soon invested in the story of Anthony Patch and the glamorous life I am supposed to condemn. I read, he eats; he reads, I listen. On the third day I bring myself a glass of water to ease the dryness of my mouth, and on the fourth I bring four fresh-baked cookies — two for him, two for me.

Every day, before Ariel comes downstairs, before Russ can interrupt our story with the ringing of the shop bell, Jim slips in the scrap of cardboard to mark our place and I slip the book deep in the back of one of the drawers where we keep the files of customer accounts. With times so hard, Russ has all but given up on expecting payment from anybody, so I know he'll not likely find it there.

And that, of course, means he doesn't

97

know. About the meal, yes. It is Jim's payment for watching the store in the afternoons. But not about the book, and not about my presence.

Perhaps there'd be no harm had I said, on any given day, when he asked what I did with myself all afternoon, *"Oh, nothing much. Your friend who's been watching the store? That Jim? He and I have developed a little lunch routine of reading an F. Scott Fitzgerald novel together."* There are times when such a confession burns at the base of my throat, especially when Russ's voice tugs at the edge of my thoughts, asking me where I've gone away to, and I have to come up with an answer that has nothing to do with beautiful, damned people.

It is dangerous enough how often he invades my thoughts, how I find myself structuring my day in terms of before and after lunch. My salvation has been knowing that when Russ comes home, Jim goes away. Out there, somewhere in the dusty streets of our little town. I have no idea where he comes from in the midmorning, or where he goes at night — an ignorance that keeps my feet on solid ground when thoughts of him threaten to uproot me.

"No," I tell Russ. It is late at night — dark,

at least, and we are sharing a last piece of pie, which itself is the last of the meal we shared with Jim that evening. It has taken nearly two weeks for me to fulfill my promise. Finally, though, I found time to spend an afternoon at Rosalie's getting my hair freshly set and spent half our weekly grocery budget on a beef roast and enough potatoes that none of us would have to share. I used the money from my kitchen purse to pay the grocer, leaving Jim's half dollar hidden at the bottom of my talcum powder, for reasons I cannot even explain to myself.

Ronnie sits at the table with us, fretting over a math problem. Ariel busies herself on the sofa in the front room, cutting out newspaper furniture for her paper dolls.

"He doesn't have anyplace else to go. There's no choice."

The subject of our disagreement is Jim Brace, who at that moment sits downstairs, having been sent there with his battered duffel bag slung across his back.

"Where has he been staying until now?"

"He's been renting a room at Bernice's," Russ says, an odd impatience to his reply.

"So why can't he stay there?"

Russ looks at me, his brows knit together. "I told you last Sunday that Bernice was leaving town. Going to live with her sister in Oklahoma City."

"Sorry." I pick up our plate and rinse it in the sink. "So many of our people are leaving, it's hard to keep track. My mind clouds up with everybody's stories. It's a shame she can't let him stay there, look after the place until . . ."

"Until when? He decides to move on?"

"Well, how long are we going to keep him here?" I keep my back to Russ and train my words to hide my thoughts. "Do you think it's a good idea to keep a drifter under our roof? Aren't you worried about the children?"

"He ain't a drifter, Ma," Ronnie says.

"I don't know what else you'd call him." I scrub the plate harder. "Man who can carry his life around in a duffel bag. Blowing into town like the wind, stirring everything up."

Russ asks, "What has he stirred up?" and I turn the tap on stronger to rinse the dish.

"We're stretched thin enough already. I suppose taking him in will mean breakfast and supper. Inviting him upstairs to listen to the radio of an evening."

"Gee, you sound like Paw-Paw," Ronnie says, and the very tone of his voice makes me too ashamed to face him. "It's a matter of hospitality."

"We have enough," Russ says, now behind

100

me, reaching around to take the too-clean dish from my hand and set it on a towel to dry. "We'll always have enough, and since when are we unable to share our blessings with those in need?"

I will myself to relax in his embrace and lean my head back against his chest. "You're right, of course."

"That's my girl," Russ says with a kiss against my temple. "So if you can round up some sheets and blankets, I'll get him settled in the storeroom. He'll need help setting up that cot."

Ronnie closes his math book and his pencil rolls across the tabletop. "I'll help too. If that's okay."

Russ and I both turn to look at him, surprised at his willingness to do anything unprompted.

"He's interesting. He's the only person I know who isn't from here."

"Don't ask him about the war," I say, wanting to protect them both. "He might not feel comfortable telling those stories, and I don't know that I want you to hear them."

Russ skirts my instruction. "Just tell him we're on our way down."

And with a scrape of a chair Ronnie's gone.

I glance back at Ariel, ensuring that she is still engaged in her play, then lead Russ back into our bedroom, where a tall armoire holds our extra linens.

"Why is it so important to you to help this man?"

Russ stands back, ready to take whatever I hand to him. "It's a hurting time, Nola. We have to do what we can."

"No." I run my hand down the neatly stacked sheets, wanting to avoid giving him those that have been overused of late as nothing more than protective covers. The cot, I know, is narrow, and not made to be fitted with proper bedding, but I want him to feel comfortable. And welcome, no matter how much I protest to my husband. How much I protest to myself. "It's more than that. This town is full of people, some from our church that you've suffered right alongside, and we're not taking any of them in. Or feeding them every day for doing nothing."

"He's watching the store."

"There's nothing to watch and you know that. I can't remember the last time so much as a nickel went into the till. We may as well prop open the door and let the whole town loot us like we do every other abandoned home."

"We're keeping an account. Things will turn around."

"Why him?" Satisfied with a faded set of blue sheets, I hold them to my face and breathe in, ensuring they are clean. Nothing these days is ever as sweet and crisp as in the days before the storms, but I still take in a hint of borax and last week's sunshine before handing them over to Russ and returning to look for a blanket.

"He needs help."

"Everybody needs help." It takes far less time to find a thin afghan, crocheted myself the previous winter.

"He went to war."

"Lots of men went to war."

"I didn't."

And there's the truth of it.

"Oh, Russ . . ." He tries to look away, but as he is somewhat trapped against the linens, arms full, I take his face in my hands. It is soft, even at this time of night, when other men might have cheeks shadowed with stubble. "You don't owe him for that. He didn't go in your place. It's not right for him to come here and make you feel . . . uneasy."

Russ shifts his bundle to one arm, captures my hand in his, and draws it away, kissing the tips of my fingers. If that were the only

103

gesture of affection ever exchanged between the two of us, it would capture his love for me. Tender, protective, and enough to steel me for the question that follows.

"Does he make *you* feel uneasy, Nola?"

"Of course not." My reply is a little too glib, covering a multitude of fears. "But really, darling, how well do you know the man?"

"As much as I know any man, I suppose. I didn't even think of us as friends. He was just the nice, smart guy who worked cleaning up the campus. Truth is, I thought he might have been on some sort of work scholarship; he was smart enough. Then when he asked if he could write to me, I realized — he must not have anyone else. Not a single soul to know or care if he lived or died. I thought, how am I ever going to be able to shepherd a flock if I can't be a friend to this one man? He wrote me once from over there, and a letter every year or so since then."

He drops the bundle of sheets and blanket on the edge of our bed and goes into the bathroom, causing me to raise my voice with the next question.

"So, you wrote back to him?"

There is a beat of silence before he comes back with a clean towel and washcloth, as there is a tiny water closet and sink attached to the storeroom. For Jim to take a shower, though, he will have to come up here — a thought I can't bring myself to consider at the moment.

"When I could. When I had an address, the times he stayed in one place long enough to get a letter."

"Did you tell him about me?" I don't know why I have to know, but I do. Without an immediate task to busy my hands, I ram them deep into the pockets of my apron.

"Of course I did. Even sent him a picture a while back. An old one, from our wedding."

His back is to me while he's bundling the linens together, as if what he says had no consequence. I know the picture in question. Russ looks handsome, if bewildered, wearing a dark suit, with the waves of his hair held in slick submission. I'm wearing a pale-peach dress, though we only had the color tinted in the single print framed in our bedroom. I stand within three inches of Russ's height, and had refused the photographer's suggestion to sit with Russ's hand on my shoulder, or to have him stand on a slight rise so that my head would barely come to his chin. I look tall and strong, my hair all soft curls with a coronet of wildflowers. My figure is full, though nobody would look at the photograph now and know that the bouquet in my hands rests on the beginnings of the tiny life within. I'm looking straight into the camera's lens, my eyes dark — my lips, too, and lifted into a smile I've never replicated since. There is humor and peace, but also a challenge to anyone who could somehow break through the frame and take me away from the inevitable future of this beautiful bride.

"Why would you do that? Send him that picture?"

"Oh, I don't know. He'd ribbed me a little in a letter, after I'd told him how smart you were. He said no woman could be beautiful *and* smart. He wanted proof, and I knew we had plenty of copies of that picture, so I sent it."

I've grown cold during the course of this conversation, and perhaps pale, too, because Russ cocks his head in concern. "Are you all right?"

"You should have asked me," I say, my words like ice. "Before sending my picture to some total stranger. You had no right."

"Darling —" he folds me in his arms, pressing my body against Jim's bedding — "you've never looked more beautiful than the day we married. And it's my picture too.

Not that anybody would notice me. I suppose I wanted to show you off a little."

"Still —"

He squelches my protest with a kiss.

"It was years ago," he says when he pulls away. "I don't know if he even got it. He's never mentioned it, and to tell the truth, I'd plumb forgotten until this conversation."

"Don't ask him about it." To my relief, Russ doesn't demand an explanation for my request. Because I know full well Jim Brace received that picture. It explains the imbalance I felt the moment I met him, that unsettling feeling that we'd met before. That familiarity came from Jim, strong enough to wrap me in it.

Later, much later — in fact, the first hours of the next day — I lie stock-still beside my sleeping husband. We made love the minute we hit the bed, my participation more enthusiastic than anytime in recent memory. He is now at deep, enviable peace while I rage with the silent conflict of the physical satisfaction of my husband, and the constant mental intrusion of the stranger he invited into our home. I attempt to placate myself with assurances that he is not exactly *in* our home, only to wage a new battle with the realization that neither is he a stranger.

Any other sleepless night would send me out for a stolen cigarette, but my pack, newly purchased three days ago, sits fat and square in the pocket of my cardigan, which, last I knew, still hangs on its hook in the storeroom where Jim now sleeps. I like to think my husband would have moved it, not wanting his wife's garment to share a room with another man, but Russ seems far too trusting to even think of such a breach. And Ronnie? Russ reported that his idea of helping had been to pester Jim for story after story about all the places he'd been, until Russ had to herd him out like a wayward calf.

I fixate on the thought of my cardigan, hanging in the darkness. Wondering if Jim has touched a sleeve. Or if he found the cigarettes in the pocket — and possibly smoked one. Giving us another secret to share.

Secret.

Something Russ said in our earlier embrace, after bringing his mouth away from a deep kiss to bury it in the warm recess of my neck.

Don't worry. Your secret's safe, waiting on the bathroom shelf.

I'd misunderstood, thinking he meant my little pink box, covertly delivered in plain brown wrapping a year after Ariel was born. My small, perfect shield against another pregnancy. Russ hated the thing — what it meant, at least — and we never spoke of it by name. Rarely did he initiate its use, and on this night, I dared not let any cautionary space between us.

Thinking back, though, I hear his teasing tone, and I know he found my sweater, its pocketful of cigarettes, and I slide out of bed. Sure enough, on the shelf of the cabinet above the sink, a fresh box of Lucky Strikes, and the lighter I use to soften the tip of my kohl pencil whenever an occasion is special enough for me to line my eyes. I draw out two cigarettes, stash them and the lighter in the pocket of my robe, and make my way through the dark house.

Surely he will be asleep, back in the room-behind-the-room, leaving a clear path to the back door. I pad across, quick and silent, slide the bolt more noiselessly than usual, and slip outside.

No moon. Pure dark, but windy, and my robe and nightgown wrap around my legs. I have to cup my hand around the flame of the lighter, and still need three attempts before I successfully touch it to the tobacco. I breathe in deep, filling myself with smoke and heat, holding both as long as I dare before letting them out in a puff that blows straight back into my face.

"Can I get one of those?"

He speaks from behind me, and for the first time I admit to myself that this is what I wanted. When Russ sent him out of our kitchen, duffel over his shoulder, with the promise of our storeroom, I envisioned just this — a clandestine meeting. Bringing him into my night. Now that we've arrived, I don't know whom I hate more.

"I've only got one," I say, handing him the second cigarette from my pocket. He puts it between his lips and takes the lighter. Expertly, he turns his back to the wind, tucks his head down, and lights the tip on the first try before handing the lighter back to me.

"You shouldn't be here," I say, breaking our smoking silence.

"Should you?"

I don't dare look at him, because I know the answer. "In our home, I mean."

"It's a back storage room. Hardly your home."

"It's too close." I turn to him now. He leans against the door, the tip of his cigarette glowing red, blocking my way.

"Too close for what?"

A challenge, and I won't answer. I refuse

to voice a pathway to my fears.

"You can't show up from out of nowhere and expect to stay on. Not like this. It's not what people do."

"What kind of people?"

"Good people."

"And you're good people?" Amused now; I sense a smile in the darkness.

"Russ is. You wouldn't be here at all if he wasn't."

"For which I'm grateful. He's a good friend."

"He's not your friend. At least he wouldn't be, if he knew . . ."

"Knew what?"

I take a final drag on my cigarette and stub it out — half-smoked — on the railing.

"Nothing. I'm going back inside." But there is no way to go inside except through him, and he doesn't seem willing to move, even though I say, "Excuse me," and "Let me pass, please."

"What does he need to know, Nola?"

His words are smoke and I breathe them in. *Why you're here,* I answer silently. *How you saw my picture and had to meet me.* But then I seize with a fear of being wrong, that he never saw the picture at all, and there's no way for me to not sound crazy, or worse, vain.

"Nothing," I say, feeling foolish. "It's silly."

To my relief, he moves aside, but catches my arm as I walk past. "I'll go. Tomorrow if you want. But I'd like to stay — if nothin' else, long enough to finish the job Russ has for me. Then, trust me, I'll move on."

I resist the urge to thank him and walk over the threshold, through the nearly empty storeroom and empty shop. His touch, still, burns at my wrist, somehow smothering every touch from my husband. Not until I'm halfway up the stairs do I stop.

"The job Russ has for me."

Apparently my husband has a secret too.

Chapter 7

Three more storms over the next two weeks. Four, if you count the one that blew for just an hour or so over the span of an afternoon. Most wouldn't, because we hadn't the time to clean up after the previous one before it rose up, so we let the dust mingle as one adulterous mess.

Greg told us in his last letter that experts — men who hadn't spent a day in this region before earth rose up — can trace the origin of the dust by its color. Red dust is from Oklahoma. Black, Kansas. Yellow, Texas — to the point the very sky loomed green. State by state, the whole world is shifting, one grain at a time. I remain, watching that which blows away, and cleaning up what stays behind.

Another family leaves at the next dust-free dawn — the Gillicks — but I don't bother to go pick through what they left behind. They were poorer than poor to begin with, and the best I can hope for is to recover items I'd given them in better days. They drive away, abandoning a dried-up farm and five chickens that some kind soul rustles up and fries for an impromptu congregational dinner. Seems we all look as thin and bedraggled as those chickens, and it is a meager offering of dishes that line the table in accompaniment. Our plates are sparse, with tiny spoonfuls of this and that, the women filling up on biscuits, leaving most of the meat for the men. Russ partakes of nothing, busying himself with pastoral duties, shaking hands and hugging children. I assume the responsibility of ladling punch, my stomach too twisted in knots to enjoy so much as one slice of Merrilou Brown's white cherry pie.

Jim is here, too, on the outskirts of everything, drinking a Coca-Cola, and anybody who happens to catch the two of us in a single glance would never think we are anything more than strangers. They wouldn't know that, while their pastor prays at the bedsides of their sick, this man and I pass a novel back and forth between us, reading fewer and fewer pages each day in favor of conversations about what life would be like with unlimited access to riches and beautiful things.

The air is warm with the promise of summer and, for once, completely still. We're gathered on what used to be a green lawn on the side of the church, the grass now sickly and scant. Pa is due to arrive for our regular Sunday gathering, and I've positioned Ronnie and some of his friends at the head of the street to watch for him and bring him here when he arrives, not that there will be much left to feed him. When it's almost two o'clock and there's still no sign, I pull Russ away from the latest chapter in the story of Miss Lana's ever-growing thyroid and tell him I'm worried.

"He didn't go to the house?" Russ asks.

"No, I sent Ronnie to check."

"What do you think we should do?"

He's shuffling in place, hands in his pockets, because he knows exactly what we should do. It falls on me to voice it.

"We need to go out there — to his place — and check on him."

"He won't like that."

It's true, he won't. My pa took a dislike to Russ the first time I brought him to dinner and hasn't let up much since. Not through the wedding, nor the birth of Ronnie just a few months later, nor all the years since. The day Russ and I took up living above the store, Pa said there wasn't a need to gather again at his table, and our visits there have been rare at best, and only when one of the hands he used to employ came into town to tell us of a need. Like the time Pa split his head clean open after falling off a ladder, or when Boo, his favorite hound, was found dead under the porch, and Pa sat up for two days straight. He mourned more for that dog than he ever did for my mother, something only he and I know.

"It doesn't matter if he'll like it or not." Here I am, in the midst of the sheep, raising my voice to the shepherd. His cautionary glance gentles my spirit, not to mention the fear that is growing with every word I speak. "The roads are fine, aren't they? There's no reason for him not to be here unless — unless something is bad wrong. Take me out there."

"I will." He tries to calm me with a touch, and I stand still for it. "We can go, as soon as everything is cleared up here."

"Now, Russ."

"Go home. Make up some dinner for him. Or better yet, put together a plate here. Let me say my good-byes, and we'll leave."

I scan the faces of our people, his church. They are what we both have for family these days, our brothers and sisters in Christ playing the roles of cousins and uncles and

116

parents. Russ is the final branch of his family, my brother is a contented bachelor in a faraway land, and my father won't step a foot across the threshold as long as Russ is behind the pulpit. Despite our familiarity, the congregation has never seen us in such a display of near disagreement, and I offer my cheek for an affectionate kiss to demonstrate to all that Russ and I are of one accord.

I send Ronnie back to the house to get our car ready for the drive, and while he's gone I fill a plate with the remnants of our feast.

"Is that for your father?" Jim asks. He's come up beside me and holds the plate while I wrap three biscuits in a scrap of napkin.

"Yes," I say, not daring to look directly at him in front of all our people. "Russ and I are going to drive out there in a bit. I'm worried he didn't come into town."

"Shall I go along with you?"

"Why would you do that?" I find the shallow cake pan I brought with one small square remaining and nestle the overflowing plate beside it, with the bundle of biscuits on top. Jim doesn't leave my side.

"In case there's a problem. In case there's somethin' wrong and you need help."

"Russ will be there."

But even as I say it, one scenario after another rushes through my mind. Pa's car, slid off the road, wheels dug into drifts of dirt. Or Pa himself, caught in the last storm — lost, disoriented, entombed. These are not figments of fear, but stories we've heard from people who have witnessed such tragedy. Children not more than a mother's reach away from the house, buried to their necks, suffocated with soil. Ranchers found with stiff arms wrapped around wayward calves. Entire families burned from the inside out when the electrical forces hit their automobiles. The wind brings nothing but death upon death, and there's a dry, hard stone in the pit of me that knows my father is on his way to ashes and dust.

"Come to think of it, that might be a good idea," I say, looking straight into his eyes. They're rich and brown with the health of promise, and blur in the face of my own tears. "Pa needs to see a friendly face."

"He's never met me."

"That's why you can be friendly."

His smile is purely for my benefit, I'm sure. He's not been invited up to share our Sunday dinners since that first week, and I've told him little about my father. I feel a bittersweet tug on my own lips, a response

118

to his comfort. I want somebody to touch me for reassurance, to ground me before an impending shock, and with Russ encouraging everyone else around, I go limp and still, preparing myself for Jim's embrace.

He does not disappoint. His hand comes to rest in the soft curve of my neck, his palm warm and encompassing. I can feel my pulse throb against its heel, his fingers curl down the crest of my back, his thumb at the tip of my jaw. This he strokes, in punctuation with his words — "It's all gonna be fine, Nola. I'm sure your pa's fine."

There is a horrible, irrational, and paralyzing desire within me, and I know if I nod or speak or breathe I will be lost to a newer touch. As it is, I cannot stop the new flood of tears streaming down my cheeks, and to my near destruction, he wipes these away.

"I have to find Russ," I say the moment I know my mouth will not move against him. "Hope to be leaving in the next few minutes."

To my relief, he puts his cap on and turns away, because I don't know that I have the strength to break from whatever was binding us up in that moment. My legs have turned to water, enough to bring rain to a million acres, and my body is chilled except for those points of fire where he touched me.

"You all right, dear?"

As always, Merrilou Brown's appearance is a surprise, and what has been liquid within me turns to ice-cold fear. When I look down, I see her eyes following what mine had been — Jim's broad shoulders receding into the crowd.

"I'm worried about my father." It's enough of a truth to suffice. "He usually comes in for Sunday dinner."

She turns her gaze to me. "I can see you're upset. And right to be, in these times. Everything so uncertain. Can we do anything to help?"

"Pray." It's what Russ would have said. "And look in on the children if we're not back by dark?"

"Of course!" She claps her little hands. "Tell them to come over for supper. I'll make butter cookies."

I'm promising to relay the invitation to Ronnie when Russ arrives next to me, his arm around my waist, too late to help me stand. He kisses my temple. "Are you ready?"

"Look at you two," Merrilou says. She steps back and cocks her head as if studying a work of art. "Like you should be in a magazine. Cover of *Life.* Can't imagine a couple more attractive. Might as well be your wedding day — especially you, Nola. You look just as pink and pretty."

I should thank her, but we both know it's not a compliment. Or even the truth. I'm flushed and gaunt, tearstained and haggard. There's a fine layer of dust robbing my hair of its natural sheen, turning it two shades lighter and giving it the texture of sand. I'd be hard-pressed to find the kind of flowers that formed my bridal coronet. More than that, I don't remember any such appreciation on our wedding day. Politeness, yes, as an afterthought over the rumbling of rumors, but nothing close to an open-armed welcome. I'm sure I'm not imagining things. Even though she hasn't mentioned it, she watched the moment that passed between Jim and me. I prepare myself for suspicious accusations — the likes of which my father would send had he witnessed the scene. Instead, she offers a glance cloaked in a caution only she and I could understand.

Russ tugs me closer. "More beautiful every day, isn't she?"

"Indeed," Merrilou says. "And isn't it amazing how time can leave someone so unchanged." She winks. "You let those little ones of yours know they can come over for supper. Though I don't suppose that boy of yours is exactly little anymore, is he?"

"That's kind of you," Russ says, and the following thank-you bears his trademark tone of gracious dismissal.

Our 1928 Chevrolet sedan was given to our family when its owner, a man who died still rich from Oklahoma wheat, willed it to Russ. He'd been a broker, not a farmer, or we might have inherited enough land to choke the life out of us.

I'm sitting in the backseat, half-listening to Russ and Jim narrate the land as it unfolds.

"More than a million acres," Russ says, quoting Greg's last letter. "Gone." He goes on about falling prices, eroded soil, plowed-under grasslands. I look out the window, and everything I see bears witness to man's greed and God's judgment. I can't separate the two.

I'm thankful that Jim is here to absorb the brunt of the conversation because I don't know that I'd be able to contribute much more than mewling agreement. I have my own greed to contend with, and with every passing drift, I fear God's punishment will be revealed.

Under the best of circumstances, the drive

out to Pa's farm takes a little over an hour. Pa has it down to the second, knowing exactly how long he can linger at the dinner table before leaving in time to be home for the five o'clock gospel hour on the radio. We've been in the car nearly two hours already, as Russ has to stop intermittently when the road disappears beneath the shifting soil. The car comes to a soft stop, and he and Jim get out — each with a shovel — to dig what they hope will be a clear path in the right direction. Despite his amputation, Jim handles the shovel with equal power, matching Russ in every way, and if either man views the chore as a competition, he makes no comment.

Once or twice, when we don't meet up with a clean patch of road, Jim uses his compass to determine that we're off track, maybe a good quarter of a mile, leading Russ to turn the car around, find our digging spot, and start over again.

It is a slow, frustrating, and frightening process, given that we've only seen three or four other vehicles all afternoon. Russ, somehow, takes it as something encouraging.

"You see, darling?" He turns his head to speak over his shoulder. "I'm sure your pa got word how bad the road is and stayed home. Most sensible thing to do."

I can't help but think that last bit was a dig at me, and I lean my head against the warm window in silent response.

"Doesn't hurt to check," Jim says and asks, without turning his head, "What's he drive?"

"Old rust-bucket truck," I say. "I think it was blue once, wasn't it, Russ? Do you remember?"

"Sounds right." He joins us in scanning the barren prairie for such a landmark.

"He wouldn't leave it, would he?" Jim asks. "Get it stuck and take off walkin' on his own?"

I say, "No," but Russ simultaneously says, "Maybe, given what a stubborn cuss of a man he can be."

Now Jim looks to me for confirmation. I'm sitting directly behind him, and he turns his head to the right so his eyes don't have to cross my husband's path. He can't look right at me, not without turning his entire body in the seat, so I settle with a little more than a profile. He repeats the question: "Would he walk?"

"I don't know." It's the most honest answer I can give. These days, who among us can claim to act with anything close to reason? Three years ago I would never have taken valuables from a neighbor's abandoned home. Ten years ago I might not have cared if my father lived or died. And last winter — or even early spring — I would have laughed in the face of anyone who said that I would ever burn from another man's touch. Not with a man like Russ Merrill, bound to me in love and matrimony, in the eyes of God and all of his creation. "If so, it would be just this afternoon. He doesn't leave his place ever except for Sunday dinner."

"Any reason he might choose not to come?"

"Not that I know." In fact, I've begun to think that his visits are something more than grudging obligation. Ariel, I know, has captured his heart, bringing out a softness in him that Mother and I could never reach. On his last visit he played a game of Old Maid with her while I mashed the potatoes for our supper, teasing her that she was destined to become an old maid herself, with all that red hair. *"Who wants to marry a carrottop princess?"* he said, and we all — even Ariel — knew he was teasing, and decided the most likely husband would be the redheaded son of a pirate.

"We're close," Russ says, easing me out of my reverie and pulling Jim's attention to

125

the road ahead.

I crane my neck, looking for any kind of a familiar landmark, but there are none. No furrowed fields, rippling grass, no head of cattle wandered far from the gate. All the time growing up here, what I liked best was that our family house sat in the deepest part of a shallow valley. Coming in on the road, you might think there was nothing to be found, but then one, two more turns of the tire, and there it was — spread out like the preface art in a storybook. Our little stone house, surrounded by a picket fence, with Mother's well-tended garden along one side. A red barn with a gray shingled roof, a chicken coop, Pa's hay wagon and blue truck — yes, it was most definitely blue — parked side by side, waiting to be proclaimed the favorite.

That's the picture I've held in my mind, anyway. It's the image I picture every Sunday afternoon, when Pa says good-bye and claps his hat on his head before ducking out of our apartment above the dying feed and tool store. It's what I've held in my prayers every time we made another mile without seeing evidence of a dead man on the side of a hidden road. But as we crest the final hill, I look out through the grimy windshield, and I can see that my memories have been overtaken by the dust.

There is some relief, I suppose, in seeing Pa's rusty truck stationed between the barn and the house, but as we get closer, hope seems a frivolous pursuit. Dirt has drifted more than halfway up the tires. The barn door hangs open, a clear testimony to the fact that there's no livestock left to escape. The picket fence is blown over, as are half the fence posts surrounding the property itself. The stairs leading up to the front porch are obscured, the door ajar, and three windows on the second floor broken clean out.

I clap my hand over my mouth to keep from crying out. When Russ stops the car, worried we'll get stuck in a drift, I ignore his admonishment, throw the door open, and run to my father's house. My feet slip in the sand, making my gait clumsy and slower than I can bear. I call out, "Pa! Pa!" intermingled with quieter prayers to God to have kept him safe. When I get to the spot I remember the stairs to be, I bend over, climbing. To my relief, I see where the dust has been moved by the opening of the door, so someone has been here. Here and gone, perhaps.

When I cross the threshold inside, my heart stops. Everything is brown. Shapes of furniture — sofa, rocking chair, wood box, side table, lamp, mantelpiece, footstool, radio — all of it covered in not merely a fine layer but a solid coat of dirt. As if somebody turned the room inside out, rolled it in mud, and set it back again. Particles dance in the air, stinging my eyes. I choke out, "Pa!" but the single syllable sends me into a spasm of coughing.

I go back to the door and see Russ and Jim making their way in from the car, and to my relief they're each carrying a jug of water. I take the kerchief from around my neck and hold it over my mouth and nose, and turn toward the parlor, moving slowly so as to disturb the dust as little as possible.

"Pa?" My call is muffled now, as are the sounds of my footsteps. It's what I imagine walking on a beach would be like, only with blue skies above and bare feet below. I make my way into the kitchen, and there, at the table, just another shape painted the same gritty shade, my father sits, still as a sepia photograph.

CHAPTER 8

I call out to him again, and he turns his head. "Is that you, girl?"

I drop my handkerchief, exposing my face. Oh, how I want to run to him, to fall at his feet, bury my head in his lap, and forgive or repent — whatever God wants in exchange for this reprieve.

Russ is standing in the doorway, and I walk back to him. Wordlessly, I uncork the jug and tip it over, soaking my kerchief. Without any attempt to wring it out, I carry the kerchief back to my father. My intent is to wipe his face clean, but at the first touch of the cotton to his lips, he opens his mouth and takes the whole cloth in, sucking at it like a starving child.

"Oh, Pa." I look away to see Russ has done the same. I leave my father's side and go to my husband. "What do you think happened?"

"No telling."

I feel a hint of frustration at his overly calm demeanor, thinking if this had been one of our parishioners, he would have been much quicker to spring into some kind of action. Assessing, fixing, comforting. Instead, his hands are buried in his pockets as he pivots, taking in the disaster that had been my home.

"Do you think he got caught unprepared?" I ask. "There's usually plenty of warning time to seal up the house."

"This looks to be more than one storm's doin'," Jim says. He stands right inside the front door, a respectable distance for a man not officially invited as a guest. "You seen him just last week?"

He speaks softly, as if not wanting my father to know about his presence.

"Yes. He came to dinner last Sunday."

"How did he seem?"

"Fine." But that's not exactly true. I remember thinking then that he seemed . . . well, dirty. Unkempt — more than usual. But there had been a storm two days before, and I figured he hadn't cleaned everything up yet. In my mind, he'd been following the same pattern of behavior as everybody else I knew: hunker down while the winds blow, restore what you can in the clear days that follow, and pray that the next assault from the sky would be nothing but cool, wet rain.

Obviously, Pa had been doing none of that. Not for a long time, anyway, and living out here alone as he does, there's nobody to help him do otherwise. He's been burying himself. A slow, gradual entombment.

"Stubborn old fool," I say — under my breath, not wanting confirmation. I walk back into the kitchen, holding my tears in check. Pa has taken the kerchief out of his mouth and twists it listlessly in his hands. He looks frightened — caught and confused. I ask, "What's happened here, Pa?"

"What are you doing in my house?"

"It's Sunday. You didn't come to dinner." The complaint seems so trivial, given our surroundings. In this moment, I doubt Pa knows it's Sunday, or that he's supposed to be in my home, or who I am, exactly.

"You're not supposed to come here." His eyes are wild, searching, and his mouth is loose, overworking itself around each syllable.

"I know, but when you didn't —"

"And that, that worthless —" He erupts into a fit of coughing, like nothing I've ever seen before. I call for Russ to bring me the jug of water and tip it to my father's lips. He fights me at first, twisting his head from left to right, rejecting the little bit that lands in his mouth by spitting it straight in my face. Finally, he knocks the jug clean out of my hands, and I rush to pick it up as it makes a mud stream on the kitchen floor. When I stand up again to put it on the table, Pa rises out of his chair and smacks me — hard — across my face. The force is almost enough to take me to the floor again, but I grasp the edge of the table and hold up my hand against a raging Russ who is charging in, fist clenched and ready to return a blow on my behalf.

"No," I say, my cheek cold with pain. "He doesn't know what he's doing." Even as I speak, Pa falls back in his chair.

"All your fault." His voice is hoarse but strong. "Whorin' around. Knew it the first night you come sneakin' in."

"Let's go, Nola," Russ says. "You don't need to listen to this."

By now my face is almost numb, and I've heard this speech from my father so many times, I should be numb to it too. But now Jim is in the kitchen, asking if there's anything he can do to help, and everything Pa says takes on a new shadow.

"He's not in his right mind." The fact that I can say such a thing without incurring further wrath proves my words to be true. I go to the corner cupboard and reach to the very back, where Mother kept the two wineglasses given to my parents at their wedding. As I expected, they are relatively clean, stored rim-side down. I claim my handkerchief once again, dampen it, wipe one of the glasses, and fill it with water.

"Drink." I set it in front of Pa.

"Is the glass clean?"

"It's clean."

He stares at it, and I know the longer he waits, the more free-floating particles will settle along the rim and fall into the water. Then he'll blame me for the grit. I pull out a chair and sit across from him, hoping to make him think this is just another afternoon, the two of us, from a time before Russ took me away.

"It's the judgment." Pa wraps his dry, dirt-encrusted fist around the thin stem of the glass and swirls the water within. "For what you done. God's takin' it all away 'cause of your ungratefulness and sin." A thick paste forms at the corners of his mouth.

"Pa, please. Drink."

"This was good land. All of it. An' the Lord gave us plenty. But then I have a son who won't come back to it. And you, wrigglin' your way until . . . I guess I ain't a good-enough man."

"You're a good man, Pa." I speak the lie

for everybody in the room.

"I ain't. I try but I ain't . . ." And he drifts into a different vocalization. It's strained and rough, like two pieces of fence post rubbing together. His face contorts, and I realize he's crying, but there's nothing in him to produce a single tear.

I reach over and uncurl his fingers from the glass, gently setting it on the table before gripping his hands in my own. I try not to wince at the dryness of his flesh, like a pair of old work boots, and try to connect to his mind with my touch.

"Pa, it's me. Nola."

"Ain't a good man . . ."

"Me, Nola. And Russ." Saying his name is a risk, and I'm relieved when Pa doesn't react.

"And the Lord, he's gonna bury us under for it. For all we done. . . ."

"And Ariel, Pa. She's waiting for you." The mention of my daughter's name quiets him, and in that moment, I know he sees me.

"Ariel? Where is she? She can't be here. Can't see this. Oh, don't let her —"

"It's all right, Pa." I'm hoping to soothe him with my words, because I have no idea how to do so with my touch. "It's Sunday.

Sunday dinner? She's waiting for you at home."

Bits and pieces are coming together in his mind, and he tugs himself away. He looks at the water.

"Is the glass clean?"

"Cleanest you've got."

He drinks it down in one ungrateful swallow.

Russ is beside me now, his hand on my shoulder. I sit up straight, thinking by now we must both look like a grim pioneer couple.

"You had us worried, Lee." His voice is gentle, filled with more kindness and compassion than my father could deserve in a lifetime. "I think it's best you come home with us."

"Can't." His eyes dart to the window. "Truck's been stuck more'n —" He looks to be calculating, but abandons the pursuit. Russ graciously moves on.

"We'll take you with us." His fingers squeeze my shoulders, telling me that we've already discussed this, and I've agreed. Now it's a matter of convincing Pa.

"Ain't leavin' my home. I seen what happens. People leave, and they don't come back. Ever' man I had workin' for me, gone. Neighbors pulled up, drivin' off without so much as a fare-thee-well. An' ever'thing they worked for? Blowin' away."

"It's only for a little while," I say. Anybody would think that Russ and I have spent countless sleepless nights preparing for this moment. Long conversations about how we would approach the subject, who would say what. I suppose, had he the clarity of mind to do so, Pa might have seen this as some kind of an ambush. A kidnapping with nothing less than rain as ransom. I guess Russ and I have a long history of figuring out life as it comes along, though, and this is another one of those moments when we are in perfect concert. Or, at least, he thinks we are. I've got a bit of an off note in my mind, because what Russ sees as an escape for Pa spells escape for me, too. There's no place in our apartment to set him up. No room anywhere, except for that little room behind the storeroom, where there's a cot and a washstand. Jim's room, meaning now he'll have to go.

I glance over to where he's standing in the kitchen doorway, and with the same suspicions that have followed me since I was sixteen years old, my father's eyes follow.

"Who's this?" He asks the question with the same sneer as every time I ever brought a boy home.

I jump in. "This is Russ's friend from before the war. Remember we mentioned him a few weeks back?"

Jim approaches, holding his hand out as if the two men were meeting under normal, cordial circumstances. Pa stands, mustering a dignity that makes me feel both sad and sick. He touches the tips of his fingers to the tabletop, as if none of us will notice his need for support, and returns the gesture. As he introduces himself, he juts his chin toward Jim's empty sleeve.

"That happen in the war?"

"Yessir."

Immediately there's a respect and rapport between the two that I've never seen with Russ. My mind sends silent showers of gratitude to Jim for treating Pa like a man, and not the quivering, raging being that had been present only moments ago.

"And if it's all right with you," I press on, "Jim's going to stay on out here for a bit, while you come home with us."

I declare it with the authority of being the only woman in the room, my voice carrying the same facade as before, as if this arrangement is the pick of a dozen scenarios the three of us spun during the drive out from Featherling.

"What's he gonna do with that one arm?"

Pa speaks as if the man himself isn't standing right in front of him.

"I can do more work with one arm than most could with five. Worked my way across this country once I got dropped off back east. Railroad. Farmhand. You can't name a job that I ain't done."

A response grows in the eyes of my father — eyes that were empty a few moments ago. This is the man he would have chosen for me. A laborer, a soldier, not some college boy who skipped the war to cower behind a pulpit. Even worse, one who'd ruin his daughter and give credence to the cloud of gossip that had surrounded me all my life.

"Why don't you go to your room and pack up a few things?" I speak gently, not wanting to renew his ire. "Russ will go with you to help."

Neither man looks pleased at the prospect, but Pa makes his halting way out of the kitchen, and Russ follows at a respectful distance, sending me a final smile that, in his mind I'm sure, is meant to bring me comfort.

"You don't have to do this," I say as soon as Jim and I are alone. Immediately we drop into the ease of posture and conversation that marks our afternoons together. Pa and Russ might as well be on the other side of some rolling wall of dirt, and not just down a dark, narrow hall. "I was speaking off the cuff."

"Kinda sounds like you're tryin' to get rid of me, Nola. Why would you want to do that?"

His look challenges me, and I lower my voice, hoping he will follow suit. "I think Pa would rest easier knowing someone's here. To watch over things."

He dislodges his feet to take a slow turn about the kitchen. "This place is done for."

"Don't say that. This is — rather, *was* — my home. Pa just hasn't been able to keep help for a while, and he won't take any kind of charity. But if he doesn't know . . ."

My words trail off because he is right beside me, and I need all my breath to do battle against the thickness of the air.

"Another secret?" He traces the word in the dust of my childhood kitchen table.

"I don't think of it that way."

"What do you think about?"

He covers my hand with his, forms it until I, too, am tracing the word. *Secret.* I can hear Russ and Pa grumbling with each other in the next room, and I figure I can remain here in his grip at least until the end of the word. Never before in our afternoons together have I allowed such proximity. We've

139

always shared a common, tacit agreement that our intimacy must be confined to conversation. Ideas and shared, impossible desires.

"Sometimes," I say, when we've finished our spelling and I've drawn my hand back to my side, "I think about what kind of work Russ has you doing for him in the shop."

"He hasn't told you?"

"Not a word, but I guess if you're going to stay out here, he'll have to learn to get along without your help, just like he did before."

"What if I want to come back home? With you?"

Something rises within me, the inner hackles of a dog set on protecting her pups, and I all but growl, "It's not your *home.*"

He is unfazed. "To my *room,* then. Where my things are, or has it been your plan all along to rob a poor one-armed stranger of all his worldly possessions?"

I immediately feel ashamed and apologize with my tone if not my words. "I'll have Russ bring you your things. And then, as you please, you can stay here or move on. Head out to California with all the other Okies. Please, Jim." I reach out, touch his arm, laying my hand on that place that some might say makes him less than a man. "I

know you're a friend to Russ, and for that
—"

We hear their voices and I take my hand
away, swiping our secret off the table as
Russ and my father — both looking consid-
erably more haggard for their excursion —
pause in the doorway.

"Are we ready?" Russ asks, giving no
room for any answer other than one affirma-
tive. Pa, again, seems vacant, but no less
angry. He clutches a small canvas bag with
both hands.

"I think I can do some good here," Jim
says, as if wrapping up our conversation.
He's speaking directly to me, his words
intended to elude Pa's hearing. "Sweep up.
Seal the windows. Don't know what the rest
of the house looks like, but I'll do what I
can."

"There's no electricity and no running
water in the house. You have to use the
pump outside."

"I've pumped water before."

"And the wash — all the bedding must be
filthy."

"I've slept on dirt before. Hard-packed on
the ground."

"And food." Already I'm regretting this
decision, trying to lure him back under
Russ's very eye. "I don't know what he

has. . . ."

"He can have what you brought from the church supper." I sense a hint of impatience in Russ's contribution.

"And when that's gone?" Jim's question is directed at me, and it takes all I have to hold my voice steady in reply.

"I'll send some out. With Russ, later, when we send your things."

Pa seems clueless as to the immediate circumstances, let alone the discussion of his home, but something prompts a hoarse thank-you from his cracked lips, and Jim strides across the room, hand extended.

"Thank you, sir," he says, drawing us all into his ruse, "for the opportunity. It's a hard time comin' across good, honest work these days."

CHAPTER 9

We bring him home with his body full of desert, empty and dry in mind and spirit. First thing, Russ takes him to the shower, helping him out of his clothes as he would a child, and stays close on the other side of the curtain while Pa stands under the cleansing stream. We don't have any kind of running water back at the farm; Pa always said such a thing made a man weak and a woman lazy. So this is new to him, raising his face to the warmth, the water creating a fine film of mud — like Adam in the garden — before, eventually, rinsing it all away.

"Told me he didn't remember ever being clean all over at once," Russ will confide in me later.

That cleanliness seems to be not only unfamiliar but unsettling. He wraps himself in Russ's blue robe and wanders into the front room, his bare feet taking unsure steps. I've never seen him barefoot before.

He wore his boots to work, his brogans to church, and his slippers to bed, for all I knew. I wince at the sight, embarrassed for his vulnerability. I know my floor holds a certain amount of grit to it — impossible to keep anything truly clean — and I feel myself poised to take the blame for the resurgence of dirt on his body. But he says nothing. Only asks for a glass of water.

"Of course, Pa," I say. "Why don't you sit down?" But until I physically take his arm and guide him to the chair he sits in every Sunday afternoon, he simply stands with a vacant face and searching eyes.

When it is time for Russ to lead the Sunday evening service, we are met with a conundrum. Preparations have to be made in the room downstairs — fresh bedding and towels; Jim's things packed away — but I can't leave him sitting upstairs in the living room alone. I have a horrible vision of his awakening, confused, and walking straight out our front door, off the balcony, and landing in a soft drift of dirt below.

"I'll stay with him," Ronnie volunteers a little too eagerly. "We can listen to the *Hour of Prayer* on the radio."

It seems the best solution. We find a pair of soft, clean pajamas for Pa to wear, and as soon as Russ is out the door, I settle the three — Ronnie, Pa, and Ariel — in front of the radio with slices of sugar-buttered bread and warm milk.

"I'm downstairs if you need me." I speak directly to Ronnie, who all of a sudden seems like such a grown-up young man. Strong and responsible, carefully admonishing his little sister not to slurp her milk, and discreetly offering his grandfather a napkin to wipe his grizzled chin. In that moment, the sight of them, together, terrifies me. It isn't the maturity of my son that stirs that storm of fear; I've been watching him grow, minute by each minute of his life, since he was nothing more than a heart-stopping awareness.

No, it is my father, instantly ancient, infirm, transforming me into one of those women. Soft, matronly, cooking rice pudding and mashed peas, speaking with a steady increase in volume, the roles of parent and child reversed. It is the age of my father that makes me old; his decline, my decline.

What a fool. Teasing myself with an idea of what I used to be, what I could have been, back when my father was young. Shameless flirtation with cautious steps outside the edge of my family, the family where I am wedged so squarely in the middle.

I go back to our armoire to find a set of clean sheets — the cleanest we have — before rummaging through the bureau to find clothing for him to wear when his strength returns, as everything he brought with him will need three washings at least before it can be worn. All of this I drape over my arm and take downstairs, through the shop, and into the back room. I haven't been in here, not once, since the day Jim took to sleeping on the narrow cot tucked within. I keep my cigarettes stashed in the bathroom cabinet, and I smoke them on the front balcony. He tried to join me once, but I held him on the third step with a simple no, punctuated by a pinpoint glowing orange. He left me to hide in my shadows, never approaching me again.

Now I find myself in a different darkness, no longer as familiar as it used to be. I am the stranger, the intruder, and I cannot predict what I would find were I to blindly feel my way through it. The light is a single bulb in the middle of the ceiling, and when I pull the chain, an explosion of light reveals everything about him.

While my bundle from upstairs remains a neat, folded cube within my grip, Jim Brace spills out all around me. Shirts draped over empty crates, books lined up sloppily on a shelf. A narrow bed — the cot having been replaced at some point, without my knowledge — unevenly made, the loose rippling blanket not quite pulled, not tucked. And a pillow, with a soft dent.

An empty chair sits in the corner, and I set Pa's things on its seat. I've stashed two cigarettes in my apron pocket, and with a shaking hand I light the first, inhaling the smoke and blowing it out. Stalling, yes, but also reveling in unforeseen victory.

He is gone. Blown away before he can take me with him.

Spying a worn leather bag in the corner by a box of out-of-date almanacs, I'm galled by its familiarity. I remember it from that first night, slung over his shoulder in our kitchen doorway. My cigarette burns away in three deep drags before I grind it straight into the floor to be swept away later. The metal clasps of the bag are smooth and silent, its cavernous center smaller than I imagined. A few items lurk in the darkness, and a power other than my own guides my hand in exploration. Another book — a small Bible by the feel of it. A glass bottle. Socks. A comb. All the bits and pieces that make a man.

Were he a traveler, Russ would have the same things.

That thought emboldens me further to take liberties I've no right to claim. It isn't a Bible but a thin volume of poetry, and a thumb through the pages unearths notes written in fading pencil.

August 9, 1928.
    Chicago, in the Park.
    Something to read at sunrise.

The glass bottle holds a scent so familiar, I see his face the moment I uncork the lid. I've no right to such recognition, and even less to run my finger inside the neck, bringing a hint of it to my own skin, transferring it to the inside of my wrist, right at my pulse.

The horror of my action jolts me to where I nearly drop the bottle, and I shove the cork back in with double strength. I don't want to run the risk of its breaking in the bag, so I take a shirt, a blue one, and hastily wrap it protectively around the glass. Before I can succumb again to any such brazen impropriety, I stride around the room, snatching up clothing and keeping it at arm's length while folding it sloppily before shoving it in. I wrap his safety razor in a scrap of towel, and search for a case to protect the pair of thin, gold-rimmed reading glasses found on the small table next to the bed, thinking it strange that he never wore them in our afternoons reading together. The thought that he would hide such a thing makes me smile, and I lift them up to my eyes to test their strength. Doing so brings the spot on my wrist where I'd rubbed the tonic. With a simple turn, I touch my cheek to his scent and breathe him in.

I chastise myself out loud. "Stop it. Stop being such a fool. Stop." And still I feel a ridiculous smile tugging at my lips.

Three books are stacked haphazardly on the overturned crate on the other side of the bed, and I have to put one knee on the thin mattress and crawl over to get them. One is a copy of *Jude the Obscure* with a stamp proclaiming it the property of the Dennison City Public Library. I think back to his telling me he wasn't much of a library guy, and after an initial twinge of betrayal, decide that this might be the reason why. The other is a well-battered pocket-size road atlas. I turn the pages, following the red wax pencil paths with my finger, touching the places he's been.

The third, I discover, isn't a book at all, but a clever little cardboard box designed to look like one. The word *Treasures* is stamped where the title would be, and a piece of blue silk ribbon is tied around it to keep the lid down. With less than a breath's hesitation, the ribbon is slipped away, and the thin cover opened. Inside, a modest amount of money — less than ten dollars, I'd guess — and a handful of train ticket stubs. Philadelphia, Cincinnati, Chicago, Detroit. There is a heart-shaped medal on a purple ribbon, three shirt buttons, and four packets of headache powder. And then, just when my conscience pricks at me for such bald-faced snooping, something catches my eye.

I drop the books onto the bed and sit down, the squeak of the springs threatening to expose me. I push the corner of a headache powder packet aside, and find my own face behind it.

The back of my neck turns ice cold in recognition, knowing before I even take the photograph out from the bottom of the box what it will be. Hidden behind what looks like a trusting Dennison City Public Library card is Russ's face. He looking lovingly at me on the day of our wedding.

"He . . ." But I don't know what I want to say to myself. I don't even know which *he* I mean. "And how . . . ?" But of course, Russ

150

had sent it. He told me as much — corresponding with a buddy; wanting to show me off.

A note.

Somewhere, there might be letters. Words that passed between them. What had he said? What did he know?

I put the box back on the crate and begin a thorough search. First, through everything in his bag, digging with vain hope, the meager contents already inventoried in my mind. I lift the mattress, get on my hands and knees to look under the bed. I flip through every page of every book, return to the shirts to check the pockets, turn every leaf in the volume of poetry.

None.

Sitting on the now-tousled bed, with trembling fingers I dig the picture out from the bottom of the box. The thick paper is worn along one side, and I know this is how he holds it. I can see the place where his thumb has dented the image. I put on his glasses, smell his skin, and look at myself.

I am beautiful in my peach-tinted gown, though this print shows no color. My neck is long and smooth, my hair shines like dark waves with a single white rose pinned behind my ear. I remember the photographer wanting Russ and me to stand facing each other, gazing into each other's eyes, but my rounded stomach in profile must have made my condition too obvious for his practiced eye, and with an embarrassed stammer, he'd suggested I turn and face the camera head-on, maybe hold the bouquet a little lower.

I look into my own eyes, remembering this woman. A year before this picture, she thought she might attend a university, or be somewhere — anywhere — away from Oklahoma. Then, months before this picture, she met Russ Merrill. Years have passed, lives have been lived and lost between the woman in the peach-colored lace dress and the woman with a single cigarette waiting in her apron pocket.

But Jim didn't know that. Or he did, and he came anyway. Looking closer, I see a telling indentation along the top of the photograph and turn it over. There, in the now indecorously familiar handwriting, are three words: *Denola, Featherling Oklahoma.*

I know if I were to look at the road atlas closely, I'd see a circle in the spot where our town would be if it were big enough to warrant attention from Rand McNally.

All of this revelation brings a certain thrilling nausea to the pit of my empty stomach. My hands as steady as I can will them to be, I tuck all of the dislodged items back into the box and replace the ribbon, going so far as to position the knot above the *r* in *Treasures*, just as it had been. I even place his reading glasses within, to keep them safe, as I toss the box onto the top of the other belongings in the satchel. The flap is closed, the worn latches latched. For all I know, everything in the world Jim Brace owns is in that bag.

Almost everything. Because one of his possessions is actually mine, and I've stuffed it into my apron pocket.

I pick up the satchel — heavy, but not too — and deposit it behind the counter in the shop. I should go straight upstairs to check on Pa and the kids, but outside the night is cool and clear, so I find myself on our loading dock, cigarette between my lips, lighter touched to its tip. After the first drag, the flame still dances in the lighter. With my free hand, I take the photograph out of my pocket and examine it in the light.

I can see my sin behind the fire. I drew him here, luring in my own temptation. Pa would've said I cast a spell, much as I had on Russ, lying with a man pledged to follow God in a holiness too pure for war. Same as my mother had done Pa, when he'd been drawn into her darkness.

I touch the flame to the corner of the photograph and watch it recoil. Gone is the dress, the bouquet, as I twist the paper to burn myself away first. Russ looks on, standing steady and tall, impervious to such destruction.

"I'm so sorry, Russ." I pucker my lips and blow to fan the flame, watching my husband disappear before my eyes. I look up to the sky. "Forgive me, Lord," though I can't articulate any action that would warrant God's mercy. The afternoons spent with Jim were in harmless conversation — literature and art and dreams, all things Russ neither condoned nor understood. "Forgive me," I start again, "for *wanting* . . ." But I haven't the words to voice what I wanted. What I still do, but to no avail. Because it's over. He's gone and not coming back, and for this I conclude my prayer with thanksgiving.

Throughout my prayer the photograph burns, until the flame licks at my fingers. I drop the final scrap, stamp it out with my foot, and nudge it to disappear between the boards of the loading dock.

"I caught you."

It's Russ, home from church, newly round the corner and fast approaching. The dock is only three shallow steps above the ground, and in an amazing feat of limberness, he grasps the side rail and ascends with a single step.

"Your pa already fraying your nerves?"

"I'm so sorry." The words of my apology have not varied from the one I spoke moments before, but now it is carried out with tears that seem to spring up from a deep, hidden well. "I try — I've tried to be a good woman. But sometimes —"

His smile is soft and indulgent, as is the first kiss, after which he says, "It's okay," before kissing me again, deep and searching. I might have gone on to grant approval had we not been interrupted by the chirping intrusion of Merrilou Brown saying, "Oh, you lovebirds!" before steering little Luther down a different path.

We pull apart and I run my hands down my apron, straightening it, feeling the weight of the lighter in its pocket. "I was getting the room ready for Pa. I had no idea there was a bed in there. It's nice."

"From the Gillicks'."

I don't ask how it came to be in our storeroom. I want to tell him that I was packing up Jim's things, but I can't bring myself to put words together in my head, let alone across my tongue and to the space between us. The best I can muster are a few stammering starts: "I was — I just —"

"Darling, there's no hurry."

I create a silent inventory. Books, glasses, shirts — things he needs.

"About your father, I mean. Let him stay in Ronnie's bed for a while, and let Ronnie sleep down here. The boy will enjoy the independence, and I'm pretty worried about Lee."

"Keep Pa upstairs at our place?" I laugh, a strange, strangled sound. "The two of you can barely stand each other's company of a Sunday afternoon."

"True, but he's not quite himself. Maybe this new incarnation can be more tolerant."

"But he's always been so terrible to you."

"How can I ever appreciate the forgiveness of Christ if I can't practice forgiveness myself? I worry that it will be harder on you, but maybe you need more time together to heal."

My fingers still sting from the flame, and I bring them to my lips, but not before Russ captures them and brings them to his. I want to pull away, knowing they bear the trace of Jim's scent, but it's too late.

Russ wrinkles his nose. "Smells like smoke?"

"I wasn't thinking. Lost track and let the cigarette burn too low. Singed my fingers."

He kissed them. "Next time, be more careful."

I promise that I will, and more. "There won't be a next time. I'll stop, I promise. Give them up completely. No more secrets." It is the least I can give, this promise I can measure and keep.

"Even better," he says, and together we go inside.

CHAPTER 10

On that first next day after Pa came home, the morning after my promise, Russ asks, "What about Jim?"

"What about him?" I'm stirring a pot of grits, thankful to have something to command my attention.

"We can't leave him out at the farm."

He speaks to me the way I speak to Ariel when I'm trying to reason her away from whimsy, and I respond with childish obduracy.

"It's more of a home than he had when he came here."

"It's an abandoned farmhouse."

"It's not abandoned. Pa owns that land flat-out."

"He can't live there anymore, Nola." He's behind me now, one hand on my shoulder, speaking softly to spare my father's pride. "Nobody can. He has a home here with us."

"Don't you think I should have some say

in this?" My wooden spoon scrapes the bottom of the pot, perhaps more strongly than is necessary. "He'll be fine. He's just sick and confused right now. He won't want to stay here. He's too proud."

"We'll see," Russ says in that way he has. Not condescending, exactly, because we share the same stake. But authoritative, in that I understand the need to walk away.

I return to the original conversation. "And as for him —" I don't trust myself to say his name — "take his things to him. I put everything in his bag." I spoon the grits into five shallow bowls and go to the icebox to get the butter and sugar. "You could drive it out there today."

"Can't today. Meeting with the deacons. But you —"

"I can't leave Pa."

And so we live that day, and the next, with Russ insisting that we must check on the welfare of his friend, who — until recently — had been his guest.

"It's a matter of hospitality," he says when I dismiss the conversation. "It's not biblical —"

"He's a grown man," I say. "A veteran of war who's traveled the breadth of this country. He'll survive." Then I distract him with my womanly ways, pulling him into an unoccupied corner of our house to kiss him with abandon, or whispering about the anticipated night without worrying about our son listening on the other side of the wall. I pour my distraction and my guilt into my husband, with a double measure of passion and intent, using my body to push away my thoughts.

The day Russ is insistent enough to toss Jim's bag in the backseat of the car and gather supplies for the drive, a familiar dark cloud threatens on the horizon.

"Don't go," I say.

"Look how high and far off," Russ counters. "That's not going to make it within ten miles of here."

"You can't take that chance."

He is right about the storm, but I buy one more day.

That night, in bed, Russ snores beside me, and I lie awake, trying to stay still and not wake him. It is just a matter of time — very little time, I know — before my husband will act on his compassion, fetching Jim right back here. Let him sleep on the sofa, or a cot in Pa's room. A pew in the back of the church, even.

I cannot let that happen.

God knows — and he *alone* knows — the depth of my temptation and the shallowness of my strength. I pray silently, *Keep him away. Find him a home.* Like the sparrows and the foxes. A nest, a den, a smooth stone for his head — only far away from me.

I know I can never tell Russ why there could be no place for his long-lost friend in *this* home — adding that to the long list of what I cannot say. Not about the lunch hours we share, or the time he touched me, or that I'd rummaged through his box of treasures, or the picture I found there. The one reduced to ashes. Part of me tingles with a delicious fear, thinking about my image traveling the country like some hidden inspiration, but there is an unease there too. Like I might be something more akin to prey. How can I present either to my kind, generous husband without betraying all three of us at once?

I swing my feet over the side of the bed and sit up. I don't dare stand. If I do, I'll break my promise. I bring my itching fingers to my mouth, imagining the taste of tobacco. Fighting the urge to slip away, I go instead to my knees, burying my face in my hands.

"Spare me." My lips brush the softness of the worn cotton sheet. "Spare us." I reach across the mattress and grasp Russ's hand.

"Spare us."

He makes an inquisitive, sleepy sound and shifts to his side.

"From this storm," I add, in case he can hear me, and I realize that if Jim ever returns, there will never be complete truth in my marriage. To make the paradox complete, I can never be completely truthful about why he must stay away. I dare not entrust my husband with the task of protecting me from this danger, so it falls to me to protect myself. To protect us.

And then it seems so simple. No other way, really.

I must go alone.

The next morning moves to the rhythm of every other. Coffee, grits. A check to the sky, hoping for a clear horizon. Russ and I sit at the table, hands clasped, reading aloud from the Psalms and praying for God's blessing on the day. I ignore the lie at the back of my throat — that unsettling mix of dishonesty and silence.

He kisses me on his way out the door, a full slate of visitation ahead. Given how small our congregation has become, each family gets its own personal attention. Prayer time, a few words of comfort, a few jokes, and sharing cake and coffee. He'll come home later in the afternoon, patting his soft, rounded stomach, humbled at the knowledge that these people have given him their best, and unable to eat a bite of what I've prepared.

The second round of breakfast goes to Pa and Ronnie and Ariel. In between I slip out to the car with three canteens of water, two blankets, and one well-worn satchel.

I corner Ronnie in the bathroom as he splashes his face with warm water — the boy has still not developed a daily habit of soap.

"I need to take a drive out to Pa's house." I keep my voice soft enough to go undetected, but not so soft as to imply a secret. "Just to check on things."

His face lights up. "Can we all go?" He's spent so much of his childhood begging to go to Paw-Paw's farm, a request so rarely granted. And here I disappoint him once again.

"No, sweetie. I think it would upset Pa too much right now. And I need you to stay here and watch after him."

"And Ariel?"

I've thought about this, and become uneasy with what seems like a devious instinct. "No, I'm going to take Ariel with me." Her presence will be my shield.

"But that's not fair."

"I don't want you to feel too burdened. I'm a grown-up woman and sometimes it can be hard even for me to take care of all who need tending."

"Ain't a problem for me. Seems Ariel's a true comfort to Paw-Paw."

I smooth his hair. "We're barely even going to get out of the car. I need to make sure it's still standing is all. Maybe get some of his things. Clothes and such. I'll pick you up some Hershey's at the store when we get his mail. Deal?"

He shakes my hand, so grown-up. "Deal. But can you make mine a Clark Bar?"

I agree.

With a flat cardboard box full of enough paper dolls to keep her occupied for the drive, Ariel settles on the seat beside me. The dolls carry on a long, lyrical conversation among themselves, freeing me from the responsibility of explaining to my daughter why she's been uprooted for this little jaunt.

The roads have been cleared since Sunday. The same wind that threatened our very lives has cleared this path, with drifts piled up against the weeds and grasses along the side. The wind, I suppose, and our people, driving through, forcing the renewed passage. Intentional, incremental restoration.

The ease of driving gives me time to plan

the whole conversation in my head. I don't envision the house, or the farm. Only his face, as I'd last seen it. Looking at my father — and me — with compassion. And promise.

I'll walk up to the front porch, through the front door, and hand over his satchel, saying, "It's best you not come back to Featherling, Jim. I think we both know that." Then I'll tell him he can stay on Pa's property as long as he likes, or at least until we decide what to do.

No, better, I'll slip the bag inside the front door. Leave, saying nothing. Even if I hear him calling my name — and in my imagination he calls to me — I'll keep walking. Head high, not looking back.

Better still, I'll stop at the front gate. Leave the bag. Drive away.

The minute I reach the turn to Pa's property, something begins to pulsate at the base of my spine. Excitement. Anticipation. Glancing over at Ariel, happily absorbed in her dolls, I'm so thankful that I've thought to bring her with me. No need, really, to leave his bag at the gate and drive off like a thief in the day. If nothing else, how would he know it had been delivered? Was I to assume he made this pilgrimage of a day in hopes of a reunion with his worldly possessions? I need to see him, to hand them over in person, if only for my own satisfaction.

But I will not stay. *Will not stay.* Not even for a conversation. Or a glass of water. Because I have Ariel, our timekeeper. I have to get her home. Have to get myself home. Back along that new, cleared path.

I am still tempted to follow through with my idea of leaving the bag on the front porch, though, and skulking away anonymously, when I see him, sitting on Pa's swing, arm stretched out beside him. Waiting.

Had anyone told me less than a week before, when Pa's farm looked like an abandoned wasteland, that it would reveal itself to me as a recognizable shadow of the home I remembered, I would have refused to believe it. And yet — here is a porch, swept clean. Window shutters, level, closed, and possibly painted. The truck set free from the drifts that held it prisoner. Beside the swing sits a small, round table, and on that table a clear glass pitcher filled with clean water, an empty glass beside it.

He stands as I approach. I notice he wears the same overalls and shirt as the day we left him here, but they seem none the worse for what must have been continual wear. I glance down at Ariel, whose attention is piqued by the slowing of the car. Paper dolls abandoned, she rises to her knees and plasters her face to the window.

"Where are we?" My sweet girl hadn't thought to ask when we first got in the car, and I hadn't bothered to tell her. To be safe, I don't tell her now, either, lest she mention it to Pa and upset him.

"Visiting a friend. I need to bring him something."

"Mr. Jim?"

It occurs to me, briefly, that it might actually be more dangerous for her to be in possession of *that* knowledge, but I will have to explain to Russ eventually.

"Yes. Now sit down before you tumble."

"We're driving in a cloud!"

Indeed, loose dust kicks up all around the car, and I suppose to some imagination it might look as if we are appearing out of a fine, brown mist, but my eyes focus on the man standing on the porch. Leaning, now, against the newel, arms crossed so he looks completely whole. His face is set in an indefinable expression — expectant, amused, maybe even relieved — and if I were to allow myself a smile, it would be big enough to cut through the dust.

I bring the car past Pa's truck, stopping right in front of the steps. Ariel shoots out, dolls forgotten, hollering an urgent request to milk a cow, or feed a goat, or take a ride on a horse.

" 'Fraid none of that's possible," Jim says, and he looks at my little girl with an expression of limitless indulgence. "None of them around here anymore."

Ariel turns to me, betrayed. "You said it was a farm."

"It was," I said. "But everything's changed now."

"But what can I *do*?" She whines the last word.

"There's kittens in the barn," Jim says. "Four or five — tiny things. Why don't you go play with them?"

She clasps her hands, pleading. "Can I, Mama?"

"Barn cats'll scratch," I say, more cautionary than disapproving.

"These are gentle. House cat took them outside. Think I was stirrin' up too much dust in here."

Ariel prances on her toes. "Please, please, please, please, please?"

"Go," I say after mock consideration. "But be gentle."

She races for the barn, as if she's been here for regular visits all her life. I wish she could know the place as I remember, green and vibrant. Creating and sustaining life . . . outwardly, at least.

When she is out of view, I reach behind the seat and produce Jim's bag. His expression changes so little at the sight, I wonder briefly if he recognizes it.

"I've brought your things." I stand immobile next to the car, the satchel a weight at the end of my arm. "I assume you've been missing them?"

"Somewhat."

Again, no definable expression and nothing in his voice to let me know if he is amused or annoyed at my gesture. His inscrutability works against my plan to drop the bag and disappear. Instead, he draws me in, until I find myself climbing the porch steps, bag in hand.

When I ascend to his level, he asks, "Would you like to come inside?" as if this is his house to invite me into. "See what I've accomplished since you left me here like an unwelcome dog?"

His words hurt. "Don't say that. You could have —"

He takes the bag from me, the touch of his hand bringing me to silence.

"Come on." His words speak a welcome; his eyes, forgiveness. He opens the front screen door, its silence surprising. "Oiled it yesterday. Can't imagine how he could stand to let it squeak on like that."

"He didn't have a lot of visitors."

"Well, neither did I. Not a one, but the sound of my own comin's and goin's like to set my teeth on edge."

He holds the door open, and I leave all of my plans for escape on the front porch as I walk through.

"My goodness," I say, taking a deep breath and a look around, "haven't you been hard at work?"

To say that the front room gleams would not be truthful, as its capacity for gleaming has long since passed. But it is clean — almost impeccably so — and given its state of destruction just a few days ago, what meets my eyes is a near miracle. The floor, stripped of the worn rugs that normally dotted its surface, is smooth and clean, with the texture of silk beneath my steps.

"Took out the rugs," he says, "an' fixed a strip of tire rubber to a push broom. Shoulda seen how much piled up. Hauled it out with a shovel." As he speaks, his eyes travel up the length of my leg, starting with the point where my toe tests the unvarnished surface and not stopping until our eyes meet, at which time I shift my attention to the mantel.

"Mopped down the walls," he continues, now taking a slow turn around the room, pointing out each accomplishment, "just with water over the stones. Didn't look like that had been done in about twenty years, storms or not. Then linseed oil on the wood-work."

"But how . . . ?" I pause, not really knowing what I wonder.

"You mean with this?" He holds up the arm with the sleeve pinned below his elbow. "You don't think a one-armed man can push a broom?"

"I didn't mean that. It's just — it's only been three days."

"Well, let me tell you, Mrs. Merrill. I ain't never been a man for sittin' around bein' idle. Not even when I find myself dumped off like so much trash."

"That isn't what we —"

"So, I admit. I waited around for the first hour or so, thinkin' surely they're going to come back. Can't just leave a man with half a jug of water and nothin' else. But then when it started to get dark, and I knew I was here for the night, I figured I best get myself comfortable."

"I'm sorry," I whisper. "We were just — I was so confused. You saw my father, and the state he was in. I didn't think."

"Didn't pay too much attention to the clock. Just worked, slept when I couldn't work no more. Lucky your pa has a few cans of soup, but they're run out today, so I was figurin' how I was goin' to get into town."

"You're welcome to use his truck."

"Figured that already. Spent the mornin' tryin' to dig it out." He drops the bag on one of the upholstered chairs, and a faint puff of dust rises from beneath it. With a look of chagrin, he says, "Goin' to have to take that out for another beatin'."

"That's the hardest to clean," I commiserate. There's a sheet draped over the narrow sofa.

"Been sleepin' there," he says. "Wind knocked out the windows in the other bedrooms, and didn't want to take over your pa's bed. I got these, though." He picks up a bundle of mismatched papers. "Didn't go through them all, for privacy. They was piled on top of a desk in his room, and I'm thinkin' they might be important."

"Thank you." I, too, dislike the idea of airing all of my father's affairs, so I stash the papers in my pocketbook.

"You wanna see the kitchen?"

The pride in his voice is infectious, and, forgetting that I have accomplished my errand, I nod in agreement and follow. Here, too, evidence of the disaster that had been is gone. Wiped clean, to a degree even my mother would approve.

"Dishes, too," he says.

At his prompting, I open the cabinets to reveal glasses, plates, bowls — all sparkling.

"How did you get all of this done?"

"Liquid soap and vinegar. I reckon I pumped more buckets of water these last few days than all my life combined."

"Vinegar," I muse. "How did you know to use vinegar?"

"You think this is my first time to clean a kitchen? Don't forget, when your husband and his fancy friends were doin' their studies, I was the one pushin' the mop."

"Don't talk like that." I inch a drawer open enough to see a glint of gleaming cutlery and immediately close it, keeping my fingers wrapped around the handle even as I turn to face him. "Makes you sound bitter."

"Maybe I am bitter." He's been leaning in the doorframe but begins a slow, purposeful walk toward me, his footfall silent on the clean floor. A panic rises in my throat as I remember the message I have to give him.

"I think it's best you don't come back."

He stops, steps away, and tilts his head to

one side. "Come back where? To your home?"

I stare him down, doubling the strength of my grip on the drawer's handle.

"The town? Are you tryin' to say I can't come back to the *town* of Featherling, Oklahoma?" He seems amused, making no attempt to hide his smile. "That what Russ says?"

I shake my head. "No. He doesn't even know — doesn't even know that I'm here."

Jim cocks one eyebrow and takes another advancing step. "Where does he think you are?"

"Nowhere. I mean, I didn't tell him. Anything, about my coming out here, to bring your things. He doesn't know."

"Why'd you come out here alone, Nola?"

He is closer now, so close that if I put my arms out straight in front of me, my palms would brace themselves against him, creating a physical barrier. Still, I keep them at my sides, not wanting to admit the need for such a thing. My ears ring with the rushing of my blood, and I know my skin is a flush rising from my collarbone to my cheeks. I try to control my breathing — heavy, yet shallow, my body physically heaving with each exhalation. I determine to keep him at bay with my words alone.

"I came alone so I could tell you to stay away."

"From Featherling?"

"From me."

He stops. "It doesn't seem to make a lot of sense for you to come out alone if 'n you're so afraid."

"You know what I mean."

"Do I?"

He is baiting me, close enough now that I can still ward him away with the palms of my hands, but doing so would put me halfway to an embrace. Instead, I press backward, the ridge of the countertop digging into my spine. "I saw it."

"What did you see, Nola?"

"The picture." No response. "My picture, when I was packing up your things."

He closes his eyes, lashes resting against his cheeks, and when he opens them again, I can tell he means his gaze to be kind. Indulgent, even, and it churns a sickness in my stomach.

"That's your weddin' picture, Nola."

"I know." I wish I hadn't said anything. Wish I hadn't seen it in the first place.

"Russ sent that to me years ago."

"It startled me, is all. That you had it."

"What should I have done with it?" He angles his head toward me. "What did *you*

175

do with it?"

He's caught me, as sure as if he'd been with me that night, seeing my younger face consumed by heat and turned to ash. I won't admit to the destruction, though. Not now. Let him figure that out for himself. Later, as he riffles through his things, looking. I fancy myself holding the higher ground, knowing something he doesn't. My own secret to keep.

"Don't come any closer." The words come from the back of my throat. Finally, I let go of the drawer handle and hold my hands up in what I hope conveys a message of threat rather than defense. "And don't come back."

He looks at my hands, then into my eyes. "Where do you think I ought to go?"

"I don't care."

"Where do you think you're going to go?"

"I'm going home." But immediately, from his smirk, I know I've misunderstood the question.

"You still don't know?"

He takes a full step back, and the tension that stretches within our proximity goes slack. My exhalation starts at the base of my spine, taking all my breath, so when I repeat, "Don't come back," I sound weak, and already wounded.

"Talk to your husband."

"Leave us alone." And I am going to say something else — maybe something like an expression of gratitude for cleaning my father's house, or an invitation to say good-bye to Russ before he leaves, or maybe even something akin to wishing him well. A benediction of sorts. But I say nothing because, at the same moment I take a breath, gathering my thoughts, he kisses me.

Not soft, not gentle, not with any hint of hesitation. I've been spared the torture of knowing what I would have done had I been given any warning. Would I have ducked aside? Turned my head? Uttered *no* in the spot of space before our mouths touched? Unlikely, as I had brought myself to this place. Orchestrated circumstances to allow secrecy and solitude. He keeps his hand at the small of my back, and though the other is invisible, it no less wields the power to lock me in this embrace.

In this moment, my identity strips away. His final words, *"Talk to your husband,"* hold no meaning. What husband? And my last words, *"Leave us alone,"* take on new life. A new us. This man becomes my counterpart, and we stand together in a place so pristine and clean — our soft sounds echoing in the dust-free air.

It is he who tears away, saying, "I'm sorry."

I put my hand to my lips, surprised to find they feel much the same, and say nothing.

Something tugs at the remnant of the woman I used to be. A voice, high, sweet, and — thankfully — far off, calling, "Mama!"

Ariel.

I should chastise her for tracking in so much dirt and straw and who knows whatever filth from the barn, but I can only stare at this beautiful creature and try madly to remember exactly who she is, and what she means to me.

"I see you found a kitten," Jim says.

She holds up the little thing in triumph. "Look at all the colors. Orange and black and brown and white and orange again and —"

"It's called a calico," I say, grateful for any sort of words.

"Can I keep it?"

I know instinctively that any protest on my part would only prolong our time here, and I long to clog myself with the dust that has been expelled from this place.

"Of course. Get some dry straw and put it on the floorboard in the car. I'll be right there."

She has a suspicious tinge to her surprise,

but soon enough total joy engulfs her as she skips out of the kitchen, leaving a trail of small, dark footprints on the floor. I move to follow, but feel a strong arm catch me above my elbow.

"I'm sorry," he repeats, but when I turn to look into his eyes, he doesn't seem sorry at all.

"You need to stay away." I speak through gritted teeth.

I feel his thumb move in three strong circles before he lets me go. "So do you."

CHAPTER 11

I drive home, somehow, watching the road beyond the white-knuckle peaks of my grip on the steering wheel. Beside me, Ariel babbles incessantly to the kitten, leaving me guiltily grateful for the small creature. Had I been alone, I might have cried, but every time I feel the threat of tears, I imagine having to give an explanation, and they turn to frost within me.

For a brief moment — well, for a mile, at least — I consider the possibility of staying in the car. Driving forever. Through the year past, I've been watching friends and neighbors drive away, never to be seen again, and I know no reason why Ariel and the kitten and I couldn't do the same. After all, haven't I lost two homes in the course of an afternoon? Behind me, Pa's farm, the place of my memories, no matter how bitter, is as good as lost to the bank. The kiss I shared in his kitchen — the first of such a thing to occur there — has killed a bit of the home that lies ahead. The three of us barrel somewhere in between. Lost.

"What kind of a cat did you say it was, Mama? California?"

"Calico," I correct absently.

"Calico," she repeats, stretching each syllable. "What shall we name it?"

"That's up to you, sweetie."

"I'm going to name it Barney, because it came from a barn."

It strikes me as funny, and I relish the small laugh. "That's a boy's name."

"Maybe it's a boy kitten."

"No, she's a she. Boys don't come in that color."

"Why not?"

I shrug. "The way it is. The way God decided."

"I'm still going to name her Barney, because that's where she came from. And where you come from is what you are. That's what Paw-Paw says."

"It is, indeed." And I hear nothing else for the rest of the drive.

Home.

I bring the car around to the alley, park it, and instruct Ariel to entrust the kitten to me so she can carry her paper dolls inside. Somewhere in the store, I say, we must have a shallow crate to make a sandbox.

Her eyes go wide. "What for?"

I wink. "You'll see. We'll send Ronnie out to dig some up for us."

"Because it's everywhere?"

"Because it's everywhere."

She hands the tiny creature over to me and my hand closes around its body. We walk into the store together through the back door, Ariel with instructions to go right upstairs, change her dress, and wash her hands and face. The instant her foot hits the first step, I set the kitten on the floor and watch, mesmerized by its slow, cautious movement.

"New addition to the family?"

Russ's voice gives me such a start, he gets only a strangled gasp for a reply. He stands behind the counter, three ledgers open in front of him, taking a handful of coins from Merrilou Brown in exchange for a new set of gardening shears. It is a purchase born of pity, as none of us have anything to cut down, but she is faithful to buy at least one small item at intervals regular enough to measure.

My eyes fix on my husband, and my heart nearly bursts with the irrational relief that he is actually *here.* As if my betrayal could have made him disappear. Every ounce of essence within me swarms with grains of confession, and I know only his embrace can bind me. Return me to something solid and true. Heedless of my neighbor's watchful eye, I run to him, throwing myself into his surprised arms.

"Hey, there." He sounds cautiously amused, but he holds me tight against him, one hand steady on my back, the other buried in my hair. I cry hot tears into his strong shoulder. He makes soft, deep hushing sounds, and then I feel more than hear him tell Merrilou that he is sure everything is all right before wishing her a nice day.

Whatever she says is lost to the rushing in my ears, but the sharp ding of the bell above the door rings through. Russ doesn't let go. Not even a bit, and with each breath, I feel closer to being whole.

"You've been out to your dad's?"

"Mm-hmm." I'm not ready, yet, to open my mouth or show my face.

"The house. Is it worse? I thought Jim wouldn't mind trying to clean it up a bit. See what we could salvage."

I pull away, just enough to speak, but keep my eyes trained on the floor. "No, it's not that. He — Jim — actually did a fine job." There, I didn't burst into fire at the saying of his name.

"Then what is it?"

"I don't even know where to start."

Russ steps back and grips my shoulders. "Nola." The power of his voice forces my eyes to meet his, blue and open as a promise. "It's over, isn't it?"

So many answers race through my mind. Yes, it's over, my facade of being a good and worthy woman. Yes, it's over, this dangerous journey, this trap. And it ended badly, and I should never have gone there alone, but it's over. Never again. Not a moment. Just forgive me, please. Forgive me.

I don't know how long it takes me to realize he's been talking during my unspoken revelation, but bits and pieces begin to make their way through. Two growing seasons without a crop. Anywhere. The last of his cattle sold for a dollar a head and killed. Even the babies. Nothing left in the land or in the barn. Nothing but walls, dirt, and taxes.

A new, open door.

"Wh— what are you saying?"

"Your pa's farm. He's lost it, hasn't he?"

I'd dropped my handbag on the counter in my haste to unite with my husband, and without releasing myself from his touch, I reach for it. With shaking hands I pull out the gritty bundle of papers. "It's all here."

Russ takes them from me, and I stand back to watch him set each document side by side on top of the already-cluttered counter. "Tax bills . . . extensions . . ." He wraps an arm around my waist and draws me close. "Looks like there's nothing left to do. It's gone, darling."

"That's not possible. He owns that farm outright. No mortgage." He's always been so proud of that.

"You know that's not enough."

"But what is he going to do?"

Russ leans in, kisses my temple. "He always has a place here."

"In a storeroom?"

"We'll see what more we can do. Knock down a wall, maybe. Put in a proper wash-room. Make it something better."

I allow myself to get caught up in that vision. All of my family — save my brother — gathered under one roof. My father, dependent on me, humbled to a place where he would have to accept my husband. Perhaps the blowing sand will chip away the sharp edges, softening him to be the man I've always needed.

"But then," I say, as the vision becomes more clear and complete, "how could we possibly keep the store? It's one thing to have our family upstairs, but we couldn't very well conduct business . . ."

As I speak, Russ looks away, and not even my most intentional maneuvering brings me back into his line of vision. This, my confirmation that he is hiding something too. Just like Jim said. A measure of my own burden lifts, and I take my first shaky step on an undeserved higher ground. In this moment lives a mutually acknowledged deceit, and I invite it into the light with a single word.

"Russ?"

"Honestly, Nola. How much business are we doing? Merrilou's been our only customer all day."

"Times are hard for everybody."

"But we're sinking, darling. Deeper than anyone should have to. People can't afford to buy, and we can't afford to give it away. Less stock to feed, no crops, no rain, and everybody picking off the bones of what others leave behind."

"It can't be that bad. We're still here."

"It's that bad. We're owed thousands of dollars."

"These are good people, Russ. They'll pay when they can."

"Not if they're gone. Every time someone comes in here and walks out with anything, it's money walking out the door. And our creditors don't care. It's all blowing out from under us. We're wise men who didn't know we were building our house on shifting sand." This he says with the sweet smile he gets whenever he can take a clever twist on Scripture.

"So, wise man." I touch his face with the backs of my fingers, hoping to send comfort and assurance, seeing he is consumed with nervousness at what he is about to say. There would, after all, come a time when I would be dependent on such grace. "On what rock are you going to build?"

"No more building." He gathers up the stack of my father's papers and sets them aside, revealing to me a vast array of lists and numbers, and one particular clipped bundle of papers with neatly typed columns. "This is what Jim's been working on, this whole time. A complete inventory of everything we have. Down to the number of nails."

"Minus one set of gardening shears?" I ask.

"Exactly."

"And then what?"

He closes his eyes, gathering his thoughts, and blows out one long breath before opening them again. "I haven't been exactly honest with you, Nola."

I lean in, touch his arm, prepared to

forgive whatever he will say.

"There's been times, a few in the past weeks, when I haven't exactly been gone on church business. Not the whole time, anyway. I went to the school and used their mimeograph to make some copies, then into the library in Boise City to look up addresses . . ."

He speaks in snippets, making it hard for me to follow what he is confessing to, or how I should react.

"Russ, what are you saying, exactly?"

"I've been trying to find a buyer."

"For the store?" My resolve to forgive falters. "This is not your decision to make. Not alone. This belongs to us — my brother and me — left to us by our uncle. This belongs to my *family*."

"I am your family."

"Of course you are." Another touch, this time with a reassuring squeeze, to make up for the fact that twice today, in so many hours, I'd abandoned such loyalty. "I'm thinking more along the lines of the names on the papers. This all still belongs to Greg, doesn't it? Shouldn't he be the one to decide to sell?"

"It's just the inventory. I'm trying to find someone who will buy us out. Everything in one purchase. A reasonable price, too.

Enough to satisfy what's owed to us by our neighbors, and give us a little left to live on."

"And then?" As idyllic as the fantasy of setting up house with my reformed father in an apartment downstairs might be, even better is the idea of leaving Featherling altogether, free from this millstone. Away from gossipy women and whatever fodder I might generate for them to gossip about.

"And then, what?"

"Where do we go?"

"Go?" He looks genuinely confused. "Why, we don't go anywhere. There's still the church. I couldn't just leave. Now when so many people are hurting."

"Doesn't seem like anybody else is willing to do you the same courtesy."

"I'll stay until I'm called by God to do otherwise. That's what I signed up for when I became a minister. What if every preacher left his post because things got a little rough? These are my people. My family."

"I am your family." I try to match his tone.

"You're my wife. If I stay, we stay."

We are distracted then by the appearance of little Barney, clawing her way up Russ's pant leg. He winces at the digging of her tiny razorlike claws and plucks her off somewhere below his knee. "Care to explain this?"

"Ariel wanted her."

"Ah." It is enough. Our daughter rarely doesn't get what she's set her mind to, if it's within our means to grant it.

I pick up the typed list and run my fingers down the evidence of Jim's handiwork. Perfect, precise entries. "This is everything?"

"Everything."

"Have you found a buyer yet?"

"Not yet." He hesitates long enough for me to have my doubts.

"Would you tell me if you did?"

"Not yet."

I find the last shred of righteousness within me. "It isn't right that you didn't tell me. This place is more mine than yours."

"And when have you ever expressed the least interest in it?" His indulgent tone matches my petulance. "You resented having to mind the counter when you were in high school, remember? You hate this place. Always wanted to get away."

"Exactly." I take the kitten from him, indulge myself for a moment in her purrs, then set her on the counter to bat her paw at the pages before I turn to Russ, grabbing his hands to bolster my plea. "Which is why we shouldn't waste this opportunity to go.

Use whatever we get to start all over. Put this — all of this — behind us. Someplace exciting. Chicago, maybe? You've always wanted to study at the Moody Institute there. We could forget everything. Make a fresh start."

"Nola, darling. I don't have anything I want to forget. We haven't failed, and God hasn't failed us. This is just —" he shrugs and looks up for the proper word — "not even a setback. More like a set-aside. Buying some time, and a little cash. You know, my church salary isn't what it was, but I still need to be able to fully focus on those who remain here."

"How could you possibly do more than you are now? I already feel like I have to share you with every other family in town."

He tucks his knuckle under my chin and raises my face to look at him. "I told you that before we got married. When I first knew that I loved you, I said I was afraid there'd be a day when I would have to prioritize my loyalty. Divide my affection."

"And now?" I fight to keep my chin from quivering against his touch. "Have I lost?"

"Ah, sweetheart."

He kisses me soft, then deep as I cling to him, pulling him closer, wanting to meld ourselves together. Because I know, as much as I know anything, this could be our last kiss. He will taste my betrayal, pull away, and never touch me again. I move my body against his, diverting his attention, banking his passion in my favor. Finally, with ragged breath, and against my whimpering protest, he pulls away. His eyes are hooded with desire — a look I've come to know well after thirteen years of marriage. He loves me. With his body and his soul and his heart. He loves me, as I do him. Never more so than this moment. We regard each other, our breath in sync, each wishing we were somewhere — anywhere — else. He, upstairs in our bedroom. Me, back in my father's kitchen, so I could have a chance to walk away unscathed.

"Remember this moment," I say at last, punctuating my command with a soft kiss. When I draw back, he is smiling.

"I think I will. Should I lock the door? Close up the shop?"

"No." I swat his arm like a schoolgirl. "When the time comes — if the time comes — when you have to choose. Not between the church and me, but if you ever have to decide if you love me enough."

"Enough for what? Nola, what's happened?"

"Nothing." I answer too quickly and back

away, disturbing the papers on the counter and startling the kitten straight up into the air. "Nothing's happened, except you're here, with me. And the time might come when you'll have to wonder, *Do I love her? Really, truly love her?* Think about this moment and remember that you do."

The last of my words are guttural, salt-ridden, and wet with tears.

"My sweet Denola. I will remember this moment. I remember every single one."

■ ■ ■ ■

Part III

■ ■ ■ ■

I have sinned;
what shall I do unto thee,
O thou preserver of men?
why hast thou set me as a
mark against thee,
so that I am a burden to myself?
And why dost thou not pardon my
    transgression,
and take away my iniquity?
for now shall I sleep
in the dust;
and thou shalt seek me in the morning,
but I shall not be.

JOB 7:20-21

Chapter 12

It is more than a week before my father returns to the land of the living. In those days between, he was a lost-looking shadow of the man I knew, spending long hours in the rocker in the front room. Familiar, I suppose, because he has a chair like it back in his own home. We keep the radio on almost continuously, as it seems to soothe him. He joins us at the table for meals, eating a little more each day. And he drinks water, glass after glass, as he claws his way out of his own drought. This, more than anything, brings him back to us.

As Pa recovers upstairs, I make a home for him downstairs. I briefly consider getting him a small radio of his own, but I don't want him to feel like he's been imprisoned in some basement room. As he floats closer and closer to the surface of himself, he emerges a softer man than I've ever known. I credit my Ariel with much of this

197

reincarnation. She is constantly at his side, bringing him sips of water in her tiny teacups, singing him songs she's learned in Sunday school, and whispering in his ear how happy she is to see her paw-paw every day.

In the early days, he was confused, calling her Denola more often than not, but with a gentleness I'd never heard directed toward me. *"Denola, darlin' . . . ,"* at which my sweet girl would correct him, calling him *"silly Paw-Paw,"* and I would hush her, just so I could hear him say my name that way again.

Summer has descended, hot and dry. So much so there is no need to bring it up in conversation. We walk with our eyes averted, mostly in defense against the glaring sun, but also because it hurts to witness the despair in the faces of friends and neighbors. No need to ask, "How are you doing today?" because we know. We are hungry. We are thirsty. Every surface of our homes is lined with dust. The dirt wedges itself in our collars, forcing us to walk about the streets with dirty necks. We feel the grit against our gums and swallow mud with water.

On bad days — which are more common than not — children romp through the street with dampened handkerchiefs tied around their noses and mouths, looking like filthy little bandits in their games of tag and chase.

Five more families leave our fold, meaning one entire side of our church could be empty if we didn't choose to scatter ourselves about. The board on the wall to the left of the pulpit shows a decreasing number week after week, both in number of attendees and offering collected. Often the latter is half the former, and a mere percentage of Russ's former salary. I look at that display, white numbers on black cards, dutifully slid into place by a faithful deacon, and wonder how we are going to feed our family for the week.

Still, every Sunday morning, Russ looks out among us, now greeting each family — each *member* of each family — by name.

"So glad you're here, Mr. and Mrs. Anderson."

"Good morning, Ralphie! I see you've brought your parents with you this morning."

"Wonderful to see you, Mrs. Whitford. Is Mr. Whitford feeling any better this morning?"

I bother him about it at first, saying it robs him of the time he could spend delivering his sermon, but he counters that people want to feel welcomed. Needed. Loved. Nobody seems to mind that we release late — there is no place else to go. Nothing else to do. Moreover, the first Sunday after the personalized greetings, the offering went up $1.37 from the previous week.

We continue to gather after the storms too. No matter the time or duration, even though that means assembling for six days in a row at one point. At those times, Russ doesn't preach, really. We sing, though the onslaught of dust keeps our piano from being in perfect tune. Sometimes one of our few remaining choir members, Kay Lindstrom, stands alone and sings with a clear soprano voice that shines through, beautiful and sweet and clean.

One evening, after a storm that blew particularly thick and black, we gather — all of us dusty and worn, greeting one another with this strange sense of shame that plagues us. As is his habit, Russ greets each family at the door with a prayer of thanks for their deliverance. We look around, counting. I have Ariel and Ronnie by my side, and Pa, too, by this time, though only because Ariel insisted. As I hoped, his dependence upon us has brought forth a gentler man, as if he's forgotten a measure of his former anger.

A murmur comes up around us.

"The Harris family? Have you seen them? Aren't you neighbors?"

"Must be running late," I say, reassuring Merrilou Brown, who seems particularly concerned. "Rosalie has that baby, sometimes makes it tougher to get out of the house."

Cutting through the chatter, Kay walks silently to the front of the church, sending Russ back to sit with me, and she sings.

"Come, thou fount of every blessing,
tune my heart to sing thy grace;
streams of mercy, never ceasing,
call for songs of loudest praise."

It is a hymn that has become our favorite of late, Rosalie's especially, and the melody takes on a certain haunting quality that brings new urgency to my prayers.

On the third verse, Ben Harris walks in. Without Rosalie, without his son, both of whom, he says, were out looking for the family dog that had jumped their fence before the storm hit.

We all leap to our feet in one accord, poised to go find them, but he holds up his hand. They've been found already. By him, their mouths and lungs filled with dust. Drowned in it. And he's brought them home, carrying each the mere fifty yards from their back door.

The news strikes me dry. I tell myself to weep; my eyes sting with salt and grit, but there's nothing left to pour down my face. I've been slowly evaporating for weeks now, since Jim siphoned the first bit of my essence through his kiss. I picture my very blood as something grainy, pouring through my veins like sand in an elongated hourglass. And this moment stretches long enough for a lifetime.

Others, too, are similarly afflicted. Ben Harris, the man who has been alongside all of us in times of worship and praise and pain, stands in the doorway of our church, hat in hand, hair caked with Oklahoma soil, telling us of the discovery of his wife and child buried alive in the open air, and not a single tear is shed. Not on his part nor ours. We shuffle, we cough, until finally Merrilou Brown rises from her pew and goes to him. She, not much bigger than the boy he lost, opens her arms, and Ben Harris — a looming bear of a man — collapses within them, heaving great, dry sobs.

Pa catches my eye above Ariel's curls and motions for us to leave.

"We can't," I whisper, though I don't know if I'll be able to stand the display. "Russ is the *pastor.*"

"Well, the kids don't need to see this." Pa

stands and scoops Ariel up with him. I look to Russ for his blessing, which he gives, silently, and usher Ronnie out of the pew.

Others are leaving too, offering raspy condolences as they pass by. I stop long enough to put one hand on Merrilou Brown's shoulder, the other on Ben's, and whisper a brief "May Jesus grant you peace" before joining my father and my children on the church house steps.

Once we are back home, I tell Ronnie to help his sister strip down the beds and put on fresh sheets. Even ours and Pa's downstairs. These days the clean linens are wrapped tight in oilcloth in a trunk wedged into the bathroom closet. Sometimes, I think, I can put up with all matter of dirt and dust as long as I have the promise of a clean bed at night. It soothes my conscience, almost, to think I can give Russ at least that much.

And there'll have to be some supper too. Our regular mealtimes have been disrupted by both the unpredictability of the storms and the constant struggle to find food for the table. The local grocer has become more of a general store, with sparse dry goods and erratic stock. Rice, canned fruit, crackers, coffee. Flour and sugar, too, but all at a price that would have been unimaginably high only a few years ago. We still have a bakery, and can depend on good, fresh bread every day, but no longer are there tall cakes with swirled icing in the front window to tempt the passerby.

With the children occupied, I set about putting a meal together, the first step being to run a sink of soapy water to wash whatever dishes we'll use. To my utter surprise, Pa comes to stand beside me, and as I pass the first clean plate out of the rinse water, he takes it from me to dry.

"Well, thank you," I say, not wanting to ruin the miracle of this moment with unnecessary commentary. I've watched him grow in appreciation for running water, but this is the first I've seen him use it for any practical chore.

"Did you know that woman? The one that died."

I run my dishrag along another plate, wanting to keep my friendship to myself for a little longer, but unable to resist a civil moment with my father. "We were friends, yes. She was a bit younger than me. Used to set my hair." I have no idea what Pa could gain from these details, but they mean everything to me. She was still in high school when Russ and I married, and grew into her own not knowing enough to shun me. "She always brought a macaroni salad to potluck suppers. Some of the women teased her about it once, and hurt her feelings, I guess. Maybe that's all she knew to make."

"And the boy?"

"Nice boy. In between Ariel and Ronnie. Eight, maybe? And there's a baby girl, too."

Pa stacks the clean plates carefully. "I like macaroni salad."

"I'll make it for you sometime."

We continue until there are four clean plates, four clean glasses, and two pots ready for the stove. I open the cabinet to find two cans of lima beans, and I have some bacon in the icebox. With that, and some rice, I figure I can stretch the meal with just one can of beans. Save the other for a meal later in the week — long enough away so the kids won't complain. Already I set my mind to not be hungry.

"They the first ones, then?"

"First ones, what?" I take the cloth off of the table and wipe the wood surface beneath.

"First killed by it."

"Oh, I don't know." But I do know, and they aren't. Maybe the first in our little town, first from our church family, but I'd read reports in the newspapers from all over. People lost, buried, electrocuted, burned to ashes in their own homes. "Now you can see, can't you, Pa? Why we didn't want you left alone out at your place. We need to stick together. Families, I mean. We need to keep track of one another, or it's too easy to get . . . lost."

"I reckon." He picks up a glass and holds it up to the window. "This glass clean?"

I sigh but decide not to remind him that he himself has cleaned it. "Yes, Pa."

He fills it with water from the tap, dumps the water out, refills it, then goes to sit at the table. "That man still at my house?"

I measure rice and water. A few pinches of salt, and light the burner. "I suppose so. Don't know for sure."

"Don't think he's out there robbin' me blind, do ya?"

"I'm sure he's not, Pa. He's more of a drifter than a thief. I think he'll keep a good eye on the place until we decide what to do." I am talking fast, bustling between the stove and the sink and the icebox — a well-practiced habit, creating the illusion that our meal is somehow time-consuming and complicated. Most days I was just trying to make the meal itself seem *more*. But this evening, my shuffling serves as a shield, protecting me from the questions and thoughts I've done such a good job of hiding these past weeks.

"What's to decide?"

I glance over my shoulder as I dice the bacon. "Oh, now, Pa. You know. It's only a matter of time before —"

"Shoulda left me out there." He takes a long swallow of his water and sets the glass down with a shaking hand. "Man oughta die on his land. With his land."

I don't know why the thought hasn't occurred to me before, but suddenly I recall my father sitting — like he is now — at his own table, covered in dirt, dust drifted through open windows. He hadn't been caught unaware. Not at all. He'd been burying himself, one breath at a time.

"You shouldn't say such things." I make no interruption in my task.

"Don't get me wrong, girl. I'm grateful for what you done, bringin' me here, takin' me in. But I don't belong in town. Never have. That was for my brother, and yours, I guess. I need to go back, pay for what I done."

I am about to open up the drawer to paw through, looking for the key to open the can of beans, but I stop. Instead, I take Pa's glass, refill it, and join him at the table.

"We talked about this, Pa. A few times.

There's no going back. No money to be made there now, not until this dryness breaks. And then it might take years."

"My house still standin'?"

"Far as I know."

"I know you been out there."

"Just the once." I wish I had kept to my supper preparations, because my father's eyes bore into me — suspicious, steely gray drill bits.

"And not since?"

"No." I speak too quickly, too loudly, to ease my father's mind.

"You sure about that?"

"Pa, I've been *here* every day; you know that. Taking care of you, and the house, and the kids."

"You been known to sneak off before, if I remember."

"Oh, you remember. I was a kid, Pa."

"Seems you thought you was woman enough."

"Well, now I've had enough of this." I back my chair away from the table and return to my stove top, lighting a second burner and slamming a pan on top of it, throwing in handfuls of the diced bacon.

"We need to be mindful of what our sin brings back to haunt us, Denola Grace."

Pa only uses my full name in times of

extreme anger, or extreme tenderness, and as far as I know, this moment calls for neither. Now his words come as a distinct, unprecedented omen, and they compel me to turn and face him.

"What are you talking about, Pa?"

"We sinned against this land, all of us. Just like your brother says. All that — what do they call it — the science? Mowin' down the grasses. Harvestin' too much. We got greedy, and God has humbled us. It's his judgment."

"I don't think —"

"Just you listen."

He stands and comes closer, lowering his voice at the sound of Ronnie and Ariel clomping up the stairs. They burst in holding the kitten, with Ariel asking if she can give her a bath in the sink since she is so dusty. I tell her no, that kittens have a way of cleaning themselves, but when Ronnie promises he'll help his sister be gentle, I send them off to try. I hoped the interruption would derail my father's thoughts, but no. He only leans closer, so close I can smell the dust that still clings to his breath. That's when I realize Pa hasn't lost a mite of his anger. It's been shifted, is all. Gathered and honed and sharpened to slice me with new precision.

"Your head ain't here, girl. You never been a-one to own up to your sin. So pretty and proud marryin' that man, all that shame you was carryin'. And you been takin' everything. Pilin' it up. That store, most of all. Our family store, down to nothin'."

"Haven't you noticed, Pa? The whole country's down to nothing."

"The judgment, I say. For our sin. But yours'll hit closer, girl. I knew when you started runnin' around with that boy, what you wanted was to run away. Didn't want none of this."

"Why would I? I was smart, Pa. I *am* smart, and I could've done anything I wanted. Greg said so. Said there were lots of girls at college, but you wouldn't have any of it. Had to beg you to let me finish high school."

"You almost ruined that yourself with that baby."

"Don't," I warn.

"You thought that preacher boy would take you away, didn't you? Run off with you somewheres to spare his name? And when he didn't . . ." He contorts his bone-thin frame, forcing me to look at him. "You got that cagey look. Like you do right now, and since I come here. Like you want to get away."

"It's because I want to get away from *you.*"

"Git on then." A drop of spittle flies from his mouth, and I regret every drink I ever gave him.

It is a short, silent dinner. The few grains of rice I manage to swallow stick like glue in my throat. Later, in bed, I ask Russ how much he heard.

"Just that you want to get away."

I prop up on my elbow and study his profile in shadow. "It's not true, you know. At least not away from you."

"Well, there's some comfort, at least."

"It was a mistake. Bringing him here. I thought it would be fine. That he'd changed, gone softer. But now it's almost worse, because he'll be sweet enough one moment, and a snake the next, and there's no knowing which is going to come out."

"What choice did we have?" He shifts too, and we are parallel. "And when you look at what happened today. Dear, sweet Rosalie, and the boy. I'm so sorry about your friend." He reaches out and grasps my arm. "But don't you see? That could have happened to him."

"I think that might be what he wanted all along."

"Well then —" he gives me a familiar, perfunctory kiss — "all the more reason to make this his home now."

He lies back, preparing to sleep, but I stay awake long into the night. Thinking about Rosalie. Not reliving memories of our friendship or mourning on behalf of her husband and little girl. I don't even think about the boy, whose name and age escapes me. When I think about Rosalie, all I can picture is a woman leaving. Away from her house, only for a moment, and never making it back again.

Chapter 13

I awake the next morning to a gentle nudging of my shoulder. A glimpse toward the window tells me the sun is high — higher than it should be for newly waking. When my eyes finally, fully open, I see Russ sitting on the edge of the bed, looking at me, bemused.

"You were talking up a storm." He traces a finger along my jaw as if to recapture my words.

"Was I?" My mind searches frantically for the dream that dissipated upon awaking. I am usually much more careful with unguarded moments. More than once — nearly every day, in fact — I find myself standing at some abandoned task. I've scorched three shirts, letting the iron burn through cotton. I get light-headed, dizzy, and Russ pesters me to eat something. Only once before can I remember Jim entering my dream, and that morning I woke up entwined in Russ's compliant arms. My silence has been my protection, wrapping itself around the details of my sin. But unguarded? From the depths of sleep? Perhaps this is how my soul will unburden itself.

"What was I saying?"

"Gibberish, mostly. But kind of moanful. You sounded sad."

While I may not be able to recall my dreams, I do remember every moment of wakefulness, and those hours in the dark haunt me more than any nightmare could.

"It was a sad night."

"True." He leans down and kisses my forehead. The smell of his shaving soap fills my senses, and as I touch my cheek to his soft-shaven face, fragments of the dream return.

"I was dreaming about her." My mouth is dry, my words thick. Already a slow-spreading ache manifests itself beneath my scalp.

"Rosalie?"

"Yes."

His face takes on a cool, careful expression, and he shifts his weight away from me to slip his foot into a boot. "I'm taking Ben in to Boise City to break the news to her parents."

"They don't know?"

"He wanted to tell them in person. We're going to have the funeral tomorrow."

"So soon?"

"There's no other family to bring in besides them. If we get a dust-free day, best not to waste it."

"I suppose." But I hate the thought of her being so quickly buried again. "I don't remember much, but I dreamed they found her. No, *you* found her. And cleaned her up. And she was alive."

"Well, that doesn't sound like a sad dream at all." His boots are on, and he is mine again.

"I guess it's sad because it isn't so."

"She's with the Lord now. She and her boy, clean and white as snow."

"Wouldn't that be nice?" I sit up, first propped on my elbows, then fully, bringing myself close enough to put my head on his shoulder. Looking down, I see a familiar shadow on the pillowcase where I'd been resting. It happens about every night, no matter how clean the linens or how carefully I wash my hair. Embarrassed to have Russ notice, I flip the pillow over and lean against it on my elbow. "What time is it, anyway?"

"Almost ten."

Disgruntled, I push against him. "Move, and let me up. Pa'll be having a fit for his breakfast."

"Already took care of that." Russ stands, and that's when I notice he is wearing his nicest suit pants. "Mrs. Brown brought over some rolls and sausage. Said to ask you if you'd be up to helping the women get the Harrises' house in order. Cleaned up, for after the service tomorrow."

"I suppose." Though nothing could be more unpleasant. "Is there any breakfast left?"

"Only because I saved some for you." He indicates a napkin-covered plate while tying his tie. "Now —" he bends to plant another kiss on top of my head; I remember the stain on my pillow, and fight to keep myself still beneath it — "I'll leave you to your breakfast, m'lady. And I shall strive to be home by supper."

"I should see to Pa and the kids."

"They're fine. Listening to the radio and wiping down dishes."

"Even Pa?"

"I think — I *know* — he said some hurtful things to you last night."

"Nothing more than usual."

"But I think he wants peace. He's more frightened than anything. Everything he's ever known about life is coming to an end — blowing away — and he doesn't know his place anymore. Let's be patient. Humbling is a painful process."

Even as he speaks, I feel some of my own pain smooth away. Russ has always been quick to forgive my father for his cutting remarks and hateful spirit. He makes grace sound so easy, almost painless, and it gives me hope that he will extend the same to me. When it's time. When the heat of my father's accusations has once again cooled. When we don't have to think about burying a young mother killed by God's wrath upon our land.

"Remember this," he says, taking my hand. "I love you. I have since the moment I saw you, and nothing he's said has ever been able to touch that."

"But he's right. He knows —"

"Your father has never seen the girl I fell in love with."

I smile weakly. "Maybe you've never seen the girl *he* knows."

Russ kisses my fingers. "Maybe not, but I'm glad for it. If I have to suffer a kind of blindness, I'd rather suffer with the one God gave me. I know this might be hard for you, but as long as he is here, try to see yourself through my eyes instead of his. Love your-

217

self the way I love you, the way *God* loves you."

He can't imagine how hard that is for me to do. I've always taken Russ's love for me as fact, like knowing the ground will be beneath my feet when I stand. It is knowledge that has thrived without faith, never tested. And now, with threats coming from two directions, I wonder if it is strong enough. Complete enough. It's always been around me, keeping me safe, but I don't know if I've let it infuse me — as if I've kept myself too full of shame to feel anything else.

"I'll try," I say, hoping to appease him.

He kisses my fingers, and I offer a delicate wave as he leaves. For a full minute, at least, I stare at the door that has shut behind him. Then, slowly, like a woman three times my age, I bring myself out of bed and take the few steps over to where my breakfast waits. I reach for the coffee, hoping the first sip will help alleviate the pain in my head. It is warm, but not steaming, and I end up gulping half the cup before setting it down. I pinch a bite of the sausage, realizing long before I taste it that it has gone cold. But it is good, and palatable, especially when wrapped in a piece of the sweet yeast roll. Still, after less than half of it, my stomach cramps, refusing any more.

Later that afternoon, I work with a small army of women doing service for the Lord by cleaning Rosalie's house. Our sacrifice is to scrub every surface, making it cleaner than our own homes. Buckets of mud-dark water are dumped into the street, and rather than wash the curtains and cloths that Rosalie had so carefully draped over her furniture, we contribute our own — those that languish in hampers and trunks, as well as others taken and laundered from homes long abandoned.

All around me, women chatter the way women will, about how the poor man will manage all alone with the baby, and that it might be best if he remarries quickly, so the littl'un will grow up knowing a mother. Soon follows a listing of suitable candidates to be the next Mrs. Harris. These musings come with the same authority and confidence as how to best scrub the stain from the porcelain sink, and the benefits of an electric sweeper over beating a rug on a clothesline outside.

I hear little of it and contribute even less. My mind is miles away from the tragic young widower and his motherless child. I resent the fact that my own house is filthy, and I walked out of it this morning to the sound of my father's complaint. Every inch of me is covered by the filth of his hateful words. Always has been.

I remember going to Jesus, believing — *knowing* — he could make me clean. I'd pray a confession about a boy I'd kissed, or a man I'd flirted with. I'd close my eyes and pray, asking forgiveness whenever I winked at a ranch hand or let some schoolmate take liberties with me behind the bleachers. And I'd feel better, for a time. Then Pa would give me a look. He'd sneer and sniff, ask pestering questions about where I'd been so late at night, even if I was at the library. I'd learned in Sunday school that God is faithful and just to forgive our sins. I can still recite the verse, 1 John 1:9: "If we confess our sins, he is faithful and just to forgive us our sins, and to cleanse us from all unrighteousness." But it was hard to feel clean whenever Pa looked at me like that. He always said nothing was a truth unless two people saw it. Even if I saw myself as clean, he never would, so I couldn't believe it to be so. I always felt dirty, and Pa made me believe that I was. And here I am, bringing up all of those old, buried stains again.

Should've been me instead of poor Rosalie Harris, and Jim in the place of her boy.

If God has to take two lives, if that's the sacrifice it takes for him to lift the curse Pa claims this to be, why take such innocents? Why not the two of us, lashed back-to-back with sin?

Russ is a good man — a handsome man too, far more than moonfaced Ben. Every woman named as a candidate to be the next Mrs. Harris would likely jump at the chance to be the next Mrs. Merrill. And any woman alive would be a better mother. Seems like I've been going about it wrong since the beginning. There wasn't any planning in the first child. Not even a marriage when Ronnie was at his tiniest. Then losing one baby, and the next, made me wonder if God ever meant for me to be a mother at all. Like he kept taking them away, hoping I'd leave the idea alone. Which I do, for stretches of time, until the instinct comes on in a rush. I look at my children sometimes and remind myself, *These are mine,* and I feel equal parts frightened and reassured.

I stand useless at the kitchen sink where I've had my hair shampooed countless times. The thought of it puts me in a familiar state of reverie, to be interrupted by the appearance of Merrilou Brown.

"You're awfully quiet this afternoon, Denola. That little kitten got your tongue?"

My smile is tight-lipped at first, keeping guard over my mouth until I can conjure the perfect reply. "I don't think anybody who's been to my house would cherish my advice on how best to keep it."

This seems to satisfy her, and she climbs back onto her stool to wipe down the shelving paper on the kitchen cabinets, leaving me to wonder how she knows we've acquired a kitten. Little Barney has never been allowed outside, and Mrs. Brown has never been invited upstairs. The thought gnaws at me so, I stand beside her, the two of us eye level for once.

"You've seen our kitten?"

"Oh, not exactly." She hands me the damp cloth and, without being asked, I wipe the upper shelf. "But my little Luther has gotten to barkin' when we walk past."

"Smart dog."

She smiles and touches the tip of her nose. "Between his nose and this one? Not much happens in this place that I don't know about."

I begin to hand Merrilou the newly washed dishes to place back in the cabinet, and she furrows her brow. "We're going to need more plates. This poor woman didn't have but six, and none of them matching." She turns to me. "Seems like you're always gathering them up at the tag sales."

She's right; I am. Though most of them have been handed off to my father after our Sunday suppers. For all I know they're stacked two feet high under his kitchen sink, but the very thought of that sink, and the last time I was there, and Jim's touch, his kiss —

"I'll see what I have," I say, thankful for an excuse to leave.

"Yes, go!" Merrilou is shooing me now, her entire face crinkled in concern. "You look like you need to get some air. The smell of Lysol gets to me that way too, sometimes."

Muttering good-byes and apologies, I stumble from the overcrowded, overclean little house and out into what was once a neat, tidy, postage-stamp-size yard. I remember the sounds of Rosalie's son playing outside while I waited for my curls to set. Like a vivid dream I can see him, a towheaded boy playing on a bright-green patch of grass under a perfect blue sky in front of his pristine white house. Now, looking up and down the street, everything is the same shade of dull brown. As if the entire neighborhood has been covered with a giant sheet of dirty canvas. Only the sky retains its hue, and I suppose that should be our sign of hope, except a clear sky means no rain, and we all are in desperate need of its cleansing.

The walk from the Harris home to ours takes me past the church, where I know another team of women is wiping down the pews and sweeping the floors in preparation for tomorrow's service. I would much rather have been a part of that contingent, but Russ told me long ago that it makes people uncomfortable to see the pastor's wife thus employed.

"You should have higher responsibilities," he'd said. Leading Bible study, or prayer circles, or teaching the children. But I've never done any of that. In our earliest married days, the women who were my elders would have burned the church to the ground before allowing me anywhere near such sacred endeavors, and in the years since, I've grown complacent with my diminished role. They love Russ; they tolerate me.

Behind the church is our small cemetery — one hundred or so markers surrounded by a short, iron fence. Often I wish we'd buried my mother here, if only to give me a slab of stone to talk to on those stretches of long, friendless days. When she died, of course, we had no idea my life would be in the little town of Featherling. I don't even remember knowing about the town's existence, it being one of those settlements that sprang up with the cost of wheat after the war.

Right inside the swinging gate, at the end of a winding stone path now obscured with dust, three stone benches and a trellis wall define the children's corner. All of our infants, in tiny graves marked by simple crosses. I have two of them in there myself, each with its own tiny cross. There was a time when the trellises surrounding the children's corner were sweet with roses and strong climbing vines. Before Ariel came along, I would leave Ronnie to the attentions of his father and come here to sit in the sweet-smelling shade and beg my babies' forgiveness for denying them life. I prayed to God for one more chance, one more child, and I'd not ask for another — a promise I never shared with Russ. He wouldn't approve.

"Faith is not a bargain," he'd say. Or, *"God wants our prayers, not our promises."*

But I'd given God both, and he gave me our daughter. I haven't made a single promise since.

A canvas tent is pitched on the far north side, a sign that a fresh grave waits beneath, lest anyone accidentally stumble in. I shield my eyes against the brightness of the afternoon and notice a flurry of activity. My son is in the midst of it, along with a gaggle of boys from our congregation. What I witness, however, is not play. Instead, they move with an organized sense of purpose, an almost militaristic precision beyond their years.

Besides the relentless onslaught of dirt, the winds have brought legions of tumbleweeds into play. Dozens have ended their journey here, laying themselves to rest against the stone markers throughout the field, a perversion of the withered bouquets. A couple of the younger boys, probably the same age as the one who will be laid to rest here tomorrow, work to dislodge and carry them to where they've been aligned — piled up to make an unsightly, prickly wall along the far side of the cemetery fence. The boys, like Ronnie, wear their fathers' oversize work gloves, and those too little to carry the bigger weeds roll them with all the solemn purpose of executioners. At the fence, a few work to contain the tumbleweeds in a somewhat-straight line. Others hack away at the dry ground, leaving a line of overturned earth between the weeds and the equally brown, dry grass.

I might not have recognized Ronnie right

away if not for the way the sunlight brings out the peculiar tint of his hair. Dark like mine, but with the tint of Merrill cinnamon from his father. His face, like those of the other boys, is obscured by a white kerchief, and I can picture his eyes furrowed in concentration above it. My little man, the man Rosalie's son will never grow to be. Never before have I felt such an intertwining of guilt and pride and fear.

The biggest boy, Clarence Wallis, I know only from following Russ's disapproving glare nearly every Sunday morning. The undeniable leader in labor and mischief, his muffled voice carries as he orders the boys to drench the earth with water from the dozen buckets — carried from who knows where — waiting on the side. They obey, adjusting their sloshing at his intermittent instruction. Then, after the boys take a single, collective step away, my Ronnie strikes a match, touches it to a long-handled torch, and hands the torch to Clarence, who in turn ignites the first of the tumbleweeds along the fence.

I hear the crackle of the fire before I see the flame. On either side, two boys stand holding between them a blanket, heavy and dark with water, meant to be a deterrent should the flames decide to jump the muddy path and devour the dry grasses that protect our dead.

My throat burns with warning. He is but a child, after all. They all are. And my eyes burn with tears — not from the acrid tendrils of smoke beginning to drift my way, but from the thought of our children being given over to such a task.

A slight shift in the wind lifts the corner of my skirt, and I bat it down, mindful of how such a little thing could pick up the smallest spark. I know the fire is louder at its source, and my words will never carry. Still, I cup my hands around my mouth to shout, "Be careful, boys!"

It captures Ronnie's attention, and he lifts his arm to wave.

I wave back, shouting again, "Be careful!"

He sends back a gesture of assurance before returning his attention to the growing fire, and I know I've been dismissed.

Back home, Russ has a sign in the shop window: *CLOSED DUE TO DEATH IN THE FAMILY.* I know that's how he feels. Every soul who ever sat in our pews is as important to him as his own people. Perhaps because he has no more than a few cousins scattered around the panhandle to call his own, and I haven't given him much more.

Wearily, I climb the steps up to our apartment and open the door. A thin wall of music greets me, followed by Ariel, wild curls flying, bounding into my arms.

"Paw-Paw made a toy for Barney!" She brandishes a long, thin twig with a length of string tied at one end. From it dangles a jumble of frayed scraps of cloth. "Watch!" She whips it like a wagon master, bringing the kitten to perform all manner of acrobatics in an attempt to capture the elusive prey. "Paw-Paw says this is how she'll learn to hunt."

"Indeed." I look around the room. "Where is your paw-paw?"

She remains absorbed in the kitten's antics. "Downstairs. He says that's where he lives now. And that's where he's a-stayin'."

"And he left you up here all alone?"

"No. I was playing in the store and saw you through the window. Didn't you see me? I waved." Her words hold no hurt or accusation, and I accept my shortcoming and move on.

"Did he fix you any lunch?"

"No."

"Are you hungry?"

"Yes."

"Run downstairs and ask if he's hungry too."

"But I'm playing."

"Take Barney with you."

Satisfied, she picks up the kitten and tucks it against her side. I search the cabinets and icebox for something small and suitable. We have a few slices of baloney, and in the bread box, half a dozen of Merrilou Brown's yeast rolls. Both would be best saved for supper, especially if I fry up the baloney with eggs. For lunch, a can of soup — cream of celery, Pa's favorite — and a stack of buttered crackers. I open the can, dump the contents in my smaller saucepan, add water, and stir, nibbling on a single cracker throughout each step.

I suppose the thought has been niggling at the corner of my mind since Merrilou voiced it, but when I open my cabinet to take out two shallow bowls, it hits me again.

"Plates." I speak the word aloud, giving it legitimacy.

I bring a spoonful of soup to touch my bottom lip, testing its warmth. Satisfied, I add a bit of precious cream and a dash of black pepper before pouring it, steaming, into the bowls and calling Pa and Ariel up for lunch. They appear together, a most unlikely pairing, but her presence at his side softens my heart. It is the first my father and I have seen of each other since yesterday's ugliness, and if nothing else, my baby girl serves as a buffer against any repeat of the conversation.

"Lunch is on." I accompany my announcement with a grand gesture.

"You eating?" Pa seems almost concerned.

"I've already had mine. You two eat up, I have a short errand to run."

Before there can be any questions, I go back into our bedroom and shut the door. No, I change my plan and dash across the hall into the bathroom. Bending over the sink, I ruthlessly run a brush through my hair, attacking it from all angles, and shake my head for good measure, hoping to dislodge any particle of dirt that might be clinging there. The resulting dust proves my efforts fruitful, and when I stand straight again, the wild mass of dark waves makes me look every bit the savage my father claims me to be. Running warm water in the sink, I wash my face, rinse it, and wash again, scrubbing until I've coaxed a bit of pink into my cheeks. Instead of drying my hands, I run them damp through my hair, smoothing it into a gentler version of itself. The calm visage of the woman in the mirror does not match the woman whose hands clutch at the basin.

"You need the plates," I say to her, and

she speaks back to me. *"You need the plates."*

In my bedroom I strip off my apron, only to discover my housedress bears the telltale scorchings of my ineptitude. With shaking fingers, I unbutton it, let it drop to the floor, and toss it into the hamper with the apron. From experience I know I have a ring of dirt around the back of my neck, as well as at that place where my collar meets my throat, so it's back across to the bathroom, back to the sink. More water, more soap. This time, something with a sweeter scent, and a dusting of powder to follow.

Aricl calls out as I am midstep in the hallway. "Are you all right, Mama?"

"Yes, baby." I step through my bedroom door. "Just washing up."

From my closet I pull a clean, pressed dress. Just a housedress, its fabric soft and thin from years of laundering. It wraps around my body with a sash that ties at the waist. A dab of cream from my pretty pink jar brings life to the dullness of my skin, and after a moment's hesitation, I sit at my mirror to apply color to my lips, then my cheeks. For balance, I lick the tip of my pencil and trace it lightly around my eyes.

I grab a handbag, pull a hat on — low — take a deep breath, and attempt a sprint past the kitchen and out the door, breezing a promise to be back soon.

"Where you goin'?" Pa's question reins me back.

I don't turn around. "An errand. Something we need for tomorrow."

"What do you need, 'xactly?"

My hand grips the door in defiance. How can he possibly know? "It's nothing for you to worry about, Pa."

"Take the girl with you. I didn't sign on to be a nanny here."

Now I do turn around, and Ariel's face lights up. "You look pretty, Mama."

Pa's eyes narrow. "Maybe she should get herself dolled up too."

"I won't be long. If you don't mind, wash up the dishes? Then Ariel can lie down for a rest. No problem at all. I should be back —" I glance at the clock, but the face blurs, senseless. "I will be back. Probably not more than an hour."

That would serve as my promise to return, even if the timing is a gross exaggeration. If I told Pa the truth, he'd guess my destination. For now I can fool myself into thinking I've fooled him.

Outside, I run down our steps, fearing somehow the force of my father's suspicions might yank me back like the wobbling mass at the end of the string on Barney's toy.

Truth be told, I almost wish he would. I even slow my steps near the bottom, but nothing arises to impede my journey. Even Russ grants silent permission, having driven Ben's car into Boise City, leaving ours parked in the alley at my disposal.

At the first turn, I see Ronnie walking away from a smoldering train of ashes. His face is black with smoke and half covered with the mask. He might be fresh from doing a man's job, but he looks like a tired, hungry little boy — one who is about to track insurmountable dirt and soot on my floor.

I should stop the car, turn around, and go home. Make him strip in the shop and come upstairs straight to the shower while I make him a baloney sandwich on one of Merrilou's fresh yeast rolls. It's what Rosalie would have done — what any mother would do. At the corner I slow down, lower the window, and raise my hand to beckon him to me. The breeze fills the car with the scent of my perfume, mingling with the pungent odor of the burning weeds, and one desire trumps another.

With a wave, I shout the ingredients for lunch and orders for bathing. Then, with my window once again sealed against the smoke, I drive on.

CHAPTER 14

Once, months before, when we all lived with a lingering hope of rain and life, Pa showed up for Sunday dinner thirty minutes earlier than usual. He left at the same time. Drove at the same speed, but said it was the darndest thing. He couldn't remember a bit of the drive. Said he set his mind to get where he was going, and just went. Didn't recall a lick of the road.

I remember worrying, then. Sending him home with his plate of leftover food, watching his every step from the front window like I was the mother rather than the child.

"He's getting old," I told Russ. "It's dangerous, having him out on the roads like that."

Russ put a comforting arm across my shoulder as we watched. "He's fine. It happens. Used to happen to me all the time driving back and forth from school to visit you."

I'd leaned myself back against him, not only feeling safe, but somehow thinking that my safety would cover my father, too.

This afternoon, as the dust rolls behind me on the drive to Pa's house, I don't feel safe at all. I sit ramrod straight in the seat, hands gripping the wheel, my head filled with a fuzzy image of my mission. The plates, at least two dozen of them, stacked and irregular. A noble mission, to feed our church family as they gather around these wounded souls. I don't consider my actions as anything but innocent and noble. And if I encounter Jim, what better opportunity to let him know that what transpired between us the last time I visited must never happen again.

If I encounter him.

The deepest part of my mind wrestles with the possibility that he might have left. That's what drifters do, isn't it? Over and over since that afternoon, I've imagined the scenario wherein he delves into his belongings, looking for the photograph, only to find it missing. And he would know. The missing picture speaks of my intentions more powerfully than I could ever hope to.

"Go away."

"You shouldn't have come."

Still, in case there is any doubt, I want to

give him that message myself. So he can look at me, straight in the eye, and know. I pray that God will give me the strength to tell him.

The car barrels along, seemingly on its own power. No, not its own. Mine, but nothing of my feet or hands. Something at the core of me compels it forward. Like I could let go, close my eyes, and safely arrive at my father's house.

Slowing at the gate to his property, it seems like such a phenomenon has taken place. As I get out of the car to open the gate, a gust of wind comes on strong enough to nearly knock me off balance. But the sky is cloudless and clear in all directions. Once I've driven to the other side, I get out again to close and latch the gate behind me. No reason. Stalling, I suppose. Or forcing myself to carry through with my errand.

On the slow drive up to the house, I rehearse everything I want to say. About the funeral and the supper and the plates. If I say only that and nothing more, I will escape.

Pa's truck is still there, though it looks like it has been moved. The sight of it brings a new knot to my stomach. He is here, unless he left without the truck. But the upstairs windows are open, as is the front door, and I wrestle with the conundrum of whether or not I will knock on what used to be my own screen door.

Turns out I don't have to worry about such a thing, because the sound of the car's engine brings him out from behind the house. I go cold at this sight of him, the kind of burning cold that happens when you hold a piece of ice too long. He is shirtless, his skin burned browner than I would have imagined, testifying to the hours he must have spent out here in thankless toil. It is the first opportunity I have to get any kind of look at the true nature of his injury. I've not let myself dwell on the matter of his amputation, seeing as he never has. Never have I felt pity, or revulsion, or anything beyond curiosity. Now I see his forearm tapered, the mass of scarring at its end. The bicep above is as full and defined as that of his other arm, a testament to his strength, I suppose.

The way he looks at me, almost in challenge, frightens me, and I look away. I stare at the hands in my lap — *my* hands, though I feel no connection to them.

What am I doing here?

And then, my father's voice. *"What are you doin' here, girl?"*

A knock on the car window makes me

jump clear out of my skin. Daring to look, I see that he has put on a shirt, and that it is mostly buttoned and tucked in. He backs away, allowing room for me to open the door. He leans against the car, as if his weight alone can keep me there. "I didn't think I'd see you again."

"But you stayed."

"Nowhere else to go."

I notice little things. Touches of paint, a new screen on the door, clean windows. "And you've been working?"

He shrugs. "Nothing else to do. Come inside."

"I can't stay."

"Can't stay?" He tilts his head back, a smile spreading on his face as if he's preparing to laugh at what I'll say next. "Why are you here if you can't stay?"

"I didn't come to see you." Even as I speak, my words sound weak. "I came to get something. Some things, actually. From the kitchen."

"From the kitchen?"

"Yes."

"Then —" he stretches his arm toward the porch — "you'll need to come inside."

He turns and I follow, wordlessly, up the porch steps. Inside the front room, I notice the windows lined with twisted towels along the sills, remnants of protection from the previous storm based on the traces of dirt I can see in their folds. Once we reach the middle of the room, he invites me to sit, but I keep my ground, repeating again, "I can't stay."

"Why are you here, Nola?"

He says my name as if he has a right to it. I watch his throat because I dare not look at his face. His mouth.

"What happened last time," I say, not able to give it a name, "it can't happen again."

"Then you shouldn't have come."

I drag my eyes to meet his. "I need something."

"What do you need, Nola?" His meaning is inescapable. More than teasing, his voice carries treacherous flirtation, and I feel myself mired as if in a dream, unable to speak back to it. The scrubbed floors hold my feet, the soles of my shoes melted to it. My legs too heavy to run, my arms too heavy to lift, and my own reply so lodged in tempestuous desire I cannot trust my mouth to open.

"Plates." I speak the word without loosening my tongue.

His body relaxes in humor. "Plates?"

I nod tersely and charge past him, feeling him follow. I go to the first cabinet and pull it open, saying, "Are these clean?"

"Yep." He is behind me. "Anything special you're looking for? Because I washed so many dishes here I felt like I was back working in the university cafeteria."

"Plates," I repeat, realizing how simple-minded I must sound. "Stacks of them, from when I sent Pa home with Sunday suppers."

"Ah. *Those.*" He moves to the butcher-block table on the other side of the icebox. A curtain has been affixed to its edge, creating a hidden space beneath. This he pushes aside and pulls forth a wooden crate packed with straw, a myriad of colors and patterns poking through. "I kept findin' this stuff everywhere. Some was too far past cleanin', so I had to toss 'em. But there's near forty here." With surprisingly little effort, he hoists the crate onto the table. "Want me to carry it out to your car?"

"That would be fine." I fiddle with the sash of my dress, surprised to find my errand so soon ended. I need only take one step. Instead, "And then I think it would be best if you go."

He leans his elbow on the crate and looks at me. "Go where?"

"Wherever you want. You're obviously strong. You can work. My brother's been telling me about a new opportunity, a chance to help —"

"I don't care what your brother says, Nola."

He is coming closer, moving with as much of a stride as the limited space of the kitchen will allow. If I don't move, I'll be trapped. I don't move. Not much, anyway, just one panicked step to the left, and he stops.

"I shouldn't have come here."

"But you did. For a bunch of mismatched dishes." His gaze challenges me.

"There's a funeral tomorrow."

Instantly he softens, taking the final step to bring him close enough to touch. Yet he doesn't. "It's not your father, is it?"

"Oh, no." Nerves, and a dutiful sense of relief, bring a weird bit of laughter to my reply. "Horrible story. A young woman in our church and her son, killed. Lost out in the last storm. Rosalie Harris?"

He thinks for a moment. "I remember her. She was a nice woman."

"A good woman." My eyes well with tears.

Then his touch. On my shoulder, first, then my neck, his thumb braced against my jaw. "Were you close friends?"

"No. It's just that —" I look into his eyes and know I've come to the moment I've been waiting for since that first night. That

242

first storm. "I'm alive."

"Yes, you are."

"And I'm not a good woman."

"I don't care."

No argument. No confirmation. It's exactly what I need to hear. I turn my face to bring his calloused palm against my lips, heedless of the dirt of my father's farm. The salt of my tears mixes with the taste of my kiss before one of us — both of us, maybe — move, and there is no place left to go. He brings my mouth to his and kisses me without restraint. No nuance of control. His arms wrap around me in an imperfect embrace.

Were I ripped away at this moment, dragged out of that house with a long hook, the way they do sometimes in the comedy shows, I don't think I would be able to answer a single question about who I am, or how I've come to be there. Certainly I've forgotten that I am a married woman, bound to a man of God, mother of two children. Four, counting those in the grave. Neither do I know anything about the man to whom I am prepared to give my body. Not his name, nor his people, nor his intentions. I don't know. I don't care. I can testify only to being a woman who's stepped into a storm, just like Rosalie, looking for something elusive and lost. What does it matter that I might die? Better I should than to wander, choked but not killed by my sin.

I feel a tug, and the detached sensation of fabric being stretched against itself. My dress, wrapped around me, secured with a belt tied at my waist, and the knot's been opened, my very dress threatening to open with it, and my senses return.

"No."

But we both sense the weakness of the word, and neither heeds its portent. He responds with my name, and I stay silent. I've no right to refuse. I brought myself here. I chose this dress. If I'm to be true to myself, everything happening in this moment is a culmination of my design. Now my shoulder is bare, his hand at the hem of my slip, and all at once his intentions ring clear. The time has passed for weak denial.

"Stop." I speak the command to both of us, as I'm on the verge of my own explorations. Jim drops his touch and steps back, far enough to allow me to breathe. His eyes are trained on the floor.

"I'll carry them plates out to your car for you." He never looks up. In two swift steps, he's swept the crate up on one shoulder and leaves me to rewrap my dress, securing the knot much tighter than I did when I stood in front of my dressing mirror back home. My hat's been knocked to the floor, and though I pick it up, I choose not to put it back on. It seems silly now. Formal and pretentious. Something I would wear to church.

There's nothing left in the day that would allow me a dignified exit, so I smooth my dress, ready to settle for a brisk walk through the front room, not stopping until I'm at the property gate. The host of my father's house, however, waits at the front door.

"I ain't goin' to apologize." He says it with the finality of a farewell.

"You don't need to. I should have known better."

"An' I think it's best you don't come out here again. Least not alone."

I bristle. "This was my home."

"Ain't your home no more. Not goin' to be nobody's, once the bank takes it. I just been bidin' my time, cleanin' it up like it is."

He moves to the side, leaving enough room for me to pass by. I can see that he's started the car for me; it rumbles in anticipation of escape.

"Don't come out here again. At least not alone."

I'm on the porch now, a strong wind pushing me to leave. "Thank you for all you've done," I say — or at least, I start to say, because when I reach out to give him the smallest touch of gratitude, a shock of electricity explodes between us, sending my arm to ring with numbness up to the elbow.

Together, we look to the west and see a wall of dust — dark, but distant.

"Come back inside." He risks another touch, but I pull away.

"I'll be fine."

I run down the steps and throw myself into the car, thankful for Jim's foresight to have started the engine. Behind me, he is shouting, but I don't look back. I'll drive as far as I can — safely — then pull off the road if need be. But I cannot go back into that house.

Already, bits of dirt are plinking against the windows, a sound teasingly similar to rain. I've come to the gate, faced with no choice but to get out of the car to open it. The hot gust makes me stumble in the effort, and another electric charge tickles the soles of my feet. Before driving through the gate, I struggle to open the trunk of the car where the lengths of heavy chain are waiting. Remembering Russ's example, I pull them out so that the chains will drag along the road, grounding the vehicle against further shock.

The dirt coats my bare legs like paint; the sound of my flapping skirt joins the wind. I hold my arm across my face, protecting my eyes and mouth from the sting. Mustering the last of this measure of strength, I manage to pull the car door open enough to wedge myself in, but midway through I hear my name.

"Nola!"

Jim's followed me, clear out to the gate.

"Get back to the house!"

Turning, I see his form, imbalanced and incomplete. In a cruel reversal of time and space, he diminishes with each advancing step. Soon he is little more than a struggling shadow within darkness, and before I become the same, I'm folded into relative safety and shut the door. Even without the benefit of sight, I know an open road waits before me, and sometime after, a turn to the left, and with faith in God's guidance, safe passage home. I find myself unable to release the brake to make the first, inching progress.

There's a jolt against the car. A grappling of a handle, a burst of air, and I'm not alone.

"Don't be a fool," he says, without benefit of any pretense. "Change places with me and let me drive you back to the house while we still can."

But already, three blinks, and we're encased in darkness. The sight of him, so covered in dust he looks to be made of sand, already a memory.

"Too late now!" He's shouting. "Turn off the car."

I still have said nothing, but I obey. At least I think I do, as there's no diminishment in noise to indicate that the car's engine has shut off. We are sealed in an imperfect shelter, bits of sand blowing in through minuscule cracks around the framing of the doors, polluting the necessary air.

"Do you have water?" His voice is closer, so I know he's leaning close.

"Yes!" I turn and lean over into the backseat, trying to ignore the feel of my hip brushing against him, and blindly reach for the canteens I know await. Bringing them both to the front, I unscrew the cap off one and take a modest drink, relieved to dislodge the dirt accumulated in my mouth, even if it means swallowing it. I hold it out in Jim's direction. "Drink?"

It's taken from me, but I keep my hands outstretched for its return.

"Do you have any clean rags?" His question is sketchy and intermittent with the wind, and I don't fully understand until he's

248

repeated it a second time. I know why he asks: we need to soak them in water and cover our mouths and noses, to keep hydrated and protected from breathing in the dust. For certain, I know I didn't put any in the car at the start of this journey, and if there are scraps of anything lying around, I can't vouch for their whereabouts or cleanliness.

"No." I keep my response simple and loud.

His is the same. "My shirt!" The canteen is given over, and a new motion added to the car seat. Then, "Here!" and the garment is in my hand.

Without any further instruction, I know what I am to do. I feel for the place where the sleeve attaches at the shoulder and tear, separating the two completely before ripping along the length of the sleeve, creating one long strip. Fumbling in the dark, I take the lid off the canteen once more and, careful not to spill any more than necessary, soak the cloth before recapping it.

"Here." I hold out the wet cotton strip, and am preparing to rip off the second sleeve when he speaks. Too soft to be heard, and I ask him to say it again.

"You'll have to help me tie it. I can't . . ."

Of course. Never mind that he could shovel half of a farm out of a house, or upright a fence, or fix a door, or carry a crate on his shoulder. This he cannot do.

I set the canteen down and inch toward him. The storm has stolen all our senses. I am blind to anything but darkness, hear nothing but the raging wind, smell only iron, taste only dryness. Touch is all that remains intact. Unable to see my hand, I reach it toward his face, and feel a sensorial flood when I find it. Nothing of the world around me, only him.

A new wind buffets the car, and I am thrown toward him. He catches me as if I've fallen a great distance, pulls me closer without risk of protest. All I can think is that God has blocked the sun, denied me even the tiniest sliver of light. Turned his back, leaving me to cloak myself in sin. And like my dear friend, a wife and mother whose grave awaits, I bury myself. Alive.

Chapter 15

Every kiss, every touch — all of it utterly wordless. My mind releases its memories into my skin, and I relive each moment on the drive home. The storm left the roads miraculously clear, and I keep my eyes trained straight ahead. If there are stranded motorists, abandoned cars, or wandering souls, I see none. In fact, I have no recollection of the intervening miles between my father's gate and the battered, hand-painted sign welcoming me to Featherling.

An odd sight greets me as I creep up on the early outskirts of our town. Actually, starting about a mile outside of what we consider our territory, two or three cars are scattered beside the road. Not stranded, nor weighted down with chains, but parked. And now, beyond them, half a dozen people, marching straight out in a line. *Searching.* My heart leaps to my throat. Someone else is missing, and without rolling down my car's window to hear their shouting, I know they are looking for me. None, however, bother to turn around to observe the dust-covered car driving straight between their ranks. I'm not so fortunate, however, to be ignored once I arrive in the town proper. Turning onto the first street, a scattering of familiar faces see me, registering what I take to be anything from relief to elation. They point and shout — to me and to each other. Men and women run out from alleys and storefronts, clutching the hands of their children.

My eyes flit from one face to the next, reaching their eyes, acknowledging their presence, but making no communication with my own. One woman stares with such incredulity that I fear I'll run her over unless I offer a wave, which she returns. Hers is a slow, full-palmed response to the mere flicker of my wrist before I turn yet another corner, onto our street, where the white steeple of the church beckons at the end.

I've arrived at our congregation's agreed-upon time, about three hours after the storm's end, at which point I expect to see the parishioners walking with a singular purpose to gather in the pews for rejoicing and accounting. They are there in dutiful clusters, but wandering in every direction.

Embracing one another, their faces awash with worry. Then Kay Lindstrom sees me. Her face turns rapturous, her eyes search the clear sky now darkened only by dusk.

One by one they find me, and soon are racing — staggering — toward the car. I force a smile, as if merely returning a greeting, and keep a slow, even speed, fearful to stop lest they all converge like two-legged tumbleweeds. With each turn of my tires, I realize I'll eventually have to bring my cocoon to a stop, emerge, and expose myself to their elation. Their joy over the lost being found. Their questions about just where she has wandered.

But of course, theirs aren't the questions I fear. Somewhere their leader, my husband, must be playing a part in the search. I want to scan the streets, looking, but every moment I avoid his eyes is a moment he can still love the woman he kissed this morning.

I pull around into the alley behind the shop, cut the engine, and rest my head against the steering wheel. Every breath taken since leaving this very spot hours before builds up and finds release in the long, muffled scream I wail into my clenched fist. I suck it back in, then out again, my teeth bearing down on my knuckles.

We've heard stories of people being picked up by storms — not the kind of late, but tornadoes, great violent cones of wind that rip across the land, tearing people from their homes and depositing them miles away. Sometimes crushed like rag dolls, but other times mercifully intact, only confused and unsure as to which world was real — the one they left, or the one they landed in. I have only a matter of minutes to decide which world I will live in when I open this car door.

I grip the handle and breathe in and out, wishing I could pray for strength. By now a semicircle of neighbors surrounds me, ready, no doubt, to shower me with attention and praise — relief that I've come home at all. Door open, one foot out, and then the swarm.

"We've been searching everywhere!"

"Praise the Lord!"

"Somebody go find the pastor!"

Nobody, it turns out, has to go anywhere to find Russ. Steps away from the car, the crowd — those wanting to lay their hands on the wayward lamb — parts, and he is revealed. His skin ashen with worry and dust, he strides to me, taking me up and crushing me against his chest in one swift, smooth motion. At once the ground disappears from my feet as his two strong arms hold me aloft. I bury my face in that warm space between his shirt collar and his neck.

"I'm sorry." It is all I manage to say. "I'm sorry. I'm sorry." My lips move against his skin, and I taste the grit of dirt with each repetition.

He hushes me, holds me tighter, and plants kisses in my hair. I recognize his words as prayer, thanking God for my safe return. Thanking God for preserving our family. I listen, concealing my betrayal in silence. If I cannot voice my own prayer, even one of silent confession, then I must be content to ride along on those of my husband. He will be my strength until I am strong enough on my own.

My feet touch the ground. Russ grips my shoulders and steps away, drinking in the sight of me. He searches the top of my head, my disheveled clothing, my bare legs. Then back up to my face.

"Nola, darling. Where did you go?"

"Out. Out to Pa's."

"But why in heaven's name — ? We were all . . . all of us worried sick about you."

"Plates." That truth rolls out, seeming strong enough to stand alone. "For the dinner tomorrow. Merrilou said we needed —"

"Plates." Russ's brow furrows in something I don't recognize. Displeasure, at the very least. "Why didn't you say something before you left? You can't take off like that."

"I'm sorry." The phrase sounds so much smaller in this utterance. "I told Pa I had an errand."

"You didn't say —" He stops, seeming to notice the crowd for the first time. There is a stir, and my Ariel emerges, calling for me and launching herself into my embrace as I stoop to catch her.

"We thought you were lost!" Her face, red and blotched with tears, presses hard against my cheek.

"Never lost," I say, the words twisting up out of me. "Only away for a bit."

"Don't go away again. Promise me."

I look up to see Russ with a new tightness in his jaw. Ronnie emerges from the crowd. My big boy with red-rimmed eyes has his hands plunged in his pockets and shoulders hunched. He goes to his father's side, clearly angry with me for bringing him to the threshold of such emotion.

"I promise," I say, relinquishing half of my grip to reach out to him. He takes my hand, uniting us. It is enough for now, and in affirmation, our neighbors and friends reward us with a smattering of applause, as if witnessing the final act in a staged melodrama. I stand upright, bringing my little girl up with me, and acknowledge them all with what I hope is a fitting smile of gratitude.

But then, in the center of the adulation, two faces refuse to smile back. One, of course, belongs to Ben Harris, who can only wait for such a blessed reunion with his wife on the other side of heaven. The other is my father's.

Pa stands with his arms folded across his sunken chest, his narrowed gaze seeing straight through patches of my untold story. A certain chill runs down my neck, and I swallow against the soured bile in my throat.

"Come on," Russ says, taking Ariel from me. "Let's gather at the church."

I take the first few steps, then reach for his sleeve, bringing him close.

"I can't." The mere thought of walking into the house of God, sitting on the pew where I hold my place as the wife of its leader, hearing my name echoed in prayers of thanksgiving fills me with a burden I can't carry another step. Our gatherings are meant to hold an accounting of one another, to show that all are well, all restored. I am neither. I haven't survived at all. The death of all I know to be good and faithful festers, threatening to burst and bleed in public confession.

"I understand." The softness of Russ's voice heaps salt. "Go home, clean up, and rest."

All I can hear is the voice of Jesus, his words vocalized from the pulpit, saying to the adulterous woman at the well, *"Go, and sin no more."* Release, if only for a short time. Sanctuary from prying, if well-meaning, eyes and potential inquisition.

I bow my head and manage to choke out a thank-you, followed by a final "I'm sorry," before heading for the stairs leading up to the front door of our apartment. A tiny hand covers mine as I grip the railing before taking the first step.

"You'll let us know if there's anything we can do for you, won't you, dearie?" Merri-lou Brown's sweet, smiling face, its creases highlighted with Oklahoma soil, sets a new fire to my steps.

I half worry that Pa will want to stay home with me, as he sometimes has to be cajoled into accompanying us to the after-storm meetings, but his heavy footstep does not follow. I slam the door behind me and push the latch. That moment, with my back against the door, the last of my strength leaves me, and I crumple to a heap. The very air within the walls pushes against me, restricting me to the few square feet of floor reserved for strangers and unwanted guests.

"Oh, God." I bury the heels of my hands in my eyes, deep enough that the initial darkness turns into dancing bits of light. No other words come, so I simply plead his name over and over, waiting for some wash of mercy to take away the filth I've carried into my home. How can I ask forgiveness for a sin so willingly committed? How do I claim repentance when, even now, were I to give half a breath to the memory, I'd long for his touch again? Still, I speak aloud to the empty room, "Forgive me, sweet Jesus," and I wait for some sense of grace.

There is none.

Instead, I open my eyes to find the room has grown darker in these passing minutes, and I know it is a real possibility that Russ and the children might be home at any time, as he tries not to keep his people out much after dark. They mustn't find me here, heaped upon the floor. I need time to think, time to compose my response to the inevitable questions. Where was I? How did I take shelter? Was I alone?

These, I know, might be the last minutes of my marriage.

Slowly, I rise to my feet. Leaving the door latched, I make my way through the parlor, running my finger over the surfaces covered with a fine layer of the afternoon's onslaught. Tomorrow will be full to overflowing with Rosalie's service. But the day after, I will take a rag and polish every piece of furniture, bringing it to a gleam bright enough to reflect the sun, should it choose to shine. Ariel will be charged with running a dry mop across the floors, Ronnie with beating the rugs. Russ can take Pa out for a drive — if the air seems safe — while I restore our home, the way I do after every storm. The never-ending battle of cleaning, reclaiming, restoring.

And then. Then. With everything in place, I will tell him. I will confess to my husband my weakness. I will tell him my sin, leaving no detail hidden, laying the blame solely on my head.

I went to him. To Jim, because I wanted to. And I was leaving. Really, truly, intending to leave, but then he got in the car, and the storm hit, and then, somehow, in the dark . . .

Even alone, I can't bring myself to say the words. To *think* them. What we'd done in the dark. When I try, every sensation returns, bringing me back to that darkness. Reliving.

I need to hate him. More than that, I need to hate myself. Hate our sin. I need, somehow, to rid myself of it. A physical repentance, cleansing the memory of his touch. His kiss. Scraping away that layer so I can offer myself clean and whole to both my Lord and my husband.

I wander through the darkening house into our bathroom, where I instinctively reach for the switch that brings the bright, white light. Door closed, I slide the latch and begin to fill the tub with water hot enough to create an intimidating cloud of steam. I assemble necessities along the edge: nail brush, washcloth. A new bar of Ivory soap. My Drene shampoo, normally reserved for Saturday night.

I wipe the accumulating steam off the mirror and lean in close to study my face, certain there will be telling signs of betrayal. My lips still feel swollen from his kiss. My neck burns with the memory of his rough, unshaven face moving against it.

But nothing.

With shaking hands I untie my dress, letting it drop to a puddle on the floor. Undergarments follow. I dip one foot into the scalding water and watch the dirt float away from my skin. When I pull it out, a clear, clean line divides pink, scalded flesh from gritty brown. Already the bath is clouded, making it a fruitless endeavor to become truly clean from revisiting it. Still, I brave the pain and step over the edge, sitting down to bring the water level up above my waist. Dirt flees, turning the bath to the color of weak tea. My legs are bent, bringing my knees up like twin peaks of bony rock. I scoop water into my hair and feel something near to mud between my fingers.

Every inch of me burns. Fire and water combined, refining. Cleansing. Purging.

I remember what Greg said about the soil carrying the color of its home. I can't say for sure what lands I wash away, but in the end my skin shines through, pure Oklahoma red.

When I stand, the water roils and laps above my ankles. I reach down and pull the metal stopper out of the drain and watch it swirl away, leaving a brown rim around the porcelain walls of the tub. I turn on the water again and pull the chain to bring it trickling from the showerhead.

Standing under the warm spring, I lather my hair with shampoo, trying to forget the feel of his fingers gripping the back of my head, pulling me into his kiss. I rub the bar of Ivory soap against the washcloth and scrub every inch of my skin, erasing his touch. And when I feel it still, I scrub again. Turning, I lift my face to the water, open my mouth, fill it. Spit, fill it again. Spit. By now the shower has turned cold, bringing with it a new sting more punishing than any heat.

I've been a fool.

I am an adulteress. I am nothing but a filthy, whorish wife. Everything my father suspected. Everything that lured my husband away from his original, sinless path. Rubbish. The ruination of this family, destroyed by my offense.

The shower, now nearly icy cold, threatens to take my breath, and with clumsy hands I twist the tap. The noises I make sound like the cries of some wounded animal as they echo off the walls of the tub. I never want to leave this hole. I cling to the sides wishing — only in the next breath — to die. To take my secrets straight to the seat of judgment. Spare Russ the necessity of passing his own.

But I cannot die. Not at this moment, anyway. Because somewhere, on the other side of the tub, on the other side of the bathroom door, I hear the voices of my family. My husband, my father, my children. They are still mine, and they are hungry.

CHAPTER 16

I survive the rest of that night by caring for my family — whipping up a late supper of eggs and biscuits before all of us collapse into stripped-down beds. I let Russ hold me, my cheek against his chest, rising and falling with his breath, until he falls asleep, and then I slip out and away. If Pa weren't living in the storeroom, I might sneak out to the alley for a cigarette. A few are still stashed away under the cash register — a trick I learned from my uncle. Back in the good days, when the farmers were bringing in money like laundry in a rainstorm, he used to offer them a cigarette right before they paid for their purchases. A good smoke and conversation, and they might be persuaded to buy something else. Another ax blade, just in case. Or some new seeds for the wife's garden. He kept the cigarettes in a long, flat box, laid out so the customers would know there was plenty to be had.

More to smoke, more to buy.

Of course, by now they'd be stale. Like setting fire to paper and dust. And I'd made my promise.

I survive the next day only because we — meaning nearly everybody in town — gather for the Harris funeral. From the pulpit, Russ speaks of the strength it takes not to question God's wisdom. His choices. I can feel eyes burning clear through me, turning my flesh to lace. Why did Rosalie drown in dirt while I sit here whole?

And her little boy.

"Always so hard to lose a child," Russ says. "I've buried two of my own. And we look to God for answers, thinking such a thing will bring us peace. But his answer is always the same. . . ."

I don't hear God's answer. In truth, my mind drifts in and out through most of the service, and I have to be nudged by Ronnie when it's time for us to rise and follow the procession to the graveside. Here, God shines down his mercy on that good woman and her little boy, granting us clear skies and a soft breeze.

Back at the Harris home, we feast on each other's generosity. I pinch and nibble from Russ's plate, and that only out of politeness to the women who have brought such bounty from their kitchens. Nobody can know how sickened I am to see the mismatched stack of plates at the head of the table, each having been carefully wiped down by a loving sister. I whisper in Ronnie's ear to take double portions, giving to him what I cannot take. I keep a glass of water in my hand, making way to refill it whenever somebody seems intent on cornering me in conversation.

I endure their pitying looks. Their whispers about how she doesn't look well at all. Too skinny, they say. And frightened because — poor thing — it could have been her.

More than once, Russ catches my eye from across the room and gives me an encouraging smile over the shoulder of one of his sheep. Any other time, I would have sidled up next to him, laid my hand on his arm, and made an excuse to go home. A headache. Or Ariel's needing a nap. But this day, standing upright and alert, listening to a dozen distorted conversations, feeling my body turn into a knot within itself — all of it serves as a buffer between my sin of yesterday and the inevitable confession.

For the first time since our marriage, I don't resent watching Russ minister to his people, healing their hurts while I nurse my own. Let them tell him of their troubles.

266

The bills they can't pay. The weakness they feel with every passing breath. Their hunger and hopelessness. Let them talk of a better life in California, or Texas. When I see him smile, I know he is listening to a story of the good old days, when the land was green, then gold, then moist and rich and brown. I watch women weep into his sleeve and more than one man poised to do the same. Others point dirty, gnarled fingers in his face. Accusing, almost, because our prayers aren't enough. Our faith has faltered, somehow. These are the ones who still resent having a piano next to the pulpit.

Most, though — the women — stand calm and peaceful in the shadow of his strength.

They love him, and he loves them. Always before, that love left me off to the side, jealous of the time and attention it took from me. Today, though, it gives me comfort. Aren't I a member of his flock as well as his wife? Don't I deserve at least a measure of the grace he seems always ready to give to them?

After a time, my legs ready to give way, I spy poor Ben sitting alone on the threadbare sofa beneath the window. His precious little girl is in the arms of a well-meaning woman who cuddles and coos the poor thing in an effort to put in an early bid for mothering.

Ben seems not to see or hear a thing, not of her nor me as I sit beside him, sliding in just ahead of another woman who approaches with a plate of food, probably in an effort to put in an early bid for marriage.

He and I sit for a while. He stares forward, I stare at him, both of us shells of the people we were a few days before.

Finally he turns toward me. He is a big, dough-faced man, and I can tell his demeanor would not change if we all were to pick up and go away at this very moment. Tentatively, I reach my hand out to touch the sleeve of his too-small jacket. He blinks no fewer than ten times, not saying a word, and I know his mind is as far away from this place as mine is. I am tempted to pull him close and unburden my soul, rehearsing the very confession I have to give my husband. He wouldn't hear a thing. I go so far as to lean over and, pitching my voice in such a way as to cut through the din, say, "I wish I were half as good a woman as Rosalie."

"Cain't never be," he says, before standing up and leaving me alone.

The day after the funeral, I attack our home with new fervor, dumping buckets of mud-brown wash water into the street and consuming two entire bedsheets as cleaning rags. I take on the bulk of the labor myself, leaving Ariel to play endless games of jump and chase with Barney, and giving Ronnie leave to spend the day playing baseball with his friends after contributing nothing more than a wipe-down of his room. Pa stays downstairs; much as he insists on having a clean house, he's never been one to watch exactly how it gets that way. And when Russ comes upstairs and volunteers to pitch in, I practically chase him away with my broom.

"Go mind the shop," I say, shooing him away with comic exaggeration. "For all we know, people are lined up right now ready to pick the shelves clean. Or maybe pay a little on their accounts. Wouldn't that be nice?" Never mind that he's been downstairs all morning and I haven't heard the bell ring once.

I feel his eyes on me with every move, and I keep my line of vision confined to the bucket of fresh water into which I pour half a bottle of Lysol, swirling it in with my bare hand, mindless of the toll it might take on my skin. I plunge in the rag, wring it out, and begin a methodic washing of the kitchen countertop.

"Nola."

I make a small sound of acknowledgment,

avoiding his eyes as I've managed to do since coming home. Always there was a reason. I was exhausted, I was mournful, I was busy. I've spoken as little as possible, too. Every time I open my mouth, even to ask if he wants a second cup of coffee, I feel a confession ready to spill from my lips. But I haven't had the words yet to make him understand. And I don't have things in order, not with the house in this sort of state. The time will come to reveal my failings as a wife — that I've given my body over to another. I'll tell him everything tonight, all those little moments that led up to my betrayal. Maybe even the first moment of betrayal. The first storm. Byron's riddle. Fifty cents. I'll tell him right here at our table. Late, with the children in bed and the kitchen cast in shadows. I'll tell him, and as I speak, he'll see the kitchen glimmering in candlelight, and he'll know I love him. Love our family. That there's nothing that can't be fixed. Cleaned. Scrubbed.

"Stop. Look at me."

I stop.

"Look at me."

I turn.

"There's something I need to show you," he says. "Downstairs."

"I need to finish —"

"Downstairs." His note of finality compels me to lay the wet rag across the rim of the bucket and wipe my hands on my apron.

I find Ariel, tell her to be a good girl and come find us if she needs to, and follow my husband downstairs. Perhaps *follow* isn't the best word. He waits at the door and stands aside as I proceed down into the shop, his purposeful step behind me. To my surprise, Pa sits behind the counter; I can't remember ever seeing him there before. Lately, if he spends time in the store at all, he spends it whiling away an hour or so with one of the other men — often Mr. Brown — playing checkers and narrating Oklahoma's slow descent into hell.

Now as Russ passes me up, walking ahead and standing alongside him, they manage to present a united front, without really looking at me at all. For the first time in my memory, the counter isn't gleaming. Always, since the first day a wall of dust blew through our town, cleaning the counter — wiping away the dirt with an oiled rag — has been the first priority, before spilling a drop of water in our home or sweeping up the floor. It has been a sacred place of transaction, a point of exchange: necessary goods exchanged for hard-earned cash or, later, goodwill promises. Beneath the residue, I know the wood to be like silk. Any other day, Pa and Russ would look at me double-fold, their faces reflected off the glossy surface.

My stomach clenches at the single purpose of their expressions. I try to pass off the threatening nausea to the fact that I've yet to eat anything today, that it is the resurgence of hunger, but I can't deny the fear pricking along its edge.

"Why do I feel like a canary walking into a cat convention?"

Russ chuckles at my feeble attempt at a joke, but not Pa. His eyes remain gray and hard as stone. Disapproving, and I know. *He knows.* Not the details, maybe, but Pa could always read my heart. Could always ferret out my sin. He just never loved me enough to grant it grace, not that I deserve it now.

I have a sliver of a second to prepare myself for the accusations to come. Russ holds his hand out to me as I approach, reassuring me that — for the next few minutes, at least — my place is still beside him.

"There's something I need to tell you," Russ says before correcting himself. "Rather, ask you."

I look at him — only him. "Anything, darling."

"I've been in contact with Greg — he's been working closely with some of the CCC efforts —"

At this my father sniffs his disapproval, and I feel a few drops of sweet relief that I can at least share the burden of his disappointment with my brother.

Russ ignores him. "They're buying us out. Everything we have, down to the last two-penny nail. We're boxing it up and taking it to a camp outside of Tulsa. Once it's been delivered, we'll get a check."

Pa sniffs again. "Check ain't nothin' but a piece of paper."

"This one will be from the federal government."

"Cain't trust them more'n anybody."

"How much?" I interject, ignoring everything I've ever been taught about financial conversations.

"Enough," Russ says. "Enough that we can cancel all of our customers' debts to us, those that are still in town anyway."

"And then? What'll the store be?"

"Gone," Pa says. "Like everything else in this godforsaken place. Just blown away to nothin'." And that's when I know his dourness has little to do with me, but more with the wounding of his pride, seeing everything his family had built — his farm, this store, the very life of this country — stripped away for nothing more than a slip of government paper.

Russ clears his throat. "There'd be enough, too, to pay up the taxes on your father's land. Keep it for another year, at least. It's not fit to farm just yet, but when the drought ends —"

"Ain't gonna live to see that day," Pa says.

"Don't say such things," I chastise, then turn to Russ. "If we don't have the burden of the store, we could all — maybe, if Pa approves — move out to the farm. There'd be so much more room. Ronnie would be a wonderful help, and Ariel — can't you see her? We'll put her in charge of the chickens."

"None of that was good enough for you before," Pa says, a myriad of meanings behind *before.* Before I married Russ? Before we had the children? Before the dust came to strip down bare everything I loved and hated? Maybe, even, a hint of *before* I took action to risk losing all the intangibles that no government check could ever replace.

"Nothing is like it was *before,* Pa."

Russ intervenes. "The first step, Nola, is to sign your approval for the sale. This place is yours and Greg's, after all. He had the document drawn up, signed it, and mailed it here."

"Well, my goodness . . ." I take the ink pen from Russ and step over to take a good look at the single sheet of paper sitting on the gritty counter. The letterhead looks official and important, but the text is a single paragraph, stating that Greg and I, the undersigned, agree to the proposed transaction of the documented inventory of goods for the proposed price. A wave of dizziness sweeps over me, and I steady myself with a touch to Russ's arm.

"That's too much."

"It's what he offered. I didn't suggest any price."

My eyes roam the meager offerings of our shelves. If we sold everything to our neighbors at triple the price, it wouldn't come close to what Greg proposed. "It's a fraud."

"It's an investment."

"It's leavin' the two of you with nothin'," Pa interjected.

"We'll have everything we need," Russ counters. "A roof over our heads, land —"

"For the time bein'."

"That's all we're ever guaranteed, isn't it? God instructs us to ask for our daily bread. 'Take therefore no thought for the morrow: for the morrow shall take thought for the things of itself. Sufficient unto the day is the evil thereof.' Besides, it wouldn't be the first time for the government to step in and help. You know they've been buying up cattle left and right."

"Dollar a head," Pa spits. "Nothin' for nothin' after they killed 'em off. Babies, too. Buryin' good beef like trash."

"Are you sure it's the best thing to do?" I search my husband's face for reassurance, trying to ignore the pull to some other loyalty. Not to some passive allegiance to family legacy, but to the grizzled man himself, the keeper of my secret.

"Ultimately, it's your decision, darling."

"We'll still own the building?"

"Yes, the ownership is shared by you and Greg equally."

"And what about you?"

He looks at me in that way that makes everything else fade into blackness — past and present — holding me in the moment. "I'll have you, my love. And our children. And our church, and whatever else the Lord chooses to bring our way."

"An' my land," Pa says.

"No, Lee. That's yours. I'd never take that away from you."

I focus again on the price, my mind reeling with the possibilities. Our debts paid. Our neighbors' debts paid. My father's debts paid. And then, maybe, a little left over. More food for the table, new pants for Ronnie, who seems determined to keep growing, some little luxury for Ariel . . . and then his name pinches at the corner of my musings.

Jim.

"What did you say?" I ask, unclear how his name came into the conversation.

"We'll fetch him back into town to help pack up. Your pa says we can use his truck to haul the inventory to Tulsa."

"Hafta clean out one of the trailers first," Pa said. "Don't want all these nice things smellin' like what come out of the business side of all that cattle they destroyed."

"So, my love," Russ speaks right past him, "how do you feel about a drive out into the country today?"

There, again, the knot in my stomach as I feel my father waiting for an answer. "Why would we have to go out there?"

"Well, we wouldn't, if your Pa had a telephone. And these days I don't know we can count on any of his neighbors still being around to take a message."

"I — I can't."

"We could have a picnic on the way. It's a beautiful afternoon."

"Now it is." I drop the pen onto Greg's

letter and wrap my arms in defense against his cajoling touch. "It was a beautiful afternoon the other day, too, when I went out there. And then —"

"Just what are you afraid of, girl?" Pa's question holds no compassion.

"It's all right," Russ says softly. "You stay here. Lee and I can go."

"I ain't goin' out there. Not for nothin'."

"You'll have to sometime, Pa." I wish I could tell him of all that Jim has accomplished in his time — the cleaning, the restoration. But I don't dare open my mouth to speak his name.

"Not until it's mine outright. Not until I can work it."

"I'll go alone." Russ, ever the peacemaker, could not have come up with a solution to make me less at ease. I trust my silence, given my desire to somehow survive my betrayal. But Jim has no such stake.

"Don't." I speak too quickly, too vehemently, to avoid Pa's suspicion. "What if you get caught — ?"

"Caught with what?" Pa interrupts.

"Sweetheart . . ." Ignoring my barriers, Russ folds me in his embrace, kisses the top of my head, and lets me go. "I'll be fine. I know what to do if the dust kicks up. Just like you do. I don't think I've told you yet how very proud I am of you. For being so smart and brave."

I hold my breath, willing my heart to turn to stone while every other part of me threatens to crumble away. I have to tell him, and would this very moment, if I could take even a step away from my father's prying eyes. But I love Russ far too much to drag him into Pa's court of humiliation again.

"I'm not any of those things." Finally, as a consolation for the disloyalty of my flesh, I commit myself to being faithful to his wishes. I pick up the pen again and, above the space where some secretary typed my name, my shaking hand signs.

Russ drapes an arm over my shoulder. "That's done, then. You'll see, it's best."

"I hope so."

He gives me a squeeze meant to be reassuring. "I'm going to go change into some work clothes. Jim and I'll get that trailer cleaned out, but if it gets too late, I'll stay the night and we'll come back in the morning. Maybe you can round up Ronnie and a couple of his friends, get them to work packing everything up. Might have a few bits we can pay them for their labor."

"I'll make you a lunch."

One quick kiss to my cheek, and he is

gone, taking the letter with him, promising to post it on his way out of town. In his absence, a silence falls, thick enough to hold the dust motes in their suspended dance, until my father speaks.

"You never could lie."

"Pa, please —"

"What I mean to say — you was always one to tell 'em, just never too good at it. Not enough to git past me."

"I don't have to get past you, Pa." A new weariness takes hold. Part of me wants to call his bluff and ask — point-blank — exactly what he knows, or thinks he knows. To justify his smugness, even if it means confirming his suspicions. But not yet. I'm not strong enough now, not in any way. I've nourished myself with nothing but secrets for days, and one thought to the next falls away, leaving me unable to construct any path of logic. There seems only one route. I tell Pa, I die. I tell Russ, I die. And holding it in is killing me moment by moment.

"I knew he'd be trouble," Pa says. "Knowed it the first I laid eyes on him. Tell me he ain't."

I say nothing, don't even look at him, as I trail my finger listlessly in the dust on the counter.

"Well, I tell you what." He traps my hand

under his. "That no-good squatter is gonna have me to 'company him to Tulsa."

The murderous glint in his eyes disturbs me. "That's not a good idea, Pa. Your health —"

"You rather your husband go with him?"

"He — Jim — can go alone."

"With everythin' you own? Just what has he done to make you so trustin'?"

No wonder he is so adept at making toys to train a cat to hunt. He dangles the truth right in front of me, and I want to strike it down, with confession or denial — anything to bring it tight into my grip.

"Come out and say it," I say, but he refuses to accept my challenge. Only tilts his head back, pushing me away with his gaze, making me feel small. Bringing me back to a time when I was a little girl, naive enough to believe that he loved me, despite the fact that I'd never seen anything to prove it. So while his eyes remain like flint, I soften mine to shale, but keep my voice to drill to what's left of his heart.

"Pa?"

He grunts.

"I've never asked you for anything in my life." He starts to protest, but I step closer, feeling stronger. "Never. I learned early on if I needed something I got it for myself."

"True enough."

I refuse to crumble under his insult. "But I'm asking you for something now. Go ahead. I want you to go with Jim to Tulsa —"

"Already said I would —"

"And I want you to make sure he doesn't come back."

Later, in the night, even knowing I have my children and father a shout away, I imagine myself completely abandoned. Alone in our bed, alone in the dark, alone in the world. Destined for many such nights, should Jim take it upon himself to confess the betrayal of Russ's friendship and hospitality.

I curl and uncurl myself repeatedly, finding one cool spot after another. I lay flat on my back, hands folded over my breast, corpse-like in my stillness. Restless, I inch over, my movement a snail's pace that takes the better part of an hour, according to the clock face in the moonlight, until I find my way to Russ's side of the bed. My head on his pillow. I imagine the shadow of his body, a deserted silhouette. With final abandon, I drop into the furrow left in the middle of our mattress, where we meet together on extremely cold nights, or any night, really, when our bodies cannot bear thc distance even in sleep.

I've thrown all this away.

And then, at the moment when the night begins its transition to morning, still dark enough for sleep but hospitable to wakefulness, I pray. On my knees, right there in the valley that has witnessed so much love and laughter, my forehead wedged between the iron bars of the headboard. Instead of being clasped together, my hands clutch at the feathers of our pillows, so tight that I feel individual quills bending within my grip.

"Dear God," I whisper, my words and my tears falling into the space between our bed and the wall, "take this from me. Take *him* from me — out of my thoughts. And forgive me. For letting him be . . . For letting him have . . ." Even to my Creator, my Savior, I cannot articulate my sin. To think of it is to relive it. My very whisper brings it to life, dancing through my veins.

"Give me this night," I plead. "This last night, for him to know me and love me as his wife. Bring him home tomorrow." Then again, we've already slipped into the new day. "Today. Let me see him, welcome him, one more time. Spare him this pain, holy Father. Let me bear it all for a little while longer. Until —"

He will be gone.

283

"I won't see him again. I won't look at him again. Only forgive what I've done. Forgive what I *wanted*. And protect me — protect Russ . . ."

Now, a prisoner of my prayer, my hands clutch at the iron bars, shaking so that they rattle against the wall.

"Give me time. Give *us* time. I will confess to him as I am confessing to you. I'll confess to my father on earth as I am confessing to you. Only give me time, so that I can know . . ."

That's he's safely away? Far enough that I won't follow. Far enough that I won't be tempted again. For that, I will trust my father.

CHAPTER 17

I fell asleep with an unfinished prayer. My pleading incomplete. I sleep in a knot, wadded up like a mass of feathers wedged between our pillows. My eyes are swollen, my mouth dry, and my spine ready to snap with each attempt to stretch. Still, I awake to a bright, clear morning. To some, such a morning means nothing more than a day without rain, but I choose to see hope in the rays of sunlight.

Ariel bounds in, demanding to know if her papa has come home, then why he hasn't, and where he is, and why he is there, and when he'll be back, and if he might be bringing another kitten.

I answer all of her questions, bringing her into the bed with me, stretching her body alongside mine as I run absentminded fingers through her hair. When I've satisfied every facet of her curiosity, I nudge her away, telling her to set the butter out to soften, promising a breakfast of flapjacks and jam.

Alone again, I go to the window. I've asked for this day, one last day, and here it stretches before me. A deserted street. Boarded-up storefronts. Loose dirt stirring itself along the ground like a crumbly brown mist.

Pa waits in the kitchen, coffee made, when I emerge, dressed, with my hair somewhat combed and my face stinging from a cold-water scrubbing. We say little to each other as I prepare breakfast, each of us preferring to speak with Ariel, who serves as a conduit to pass along requests for syrup and eggs and cream. Ronnie joins us shortly after, his hair wild with sleep, his face crisscrossed with the markings of his sheet.

"Everything ready to go?" I ask, pouring him a glass of milk. His isn't watered down, as is Ariel's. "I think your dad was hoping to load up today."

"All but the big tools," he says, most of the words swallowed in an enormous yawn. "Unless there's some huge crate I don't know about, those'll have to go separate."

"Good boy." I kiss the top of his head, the most he will allow. "You may do as you please this morning, but stay within ear-shot."

"Can I go with Dad to Tulsa? Just to help?"

I turn back to the stove and drizzle batter on the griddle. "No. Your father's not going. Just Mr. Jim and Pa."

"Then could I go with them? It's not like I have school or anything."

"I don't think it would be a good idea."

"But why?"

"Because what if 'n we don't come back?" Pa says, and then I hear him slurp his coffee.

"Your paw-paw's joking." I shoot my father a withering look over my shoulder. "He'll be back quicker than you'll know it."

"What about Mr. Jim?" Ronnie asks.

Pa's gray eyes pin me over the rim of his cup. "Likes of him's best left to the road."

I turn my attention back to the stove.

"I'm going to miss him," Ariel says in the absentminded voice that tells me she is swirling a chunk of her scrambled eggs in her pancake syrup. "Mama's going to miss him too. They were special friends."

"You go wash up now," I say without turning around. "You're sticky nose to toes."

"But I'm still eating."

"Then finish up."

She hums a wandering tune while she eats. I stare at the batter, waiting for the bubbles to break, feeling my father's disapproval like so much spattering grease. Still midmorning, and already the kitchen shows promise of being unbearably hot. I try to think of what I can serve for a cold lunch — what I can pack away for a journey — but I don't have to look through my cupboards to know they are nearly bare. There's not much more than a handful of coins in my grocery jar, but no matter. The shelves of Featherling's grocer have grown as empty as our own. Sometimes we risk the drive to Boise City, where the stores are bigger and the prices lower. Russ doesn't like me to go on my own. But the idea of being absent upon his return — *their* return — is enough to make the risk worthwhile. Besides, I wouldn't be alone this time. Since Russ has the car, I'll have to ask for a ride.

I flip Ronnie's pancakes. "I'm going over to Mrs. Brown's. To see if she could possibly take me into town. Do you need anything, Pa?"

He leans his head back and narrows one eye, as if watching me through a spyglass. "No need for that today, girl."

"We don't have any food here, Pa. I need some groceries."

"Make do. And sit down and eat somethin'. You're lookin' skinny as a rail."

Ronnie, usually so oblivious to any conversation not about cars or guns, looks to his grandfather, then to me, his expression wary.

Three good-size pancakes are rising on the griddle, and I've scraped the mixing bowl clean to make those for the boy who just swallowed the last of the eggs.

"I'll eat later."

"Now," Pa says. "I ain't seen you take a bite in days."

"You're not with me every moment." I pile the cakes onto a wide spatula, with a thin slice of butter between each one, and carry the stack over to Ronnie.

"I can't eat all them, Mama."

"Of course you can, sweetheart. I've seen you take down twice that in a sitting."

"Maybe later, after I finish up downstairs." He takes two of the cakes and transfers them to his plate. "That one's yours."

"Good boy," Pa says, but Ronnie seems to take no pleasure in his approval.

Rather than prolong the conversation, I pull Ariel's empty plate over to my place at the table and deposit the remaining pancake amid the swipes of drying syrup. Her fork is too sticky for me to touch; instead, I rip off a quarter-sized bite, dab it in the sweet residue, and put it in my mouth. This is precisely how I've eaten nearly every pan-cake since my children were born — the last of the stack, dabbed about on a dirty plate. Russ used to tease me, calling me Scraps before planting a coffee-laced kiss on my sticky lips. But I defended my prac-tice, saying, "What does it bother you? You don't have to do the dishes." Often it was the first quiet moment of the morning, with them already off to school, or play, or out the door with Russ so I could have a few minutes' peace. I'd make a second pot of coffee, maybe read my Bible a little bit while nibbling the fluffy, sweet cake, none the worse for growing cold.

This morning, though, I might as well be nibbling a scrap of plywood. Even though it still bears the warmth of the griddle, there is nothing pleasurable about that first bite. Or the next. Were it not for my father's chal-lenging gaze, I would give the remainder over to Ronnie, who has already plundered his serving. A sip of cool coffee does noth-ing to moisten the barricade it makes in my throat, and I dread the next bite as I at-tempt to swallow the first.

"These are good, Mama," Ronnie says, sensing my discomfort. "Filling."

"Thank you, baby," I say, grateful for any

bit of conversation that will delay the next bite.

"Finish up."

That Pa echoes the exact words I said to my four-year-old only moments before is not lost on any of us. I tear off half of what remains on my plate and shove it in as one massive bite. Already my stomach seizes in anticipation, and it isn't half-chewed before I force it down my throat, silently willing it to stay there. Similarly, Ronnie shovels his food in with youthful zeal, and I fancy us in a tacit race to escape.

I win.

After I've washed up the dishes and set them to dry, I run a comb through my hair and work a thin layer of Jergens onto my hands and face, along with a touch of lipstick. With a shout to the house that I'll be back shortly, I go outside, avoiding the shop by going out the front door, down to the street. I pause midway and crane my neck, looking up and down for any sign of Russ and Jim's arrival. Seeing none, I quicken my step, across the street to the Browns' place, and knock on the door.

"Well, Denola! What a lovely surprise!" Merrilou swings the door open with enough strength to bring me in with it. The excited, welcoming look on her face, however, disappears almost immediately. "Good heavens, young lady. Are you all right?"

"Of course I am." I brighten my smile to ward off any more questions.

"You look terrible."

Merrilou Brown's blunt honesty has often been a source of amusement in our household. *"Don't ask if you don't want to know,"* Russ always says. She is the first to inform him of a tedious sermon, a misquoted Bible verse, a church need left unattended for too long. Wary as we are of her opinions, they hold no malice, and I feel no insult at her pronouncement.

"I'm fine," I reassure, lessening the smile for a more serious, convincing expression. "A bit weary is all. Like we all are."

"Looks like more than weariness." She steps back, allowing me inside. "Bone thin, them dark circles under your eyes. Sweet Moses, your skin looks like you been dipped in ashes. The rest of us brown as Indians, and you the Indian pale as a ghost. I'm going to make you a sandwich."

"No, thank you." I stand inside the door while she closes it behind me. "Just came from breakfast."

"Little late, isn't it?"

"These summer days. We tend to linger."

"Tea, then?"

I accept and follow her into the kitchen, marveling at the cleanliness that permeates the Browns' home in the same way that dirt does mine. Baseboards, crevices, the carved scrolls of her dining room furniture.

"How do you manage it?" I speak to the top of her head.

"Manage what, dear?"

"Keeping your house so clean. There's not a speck of dust anywhere."

"Well, not much to that. You can't let it get the best of you. Keep out what you can, and clean up what you can't."

She makes it sound so easy, multiplying my frustration. I have a dozen arguments to throw her way: she doesn't have little ones underfoot; she doesn't have a warehouse of a shop to clean. With just herself and Mr. Brown, they could seal off entire rooms. Who knows what drifts I might find if I sneak down the hall and open one of the doors?

Once in the kitchen, Merrilou opens the icebox, revealing something akin to a feast upon its shelves. From it she takes a pitcher, while instructing me to get two glasses from the cabinet above the sink.

"You won't need the step stool like I do," she says, closing the icebox with a bump from her hip. She pours the tea and places a plate of small, crispy cookies between us, calling them "just right for nibbling."

"Delicious." I follow her instructions with tiny, crumbly bites.

"Now." She taps a cookie on the table. "To what do I owe the honor of this visit?"

I laugh nervously. "We're neighbors, aren't we?"

"We are, but I don't know that you've ever been one to drop in."

She has me there, and I swallow another tiny bite, stalling while I wait for the right words to express my mission. "I'm . . . I mean, we're running low on a few groceries —"

"I knew it!" She pops up from the table. "You're too thin. I've been saying as much to Mr. Brown for weeks now, that I worried you might not have enough food. These days, money being what it is —"

"No!" I catch her hand, a tiny, twig-like thing. "That's not it at all. We have plenty, or the means to have plenty. I simply haven't been able to stock up on a few things, with our grocer so limited, and then the storm and the funeral. And today, Russ has the car out at Pa's place . . ."

"What's he doing out there?"

Maybe it is the magnification from the thick lenses of her glasses, but all of Merrilou's questions seem to come with two meanings: one for her curiosity, and one for my confession. I give her a brief summary of Russ's plan for the store, and she listens with sage silence, nodding and making little affirming noises throughout.

"So, he — Jim, Mr. Brace — is doing a tremendous favor for us, taking this haul into Tulsa. He and Pa. And I thought the least I could do is pack him a few meals, but I'm not finding enough in my kitchen to make a decent meal for anybody." I attempt a weak smile; she returns one equally unconvincing. "So I thought maybe you could . . . I haven't had a chance to go into town, and I'll — we'll — gladly replenish . . ."

I can't speak anymore, not with the wave of shame engulfing me, because I'm no longer asking for a ride into town. Even before I walked through her door, I knew I didn't have enough money to justify a two-hour drive. She, the angel, doesn't make me ask.

"Nola." Her voice is soft, sweet. Like talking to a mother, and in that moment I wish I had such memories of my own. "Of course, sweet girl, what we have is yours. Take whatever you need, but I know you're not telling me the truth."

"I am —"

"I can see in your face, there's something hiding there. And if we're going to survive these troubled times, we're going to have to take care of each other. Woman to woman."

"I'm fine."

"You're not. And I've learned a few things over the years. There is no need too big nor any hurt too deep to take to the Lord. But you have to go to him. Not because he doesn't know. Trust me." She waggles a tiny finger under my nose and smiles in a way I'm sure she means to be reassuring. "He knows everything. He can count every crumb in your bread box. He's tasted every bite you've taken. He follows you every minute of the day. *He* knows your hunger."

"We're not —"

A wave of her hand dismisses my protest. "I'm not talking about Pastor Russ and the kids. I'm talking about *you.* Looks to me like you've got something so swallowed up it's eating you from the inside."

Her words cut to the quick of me, wrapping themselves around the last exposed nerve, sending a pain sharp enough to make my ears ring.

"Really, there's nothing . . ." I stand and clutch at the table to steady myself within the spinning room. "Nothing . . ."

"Oh my." She's at my side. "Sit down. Let me get you some water."

"No, thank you, Merrilou. I need to get back."

"I'll make up a basket and bring it over."

"What?" I press my fingers to my temple, trying to make sense of what she is saying. At once the unfamiliar kitchen begins to blur, and for the life of me I can't remember why I've come here. The room grows smaller as Merrilou Brown's words loom large — nonsensical jabber and platitudes. All I can think to say is, "Thank you. Thank you," over and over as I stumble back through her house, now choked by its pristine perfection.

Outside, while she continues to shout for my attention, I gulp in the hot, thick air, taking comfort in the feel of the airborne grains on my skin.

"Nola?"

I hear his voice through the heat and have to hold my hand up to block the brightness of the sun to see him. Russ stands in front of the shop, closing the car door behind him. Pa's truck is nowhere to be seen, making me think that somehow the plan has fallen through. For an instant, I think maybe we can hold on to everything exactly as we have. If nothing else, he is holding his arms

297

out to me, welcoming, inviting, and a cool rush of strength sweeps through me.

He doesn't know. He can't, because no amount of godly grace would account for the quickened pace that brings him to meet me halfway across the street, take my hands, and guide me gently home.

"I missed you," I say in answer to his question about the fervency of my embrace once we were safely inside the store. I'd launched myself into his arms before the bell above the door stopped ringing.

"I can see that." A good-natured chuckle accompanies his comment. "I missed you too."

"Don't go away again?"

"Well, I don't know. If I get this kind of reception . . ."

He brings me close and nuzzles my neck. My mind fills with questions. *What do you know? What did he say?* And the blessed answer. *Nothing. Nothing. Nothing.* Here he is, my daily bread, and I thank God for the nourishment of this moment.

"Jim should be here in a minute," he says, pulling away with obvious reluctance. "Truck pulling a trailer moves a little slower, but I spotted him behind me as I was getting into town."

"It's all set, then?"

"All set." He looks around the store, inviting me to do the same. It's a ghost town, boxes stacked to varying height and depth, with nothing but empty floor space in between. "Hardly seems like a life's endeavor, does it?"

"It was never what I wanted, being a shopkeeper's wife."

"Or a farmer's wife." He grins. "Or, truth be told, a preacher's wife."

I face him full-on. "I wanted to be *your* wife, whatever that meant. And I still do. You have to believe that. No matter what we lose."

Before he can answer, the bell over the door rings, and I turn to see Jim, hat in hand.

"Mrs. Merrill," he says, cool as cream, looking right at me as if the last time we saw each other wasn't in dark, desperate embrace.

"Hello, Jim." I trust myself with nothing beyond that greeting, and even wish I could swallow those words back. Were they too soft? Too intimate? Had I ever called him Jim in Russ's presence before? The last time I spoke to him, I had my lips against his skin, my fingers entwined in his hair, and I force myself to keep my hand pulled away from my mouth in an effort to keep that memory in place.

"Back door's locked," he says, as if apologizing for coming through the front. "So this is all of it?" He keeps his gestures close and tight.

"This is it," Russ says, heaving a sigh that sinks his shoulders. "I'll go upstairs and get Ronnie to come help us load."

"I'll go," I say. "He might be out with friends. You two can start organizing a bit."

Jim catches my eye, perplexing me with the sheer blankness of his stare. His look goes straight through me, piercing, like a spear through my core, pinning me in place. I imagine bits of my flesh peeling off and landing on the floor as I step away.

Upstairs, Pa is at the window. He turns when I arrive. "He's here?"

"They are."

"Got the truck runnin'."

"Apparently."

"Saw it turn the corner and go around the back."

"Yes. I'm up here for Ronnie. It's time to start loading. Perhaps you'd like to help?"

"Reckon I could." Beneath the gruffness of his reply, I sense he is pleased to be useful.

"Where's Ariel?"

"Taggin' along after her brother. Tol' him

to check back in an hour." He glances at the clock. "Might be quicker to wait than to wander off tryin' to find him."

"I'm sure he's just a block over. Playing ball. Probably saw the car coming into town. I can just —"

"You can wait. Like I said. He'll be back directly."

Pa disappears through the kitchen door, and I listen to his slow, shuffling step down the stairs.

I exhale.

Once, when Ronnie was a very little boy, he dropped a small sack of marbles on the floor, and they scattered and rolled in all directions, and the more we tried to gather them together, the more they clacked against one another, setting off in slow, straight trajectories behind furniture, under rugs, ricocheting off walls. I'd pick one up only to have it slip through my fingers while picking up another. I knocked them away with a touch of my foot, losing some forever.

That's how I feel now. Over the course of such a short time, my life has been ripped open, everything I know and love dumped out. My affections and secrets dispersed and strewn about, every word poised to set off some dangerous reaction.

"Give me this day, Lord." I repeat the

prayer, though it gives no comfort. This day — this *afternoon,* maybe, should the weather hold — and I'll chase down all those dangers. Gather them up before they roll away. Uncover what's hidden. Everything neat and tidy again. Cinched up, safe.

It never occurred to me that he'd follow me upstairs. That he'd watch and calculate, knowing I'd be alone. So when he walks into the kitchen, just as he did that first night, and stops himself in the doorway, waiting to be beckoned, I feel the same flash of excitement, only now it is heightened by both fear and familiarity.

"You shouldn't be up here," I say, backing away though he is nowhere close.

"Apparently I shouldn't be anywhere."

"I mean it." The words eke their way out of my pinched throat. "Go back downstairs."

"I have to talk to you."

"Please." He is three steps in, and I find myself pleading to my own weakness. "Go."

He holds his hand up in a gesture of peace. "I will. I promise. Just let me say that I'm sorry."

"Stop."

He moves closer.

"And I know there's nothing I can do to ever make it right. But I promise you, I'll never say a word to Russ."

I fold my arms tight across my chest. "Why should I believe you?"

"Up to now, which of us is the liar?"

He touches my face and a shock runs through me — sharp, electric, and painful enough to make me yelp as if he slapped me. In reaction, I bring my hand to his cheek, my palm stinging with the contact, and for a moment it seems we might both catch fire on the spot.

"Go." The syllable takes the last of my strength.

"Storm's kickin' up," he says. "Won't be safe enough to leave until tomorrow."

The air crackles between us, the phenomenon stronger now with the earth so parched dry. I don't dare move, knowing the next step, the next touch of *anything* — furniture or flesh — will crisp my nerves. The best thing to do is to stay still, to settle into the moment until the surrounding energy acclimates. Jim knows this too, because he turns into a portrait before me, and I stare into him, study him, unabashed and bold, as I would study any other work of art. The defined curl of the hair on his brow, the shadow of stubble on his chin, the pox scar at the top of his cheekbone. He studies me, too, our bodies moving together in breath the way they have before. I don't need to touch him. I remember. I relive.

"Looks like I got here in the nick of time." Merrilou Brown's voice somehow cuts through the pounding sound of my own blood in my ears.

I glance around Jim's shoulder to see her standing at my table, holding a wicker basket twice the width of her shoulders.

"In time?" I slide out from Jim's gaze, telling him the glasses are in the cupboard to the left of the sink.

"Looks like we're in for a whopper. And you might want to know that your kids made it in safe and sound downstairs." She sets the hamper on the table. "Brought over enough dinner for all of us, if you don't mind me and the mister joining you."

"N-not at all. Of course, we'd love it."

"Good." She sends Jim, who calmly sips what will be the last of the good water for a while, a wink that only I can interpret as disapproving. And yet protective, like she is prepared to launch herself into battle for my honor. She knows too. Just like Pa. But I feel no shame, only gratitude. "And," she continues, taking out a stack of sandwich-shaped wax-paper bundles, "you'll be glad to know, there'll be enough left over to pack this one a meal for the road."

■ ■ ■ ■

They are gone in the predawn hours of the next day. Russ and I stand on the balcony overhanging the street and wave, his arm wrapped lightly around my waist.

"I'm still worried about Pa," I say, never losing my hopeful smile.

Russ plants a reassuring kiss on my temple. "I'd say there's nothing better for him. He's almost back to his old self. Maybe stronger. And this will give us time to make some improvements in his room."

I should say something about Jim, inquire whether Russ is going to miss his friend, maybe, or express some gratitude that Pa has a traveling companion for at least half of the journey. But I say nothing.

As soon as the truck and trailer turn the corner and disappear from view, Russ tugs at me to go back inside.

The children are asleep, and it's easy to pretend that we have the small apartment to ourselves. Last night's storm wasn't nearly as volatile as we had anticipated, and working together, Russ and I have the kitchen pretty much clean before the coffee is ready.

"We could go back to bed," he suggests

with a hopeful grin.

"No," I say, reaching for a cup. "We can have a nice breakfast while it's still cool outside. Grits and eggs?"

He agrees, and while he is washing up, I go through the motions of preparing breakfast by rote, my mind full of the moments to come. I've made a promise to God, and to myself, that I will unburden myself of this secret. And now, with the threat of Pa's judgment removed, I can go to my husband, claiming God's forgiveness of my sin, and imploring Russ to grant the same.

I stir the grits and flip the eggs, thinking, *As soon as the food is cooked.* Then, when we are seated, I know I have to wait until after the blessing. Under his watchful, concerned eye, I eat half my portion, needing every bite for strength. He looks at me with such love, such contentment, reaching the small distance across the table to touch my arm as he speaks — thankful, he says, for this moment.

"I can't imagine living the way Jim does," he says. "Drifting, unanchored."

I respond with an inarticulate sound and clear the plates. Refill the coffee. Buy a few more precious minutes. While I do, Russ takes our well-worn Bible and opens it to the place where the ribbon marks our last reading.

"Psalm 32," he says as I settle back down in my seat. "Shall I read? Or you?"

I slide the Bible toward myself, volunteering. My own words remain stuffed down, drowning in grits and coffee. I think, maybe, speaking God's Word will dislodge them, clothe them with strength I could never summon on my own. The moment my eyes scan the first words of the chapter, I feel hope.

" 'Blessed is he whose transgression is forgiven, whose sin is covered.' " I look up to see Russ in earnest agreement. " 'Blessed is the man unto whom the Lord imputeth not iniquity, and in whose spirit there is no guile.' "

Here I stop, forced to question my spirit. My guile. I've held nothing back in my confession to God. Jesus knows my duplicity, by my heart and by my words. And while I am fully prepared to confess the act of adultery to Russ, I freeze at the thought of telling him the depth of my depravity, how I've schemed and manipulated both truth and circumstance.

Still the psalm prods. " 'When I kept silence, my bones waxed old through my roaring all the day long. For day and night thy hand was heavy upon me: my moisture is turned into the drought of summer.' "

Selah.

"Maybe your pa's right," Russ says, "about the land paying for the sin of our greed."

"Maybe," I agree, thankful for the diversion from the words that seem so clearly meant for me. Russ waits patiently. Tears gather at the base of my throat, impeding my voice as I attempt to read the next verse, but I push past them. " 'I acknowledged my sin unto thee, and mine iniquity have I not hid. I said, I will confess my transgressions unto the Lord; and thou forgavest the iniquity of my sin.' "

"Darling." Russ pulls me over and brings me to sit on his lap, because I've lost the battle. Tears flow, and as he wipes them away, he says, "Your pa's not right about everything."

"Can it be that simple?" My eyes rake again over the verse, now clouded by tears. "To confess my sin and be forgiven?"

"I wouldn't say it's simple, but it's true. Think of the sins David committed. Adultery. Murder. And yet . . ."

"He was king."

"The lineage of Christ himself."

There is comfort in recalling my prayer of repentance last night and in the image this morning of watching the object of my sin being taken away. Somehow I know that, were I to come clean with Russ this very moment, he would ask, *"Have you confessed your sin before the Lord?"* Indeed, having listened in on so many pastoral conversations, I know he has posed this same question to others seeking reconciliation.

And my answer would be yes. God has forgiven my iniquity. I know I must also confess to my husband, but to do so now would destroy my assurance of grace. As fine a man as he is, Russ is a man — Christlike in every way, but not Christ himself. Capable of forgiveness, yes, but not cleansing. With the Lord's forgiveness, I am clean — a state so rare these days, I long to enjoy it just a little longer.

"Shall I finish?" Russ pulls the Bible closer and uses his finger to find the place. " 'For this shall every one that is godly pray unto thee in a time when thou mayest be found: surely in the floods of great waters they shall not come nigh unto him.' " He jiggles his leg beneath me. "That doesn't sound too bad, does it? A flood of great waters?"

I rest my head on his shoulder and feel the vibration of Scripture. " 'Thou art my hiding place; thou shalt preserve me from trouble; thou shalt compass me about with songs of deliverance.' "

For these next few days, I will hide myself in Russ. Forgiven, I will lose myself in him, his every word, spoken with love, a song of deliverance.

■ ■ ■ ■

Part IV

■ ■ ■ ■

Thine hands have made me
and fashioned me together round about;
yet thou dost destroy me.
Remember, I beseech thee,
that thou hast made me as the clay;
and wilt thou bring me into dust again?
Hast thou not poured me out as milk,
and curdled me like cheese?

JOB 10:8-10

CHAPTER 18

Until this summer, we only thought we knew misery. Never before would I have imagined that a season could attack with such a vengeful spirit, but as the weeks wear on, the wind and the heat and the dust meet each other midair in battle, and our very lives fall victim to their hate.

I can't take a single step outside without feeling my skirt twist and wrap around my legs, crippling my progress in the shortest journey. As time wears on, however, there prove to be fewer and fewer reasons to leave home at all. The number of church families dwindles so low as to leave more than half of the pews completely empty, so Russ's ministerial visits become little more than weekly social calls, kept up to encourage the remnant to remain. I go with him these days — a decision of my own making, claiming a need to get out of our stifling apartment even if it means an hour spent in

313

another home no less oppressive. We always venture out early in the day to capture the coolest hours and to better the odds of escaping a storm.

Back at home, the melancholy sets in. The unrelenting monotony of waging war against the stirred earth. Windows kept closed against the dust manage only to trap the heat. Fans moving to cool the air kick up miniature storms within the walls.

And the thirst — the dryness of our bodies keeps us from making spit or sweat or tears. The ever-present dust in our hair, our nostrils, our eyelashes. Caking in the folds of our skin. Coating our tongues; splitting our lips.

I've given up on all but the basest of housekeeping: Running a damp mop over the floors every morning. Storing the dishes upside down under a wet towel in the cupboard. Folding all our bedding and stashing it in a trunk, leaving our beds with nothing more than a barren, striped mattress during the day.

It has been six weeks since Jim and my father drove away, truck and trailer laden with the lost promise of profit. Five weeks since Pa came home, alone, with only terse answers to all of our questions. Ariel wanted to know if there were dust storms in Tulsa, to which Pa said yes. Ronnie wanted to know if the Civilian Conservation Corps camp looked like fun, to which Pa said no. Russ wanted to know if Jim decided to stay behind and get work with the CCC, to which Pa said nothing.

I took a chapter from Pa's book, holding my silence until later, when I had a chance to get him alone.

"Is he in Tulsa?" I asked, only for my own sense of comfort.

"Don't you bother 'bout where he is."

I didn't eat a thing during the week I waited for their arrival. *His* arrival — Pa's. I'd sit with the family, picking around at the food on my plate, imagining the unwanted crunch that came from the dirt no amount of careful cooking could escape. Russ and Ronnie made good-natured jokes about "living off the land," and Ariel declared she would pretend it was a crushed-up cinnamon stick from the drugstore in Boise City. I, however, couldn't bear the shame of bringing even one filthy bite past my lips. I'd smile, sip my water, chime in when the conversation allowed, and hand my plate over to my growing son the moment he asked, "Are you going to finish that?"

Once Pa returned, having survived on so little, it seemed needless to nourish myself more. Starvation, it seems, has become my only true sense of peace. The very emptiness of it fills me, and I imagine my stomach being something like a balloon, so puffed up with *nothing* that allowing even a morsel would perforate its wall, and the resulting pang would ignite not only my physical hunger but the spiritual deprivation I've chosen to deny. Feeding my body might bring to light the malnourishment of my soul. By now I've managed to transcend the appetites of both. I do not eat. I do not pray. Above all — or perhaps at the heart of all — I do not confess. Day by day, God gives our family the strength to survive, despite my selfish weakness.

It is the third week of July when I take down the dust-catching draperies from all of our windows and replace them with pull-down shades I ordered from Sears and Roebuck. They cost every penny I had stashed away in my powder box — including Jim's fifty-cent piece — and four dollars begged from the cash remainder of our inventory sale.

The day the blinds arrive, as I work to affix one above our living room window, a new kind of blackness rises up against my eyes. For a moment, I think it to be a sudden, ferocious storm, but then dizziness overtakes me and — as Ariel, who is playing nearby with the ever-growing Barney, will tell me later — I drop off my stool like a sack of potatoes.

When I wake up, two days have passed. I find myself in a clean white room, covered by a crisp white sheet. The sound that brought me out of the darkness was that of my husband's voice, brimming with prayer.

". . . and for how I've failed her, Father. How I've failed you, and the children you've given over to my care . . ."

He is praying for the restoration of our marriage and our land, seeing the two of them as coconspirators in the ravaging of my body. I lift my finger in a nascent effort to reach out, to beg him to stop. His confession rings like blasphemy in my ears, as my waking thoughts are consumed with the sin that has managed to weave itself within my bones, bringing a constant, familiar ache that springs to life not long after I've eased into consciousness.

I try to say, "Russ, stop," but the only sound that comes is a soft, snakelike hiss, which frightens me more than silence. I've willed my eyes open to the bright whiteness around me, and wonder briefly if I haven't died. If this isn't heaven, and the voice I hear that of an angel speaking a petition on

317

my behalf. But when I see his head bowed low, his shoulders slumped, hands clasped, Bible open across his knee — it is a sweeter sight than any glimpse of heaven could afford.

This, again, another day. Another chance, brought back from near death. Or so it seems. My mind hearkens back to the bits of conversation floating beyond my dreamless sleep. *"Dehydrated. Severely malnourished. Near starved."*

When my eyes are finally fully open, I find a needle plunged within the deep vein running the length of my forearm and a rubber tube attached to a glass bottle suspended from a pole beside the bed. The sight of it frightens me — like something out of that terrifying monster movie Russ and I had seen on a rare film date early in our marriage.

"What is this?" I ask, and am nearly frightened again by the immediate reaction of Russ. He springs to life, knocking the chair out from underneath him and his Bible to the floor.

"Nola!" He comes to my side, his warm, soft hand pushing the hair away from my brow before he bends low to kiss me. "Thank you, Jesus." His lips speak the prayer into my skin.

I return his kiss to my lips as best I can, given I haven't the strength to lift my head, and I don't dare embrace him lest I rip the needle out of my vein. "What happened to me?" I say the minute he settles back in his chair.

"I should get the doctor." He looks poised to jump up again.

"Not yet."

"At least the nurse."

"Russ. Just you. Tell me, what happened?"

"Oh, darling. You gave us such a scare."

"I remember falling. I heard Ariel —"

"Yes, you fell. And hit your head pretty hard. You probably feel it. . . ." He touches his fingers to his own temple, prompting me to do the same, where I find a raised, tender bump. "But that's not the worst of it."

"What's this?" I lift the arm tethered by the rubber tubing.

"The doctors estimate that you weigh under one hundred pounds. And when I saw you, when they'd stripped —" His words break away as he buries his face in his hands. Not crying, but with an anguish I've only seen twice before in those moments when he held the empty shell of a lost child. I know the gesture that will come next. His hand takes on the function of a

319

dry cloth, wiping the pain away, his face emerging inch by inch, a visage of reliable strength. This time, though, I see a man reeling from shock and devastation. "How could I not have known?"

I want to reassure him in that moment, the way I have in so many moments leading up to this one, that I am fine. A little tired, maybe. Bit of a headache, but fine. Nothing a cool drink of water and an aspirin won't set right. And when he unfailingly brings both to me, I'll smile, tuck the pill under my tongue, and spit it out once he leaves me alone to lie down with a cool rag on my brow and a fan cooling the air around me. In all those times, he was my caregiver and pleased to do so, as there'd come to be so few people for him to minister to. Now he appears beside me, a victim of some cruel twist, and a deep fear takes hold. Somehow, during my days of darkness, I've been betrayed. By my own mouth, maybe, speaking aloud in sleep as I've been known to do. Or by Merrilou Brown voicing her suspicions in those long hours when people waited and wondered. Perhaps Jim himself, lurking out of the range of my perception, breaking his vow as I've broken mine.

"Known what?" I ask, dreading the answer.

"That this happened to you. That your body — that you were *dying* right in front of me."

"I'm not dying. And even if I were, you couldn't have known. *I* didn't know."

But then, I think, maybe I did know. I must have known, disappearing meal by meal, becoming more of a shadow in the light of each day, and at night . . . those nights. Always a reason to avoid his touch. The bedroom was "unmercifully hot." My skin felt "like a field of sweat." I cooled myself with alcohol rubs, and his touch "took all the coolness away." I slept on top of the sheets, rigid and alone, a valley of emptiness between us. I dressed and undressed when he was out of the room — better, out of the house. I sated him with kisses to the back of his neck and spun out of his embrace as if I were flirting, keeping him as far away from my body as the confines of our tiny apartment would allow. And then, during those times when my defenses were down, when his arm would encircle me, and his handsome brow would frown, and he'd say, "Darling? You're getting to be so thin . . . ," I'd flash a bright smile and toss off something about his mistaking me for some Hollywood actress and playfully bump him with my hip.

321

Only Ariel hadn't been fooled. While Ronnie spent every moment he could outside the stifling confines of our home, and Pa regarded me with the same judgmental scowl he had all my life, Ariel had, on more than one occasion, looked me right in the eye and asked, "Where are you, Mama?" Once, when I complained that it was too hot for her to cuddle on my lap, she crankily retaliated, saying my lap was "too pointy, anyway."

Suddenly my arms long for the feel of her, and I ask Russ if the kids are here somewhere.

He shakes his head. "They're back home, with your dad." I must have communicated some discomfort with the idea, because he smiles and reassures me that Mr. and Mrs. Brown are keeping an eye on them as well. "All three of them."

"And you've been . . . here?"

"Day and night, dearie. Day and night." This from a bustling, white-uniformed nurse who has crept inside the room in thick, rubber-soled shoes. She is a large woman, the first genuinely fat person I've seen in years, and that alone brings me comfort. Older, too. Probably close to fifty, and she carries her girth around her as a monument to commemorate better times.

"The man slept right in that chair."

I have no time to reply, as she takes the thermometer she's been vigorously shaking and pops it into my mouth with an unmistakable, if silent, command to keep it shut.

Russ and I both obey, our eyes finding each other behind her healthy white posterior.

"Perfect," she pronounces, and I feel so pleased with myself. She turns to Russ. "Now, mister minister, time for you to skee-daddle out of here while I help her freshen up a bit. Go to that diner next door and ask for the special. Tell 'em Nurse Betty sent you, and they won't charge you but a nickel for the whole plate and all the coffee you can drink."

He starts to protest that he isn't hungry, but Nurse Betty stares him down so hard I marvel he has the strength to stand beneath it.

"I'll be back in an hour," he says, grazing his hand against my cheek. I don't think he dares bend down to kiss me. And then he is gone.

"Nice fellow you have there," Nurse Betty says. She lifts the glass bottle off its perch on the pole, detaches the rubber tube, and reattaches it to a new, full one.

"He is," I acknowledge, knowing instinc-

323

tually that she won't answer my question unless I acknowledge her. "What is that?"

"Fluid. Keepin' you hydrated. You know you're fixin' to turn yourself into a tumble-weed, don't you? Need to work on gettin' some food into you next."

"I'm fine." My reply comes automatically. "I'm not hungry."

"Don't matter." She is finished with the bottle and the tubing and helps me to sit up straight. The ache in my bones is a new, unfamiliar sensation, and I wince at her prodding. "C'mon now, stand up."

With her help, I do. I'm wearing a gown made of thin, white cotton, draped across the front of my body and tied along the back. Nurse Betty tugs at the strings before she eases my right arm out of the sleeve, leaving the entire garment to dangle off my left shoulder. Though she surely has seen her fair share of bodies in all states of undress, I curl myself against the shame of my nakedness, trying to step away from her grip.

"Now," she says, her voice brimming with no-nonsense compassion, "ain't everybody can take a look in a mirror and see what's ailin' them, but you can. So —" she makes sure I am steady on my feet before stepping away and coming back with a mirror, not unlike the one that sits on my dressing table at home — "you take a look. Bit by bit. Don't you take your eyes off the glass."

She holds it first in front of my face, and I confront my eyes, large and brown, growing enormous in the sharp planes of my face as she steps away. Prominent cheeks; thin, dry lips. My neck, thin enough to dissect the middle of the image. The hollow of my clavicle, deep enough to hold rain, should any ever fall.

Nurse Betty steps back, moves the mirror down, until I see my breasts — always small, now depleted of any purpose. They sit atop the shadow of an emerging rib cage, beneath which a concave stomach still bears the scars of stretching. Prominent hip bones jut from either side. And then —

"Stop." I look away, unable to take any more.

"Got a good two inches of daylight between your thighs," Nurse Betty says. "That man of yours said he wouldn't have recognized you if —"

"He *saw* me? Like this?" With a shaking hand I reach for the gown and cover myself, save for the aching emptiness in the back.

She ignores my question. "Said you hadn't been sick, far as he knew."

"I haven't been. I'm not."

"Well, this ain't healthy. An' I know well as anyone that times are tough, but it don't seem to me you have it so bad that you need to starve to death."

"I'm not starving to death." I turn my back as a request for her to fasten my gown, and she obliges, giving a little tug and a pat when she's finished.

"Doctor did some lookin' to see if you didn't have a worm or somethin'. That happens sometimes — people swaller some little tiny thing, and it goes on livin' in their stomach, eatin' and eatin' so's that person don't get a bit of nothin'."

"I don't have a parasite." I inch my way back to the bed, steadying myself on her arm as I sit. "But there might be something else."

She fluffs the pillow and eases me back against it.

"Thought there might be."

"Could the doctor test — is there a way he could tell me if I might be pregnant?"

She stands back, hands on her ample hips, bringing me to envy her softness. "Think you might be?"

I look down, staring at the deflated fabric of my gown.

"When's the last time you had your flow?"

"Ten weeks." I've been watching, calculating daily since that afternoon. It's the first time I've ever had such a conversation out loud. Our pastor's wife gave me a booklet when I was twelve years old, with pictures to explain the "Mysteries of Womanhood." When that mystery first came to life, I found my mother's abandoned, half-empty package of Lister's Towels and a tangle of belts. I wish I'd known Nurse Betty then.

"And you've had relations, I assume?"

"Yes."

"With your husband?" The question holds no judgment, only a deep understanding of my fear.

"Of course." But I don't fool her. She takes my answer and responds with a slight incline of her head, enough to exaggerate the roll of flesh around her neck, and she holds her tongue long enough for me to come clean with the entire truth. When it's clear I have no intention of elaborating, she offers soft congratulations, saying, "You're safe for now. Doc would have made a note of it if you weren't."

I bring my hand to my mouth to capture my prayer of relief and whisper, "Thank you, God," before another concern arises. "But then why haven't I had my time?"

"Because your body can't spare it. You're not takin' in enough to support your own life, let alone another'n."

She puts her hand on my arm, and it is the first touch since his that doesn't make me want to pull away. It is warm and dry and soft, an entire embrace in its strength.

Her hair, gray at the temples, is pulled loosely away from her face, with her crisp white nurse's cap nestled within. Before my eyes, she becomes a figure of both authority and affection as she lifts my hand and folds it between her own.

"Now you have to get yourself better so you can get yourself home."

"I'm fine now, really. Just let me rest —"

She shakes her head at the word *fine*. "You're not fine, and it's not about rest, darlin'. You need to eat. Doctor says five pounds, and you can go home."

"Bring me a steak," I say, my smile weak.

"No such luck." Nurse Betty pats my thigh as she stands. "Now that you're awake, though, I'll send the doctor in, and then I'll be back with your lunch. Gon' keep hubby out of here until you've eaten. Might hurry you along."

With that, she is gone, the curtain left slightly ajar in her wake. Not enough for me to see any of the occupants in the other beds, but I hear them. Rustling, coughing. I realize if I can hear them, they can hear me, and I commend myself for not making a full confession to Nurse Betty. Not that I needed to. It was in her eyes, a full understanding of both my fear and my relief.

"What's your name?" comes a small, thin voice from the other side of the curtain.

I decline to answer, and she goes into a low, wheezing laugh that soon turns into a wet, hacking cough that lasts nearly a minute according to the clock on the wall.

"Are you all right?" I venture once she's gone quiet again.

"Doc says it's dust pneumonia." She pronounces it NEW-monia, and without stirring a thing, I clearly picture the woman in the bed next to mine. Thin, like me. Browned by the sun, dried by the wind. An ever-present handkerchief for those moments when the cough brings up all the grains of earth she swallowed. "Prob'ly goin' to kill me, even if Doc don't say so."

"I'm sure you'll be fine." I try to work hope into my voice.

"You a doctor?"

"No."

"Well, then."

Nothing left to say, so I lie back against my pillow and stare up at the bottle releasing a slow drip . . . drip . . . drip straight into my arm. Already I can tell I feel better than I have in the last days of my memory, and I wish Nurse Betty had left the mirror at my side so I could primp a little bit before the doctor arrives. Left to my limited resources, I lick my fingertips and arrange my hair, avoiding the still-tender spot on my temple. I pinch my cheeks — a trick I learned in the girls' room at school — and tuck my lips between my teeth, biting them until the pain rings in my ears.

I hear footsteps from the far end of the long corridor of a room. The occasional "Good afternoon" punctuates a low, tuneless whistle. The curtain is slid wide, and a man steps close. He has a thin fringe of hair above his ears, with longer strands streaking across the top of his otherwise-bald head. The lenses of his dark-rimmed glasses are smudged, and even before he steps close, I can smell a faint hint of red onion, a remnant of his lunch. He clutches a clipboard in one hand and keeps a stethoscope at the ready in the other.

"Good afternoon, Mrs. —" he consults the clipboard — "Merrill. I see you are wide awake at last. That's a good sign. Breathe deep."

He places the stethoscope to my heart and listens, then instructs me to sit forward while he listens at my back.

"Sounds fine. Much better than when you arrived. And you've had a chance to speak with your nurse."

"Yes." It's the first he's invited me to speak. "She —"

"She informed me of your concern that there might be a pregnancy. From what I could tell in my initial examination, it is unlikely, though I may have overlooked. Given that you have not experienced menses in more than two months' time, I could perform a more specific test, but your advanced state of malnutrition leads me to believe that is the far more likely culprit."

This whole time he's been shining a light into my eyes, touching the tender areas behind my ears, indicating that I should open my mouth wide so he can peer down my throat.

"Sit up, please. Turn. Very good."

I follow the instruction given by his twirling finger until my legs dangle over the side of the bed, at which time he thumps my knee with the same instrument with which he stared into my eyes, bringing an involuntary kick of my leg.

"It is vital, Mrs. Merrill, that you restore your body to a state of normal nutritional health. Or I feel the consequences will be far graver than a knock to the noggin." At which point he tenderly touches the area around said knock. "We have people suffering illnesses far less preventable than this. It shames me to lose a bed to a dissatisfied housewife mired in self-pity. Lie back."

His words swirl around me, a cautionary cyclone of diagnosis and instruction, each one leaving me to wonder if he cares two bits whether I live or die in this bed. The racking cough of the woman next to me calls his attention, and he cocks an ear to her while keeping his eye on me.

"Do you hear that? That, my good woman, is a sickness worthy of a hospital bed. You, on the other hand, have done something silly to yourself, and I have very little patience with the phenomena of female hysterics." He makes another note on the clipboard. "Three days to consume everything brought to you. Five pounds. Or you will be taken to another facility."

"Another facility?"

"You are suffering from an acute case of anorexia. A disorder of the nerves. One best treated in a facility designed to meet the needs of the mentally infirm."

"I am not —"

"Sane people do not starve themselves to death. Not when there is an alternative. I've already sent a telegram to Eastern State

Hospital in Craig County advising them of your case. You may subject yourself to an extensive psychiatric evaluation, or you may avail yourself of our nutritional offerings and take yourself home. Whatever demons are plaguing you, Mrs. Merrill, rest assured you will only give them a stronger foothold in this advanced state of physical deterioration."

Obviously concluded, he makes one more note on the clipboard before replacing the cap on his pen and putting it in his white coat pocket. He wishes me good day and good luck — the warmest of all the words he has said to me — turns on his heel, and whistles away.

I don't even know his name.

I spend the next few minutes listening to the shallow, wheezing breath of the woman next to me.

"Soundin' better, Ladonna," Nurse Betty booms on her way to my bed.

Ladonna. She has a name, and knowing it makes her more than a noise. Now I'll be as aware of her own breaths as I am mine.

Nurse Betty carries a short-legged tray, which she places squarely over my lap once I'm again in a sitting position. "Beef broth," she narrates, pointing to a bowl filled with a steaming, sloshing liquid. "Cherry-flavored

Jell-O, and a big glass of milk. How does that look?"

My first answer would be *unappetizing,* with the exception of the Jell-O, which looks cool and inviting in its quivering mass, but the doctor's threats echo throughout my empty body.

"Delicious. Jell-O? What a treat."

"Thought you might like that." She unfurls a napkin, tucks it into the neckline of my gown. "Put a special request in with the cook the moment you come in."

"That was very kind of you." Finally I feel my body holding enough moisture to produce tears, but I keep them back, lest Nurse Betty see me as weak. In the wake of the doctor's visit, strength — at least the appearance of it — is vital. "I'll save it for dessert."

"That's what I'd do." She hands me a spoon. "Now, eat up, 'less you want to say a blessin' first."

Feeling her insistence, I bow my head and offer a short prayer of thanks, including a request for a blessing for all who saved me. Amen.

"That's nice." Nurse Betty sits on the chair last occupied by Russ, and it strains and creaks in response.

"You're staying?"

"Have to make sure you clean your plate. Bowl, in this case."

"Surely you have other patients to care for. This poor woman in the next bed —"

"Is doin' fine, for now at least. Lord bless her soul. We don't want none of this to go wastin'."

"I wouldn't waste a thing."

"Not with me watchin', you won't. Now, trust me when I tell you, you don't want that beef broth gettin' cold. You gonna spoon it for yerself? Or do you need some help?"

"I'm fine." I dip the spoon within the deep-brown broth and lift it to my lips. The first taste is salty and hot, leaving a savory trail trickling across my tongue and down my throat when I finally find the strength to swallow.

"Good girl," Nurse Betty says, and I know for certain she is somebody's mother.

Chapter 19

I eat. And I eat and I eat. For the first day, nothing but broth, meant to "awaken" my appetite, according to Nurse Betty. Before my first night's sleep, the needle is taken out of my arm, disconnecting me from the constant drip of fluid, and the next morning I am given a scrambled egg and a dish of canned peaches. And coffee, and milk, and Jell-O. Then a soup made with soft vegetables, and a warm roll to sop up the broth. And Jell-O. Eggs again for supper.

I tell myself I am hungry. Tell myself this food is a gift, not to be wasted. Tell myself there is nothing wrong, not really. Not anymore, now that Jim is gone, and I hardly ever think about him at all. I bask in Russ's attention, his face beaming with pride and relief every time I clean my plate. I watch him turn on his heel to chase down a nurse when I wonder if I can't get a second dish of Jell-O. The last time he was this attentive to me was during the days following my second miscarriage. He was at my side every waking moment. Sleeping moments, too, until I had to insist that he go take Ronnie out to play and leave me be for some peaceful contemplation.

During my days in the small Boise City hospital, I never contemplate sending him away.

"I was so afraid I'd lost you," he says — more than once. Holding my hand, stroking my hair. "I don't know how I couldn't see . . ."

Over and over, he asks my forgiveness, each request like a burning coal dropped at the top of my throat. I swallow my shame, though, with the same reluctance as I swallow broth and cream, and soon the nutrients take purchase.

Everything becomes clear. My thoughts run a course to completion instead of swirling upon themselves like dust devils in my mind. Even better, they run forward. Since the day of Rosalie's funeral, all of my mental discourse has circled back to that afternoon with Jim. If I tried to clean my house, I thought only of my own filth. When I willed desire for my husband's touch, I experienced the betrayal of my flesh again. When our congregation prayed for rain, I silently crept away from agreement, fearing the rebirth of Featherling might bring him back. And when I prepared food for my family, I refused it myself, thinking that if I could not bring myself to let Russ know the truth about his wife, I would make her disappear instead. Little by little. Worn down, and worn away.

On the morning of my third day, I am given a robe and allowed to walk out onto the hospital grounds. The day is hot, but clear and still. The grass on the hospital lawn might be brown, but it is still grass — brave, brittle blades like I haven't seen in over a year. The sky is dotted with the kind of white, wispy clouds that so vex the farmers as they float and taunt our parched land. My ears fill with the sounds of life — automobiles, voices, even a rhythmic pounding from a construction crew not far off. For so long I've been surrounded by silence — albeit an audible silence brought on by the constant, unbroken wind. I've seen nothing but dirt, layered an inch thick over our paved streets, drifted up against the sides of our buildings. We've seen homes buried up to their windows. Full-grown trees looking like shrubs poking out of dunes.

I can see; I can breathe — neither of

which have been reliable luxuries of late. I even welcome the immediately oppressive heat from the sun, knowing I can easily avoid its blinding power within the shade of a covered patio, where the contrasting coolness refreshes me to an unexpected degree. I'm wishing I had the foresight to bring a cool glass of water with me, when Russ comes through the screened door.

"There's my girl," he says in a way that brings back memories of courtship. Then, as if reading my mind, he presents me with a tall, white glass, sweating in the contrasting heat.

"What is this?" I ask, taking it from his grip.

"Egg cream." A taste has spilled over onto his thumb and he licks it off. "From the diner, just over there. And if the doctor gives his permission, I can bring you a hamburger for supper. How does that sound?"

I don't want to diminish his enthusiasm by telling him the truth, so I mutter an appreciative sound as I pucker my lips around the waxed-paper straw. The taste that hits me is sweet and cold, effervescent with flavor, and I am about to declare it sublime when Russ beats me to it, using the very word.

"Sublime, isn't it? I thought you deserved

a treat."

"Not all of it," I say, holding the glass to him, offering to share.

"I treated myself to one yesterday. And I've felt guilty ever since."

"Guilty?" I take another sip. "Why?"

He looks past me, out into the sky. "It's another nickel we don't have, at least not to spend on this kind of extravagance. And then, thinking, the difficulties you've had. I felt . . . disloyal."

"That's silly." Already the drink bubbles in my stomach, threatening to burn its way out, each sip diminished in sweetness.

"So you'll forgive me?"

I lay my hand on his knee. "There's nothing to forgive."

"There's so much."

"There is," I concede, "but it's me." I set the glass down on a small iron table next to the bench and go to my knees, clutching both of his hands in mine. When I look up, he appears a mountain of grace, and I know I have to take this first small step to claim it. "You have to forgive me."

The minute he parts his lips, I know it will be in protest. Even more, I know his protest will weaken my resolve, so I rush on before he can speak.

"No, Russ. *Listen* to me. What I've done —"

"You were sick."

"I wasn't sick."

"The doctor said —"

"Not the whole time. Not always. Not before."

"It's understandable. We've lost so much — the store, so many in the church, Rosalie. I know nothing's been the same since we lost her. She was such a wonderful wife, and a good friend. A good woman."

"Better than I am."

"Nola —"

"Stop. *Stop!*" The unforgiving concrete of the porch brings a distinctive pain to my knees, but I imagine it as nails, boring through my bones and anchoring me in place, not to leave until I have laid my sin at his feet. "You have to know. I have to tell you because it's killing me, Russ. It's killing me inside, and if I don't — if I don't tell you —"

"Darling." He works one hand out of my grip and cups the back of my neck, his thumb nestled into the hollow behind my ear, where I know my pulse pounds against it. "I know."

During the course of my impassioned plea, I've risen up, as if my spine has been infused, bone by bone, with steel, until I am ramrod straight before him. Those two words, *I know,* reduce my knees to something like the gelatin with which I am far too familiar, and I collapse into a puddle at his feet.

"What?"

"I know." He says it again, this time with more weight, before lifting me up to sit beside him.

Both of us now look out onto the lawn, watching two men in the standard stark-white uniform push two patients in wheelchairs along the path that winds around what must have been a flower garden at one point. They — the patients — appear to be elderly women, their faces sunken in with toothlessness and thirst. Neither speak, but one soon erupts in the familiar cough and brings a handkerchief to her mouth to trap it. Not an elderly woman, but Ladonnna, looking twice her age in the glaring light of day. Here, by the strength of sunlight, her demise looms large. I watch as the attendant parks her under a tree, while the other goes on with his charge. Within the seconds it takes me to absorb what Russ has said, a passel of children, shepherded by an exhausted-looking man in a sweat-stained blue shirt, pour themselves onto the grass around her, clambering upon her lap despite his protest.

I can sense her smile from here. Surely none of the children notice how quickly she tucks the handkerchief away, how she sits up straighter in her chair, how her body shakes with disguised spasms the minute the youngest is enticed away to fetch a ball.

This is a woman fighting for her family, facing down the demons of disease to claim one more day. Perhaps one more moment. I draw on her strength, trusting it far more than my own, as my heart has come to a crashing halt. True, I've longed for this moment to shed its burden, and yet here I am so unprepared. I envy her slow decline, her time to coach her children in the ways they will survive without her. I had no such premonition with my own mother, and now, after this conversation, neither will my own children. All they'll know is that their mother fell down, hit her head, and never returned. Because Russ knows. And because of *that,* I resolve to fight to survive — as his wife, and as their mother.

With caution, I launch my first defense. "What do you know?"

"About Jim."

I've listened to this man speak the equivalent of years, and no single word has ever

343

worked its way beneath my skin like the way he said that name. *Jim.*

About Jim.

I myself haven't uttered it once since he left, for fear that speaking it aloud would reignite the power the man held over me. Nor can I say it in this moment. Tears spill from my eyes, land salty on my lips, mixing with the lingering sweet, and I bring my free hand — the other still trapped in my husband's grip — up to wipe them away.

"It's all right," he says, his voice gentle as the breeze newly arrived to rustle the trees. On the lawn, one of the children shows his mother a picture, and it gets caught up and blown away. I can hear their laughter as the littlest one catches it.

"How — how — ?" Jim must have betrayed me after all, a bitter irony. Or perhaps Russ has simply *known.* Seen something in my eyes, felt it in the way I'd worked so hard to shrink away.

"How did I know?"

"Yes." I swallow, part of me so thankful that I didn't have to voice it all on my own.

"Mrs. Brown —"

Everything blurs as I spin my head to look at him. "Mrs. Brown?"

"Please, Nola. I don't want you to think it was any sort of gossip on her part. She

344

mentioned, a while back, actually, before your Pa came to live with us, that Jim might be inclined to — how did she put it — be *forward* with you."

"Forward." I return my gaze to Ladonna's family on the lawn. *Forward.* The word is so insulated with puritanical innocence, I know he *knows* nothing.

"I understand the temptation," Russ says. "On your part, and his. You're a beautiful woman."

"Don't say that. Don't ever say that again." Then I wonder. "What do you mean on my part?"

The wind picks up, as evidenced by the fluttering hems on the little girls' dresses. Back home we'd be feeling the first stinging bites of dust, but here on the covered porch, we are spared for a time. The father gathers his children to him — after each has given Ladonna a dutiful peck on the cheek — and the hospital attendant comes walking out at a brisk pace to retrieve her.

"We should go back inside," Russ says, preparing to stand.

I don't budge. "What do you mean *on my part*?"

He tries one more time to encourage me to get up, but then, with an obviously reluctant resolve, uses his body as a frame to protect me from the ever-strengthening wind.

"I hadn't seen him since before the war. Looking back, it seems like we were practically kids. And he said he was wounded, and drifting. Couldn't keep a job. I wanted to do what Christ would have me do. Help the weak, give shelter to the alien. I'd envisioned him as being something *less* than what he turned out to be. I thought I could somehow make up for the fact that he went and I didn't."

I've always known this to be a shame my husband carried, and until this moment, I always sought to soothe it with words of comfort and reassurance. *"Our country needed men of God too,"* I've said countless times whenever we stood — he with his head held low — watching veterans march in flag-waving parades. Not until this moment have I seen us as allies, each carrying a shame we don't dare voice for fear of accruing further judgment.

"You couldn't have known," I say, stepping right back into my role as comforter, swinging the illumination of my regret to his.

"I should have seen — how could I not *see* — the way he looked at you."

I touch his face. "Because you are a good

person. With a good heart. It's hard for the rest of us, sometimes, to live in the shadow of so much goodness."

"And that's why you wanted me to send him away?"

I nod. "Yes."

"Well, now he's gone, isn't he?"

"And he won't be back?"

"Not if I have a say. And never close enough to touch you. Say you forgive me, Nola."

I start to say, again, that there is nothing for me to forgive, but I can see in his eyes that he will accept no such answer. This will be the price of my freedom — yet another lie to carry. But as with any burden, I've grown used to the weight, and I take it on, saying, "Of course, darling Russ. I love you so much."

The wind by now blows with a familiar strength, and the forgotten egg cream glass rattles on the table. With a final "Inside, now," Russ scoops me up in his arms and carries me across the winding pathway to the door that opens to my hallway. "Don't want you to blow away."

I wrap my arms tight around him and bury my face in the hollow of his neck. With total trust, I close my eyes and feel my body fly through the storm.

■ ■ ■ ■

The doctor is kind enough to release me after I've gained only four pounds, having witnessed what he determined to be a "remarkable change in behavior and enthusiasm."

Nurse Betty announces the news after an afternoon meal consisting of a cheese sandwich and a dish of canned pears — neither of which are appealing, but which have been consumed with uncharacteristic compliments and gusto. She carries my housedress draped over her arm; it is freshly laundered and smells like the industrial detergent used on every sheet, pillowcase, and gown in the hospital.

"Somebody's goin' home!" She announces it to the room, getting very little response from the other patients. I've been surrounded by the sounds of coughing from those in with varying stages of dust pneumonia, the quiet moaning of those in with an array of "womanly concerns," and the stunned silence of women who — like me — have taken it upon themselves to seek inward solace.

"Pity I couldn't stay for supper," I say, reaching for my shoes. "I've grown a bit spoiled here."

"Doc left something for you at the front desk. Care package of sorts. Now, honey, I have to ask you —" she pulls the privacy curtain and sits on the edge of the bed, our professional interactions officially at an end — "do you have enough? At home, I mean. I know you have kids —"

"We have plenty." Which I thought was true, until I came here.

"You can't have no shame in askin' for help if you need it. People, neighbors — they want to help."

"Our neighbors have been wonderful to us." I think about Merrilou Brown and her generosity with both her pantry and her opinions.

She pats my hand. "You remember to take care of yourself. You don't want them kids growin' up motherless, do you?"

"Of course not."

"Hard enough when the good Lord takes us on his own accord — we don't need to be rushin' into his arms 'fore our time. Speaking of which, Doc wants you out of here by two. Need the bed."

"I'll be ready."

"As for your other worries," she says, step-ping closer, "there's more'n one way for a child to lose a mother. You have a good 'n' kind husband. One of the best I ever seen. Be thankful to God for blessin' you there."

I nod, unable to speak, and stay perfectly still as she draws me in. I do not remember the last time I was folded into so much softness. Surely not since I was a child. The whiteness of her uniform and the powdery essence of her skin take me to a place of my own innocence. I don't want to leave her arms. Not for Russ or for my home or for anything beyond the sound of her gentle hush.

Too soon, though, Nurse Betty senses my strength and steps away to test it.

"You're goin' to be just fine, girl." And then her soft shoes take her away.

Left alone in the white enclosure, I strip off my gown and step into my freshly clean undergarments before slipping my dress over my head. Immediately I feel the results of three days' nutrition. While it still hangs more loosely than when I first purchased it, I can feel the fabric against my back. I don't need a mirror to know my figure is more prominently and more flatteringly displayed. I do, however, seek out the washbasin at the end of the room to splash cool water — and with it, some color — onto my face and run a comb through my finger-dampened hair. Here, too, I see hints of softness beneath my cheekbones, the planes of my jaw less pronounced. Only my eyes remain the same. Too large, too brown, too many secrets behind them. If they hold my soul, they hold it down in the deepest darkness, no light pouring in or out.

"Are you ready?" Russ is wearing a suit, as if squiring me away on a date, and he hands me a small bouquet of flowers wrapped in brown paper. "I probably should have brought these sooner, but I thought you'd rather have them at home than here."

"They're sweet." I put the bouquet to my nose and inhale. "Thank you. But maybe a bit extravagant?"

"Not too. Now come on. I have the car waiting out front."

"One more thing."

I turn and make my way down the aisle between the beds to where Ladonna lies, staring blankly at the ceiling. Knowing Russ would approve, I take the prettiest of the bouquet — a single pink rose — and hold it out to her.

"Maybe," I say, "the next time your husband comes to visit, you can wear this in your hair. Ask Nurse Betty to help you. It'll bring a sweet blush to your cheeks."

She buries her nose in the petals and is smiling when she draws it away. "You goin' home, then?"

"Yes. And you're sounding much better. I'm sure you will be soon too."

"Doc says about a week. That's how it goes with this. They either decide they can save you or figure out they cain't. No use keepin' a body here to die."

"Here." I reach into my pocketbook and produce a small card I've prepared for this occasion. "My address. In Featherling. Write to me, if you like."

She takes the card, and judging by the depth of her study, I know she isn't accustomed to reading or writing much of anything. Still, she looks up, and I see for the first time in our acquaintance a hint of light in her eyes.

"What would I write about?"

"Life. After you get home. And I'll write back about mine. We both have a lot to live for."

Russ calls me away, so I offer Ladonna nothing more than a quick squeeze of her hand before joining him. Together we walk to the front lobby desk, where Nurse Betty waits with a cardboard box filled with boxes of Jell-O, cans of Campbell's soup, and a paper sack filled with apples.

"Doctor's orders," she says, though the conspiratorial smiles of the other nurses lead me to believe this is more their doing than his. "No offense, honey, but we don't want to see you back."

I interpret the next small gesture as an invitation and throw myself into her arms, surrounding myself with the final white cloud of her strength.

The car is gleaming clean — a condition I haven't seen in recent memory. Russ puts the box of supplies in the trunk alongside the requisite bottles of water and the coiled-up chain. It is a three-hour drive from Boise City to Featherling, and starting this late in the day is not ideal. For the moment, the sky is clear, and we are well prepared should a storm overtake us on the road home.

"We'll be fine," Russ says, obviously sensing my unease. "It won't be like last time."

"Last time?"

"When you were caught. Alone. If nothing else, you'll be with me."

I let him kiss me before opening my door, and then again after he's settled in beside me. The car roars to life the minute he hits the starter switch, and we pull away from the hospital with me hanging out the window, waving a final good-bye to Nurse Betty.

"They were truly wonderful to me," I say, looking forward again.

"Yep."

For the first time, I notice a tightness in Russ's jaw, and it takes little for me to discern the cause of it.

"I didn't see the final bill. Was it a lot?"

He takes one hand off the wheel to pat my leg. "Nothing to worry about."

"Of course it's something to worry about. How much was it?"

"Let's talk later. After you've had a chance to see the kids. I'll bet they can't wait to see you."

I know better than to pursue the conversation. Without ever being unkind or abrupt, Russ has a way of making it very clear when a topic has run its course. His silence is in no way reassuring. If anything, I worry more about what my indiscretion has cost us in measurable financial terms. Everything else — the intimacy, the comfort, the revitalized joy — all of that I can restore with my own efforts. But I have no way of bringing an actual cash flow into the family. And though I'd never say as much to Russ, neither does he. The money we got for the store's goods was distributed to our suppliers, enabling us to cancel the debts of our customers and to pay the outstanding taxes on the store building itself and our farm. We eked out a budget from what was left over, given that the salary from the church had all but dried up. With this — my illness — surely whatever we had left is gone.

"I'm sorry," I say, leaning my head against his shoulder. "I've cost us so much."

"God will provide." He says it with the immediacy that always comes when he speaks through his faith. "Do you believe that?"

"I suppose so."

I wait for him to chastise me for my doubt, but instead I feel his shoulder quake beneath me in what is either a sigh or a chuckle.

"Oh, darling. He already has."

CHAPTER 20

The drive from Boise City takes us through what once was lush, thriving farmland. The first time I took this drive with Russ, we'd gone into town to see a Gloria Swanson film. Not that we didn't have a theater in Featherling. We did — still do — but had we gone there, we couldn't have held hands in the darkness, or snuck kisses to coincide with those of the lovers on the screen. On the drive home, the car open to the stars and the cool spring air, we took a turn off the main road, found a grove of trees in the middle of an empty field, and gave way to the passions of our youth.

"You remember that night?" Russ has never failed to mention it, all throughout our marriage, anytime we have occasion to pass by the turn. My response is to say we'd just seen *Shifting Sands,* and from there we launch into a narrative reliving all but the most lurid of details. Once, when Ronnie was about five years old, we had to bring the story to an abrupt end, and he'd bounced on the seat all the way home, demanding to know why he couldn't go see the trees too. Russ told him that was something he'd do when he was a little older, and I punched his arm — hard — unable to imagine our little boy in such a clutch.

"Of course I remember," I say. "We'd just seen *Shifting Sands,* and . . ."

The boastful beauty of the farmland has been turned to desert, nothing but drifts and dunes of soil, punctuated by the occasional half-buried fence post. Our grove — once hidden from the road by other vegetation — now stands stark on the horizon, leafless and barren as November.

"You were so —" It is his line to say I was beautiful, but he stops short. "Alluring, I think is the word. More than beautiful; I knew plenty of beautiful girls in my time. But you — like one of those sirens we learned about in Greek mythology. Even though you were right beside me in the car, I felt like you were leading me away."

"To your doom?" I make my voice light, but I know — always have known — that I'd never given Russ any reason to feel like he'd taken advantage of my youthful innocence. We'd been innocent together, he perhaps more than I, and I'd offered him everything with our first kiss.

"Maybe. My downfall, at the very least. I knew that night I'd marry you."

"Even if you didn't have to?"

"I had to. Not because of the baby, but because — sin or not — you made me feel like a man. Like I was fulfilling what God wanted me to be. Like Solomon, or David. But I never wanted any other woman. Not before you, not since. Not ever."

I close my eyes, reducing my world to the feel of my arm entwined with his and the motion of the car around me. I know I should say something like-minded in return, but every layer of silence entombs my sin all the deeper. Instead, I mutter, "I love you, Russ," and then something about being eager to see the kids. Then I feign sleep, and within a mile or so, fall true to my slumber.

Though I've been gone from Featherling only a matter of days, I feel as if I'm returning to a place already long forgotten. It used to be that the drive home from Boise City meant passing by one farm after another, with bits of conversation about the families who lived on them — their latest tragedies and triumphs. On this day, conversation is rendered unnecessary. Dirt fields, abandoned houses, fences choked with tumbleweeds. In town, too, it seems more storefronts are boarded up, windows dark, shades drawn. Like life itself has been scraped up and taken away.

But then, as we park the car in front of our own emptied store, my little Ariel comes running down the stairs, wild, untamed curls flying.

"You're home! You're home! You're home!" She shouts it first, as if alerting the remnants of the neighborhood, and repeats it with hot tears on my shoulder. Russ's warnings about being careful, gentle, because Mama had been very, very sick go unheeded. She clings to me, demanding promises that I will never, ever go away from her again, and I make those promises with kisses trailing every inch of her sweet, wet face.

Pa and Ronnie are less enthusiastic in their welcoming. Ronnie stands at the foot of the stairs and offers me a cautious hug. Pa waits at the top and says his first words after I climb up to him.

"Had us all worried sick, you know."

"I'm sorry." I wait for him to step aside and allow me entrance to my own home.

One step over the threshold, and I long

for the stark, impeccable cleanliness of the hospital. In my absence, a fine layer of dust has been invited to coat every surface, and accumulated dirt cushions my steps. The air is close and hot, smells of grease and unwashed clothes.

"I'm glad you were here to take care of the kids, Pa." They, at least, appear to be in the same state of being as they were when I left. "I know that couldn't have been easy for you."

"They's good kids," he says in the tone I've learned to classify as praise.

I spend the rest of the afternoon trying to convince Russ that I am resting, even as I surreptitiously swipe a cleaning rag over every piece of furniture within reach. To-morrow I'll have Ronnie beat the rugs while I sweep the floors, but I have to resign myself to sleeping in grit-ridden sheets for this first night home.

Merrilou Brown shows up at the door with a covered dish of red beans and rice, a ritual I can only assume has repeated itself throughout the duration of my stay in the hospital. The minute she sets the dish on the table, I take her hands and whisper a fervent thanks.

"It's nothing." She twitches her little arms, but I hold on. "It was nice having little ones to cook for again."

"Not just for the suppers." I dart my eyes above her head to ensure a moment's privacy. "Russ told me what you said. About your worries . . ."

"Oh, that." This time she does break away. "I tried to warn you myself, you know."

Her chastisement diminishes me. "I know."

"And I'm afraid your nerves got the better of you."

"You're right."

"But the good Lord has a way of bringing all of our darkness into light, doesn't he?"

"He does." My smile is no match for her sincerity, offering neither grace nor gratitude. "And you're such a dear to bring supper, but I'm sure I'm up to the task after today."

"It'll be easier, I'm sure, once the surplus comes in."

"Surplus?"

"Pastor Russ didn't tell you? Well —" she gives my arm a quick, birdlike squeeze — "I'll let him explain. I need to get back to Mr. Brown before he takes it upon himself to scorch the biscuits."

She yodels a good-bye to Russ and the kids, and I fight back a tinge of jealousy at the warmth with which they — especially

Ronnie — see her through the door. After a deep swallow of my pride, I summon everybody to the table, running a damp rag over each plate before setting it on the fresh cloth I spread down before Merrilou's arrival.

"This glass clean?" Pa asks, inspecting it even as I hand it over. I wonder if he asked himself that same question during his years of living alone, or if he asked it of Merrilou Brown before sitting down to consume her supper, or if it is an inquiry reserved specially for me.

"Just rinsed it out, Pa." The droplets still cling to the rim.

We gather and hold hands as Russ leads us in a blessing, thanking God for the restoration of health and family, while pleading for a restoration of our land. At his amen, I heap generous amounts of Merrilou's food onto each plate, allotting a modest spoonful for myself.

"I'm still not quite up to solid food," I say, answering Russ's disapproving gaze. "I'll have a glass of milk with it, though. And how about some canned peaches with cinnamon for dessert?"

Ariel wriggles delightedly in her chair at the idea, and I nibble two beans off my fork.

"What was Mrs. Brown saying about a surplus?" My question is directed to Russ, but it's Pa who responds first with a disapproving snort and a muttered expletive directed at the government.

Russ ignores the emergent tirade. "Greg wrote to us about it a few months ago, remember?"

I shake my head. So much of what happened since that afternoon remains lost to a blur of survival and shame.

"The Agricultural Adjustment Administration —"

"Them ones what went and ruined good crops, took and slaughtered all for nothin'. Takin' a man's work and makin' it straight into trash."

Russ waits politely for Pa to finish before continuing. "Yes, there were some misguided decisions at the forefront. But now they're bringing food to many of the towns hit hard."

"Puttin' good people on the dole, without them even wantin' the charity."

"Nobody has to take anything they don't want," Russ says, his patience now coming with noticeably more effort. "But I'm offering up the shop as a distribution center." He turns to me. "I hope you don't mind, Nola."

None of his words make any sense, nor do Pa's, and I feel myself on the verge of retreating into the familiar detached fuzziness of hunger and denial. "Why should I mind?" I fight my way back, hoping my questions will bring the missing clarity.

Pa undermines my effort. "Might be you'd mind turnin' what used to be a thrivin', self-made business into a breadline."

"It's not a breadline," Russ says, speaking with the sharpness that only my father can provoke. He brings his voice to a place of gentle reason before continuing on. "I don't know what they'll have. It differs, I think, depending on what's available and the greatness of need. I got a letter last week, asking if they could distribute from the church, but I know there's a few who wouldn't be comfortable going there, so I offered the shop. Put it to some good use."

Pa keeps himself to mere noise, shoveling in a forkful of rice, his disapproval undaunted.

"I think it's a fine idea," I say, separating my own grains of rice on my plate. "And, Pa, you can stay upstairs if you've a mind to." Then, to Russ, "What do we need to do?"

Before Russ can answer, Pa makes a show of cleaning the last of his plate and dropping his fork on the table. The suddenness of his action startles Ariel, who's been following the conversation with her eyes held wide, but Ronnie seems not to notice anything at all.

"Been doin' more'n any man should of dishes these last days."

With that, he leaves, and nobody says a word until the sound of his footsteps down the stairs disappears. When it does, I lock eyes with Russ.

"When did you know about this?"

He shifts uncomfortably in his chair and looks to Ronnie for confirmation. "A few weeks ago?"

"And you didn't tell me?"

Again, Ariel's eyes are wide, in recognition of underlying conflict.

"You seemed so frail. I didn't want to burden you."

"When were you planning to tell me?"

"It's not a secret, Nola." He speaks with an infuriating mix of soothing compassion and subtle accusation, and I flinch at the thought of living with that tone for the rest of my life.

"Of course. It'll be good to help our neighbors. We haven't been able to be generous in such a long time."

"It's for our benefit too, darling."

"No." It is nearly the first Ronnie has spoken since his lukewarm welcome. "We ain't going to take charity. Bad enough people've been bringing food over every day since you went."

Ronnie stands as if to follow Pa's example, but a sharp word from Russ brings him back to his seat.

"Son, I understand your bitterness. This has all been hard on us. But they'll be setting up sometime this week, and you're going to need to help your mother. And I'll be expecting you to do so with an attitude of respect and obedience. Is that understood?"

"Yessir." Ronnie stares deep into his plate.

"I'll help too, Papa," Ariel says, laying a small hand on Russ's sleeve.

"That's a good girl," Russ says, and I might join him in his proud, parental smile, if one lingering question weren't niggling at the corner of my mind.

"Why am I going to need all this help, Russ? Where will you be?"

"I'd rather we talk about it later." He speaks with our understood emphasis when something needs to be discussed outside the earshot of the children.

"All right."

I offer second servings, but everybody declines, meaning there will be enough left over for the next day. Once the pot is safely put away in the icebox, I open a tin of peaches, dish out the servings, sprinkling sugar and cinnamon on each, and thrill the children with promises of Jell-O at all of our meals in the foreseeable future.

"And look at this," Russ says with a glance out the darkening window. "A whole day without a storm. Without much wind, even."

"And Mama's home," Ariel chimes in.

I ask the children to take their dishes to the sink, and then give each permission to listen to the radio while the other takes a bath. Ronnie volunteers to go first, so he can listen to *Amos 'n' Andy,* but Ariel declares she's listened to enough of the radio while Paw-Paw was taking care of them and opts to spend her time making Barney chase after a knotted length of yarn. Our home fills with sounds of happiness and health, and I pray the same will soon be true for Ladonna's home.

Russ comes up behind me as I stand at the sink. I know he means for me to lean back into him, but I don't. Despite the emerging contentment around me, I know there is something he is holding back, and I have to keep my guard until I know exactly what that is. Instead, I toss a comment over my shoulder, something about the quicker this chore is finished, the quicker I can spend this first night in my own bed.

I dawdle bathing Ariel, noting that the water is surprisingly clean even after giving her hair a good shampooing. I let her float her rubber boats and play pretend that the washcloth is a giant sea monster while I work a comb through her tangles. When she is ready to get out, I lift her over the side of the tub, staggering a bit under her weight, and wrap her in the cleanest towel I can find.

"Can I have some of your pretty dust?" she asks, her nose to my nose.

"Well, I suppose that would be all right." By *pretty dust,* she means my talcum powder, and I walk her across the hall to my bedroom, where the tin sits on my dressing table. I dab the soft, white puff into the powder and dust her from top to bottom. When I finish, I give her the puff and let her dab it along my neck and shoulders.

"Now we're the same," Ariel says. "And I'll be able to smell you on my pillow all night. And I won't have to miss you again. Ever."

I take her in my arms and hold her so tight, I fear one of us will crack. "That's right, my baby girl. I'm never going away again. I promise you that."

Later, in the dark stillness of our bedroom, I lie in bed, staring at the light streaming from the kitchen. I know Russ is sitting at the table, preparing his sermon, a glass of water and a short stack of saltine crackers at his elbow — a ritual he's kept for as long as I've known him. I hear the kitchen door open, and Pa's muffled voice. Brusque, Spartan, masculine conversation, before Pa goes into the bathroom to wash up. When he's finished, his shadow stands at my door, and a soft knock opens it wide.

"You awake, girl?"

"Yes, Pa." I clutch the blanket closer to me.

"Glad you're home. Think you can set things straight now?"

"I think so."

He grunts something like an approval.

Alone again, I wait with quiet, still dread. I try to ease my mind with prayer, thanking God for delivering me safely home, for my restored health. I pray for Ladonna, that she'll be home among her children soon. And for Jim to stay away. I think maybe I should get out of bed, down on my knees, because it feels like my prayers are hitting up against the ceiling and sprinkling down all around me. I picture myself getting out of bed and seeing my silhouette on the mattress, outlined by the residue of all I've offered to God.

It seems a full hour passes before Russ comes in, all washed and clean, sliding in beside me. I remain still and stiff at his side, intending to feign sleep, with the exhaustion of the day serving as a viable excuse. But then he turns, props up on his elbow, looks at me. With my eyes long adjusted to the darkness, I turn too and reach my hand up to touch his face. Two days' worth of growth, and only the slightest bit of fuzz on his jaw.

" 'Baby face,' " I sing. " 'You've got the cutest little baby face.' "

I feel him smile, then pull him toward me for a kiss that deepens immediately, and each embrace that follows carries with it the urgency of separation. I respond as one resurrected, burying the woman who would give herself so callously to another man, and emerging from a body rescued from the brink of death. Russ, I can tell, is as starved for my flesh as I've been starved for food, and I give myself to him. I keep my eyes open, filling my vision with bits and pieces of my husband, fearing the images that might come with the dark. Whispers of his name fill the silence, spoken as promises. Through sheer, passionate will, I bring his wife into our bed. The wife who didn't know the heartache of buried children. The wife who didn't know the touch of another man. The wife who didn't know the loss of her very life.

Russ loves that woman, and with each passing moment, I roll myself into her. Disappearing, hiding. Like a skin-fitting costume. Later, as he sleeps beside me, I fight back my tears, terrified I'll wash it all away.

CHAPTER 21

At the post office, I find that two letters from Greg arrived during my stay at the hospital in Boise City, the second a short note dashed off after he received the telegram telling of my collapse.

> Remember, Sis — many have found new homes away from Oklahoma.
> Perhaps it is time for you to consider the same.

I'm glad not to have kept this to read after Sunday dinner, as the mere notion of picking up stakes would be near blasphemous to my father and an unthinkable luxury to Russ. I take Greg's suggestion and tuck it away, just as I do the note, and peruse his letter for Sunday's reading.

Another envelope catches my eye as I riffle through the accumulated post. This one from the hospital, and I can only imagine it is a statement of account. Knowing it was my stay that prompted the bill, I am fully within my rights to open it and see with my own eyes the further sacrifices my family will have to make to accommodate my shortcomings. The addressee, however, is Russ Merrill, so with a strange mix of loyalty and denial, I tuck it within the other pieces of mail before heading back home.

Russ, returning from a morning visit with the Lindstroms, heralds me from across the street, and I wait for him to join me. I don't often have the chance to see him from a distance, and I'm struck by the toll these hard times have taken on him, too. While still broad-shouldered, he seems to lack the comforting softness I remember. His clothes fit with room to spare, like a layer of the man has been planed away. One hand holds his hat to his head, the other waves to a passing neighbor, and then he is at my side.

"I was planning to pick the mail up on my way home," he says by way of greeting. "I should have told you."

"I needed the air. It's fresh enough today."

"Anything for me?" His question holds expectation.

"Letters from Greg. And something from the hospital. Bill, I suspect."

"May I?" He takes the letter, opens it,

retrieves a single sheet of paper, and reads, holding the paper fast against the wind. "They've offered me a position." He looks more at me than the letter, so I know this is no surprise to him. "Letting me work as their chaplain during the week over the next three months, in exchange for forgiving your hospital bill."

"Let me see?" I don't distrust his words, but here, in the middle of our empty, dust-dancing street, they hold no meaning. He hands the letter over with some reluctance, and as I read, a plan unfolds as being clearly one of Russ's design. "You never said anything to me about this."

"I didn't know yet if it would be a possibility. I only proposed it on that last day. I didn't want to worry you."

"About how we were going to pay the bill? Or about your going away?"

"Neither."

A droplet of hope forms within me. "Does this mean we're moving?"

"Moving?"

I wave the letter, daring the wind to take it. "Away from here. Into town. You can't serve there if we don't live there."

His face fills with compassion, and I know I've lost. "Oh, Nola. We can't. Where would we live? I'm not going to draw a salary. For me, they'll have a small room. A dormitory for staff. But I can't bring all of you with me."

"We're to be left here, alone?" The idea holds more fear than he can imagine. I hand the letter back to him, and we begin a slow, strolling pace toward home.

"I'll be back every Saturday to spend the day, prepare my sermon, and go back after dinner on Sunday."

An understanding of his priorities dawns, and I cannot hold back my bitterness. "So, you'll come back for *them.*"

"They are still my church, darling — *our* church — and what they give is what's going to sustain you while I'm gone."

"I hope you didn't intend for that to be comforting. They'll eat me alive."

"That's not true."

"It is true, and you know it. They only tolerate me because they love you. Please — don't leave me alone with them."

For a moment, I think my pleas have found their purchase, but his hesitation serves only to strengthen his argument. "Three months. Next week through November, and it'll be done. We can't ignore this obligation."

"I'm sorry." I'd eaten half of a bowl of grits that morning, with butter and sugar, and I feel it churning, unwelcome, in my stomach. When we get to the front stairs, I pause for a moment, hand clapped over my mouth until I am sure they are settled. It's a reminder of how I've driven him away. "It's my fault. I got sick — I let myself get sick. To think the whole time I was so worried about failing you as a wife. And now you're leaving."

"I'm not leaving. Not you or the kids. I'm working is all, and there's a lot of people who have had to go and do the same. I'm just blessed not to have to go too far for too long."

We begin a slow ascent, me leading the way, as the stairs are too narrow for us to take them side by side. The familiar view of the street unfolds incrementally with each step. The little I'd seen of Boise City showed it to be suffering its own decline, but far from the astounding desolation laid out before me.

"But would you ever?" I ask, keeping my toe poised on hope.

"Would I ever what?"

I stop, look back and down at him. "Work. Leave here and do something else. Something different."

"I'm called to be a minister, Nola. You know that."

"You could be a minister anywhere."

He smiles. "Do you think it's that simple? Drive up and find a church?"

"No, but look at this. Being a chaplain. I know they're not paying you now, but they could."

"It's not what I'm seeking."

I grip the handle of our front door, not wanting to bring such an unresolved question inside. "But couldn't you, for once, put our needs above theirs? This town is dying all around us. This whole part of the country is blowing away. There's no high school for Ronnie next year. Do you know that? I've only ever asked you for two things during our entire marriage, and the first one was to not let that friend of yours into our home."

I was bucked up, strong against him, with only the slightest quiver in my chin to betray my fears.

"Don't bring that business up, Nola. I don't want to talk about that."

"Then I won't, except to say that you had your way, and it might have ruined us. Now, you took on this little church because you didn't have a choice, and you've been so faithful to them. But how faithful have they been to you?"

We are on full display now, brow to brow with each other on the street's stage. Russ leans closer and drops the volume of his words too low to be picked up by the breeze.

"Everything we have is because of them."

"No. We have all of this —" I wave my hands, encompassing the whole of our apartment — "because of my uncle's store. Which you sold out from underneath me."

"You agreed —"

"And it was decided and done before I did. As for this —" I grab the hand holding the letter and shake it — "you didn't solicit my opinion there, either. Everything in our lives comes to me as a done deal."

"Don't forget, darling. *You* came to me as a done deal."

He's never hit me. In all our years together, he's never raised his voice, let alone his hand, in anger. Even in this moment, his voice is calm and controlled, which makes his words cut all the deeper, inching through me with slow, deliberate expression. I can tell, even as he says the last of them, that he regrets every one. Recoiling on himself, he reaches out instantly to rescue my spirit, the same as if he meant to keep me from throwing myself off the balcony and into the street below.

"I didn't mean that."

I should soothe him. Tell him that, of course, I know he loves me. Would have married me whether he had to or not. That our lives hadn't been a second-place ribbon from the prizes we sought. But I don't. In the back of my mind, I hold words of confession that would cut far deeper than this. I let them settle and hurt beyond their intention.

"You never say what you don't mean."

We have three more days of dust before he leaves, one heavy enough that we can't see the building across the street for the better part of an hour. The second storm lasts deep into the night, yet when the wind stops blowing, Russ dresses to go to the church to greet the gathering survivors.

"You and the kids stay put," he says, speaking into my dream. "I'll let everyone know you're safe."

For the first time, though, no one else shows up. He waits an hour, lights glowing from the windows, before making his way down the empty street back home.

"You can't give up," he says from behind the pulpit after the third storm. It happened to blow itself out late on a Sunday afternoon, which accounts for the gathering of all his people. *All,* by this time, meaning fewer than twenty, even counting the children and babies. "We have to hold strong against this enemy. If we can't stand up against the natural forces that seek to slay us, how can we ever fight against those that are of the supernatural? The angels of heaven and the demons of hell battle each other daily, invisible in our midst. The next time the wind blows, imagine that cloud as the up-dusting of their battle. Satan seeks to distort and destroy, but our Savior promises us that by our faith we shall conquer."

From behind the pulpit, he preaches to an imagined crowd of thousands — or even the hundred who have been in attendance throughout our lifetime together. He runs his finger along the edge of the pulpit and brings up his hand, as if balancing an invisible china plate.

"Faith the size of a mustard seed. Faith not much more than the dirt sitting on the end of my finger." He blows, and we all see the faintest cloud puff away from his lips. "Imagine that much faith. Imagine your faith, magnified, joined together to create the walls we've seen rising out from the west. Oh, people —"

And then, something he rarely does. Something he avoids because the first time — that first Sunday — he'd lost himself to me. Or so he likes to say. He looks at me.

Speaks to me, allowing all the rest of his congregation to fade into blackness, like they used to do in the old silent movies we watched together during our courtship.

"If we were fueled by hope instead of dwellers on our hunger. If we would only cling to God's promises instead of holding on to bitterness. We could find joy, not only in every morning, but in every moment of stillness."

He closes the sermon by announcing that he will be unavailable during the week due to a ministerial opportunity in town. Nothing about the trade of time, nothing about the outstanding hospital bill, nothing that would unduly burden these people with responsibility for our livelihood.

"And," he continues, "while I know the Lord will watch over my beautiful wife and children during my times of absence, I know I can trust you to keep a neighborly eye on them as well."

There's a smattering of nervous laughter, my own included, which I use to mask my discomfort at the thought. For a moment, a single note of camaraderie fuses us, but my amusement dies off first, leaving me ensconced in silence and alone.

It's an adjustment, the absence of a person,

and for our household, having Russ gone means a new kind of quiet. I never noticed before how we each were persons content to our own devices — Ronnie out with his friends, Pa lost to his thoughts, Ariel enraptured with her kitten, now more than half grown. Not to say my girl is quiet — she's a chatterbox of swirling words, but her voice takes on a certain hum in one-sided rambling that is easy to ignore. Russ has always been the one to serve as the spirit between us. Without him, silence falls as heavy as the heat, rippling in a monosyllabic mirage of conversations.

Then, at the edges, something new. My father's cough.

Perhaps the sound is nothing new. These days, anywhere you go, a person's every third breath is a cough. We've a constant scratch at the backs of our throats, always something that needs to be expelled. It might well be that I've ascribed this to the myriad of sounds an old man makes, along with grumbling, complaining, and grunts of gruff approval. With Russ gone, though, it takes on a menacing note. It fills all the empty, silent gaps of the day. And at night, when I'm in bed alone, the window left open to the hope of a clean breeze, it wafts up, the way I used to fear my smoke would.

It's stronger at night, and I realize Pa's trying to mask it during the day, stifling its strength.

For a time, it's been his secret.

At breakfast one morning, the Friday of Russ's first week away, after the children have cleaned their plates and gone off to play, I tell Pa that he needs to go see a doctor.

"An' have 'em tell me what, 'xactly?"

"That you're sick."

"I know I'm sick."

"But to see if they can help."

"Far as you know, they got any cure for this?" His guard is down, and he erupts into a wet cough in the middle of his sentence.

I think about Ladonna, whom I like to remember as a friend, though I've not heard a word since I last saw her. In my mind, she is cured. Strong, making sandwiches for her passel of healthy, rolling children.

"No, not yet. But they could give you something, I'm sure."

"Figure I'm just gettin' what I deserve, is all. Done my part tearin' up the earth. Bad as any other farmer. Now it's come back to git its revenge on me. Ain't no kind of sin goes unanswered."

He's coughing again, the spasms bringing the coffee to slosh over the rim of the cup.

Wordlessly, I take a glass from the cupboard, run it under the tap, fill it up, and set it in front of him. He can barely exude, "Glass clean?" before accepting my assurance and taking it down in soothing, careful sips.

I turn my back, allowing him the privacy of wiping his mouth and chin, and return with a fresh drink for myself. It's not that we haven't had moments to ourselves, just the two of us, over these past months, but always before there'd been an impediment to what I am about to ask. At first the knowledge seemed too dangerous, and then, while I was wasting away, too heavy. Up until now, there's been no room for the truth, and time enough to learn it. But knowing Russ will be home tomorrow to fill up the empty spaces, and the pallor of my father's face measuring years as days, I choose to indulge my curiosity.

"What'd you do to him, Pa? What happened to Jim?"

"Thought you'd know better than to speak that name."

"Where is he?"

He takes a sip of water and wipes his mouth on his sleeve. "Decide you want him sniffin' 'round here now that your husband's outta the way?"

"No."

"Then don't ask."

"But he's —"

"A drifter. Worthless as anythin' driftin' out there. An' that's what I left him to do."

"So he's alive." It's the first I've allowed myself to contemplate the contrary.

"Does it matter?"

"Of course it does."

"Seems to me you're set on mournin' him or missin' him, and ain't either one of them proper for a wife."

"I don't miss him. I've just . . . wondered."

"If I left him for dead at the side of the road? Or popped him a little persuasion to leave my little girl alone?" This he says with his hands clutching an imaginary shotgun aimed at an invisible enemy.

"And I've worried. About him as much as you, Pa. If something happened . . . if you did something —"

"Worryin' ain't gonna add one day to your life, girl. Nor mine neither. An' here I am with naught but days left, looks like."

"Don't say that. When Russ comes home, he can take you back to the hospital with him."

Pa shakes his head. "Got no use for them places."

"Well, that's obvious enough," I say. "Maybe if you'd taken my mother to a hospital . . ." I leave the thought unfinished.

"You think I didn't try? Wouldn't none take her, Denola. An' her not welcome at the reservation, neither, half-breed that she was." He speaks with the usual irritation that accompanies all conversation about my mother, but I can hear the regret buried within. "I never could do fully right by her."

He's coughing again. Not explosive like before but a rumbling chain like traveling thunder.

"I have to go to the post office," I say, leaving him to his spasm.

Before I go, I rinse his glass and refill it, and ask him to stay upstairs for a time while the kids are out. I tie a bright floral scarf over my head to protect my hair from the dust and our neighbors from the sight of seeing me with the pins still in.

It's a teasing day, the smell of rain drifting in from somewhere, without a hint of it on any horizon. Head down against friendly salutations, I run across the street and down the half block to the Browns' house. We've given up our telephone since Russ's pastoral duties have so greatly diminished, but the Browns are kind enough to let us use theirs when we need to.

"Well, such a surprise," Merrilou says when she opens the door. "And what a pretty scarf. The colors suit you."

I thank her and ask, in a manner I hope is not too abrupt, if I could please use her telephone. "I need to call Western Union."

"Well, of course."

She responds without any overt sign of curiosity or concern, but I feel I owe her some form of reassurance.

"I need to send a telegram to my brother."

"Is everything all right, dear?"

"For now, yes. I know it'll be charged to your number." I produced the small handful of coins in my apron pocket. "I'll leave you the money today, but you'll let me know if it's enough?"

Merrilou waves off my concern saying, "Pshaw!" My impatience, though, is palpable, and she allows me to the little nook where a telephone sits on a table, both in shining perfection. There's a notepad and pencil nearby, and I use them to draft my words. Explanation will be too pricey, and vagueness ineffective. I write my message on the pad and tap the lead of the pencil on each word, counting the cost.

PA SICK. COME HOME.

CHAPTER 22

The fact that my brother returns to me looking like a man aged from a decade in battle comes not from the years spent away, but as a direct result of the seven-hour drive with Russ from Boise City — four of those hours spent pulled to the side, with chains anchoring them against the electric charges from the sky and water-soaked rags tied around their faces.

"Every politician in Washington should live through this," Greg says later at dinner. He's showered by then and is making a good effort not to be too obvious in inspecting his fork, his plate, his food as we sit around the meager feast I was able to put together while Russ briefly met with our church family, promising them an introduction the following day.

"That's all we need. 'Nother load of filth blown in," Pa says. We've set up a table and chairs down in the abandoned shop so that he won't have to climb the stairs anymore. Doing so takes a toll on his weakening breath.

Greg laughs. "That's one I'm going to tell at the next committee meeting when I get back."

"Should go over well," I say, sitting up a little taller, trying to match my brother in posture, if not position.

"They already call me the Okie. It's expected."

Looking at Greg, I can't imagine anyone calling him an Okie. He inherited few of our mother's features, leaving him with her prominent cheekbones but my father's narrow nose. He also has Pa's slate-gray eyes, and hair at least three shades lighter than mine. He wears it short and neat, and though he is shy of forty years old, the first signs of thinning are obvious at his temples. He doesn't even sound like one of us; in fact, I find myself slowing his speech in my head, stretching out the syllables to match them to our Oklahoma pace. Pa has no such patience, and already in the few hours Greg has been home, he's been told repeatedly not to talk like a rabbit is chasin' his thoughts.

Greg is an object of unabashed curiosity in church the next day, as it's been a year since our church has seen any kind of visitor. Not only does he stand out in his well-cut suit, but he is such a specimen of health and vigor. His body is not permanently bent against the wind; his eyes are wide and open, not beaten down by dust. He breathes deep and silent, no rattling from deep within his chest. When we introduce him to the church, he stands tall and looks at each person, having yet to succumb to our perpetual shame.

It is a treat, I say, to have the man himself at the Sunday dinner table, rather than a simple voice from a page, and he does not fail to entertain us with stories too complicated — and in some cases too ribald — for correspondence.

Later, in the blazing light of the afternoon, Greg and I walk the streets of Featherling arm in arm as I narrate its demise.

"People started pulling up stakes and leaving," I say as we stand in front of a boarded-up storefront that used to be a favorite women's boutique and hat shop.

"We see that." Greg takes a thin cigarette case out of his shirt pocket and offers one to me, looking incredulous when I refuse.

"Russ doesn't like it."

"Russ ain't here." As if an Oklahoma inflection will change my mind.

I shake my head again. "I promised."

Greg shrugs, lights his cigarette, and takes a long, surveying turn with the first drag. "Thing is, all those people who left? They aren't finding anything better than what you got here. California's got them piled up like dogs at the gate."

I name off five families that went to California. "Wonder if they'll come back?"

"They can't. It takes money to move, and it doesn't look like there's much here to come back to. Even if the drought ends — *when* the drought ends — it's going to take some time before this is viable country."

We start walking again, slowly so as not to kick up too much of the dust that buried the sidewalk beneath us.

"You've got to get out of here, Sis."

"And go where? Join the other dogs in California?"

"You never wanted to be here. Even when you were little, all you ever talked about was leaving."

"You did too. Unfortunately, I didn't have a war to take me away."

"So what's keeping you here now?"

"Russ. I think he feels sometimes like he's the only anchor keeping this town from blowing off the map."

Greg looks around. "Seems like a lightweight anchor."

"He has his church — what's left of it. And he wants to save what he can. The store, the building, anyway. And Pa's land, as long as we can keep up the taxes. He calls us the remnant, faithful to stand strong in the face of obliteration." I say this last part in Russ's orator's tone, not meaning to mock, but bringing a smile to Greg's face nonetheless.

"Seems to me he's only standing with one foot in town."

"We need to head back." I take his elbow and turn us toward home. "Even if the wind's not blowing, it's not good to stay out too long. Air's thick."

"I've noticed."

He takes a final puff on his cigarette and tosses it into the dirt. Despite our efforts for slow, careful steps, we walk in a perpetual cloud that will fill the cuffs of his slacks. It clings to my bare legs. We take it with us everywhere.

"Besides," I say, picking up the conversation, "we can't go anywhere until Pa gets better."

"All the more reason. Get him away from here. Take him someplace where he can breathe some fresh, clean air. Money's not a problem, at least not as big a problem as it might be for most people. I'm not a Rockefeller or anything, but I can swing a few train tickets, help set you all up in a little place."

"Where?" With that one word, I allow myself a glimpse into his vision.

"Out in DC with me. Or Baltimore, even. Some nice places there if you think you could bring yourself to live with the snow."

"I've learned to live with this, haven't I?"

That night, as Russ prepares to return to Boise City, I ask if we shouldn't send Pa back with him.

Russ shakes his head. "I don't know that there's anything they could do for him there that we can't do here. I've brought home the elixir. Sit him up as much as you can, get him walking. Let him rest. It's what I've seen the doctors do with the other patients."

"But you don't think he'd recover more quickly there? At the hospital? It seemed like everything was so much cleaner there. Even the air, I mean. Healthier."

"You know how stubborn your father is."

"Maybe not even to stay. Let a doctor examine him to see if there's anything else we should be doing."

I know Russ attributes my sense of urgency to that of a caring daughter, but my heart rings with my brother's promise. And if Pa were to get better . . .

"Go ahead." Russ draws me back from my reverie. "Ask your father if he wants to drive to Boise City and back just to visit a doctor about his cough. Darling, I think a whole day in the car would do more harm than good."

"But will you try to talk to one of the doctors? Tell him everything about Pa's symptoms. The coughing and, lately, the confusion."

"I will. I promise. And I'll call you if there's anything else you should do."

I walk with him out to the car, where he tosses his now-familiar satchel into the backseat before taking me in his arms. My cheek settled against his chest, I let myself feel the beat of his heart before lifting my face for his kiss. It is brief and sweet, as if he were only going around the block for a deacons' meeting at the church instead of seventy miles away for a week's time.

"I miss you when you're gone," I say, my finger tracing the soft edge of his jaw.

"It's a great opportunity God has given me. To do his work and meet our needs. I'll be back before you know it."

"Saturday. Noon."

"Saturday, noon. Yes. And in the meantime, isn't it nice to have your brother here for company? It'll be good for the two of you to catch up."

I offer up a sly, coy smile. "We were always able to get into some kind of mischief together, but I'll try to keep us out of trouble."

Trouble, though, soon finds us. Over the next three days, Pa's health declines rapidly, with a fever that refuses to break and breath that comes through lungs as full of dust as the constant wind outside. I wondered if he wouldn't be better off upstairs, set up in our bedroom, with a window's view to the Oklahoma sky, which, when it isn't a dusky brown, shines blue as water during the day. But Pa won't budge.

"Ain't gonna die in my daughter's bed." A racking cough envelops the last words, accompanied by brownish spume.

"You're too stubborn to die in any way," I say, gently wiping the corners of his mouth. "How about we move your bed up to the front room instead? You can listen to the radio, and Ariel could spend more time with you."

It is the mention of Ariel's name that softens his reserve, working into his heart the way she alone ever could.

I think the move can wait until Russ gets back, but Greg insists the transition is something we can handle. We allow him to make his own slow-going gait up to the apartment, where I have a tepid bath waiting, not only as a means to bring down his fever, but also to temper the sourness that comes from so many bedridden days in the heat of summer. Ronnie stays close by the door, keeping it mostly shut to protect Pa's privacy, but open enough to maintain that all is well. While Pa soaks, Greg and I work to move the bed frame and mattress, flipping it to a fresh side, and making it up with fresh linens and pillows. It fills the majority of the space in our front room, especially as it is angled to allow Pa to look out the window while keeping the kitchen out of view.

We work quickly and, for the most part, silently. While I attend to the finishing touches — a narrow side table with a pitcher of water and a stack of clean handkerchiefs — Greg goes into the bathroom to help Pa with a shave and into a pair of crisp, clean pajamas. Years of living with my father's contrary nature have me bracing myself for his disapproval at being treated like some kind of invalid, but as Greg escorts him into the room, Pa seems not to notice that he is in any kind of a new place. He climbs into the bed without question, while we pile and prop pillows behind him. When he is settled, I offer him a drink of water.

"Glass clean?" The question almost disappears in the storm of his cough, but I've anticipated it as always.

"It's clean, Pa."

He drinks it down, along with a spoonful of the elixir Russ brought home, and drifts off into a somewhat-peaceful sleep. I go into the kitchen and make a lunch of cheese sandwiches and iced tea, to which Greg adds half a chocolate bar for each of the children, as well as one for me, which I say I will eat later — maybe after supper. With lunch finished, I excuse Ronnie to go outside to play ball with his friends, making him promise to wear his mask, no matter if the wind seems dusty or not.

"Oh, Ma," he complains, as he does every time I admonish him, "none of the other kids have to wear 'em."

"Well, they should. And since you said so, I'll bring it up at the next church meeting, so all your friends know you were the one who ratted them out."

He leaves, sulking, baseball mitt in hand, with the once-white mask looped around his neck, and a promise to cover up his nose and mouth properly once he gets outside. I figure that promise is as valid as the one I'd given to eat the chocolate bar, but let him go anyway. Besides, later I'll send Ariel out to spy.

Greg and I take our tea to the sofa, where we watch Pa sleep, his once-powerful chest rising and falling with labored rhythm.

"Russ should be here," Greg says. Not accusatory, but as a point of fact. "This is too much for you to handle alone."

"He can't right now. We have bills. Obligations. There's no choice."

"There's always a choice, Sis. Is this what you want?"

I take a long drink of tea, letting it fill the void left by my unfinished sandwich. "No. Not a bit of it."

"You need to get out." He picks up the conversation as if three days haven't passed since its inception.

"We're stuck here, Greg. Buried."

"If you're that miserable, you can leave, you know."

"Spoken like a true bachelor." I laugh, hoping the sound will lighten the moment, and cool my skin against my glass.

"I'm serious. When we were kids, we talked about getting out. I meant everything

I said about wanting you to go to college, but even then I knew you wouldn't have much choice. But that's changed now. You're an adult; you're the parent. You need to do what's best for your family."

"I'm the wife, Greg. That limits me."

He considers that for a moment. As he's never had to answer to anyone since leaving home, I can understand his bluster.

"There's something wrong, Nola. I can tell."

"What can you tell? You haven't laid eyes on me but half a dozen times since the wedding."

"But I *know* you. You've always been so full of life. It's the one thing Pa was always on you about. To calm down. Slow down. And I'm looking at you now — since I got here, actually. You look defeated."

I glance pointedly at our father. "Looks like he won."

"He's not going to win. You can't let him. I won't let him. Nola, you're stronger than that. You always have been, even though I'm not sure you can see it."

I take another long, slow sip and rest my near-empty glass against my leg. "Can you keep a secret?"

"I work for the government," he says, taking his turn to joke. "It's what I do best."

"I left him once."

"Pa?"

I shake my head. "Russ. Just for a little while. For an afternoon."

"Where'd you go?"

I stare at Pa, at the tiny stream of spittle coming from the corner of his mouth. "Nowhere."

"Did you go alone?"

"No." I barely say the word aloud, but the meaning rings clear between us, and Greg asks no more questions. "It's taken a long time for me to come back. I almost didn't — that's why I had to go to the hospital. That's why Russ has to work at the hospital: because I went away and took too long coming back. And sometimes, I have to wonder if I'm really here at all. The whole world, it seems, is blowing away around me. Nothing but dirt and wind. And Russ. And the kids, and Pa. And then, for a time —"

He takes my hand, his touch cold and clammy from the glass. "You've got me, too, Sis."

"You're too far away. You're not a part of this."

"I'm sorry about that, but I'm here now. Let me help."

"How? And don't tell me to pack up and leave, because that's impossible. We have the store here, for whatever it'll be. And the farm."

"Sell it."

His words come out with such finality, it seems the deed's already done.

"We just paid the back taxes."

He shrugs. "So? We're going to buy farms all over the country."

"But why? You won't be able to grow anything. Land's dead."

"Land's never dead. It's just overworked. We can bring it back. Replant the grasslands, rotate the crops. It might take a while — years, maybe. Probably. But we can bring it back."

"It's not too late?"

"It's never too late."

"You know Pa'll never go for that."

"Then we won't tell him. Not until we have to."

We sit a little longer, until Barney's appearance heralds Ariel's arrival, her face pink from sleep and her hair askew. Pa chooses that moment, too, to open his eyes, and seems momentarily startled at his surroundings. I explain his change in venue after sending Ariel into the kitchen to fetch him the uneaten half of my sandwich and a fresh glass of tea, which she brings in, expertly balanced on a tray. Next, I've intended to send her out to call her brother home, but the sky has turned our view to a sepia tone, and I rely on Ronnie's experience to get himself inside before the wind kicks itself into something dangerous. Sure enough, the bell downstairs sounds, followed by the familiar, healthy stomp of my son's footsteps.

"Go wash up," I order, without hardly giving him a glance.

"Yes, ma'am," he complies without argument.

He'll be hungry again, so I set about cooking a small pot of rice, to which I will add sugar and butter and cinnamon, and pour out the last of the cold milk into two clean cups. I offer Greg the same snack — like Mother used to make for us when we were children — but he declines. Pa, however, perks up at the mere mention of it, and I prepare a heaping cup for him, too.

As a special treat, I allow the children to eat in the front room with Pa, where they listen to the radio. Ariel takes full advantage of the privilege, allowing Barney to nibble bits of the warm rice off her spoon. When the comedy team on the radio tells a joke, she laughs along with her brother and grandfather, though it is clear she hasn't understood. Greg and I laugh too, though I suspect more at the relief of seeing Pa so lucid and, possibly, happy.

"It's a beautiful family," Greg says.

"Thank you." I go to the sink to rinse out the rice pot.

He follows. "I'm only going to ask you this one time." His voice is so low, I barely hear it over the sound of running water. "What happened to him?"

Greg doesn't need to know his name, let alone say it. Without a single glance away from my chore, I answer.

"You'd have to ask Pa. He took him away."

I ask Pa too. Late at night, while the children sleep in their rooms — Uncle Greg in Ronnie's bed, Ronnie on the floor. I lean in close, trying to catch him in the weakness of semisleep.

"Where is he, Pa? What did you do? Did you kill him?"

But I get only garbled sounds in response.

By Thursday it is clear that Pa is bad. Worse. His breathing labored, his fever rolling and breaking. We can hear his wheezing above the wind, throughout the house, and there is no way to describe what spews forth during his fits of coughing.

"We need to take him to the hospital, Greg. It's time."

"Nola . . ." And nothing else. No other

words needed. There will be no drive to the hospital. There is nothing they can do.

Russ arrives in the wee hours of the next morning, bringing with him a small, brown paper bag from which he pulls a glass bottle that looks minuscule in his large, strong hand.

"Morphine," he says, following with the doctor's instructions for how many drops to administer. "To help him sleep."

"I don't want him to sleep. I need more time."

"We only have the time that God gives us." These words, I am sure, have been uttered at the bedside of countless people in Featherling — old and young. In this moment, he is not my husband, not the son-in-law of this dying man, but a pastor. A man of God, versed in the gift of mercy.

He brings a chair out from the kitchen and positions it at Pa's side. Folding one of the old man's hands between his own, Russ bows in prayer. "Father God, we are here in your presence, ready to do your will."

Pa's eyelids flutter in the soft light of the lamp. In a voice thick with death he says, "You took my girl. Took her away."

"Denola's right here," Russ replies, his voice gentle. He stretches out his other arm, beckoning me to his side. "I didn't take her anywhere."

"And we're all of us payin' for that sin."

"Jesus paid the price for our sins, Lee. I know you believe that."

"Jesus," Pa says, his eyes tracking along the ceiling. Then he looks at Russ. "He tried to take her, you know. Wanted to take everything. He told me. Everything."

I stand, breathless as my father, listening to him confess my sins.

"Nobody took her." Russ has looped his arm around my hip and drawn me closer.

"I ain't a good man," Pa says.

"Of course you are." I go to my knees, laying my brow on the sheet next to his arm. "Everything you've ever done, it was all to protect me. And I'm here."

Pa pulls his hand free of Russ's grip and touches my face. "You look like your ma."

I press his hand closer, turn my face to kiss his palm. "You've always said so."

"I loved your mother."

After that, there's no need to administer drops to help him sleep. There are seven more shuddering breaths, and my father's spirit is swept away.

CHAPTER 23

In his obituary, Pa is described as a success-ful Oklahoma rancher, survived by a son, a daughter, and two grandchildren. It runs five lines in a narrow column and is wired to every newspaper within a hundred miles. Greg and I both know only of the existence of distant cousins, practically nameless, from scattered comments throughout our childhood. Where they live — *if* they live — is as much a mystery as the details of their connection to our family. Neither of us have any reason to think long-lost kin will show up for Pa's funeral. Still, Greg says, we need to post the notice of his passing, lest anyone wants to lay claim to what is left of Pa's estate. Any legitimate heirs, and we won't be able to sell the land for whatever pit-tance the government is willing to give.

Greg explains all of this to me while I work an iron over Pa's best shirt. Russ is out taking care of the burial arrangements, and the children are downstairs in the shop helping Mrs. Brown prepare it for tomorrow's reception.

"None of this would be necessary if Pa had left a decent will," Greg says. "We could sell it tomorrow."

"I don't know that he ever intended to die."

"You don't think he might have one out at the house?"

I sprinkle starch along the sleeve. "Could be."

"We need to go out there to look."

The iron hisses against the fabric. "You don't want to go out there, Greg."

"Sounds more like *you* don't want to."

"You're right. I don't." I drape the shirt over the back of the chair, a towel underneath and over to protect it from the dust.

"I understand if there are painful memories for you there," Greg says. He's taken on the task of shining Pa's good shoes, and it occurs to me that the only people in this town with clean shoes are the ones in their graves.

"Do you?" I set the iron on its cooling plate and fold the board. "Because you were never around much after you got out."

"I know. I should have been. I knew you had it rough there, but I couldn't just *take* you, even if I wanted to. Remember, I was pretty young myself, and once I'd gotten away —"

"I understand. I wouldn't have come back either."

"I fought a war, Nola."

"So did I. Against *him.*"

"And you survived. You got out. Maybe just not the way we planned."

I brace my hands on my hips and look around the tiny room dominated by the bed, now stripped of its soiled linens. "And look how far I've come. I could have gone to college, you know."

"Of course you could have." No hint of condescension in my brother's voice. "You're brilliant."

"That's what I tried to tell him. Not that I was *brilliant,* but that I was smart. As smart as any boy. As smart as *you.*"

Greg gives a final buff of a shoe, then carries the pair over to where the rest of Pa's burial clothes are laid out.

"That was your mistake, comparing yourself to me. He never forgave me for leaving."

"No, he never forgave you for not coming back."

"Look, I'm sorry." He hugs me, and I let the weight of days fall against him. "I shouldn't have stayed away. At least not from you. I should have done something. Fetched you myself if I had to, but Russ beat me to it."

"Fetched," I repeat, mimicking him. For the first moment since his arrival he sounds like his Oklahoma roots — something I'm sure he's worked hard to erase.

He laughs, gives me a squeeze, and kisses the top of my head. "I always thought you were happy. Love, marriage, kids, home."

"I am happy," I say, trying to convince myself as much as him. "And there's no reason you shouldn't have a family of your own."

"Someday." His wistfulness matches mine. "But not here. I could never live here again."

To say that Pa's funeral is sparsely attended would do the occasion a kindness. As expected, no distant relatives make the journey, though they'd hardly have had time to do so, since we bury him a scant two days after his passing. With summer turning into fall, the frequency and violence of the winds is increasing, so we dare not waste a window of stillness to gather at the cemetery.

This morning, my brother, my husband, my children, the Browns, and a handful of the faithful from the church stand with us, including Ben Harris, who came to offer his condolences, having seen the notice in the scrap of a town where he and the baby now live with his parents.

Afterward, we set up the luncheon along the gleaming store counter, which seems almost disrespectful, as Pa always scorned the foodstuffs distributed from this place. There are sandwiches made from the government's ham, pickles, a macaroni salad, and pie. A modest spread by any estimation, more so than I ever remember for a funeral. I know, however, that if it weren't for these people's loyalty to Russ, I would have buried my father alone. In that light, I attribute the frugality to the shortness of notice and the limitations of time.

As we all know one another, there is no need to stand in a formal receiving line, but I do meander throughout the room, re-acquainting our church family with my brother. When they learn of his position in Washington, the room rings with questions: What's to be done? Is there any relief in sight?

Greg, for his part, speaks reassuringly.

"They know," he says over and over again. "They are watching, and they are listening. The best we can hope for is that God will send rain. But until that time, believe me,

Congress is working to send ideas. And help, where they can. You pray; they'll work."

At every conversation, Russ is at my brother's side, lending his particularly comforting presence, thereby endorsing Greg's promises. Together, they make the same demand. Faith.

Under Russ's watchful eye, I nibble at the corner of a sandwich throughout the afternoon, insisting that I want our guests to have their fill before I indulge in more. By the time everybody leaves, the trays are largely empty. I allow Ariel to take scraps of ham upstairs to feed Barney, and tell Ronnie he can listen to as much of the radio tonight as he wishes, leaving Russ, Greg, and me in the empty store, picking at the rest of the feast's remains.

"Good people here," Greg says, glancing around the room, admiring the ghosts.

"The best," Russ says. "I wish you could have seen this place five, six years ago. It was a thriving place."

"I remember working here sometimes when I was a kid. You remember that, Nola?"

I pick at the crust of my sandwich. "I do. And I hated it. But I think back to how forward-thinking Uncle Glen was, letting a girl work here at all. If I recall, he never even wanted us to have the vote."

There is a brief moment of levity before Russ clears his throat. "I haven't had the chance yet, Greg, to tell you how sorry I am that this place —"

Greg holds up his hand, deflecting any further apology. "Look around you, Russ. Can't even keep a chicken alive here, let alone a business. Now, I've been telling Nola, and I'll tell you, too. You all have got to pull up stakes and get out of here."

"Greg, please," I interject. "This isn't the time."

"It's the perfect time. You've got nothing holding you here. It's time to save your family."

Russ's face remains a placid field. He will not take umbrage with what Greg said, but I know my brother is sowing his protests in rocky soil.

"My church is holding me here. And now, my work at the hospital."

"Nola says that's temporary."

"It was," Russ says. And now he looks away.

"Was?"

"Darling, I didn't think this was the right time to tell you, but since it's come up . . ." He casts a meaningful gaze — almost a glare — at Greg, then turns his body to block him out. "Earlier this week, before we knew about your father, the director called me in. They want to hire me on full-time. I'll start drawing a paycheck after the hospital bill is paid off."

I give myself a moment to recover from the feeling of betrayal at having to learn the news in this fashion, not to mention that Russ has obviously accepted the position without even consulting me. A job. In the city. Maybe not a city, exactly, but a town. With schools and a library and a movie theater.

"Oh, Russ!" I wrap my arms around him, unashamed of such a display in front of my brother. "I'll need a few days to pack up some things from Pa's place, and maybe we can store them here, depending on how large a house we can find."

"Nola —"

"Oh, I know it won't be anything grand at first. We can find something small for now. I don't mind. But think — a *salary.*" I glance at Greg and notice immediately that he does not share my enthusiasm.

"I'll leave the two of you to hash this out," he says, grabbing one more sandwich. "Think I'll go upstairs and see if either of your children are interested in beating their uncle at a game of checkers."

Russ waits until he leaves before speaking. "We can't do anything right away, Nola. Right now things are the same as they've always been. I won't draw a salary for a while yet, and even then, it won't be enough to start up a new household."

"So what will we do?"

"Exactly what we've been doing. For a while longer."

"How much longer?"

He breaks a little then and rubs his hand across his face, the way he does when we find ourselves venturing into a conversation he never intended to have. "Until God tells me, clearly, that it's time to leave this place. To leave this church."

"It's not enough that you hear me?" My question rages thick with accusation, but he does not back down in the face of it.

"No, of course not. We can't rely on our own wisdom; you know that. We are to trust in the Lord with all our hearts, and lean not on our own understanding."

Now he accuses me, even if unknowingly, and I wither. "I *do* trust God."

"Do you? You didn't rest five seconds with this possibility before launching into plans. No prayer, no consideration, just a leap into what you desire."

"You make it sound as if I haven't been

desiring this all my life, Russ. Have you thought that maybe God took my father away right at this time to free both of us up from our obligations here? And to give us somewhere to go?"

"I still have obligations here. Or have you forgotten about our church?"

I cross my arms, press them close against me to keep my heart from exploding. "How could I? You've never given me a minute of our life to forget about it. But haven't you noticed, darling, that they've forgotten you? Why else are our children hungry? What other explanation is there for the fact that I'll have to make Ariel's school dresses out of the curtains left behind in the houses they abandoned? Are you proposing that you'll drive back here on the weekends to stand behind that pulpit and preach to me and the children?"

Somewhere in the midst of my diatribe, I've crossed from sarcasm to cruelty, and I watch Russ's jaw work to hold in the words that would pay me back in kind. If he only knew what hidden stones he cannot throw, how little right I have to mock his fidelity, I wouldn't have the strength to stand against him, let alone speak down from some ill-gotten morality. That reminder alone stills my tongue, and I turn to leave.

"Stop."

My father said the same thing to me once, when I told him that I was going to marry Russ. I was holding a secret then, too, deep within my body. And, like that afternoon, I do not obey.

Russ returns to Boise City that night. It is the first time he leaves without so much as a kiss, let alone some longer, promise-filled embrace. Not ten minutes after he drives away, I fall into our bed and into an exhausted sleep.

I wake to find Ariel curled at my side. It is her first day of school, and I hate that it has been tainted by the loss of her beloved Paw-Paw. Still, her enthusiasm has not waned, and her insistent demand that I "wake up wake up wake up" proves to be as effective as the smell of coffee wafting through the house.

I am still wearing the dutiful black dress from the previous day, and gratefully strip it off, getting some relief for my stifled, sweat-sticky skin. Wrapped in my robe, I scuttle across the hall, splash myself with cool water, and don a cool, thin housedress. In the kitchen I find my brother at the stove, spatula in hand, stirring a pan of scrambled eggs.

"Bachelor breakfast," he says, grinning at me over his shoulder. "No biscuits, just bread. I don't trust myself to toast it. But there is coffee."

"Coffee's all I need." I pour a cup, having learned to drink it without sugar or cream. "It's good."

"Thought we might head out to the farm after the kids go to school." He says it as if proposing a simple walk across the street to have coffee cake with Merrilou Brown.

"You might want to think again," I say, smiling over the rim of my coffee cup. "I'm not ready for that. And I don't think you are, either. Who knows what we'll find?"

"We'll have to face it sometime, Sis."

"Why today?"

"What would make tomorrow better?"

I have no answer that will satisfy either of us. "Let me walk Ariel to school. We'll leave when I get back."

"I want to go to Paw-Paw's farm," Ariel whines, but I put a gentle finger to her lips.

"You're finally a big girl going to school. That's much more exciting. Now, go get your mask, and remember to wear it at recess."

"I hate the mask," Ariel says.

I look to Ronnie. "You too."

"Would we have to wear masks if we lived

in town?"

"Why would you ask such a thing?"

"I heard you and Dad talking last night."

"The answer is yes," I say, "if I tell you to."

Merrilou Brown stands at the corner where the children cross the street on their way to the school. Under her watchful eye and mine, my girl makes her way with brave little steps, trying valiantly to keep up with her brother. How can she look so much smaller than she did days ago?

"Grow up fast, don't they?" Merrilou says. "Next thing you know, they're gone."

"We — my brother and I — are going out to my father's place to clear up a few things," I say, not wanting to dwell on the thought of losing another child, no matter what the circumstances. "Ariel's finished at noon. Can you see her home? In case we run late, or something comes up?"

"An honor," she says, holding a sedan to a stop with the mere display of her tiny hand. "I'll watch over her as if she were my own."

Back home, Greg has been tinkering with Pa's truck to make sure it will take us out to the farm and back, as it hasn't moved much since its journey to Tulsa.

"We need to have water," I tell him, filling a jug from the spigot in the shop. "And if you'll grab some towels from the linen closet upstairs? I think the chains are in there."

Greg complies, unquestioning, and within the hour we are on our way, creating a perpetual cloud of dust. I sit beside him, bouncing in the seat, the road seeming to have disappeared since the last time I drove it. Greg grimaces, gripping the wheel and muttering mild curses under his breath, unfamiliar with both the vehicle and the terrain.

"You'll have to let me know when I'm close to the turnoff," he says. "I don't recognize anything."

"I will."

"When's the last time you were out here?"

"A few months." I shrink away in my seat, feeling shame not only for what happened the last time I was at Pa's place, but for his death and the drought itself. "It was bad then."

"I need to see it," Greg says. "Should have come back sooner."

We brought it upon ourselves, this dust. That's what Pa said, clear up to his dying breath. The dust took that, too. His breath, his life, drowning him with lungs full of the very dirt he loved so much. He grumbled a curse on this murderous land, shaming us all for the greed that choked out the blessings. More crops, more money. All the grasses of God's creation slashed and uprooted, or plowed under, making way for wheat. We tilled, we planted, we harvested, and we started again. Never satisfied.

I point out the turnoff from the main road, and we soon see the gate that marks the drive up to the property. It hangs open, sagging on its hinges, tumbleweeds making a solid wall out of the fence.

"Pa ever see it like this?"

"Not this bad." I tell him about the day we brought him to our home, leaving Jim out of the story entirely. "I think he started dying on that day."

"I'm sorry you had to go through that alone."

"I wasn't alone. I had Russ. He was so —"

At that moment the house comes into view and takes all my words away. Left unchecked, the storms have blown in enough dirt to create a series of foothills up against and over the porch, meaning we will have to dig our way to open the front door.

Greg stops the truck as close to the house as possible, and before he can hit the switch to turn it off, I suggest we keep it running.

"Don't want to get stranded out here," I

say, not sure I want to get out of the truck at all.

"It'll be fine." Greg presses the switch, burying us in silence. "Know where we can find a shovel?"

"Maybe in the barn?"

Our gazes follow one another and see that entrance to that structure won't prove any easier.

"I have a better idea." Greg reaches into the truck's bed and produces a tire iron. Moving with a focused purpose, he scales the semipacked dirt up to the buried porch, and with a series of decisive swings, empties the front window of its glass.

"You would have gotten quite the whippin' if you'd done that in the old days," I say, tentatively poking my head across the sill.

"Careful, there." He helps me cross over, and I soon realize the inside of the house was no better protected from the ravages of the wind than the outside.

"They didn't seal it up," I say, mostly to myself.

"They?"

"Russ."

"And?"

My expression is enough to dissuade further questions.

"What are we looking for, exactly?"

"Papers," Greg says. "A will, preferably. He never mentioned one to you?"

"Never, but then, he'd never confide something like that to me."

"And he didn't bring any papers with him when he left here?"

"We had a few things — tax records, mostly. Pa barely brought his thoughts."

"Then we'll just look around. It will be assumed that the property will go to me as the eldest, but we could expedite matters with a will. Any idea where we should look?"

"The desk in his room," I suggest, along with the idea of a hurricane lamp, as the collected dirt on the windows make the light inside too dim to be of any use.

"And that would be . . . ?"

"Kitchen. Follow me."

I wait at the doorway and direct him to the lamp, the kerosene, and the matches, my mind reeling with the kiss that marked the last time I was in this room. Once the lamp is lit, the room takes on a grainy, brownish haze, and I imagine this must be what the explorers felt upon discovering the contents of Tutankhamen's tomb. Only the inner chambers of the pyramids were more protected from the residue of blowing dust than were the walls and windows of my childhood home. To my estimation there isn't a clean spot to be found. All of Jim's work to restore it to some semblance of livability has vanished beneath the drifts left behind by endless assaulting storms.

"The desk?" Greg prompts.

As far as I remember, I've never touched this piece of furniture before. Even in my weekly cleaning chores, going over every inch of exposed wood with an oiled rag, Pa's desk had been strictly off-limits, even though he kept it closed down tight, denying any access to whatever might be behind the rolling pleats.

"There must be a key," I say, touching one tentative finger to the round silver lock.

Undaunted, Greg grasps the handle and finds it not to be locked at all. He rolls the top upward, exposing an interior consisting of a pen, an inkwell, a pair of thin wire glasses, and a short stack of neat papers. Standing sentry over all of this, a framed photograph of my mother as I've never seen her. Young, radiant, wearing a high-collared white dress, her hair a shining mound of black silk adorned with a wreath of tiny flowers.

"Beautiful," Greg says, speaking over my shoulder.

I pick up the photograph and hold it

closer to study every soft, sweet feature. "He kept this from us."

"Looks like he kept it from himself."

"No, I mean this woman. Mother was never this woman. He hardened her."

"Life hardens people, Sis."

"It doesn't have to." I think about that picture Jim secreted away in his bag, and the soft, rounded woman I was on our wedding day — nothing like the thin, brittle creature I've become. "I'm keeping this, if you don't mind."

"Bring it with you if you ever have a chance to come visit. We'll find someplace to make a copy."

A quick search through the neat stack of papers yields a series of clipped, orderly receipts, tax notices, deeds, and titles. Nothing like the chaotic bundle Jim found loose on the desk, further testament to Pa's sharp decline. Finally, a single sheet within a faded envelope with *GREGORY* written in Pa's faltering block letters, the same of which fill the page with a simple message:

UPON MY DEATH, ALL I OWN IS BE-QUEATHED TO MY SON, GREGORY MITCHUM, TO DO WITH AS HE SEES FIT.

It is signed by Pa and witnessed by two people whose names I do not recognize.

"As I see fit," Greg says. "Well, that makes things easier."

He gathers all the papers in one armful, picks up the lamp, and leads the way down the hall and through the front room haunted with furniture disguised as foothills. I clutch the photograph to my breast, protecting it from the tiny clouds of dust brought to life by our footsteps. It is the only unspoiled thing in the house.

We go to the front door, forgetting the impediment of the sand hill that kept us from opening it upon arrival. Unwilling to crawl out of what is now his own home, Greg hands the sheaf of papers to me and, using his shoulder and some newfound strength, shoulders the door open, inch by inch, until he's created space enough for us to squeeze through.

"You first," he says, holding our treasures to be passed through the narrow opening once I am ankle-deep in the sand on the porch. "And head on out to the car."

I obey, taking one tentative look back over my shoulder with every few steps, waiting for him to join me. It isn't until I am standing with my hip touched up against Pa's truck that I see him snake his arm through the door. When he does, he has the hurricane lamp with him. Curious, as it is still full daylight, I am about to shout the question when he turns back to the door, slides one arm inside, and brings it out again. This time without the lamp.

In no apparent hurry, he navigates the porch and begins walking calmly toward me as the front window fills with a distinctive orange glow.

"Greg!" I shout, then lower my voice as he joins me at the truck. "What have you done?"

"As I see fit." He drops his hands in his pockets and we stand side by side, watching the flames do the first of their terrible work. "Won't be nothin' but ashes soon." In this moment, he sounds exactly like our father, and I can see the stubbornness in his profile.

"Won't we get in trouble? What if it spreads? This whole country is a tinderbox."

"We'll watch." He lowers the truck's tailgate and perches on the end, patting the iron seat beside him. I refuse, again, a proffered cigarette, and bring my knees up to my chest, resting my chin for the show. Heat bathes our faces, and I want to suggest that we move the truck farther down the drive, but there's something cleansing about the intensity, and I keep my mouth closed against it. Black smoke belches through the window and is caught up by the wind and blown away. The walls are solid stone, and I imagine my childhood home becoming a kiln, destroying its contents while remaining strong. It is a giant box of fire.

Greg says softly, "It can't hurt you anymore."

I look at him, surprised. "This place never hurt me. Made me feel a little trapped is all."

"Well, Pa then. He can't hurt you anymore. You just need to let go of all the memories."

He speaks like one who has done just that, and there isn't a doubt in my mind he's lived for days — weeks, even — without giving this place and the people in it another thought.

"So, how do you suggest I do that? I don't have the luxury of a million miles."

"You don't need a million miles, Sis. For starters, you can convince that husband of yours to take me up on the offer of moving east with me. You can get a whole new start there, find the life you were meant to live."

"Maybe this is the life I was meant to live."

He looks at me then, a searching gaze, as if trying to gauge the truth of my words. I'm not quite sure myself whether I meant them in sincerity or jest.

Finally he sighs. "Maybe it is. But I want to see you happy. Can't see how that's going to happen here. You deserve to be happy, Nola. Everyone does."

I want to say, *Not everyone,* but I don't want to tread on his graciousness, even if it is born out of guilt. I thread my arm through his and lean my head on his shoulder. "Thanks." There is nothing else to say.

After a time — nearly two hours by my estimation — the fire has gorged itself on all the fuel within. The walls and even the roof are charred but intact, and only lazy licks remain.

"I guess dust doesn't burn," I say, wiping the sweat from my brow with a kerchief darkened by soot.

"It burns enough." Greg hops down and reaches out his hand. "I'll be on a train first thing tomorrow morning."

■ ■ ■ ■

Part V

■ ■ ■ ■

He breaketh me with breach upon breach,
he runneth upon me like a giant.
I have sewed sackcloth upon my skin,
and defiled my horn in the dust.
My face is foul with weeping,
and on my eyelids is the shadow of death.

JOB 16:14-16

CHAPTER 24

Fall comes, and then winter, bringing no relief from the dust and wind. Still we have no rain, and the respite brought by cooler temperatures serves only to intensify the stinging sensation of dirt against skin. We walk from place to place assuming the posture of some primitive cripple, our backs bent, faces shielded. Our shoulders bear the weight of the earth as it moves against us, one minuscule grain at a time.

In the mornings when I walk Ariel to school, I hold tight to her hand, fearful that God might take her as he did my other children, using the brute force of nature to snatch her up from my side as punishment for my sin. On days when Ronnie walks her home at lunchtime, I insist he do the same, and at 12:04 every day I peer out the window to make sure he obeys. The sight of them together opens up a sadness that gnaws at me from my womb. Ariel, my tiny, knock-kneed girl, her beautiful hair confined to two tight plaits, her pinched little face obscured by the white mask, her eyes turned to the ground for their own protection, missing out on all the beauty the world might have to offer. Every step a struggle — to keep up with the impatient, strident pace of her brother, to keep upright against the wind. And yet, when she blows inside, I know I'll see that sweet smile etched in the patch of clean skin the mask has protected, and her eyes will come to dancing life at the sight of Barney, who rises and stretches and arches herself at the sound of our girl's arrival.

Ronnie worries me less, as he seems to be the only living thing that isn't shriveling away before my eyes. He's soon enough overcome his shame at accepting food from the crates delivered to the shop on a semi-regular basis, especially when those deliveries begin to include entire hams and slabs of bacon. I cannot keep enough bread and butter in the house to fill him up. He might well be one of the locusts or the rabbits that God added to the plague of drought and dust, eating everything that dares poke its head out of the ground. I cook for the three of us and share a portion with Ariel, doling out the rest to Ronnie in feigned discovery that there is "just a bit left." Overnight he grows to be as tall as me. In an afternoon, his shirtsleeves strain at his wrists. I blink, and his shoulders expand to such a breadth that I do not recognize him from the back. And I think, *God will snatch him away too.* But while I fight for and cling to my daughter, I would launch my son with every blessing within me. He and I share a silent desire to escape.

It becomes far too easy to live without a husband. We write each other letters, two a week, sometimes reuniting on the weekends before the letters are delivered. Mine consist of little moments throughout the day — silly things Ariel has said, Ronnie's accomplishments at school, even Barney's funny moments of destruction make their way onto my pages. Russ tells me what he can about the patients he visits. No details, of course, about their names or conditions, but tales of a woman who came in to have a baby and was surprised with triplets, or a man who was thrown through a second-story window by the sheer force of the static electricity when he touched his radiator. We sign every letter with love, and I keep them in a box on my dressing table, reading them out loud to my reflection during the long stretches of the day when I think I'll lose my mind if I don't hear some other voice above the wind.

He telephones the Browns' home every Thursday evening, an indulgence the hospital grants in exchange for his working late into that night. I spend those evenings there, where it somehow has become an opportunity for Merrilou to host the children and me for supper. I contribute what I can — pies made from canned peaches or fresh, warm biscuits — but Merrilou makes no comment if I arrive empty-handed.

"God blesses us so that we might bless in return," she says in response to my profuse thanks.

When the phone rings, she takes the children into the kitchen for additional cookies and milk, or meat scraps for Barney, leaving me alone at the lacquered telephone table for my ten-minute conversation with Russ.

Sometimes it feels a bit like being courted again. He'll say soft, sweet things that nobody would attribute to a hospital chaplain, and I return in kind, depending on how sure I am that the children are engaged in something entertaining with the Browns. I hear Russ's voice and think to myself, *One more sleep, then one more sleep, and he'll be home.*

We are together two days each week — in reality, though, little more than twenty-four hours. He'll be home midmorning Saturday, gone after dinner on Sunday, with some of the time in between spent preparing his sermon and visiting with those few souls still in town and in church.

"It won't be forever," he says, holding me in his arms each Saturday night. "I promise you. This drought will end. This Depression will end, and we'll build our life together. Just as we always have."

I sleep beside him, believing him, and wake up reassured. But Sunday morning, from behind the pulpit, I hear him say the same things, spoken above and around my head. Words swirling with promises, blown in from a distance, leaving a residue of hope. And then, after dinner, he's gone.

Christmas looms, a more unwelcome holiday than I can remember. Along with his regular weekly letter, Greg sends a colorful card depicting two children — a brother and sister, roughly the ages of my own — careening on a sled down a field of snow dotted with bright-green firs. Their cheeks are plump and pink, mittened hands raised in glee. Inside, along with the cheerful greeting in manufactured red script, two lines written in his own hand:

Merry Christmas
  Wish you were here.

Greg has come home for a Christmas visit on several occasions, when there was a new baby to celebrate or a lost one to mourn, but Pa never was one to make a big fuss over the holiday. Russ embraces it wholeheartedly, of course, secreting gifts throughout the year and clumsily wrapping them in the late hours after the children go to bed.

This year, though, we have nothing. Greg's card, propped up in the center of our kitchen table, is the only decoration. In the evenings, the children and I listen to Christmas recordings on the radio, but other than that, the same malaise that grips our little apartment seems pervasive throughout the entire town. Even as the days grow closer to the holiday, few of us remark about it when we encounter each other on the streets. The dirt has cocooned us, and most days we walk about surrounded by an ever-shifting wall.

During our Thursday telephone call, Russ delivers the good news that he will be able to stay home for the entire week from Christmas to New Year's Day.

"That itself is the perfect gift," I tell him, thinking I will present it to the children in just that way. "I'm afraid I haven't done anything in the way of decorating, but if you're going to be here, I'll see what I can do."

"I'll bring a tree," he says, and I experience an instant lifting of my spirits at the thought of something green and fresh. "A big one, and we'll set it up downstairs."

"Downstairs? In the shop?"

"The idea came to me last night. We can all use some cheering up for the holiday. Christmas is about bringing family together, isn't it? So I thought we could bring the whole family together for Christmas Eve."

Already my image of a sweet family celebration slips away. "The *whole,* as in the church?"

"As in the town. Everyone invited."

"But that's just —" I calculate — "three days away. How in the world would we organize such a thing?"

"I'll have to cut this conversation short, because I used part of my long-distance time to telephone the *Weekly* to get them to run an ad in Saturday's paper. All invited, bring food to share and a gift to exchange.

Nothing new, just something you're willing to give away. They thought it was a fine idea."

"How good of you to consult them." I instantly regret the note of sarcasm in my voice.

"I'm sorry, sweetheart, to spring it on you like this. There hasn't been time —"

"It's all right." I force a note of brightness into my voice. "It will give me and the kids something to do, getting the place cleaned up and ready."

"Ask for help," he cautions. "People will want to be a part of this."

"Of course they will." And then our time is up.

Merrilou Brown is at my elbow not long after I hang up, unusually attentive, even for her.

"Doesn't that sound like a good idea?"

Not for the first time, I suspect she might have listened to our conversation on a second, hidden phone. "You know?"

"Mr. Bradley at the *Weekly* showed me the ad copy earlier today. I wanted to let Pastor Russ share it with you himself."

I opt to echo her words. "That does sound like a good idea. We need some good cheer."

"Mr. Brown and I are here to do whatever you need. I assume the place needs some sweeping up?"

"A little, yes. And the windows washed. I suppose I could clean out my father's room for the coats and things."

Mrs. Brown lays a tiny hand on my arm. "Like I said, you let us know what you need, and we'll be there. How about first thing in the morning?"

She is at the door within an hour after I take Ariel to school, bucket and mop and broom in hand. We speak little, as she starts immediately on the large front window, standing on a stepladder to reach the top, while I go into the storeroom. It still looks like a spare bedroom, with sparse furniture and the very bed where Pa took his last laboring breath. I wish I could expedite this process as Greg had our father's house, with nothing more than a douse of kerosene and a match. Since that is not an option, I decide to simply close the door and set about hammering a series of large nails in the wall on which people can hang their coats.

"If there are too many," I say, nails perched in my lips, "they can take them upstairs."

I take it upon myself to clean and oil the counter until it shines, and Merrilou takes to hanging garland from its top. The empty shelves that were once full of tools and seeds and sundry items are also given a hard-elbow clean to prepare them for displaying the gifts to be exchanged.

"Won't that look nice?" Merrilou says. "A whole wall full of presents."

We are nowhere near finished when Ariel comes home from school, so I set her to work cutting out paper snowflakes to hang in the windows. Hours later when Ronnie comes home, I send him right back out to go from door to door finding those who will contribute a chair to set against the wall. By Friday night, with a string of red and green lights running along the ceiling, the empty shop looks ready for a celebration. To maintain this pristine condition, we twist wet sheets and line every inch of the floor and windows, doubling them at the door.

"It looks nice," I admit as Merrilou and I stand on the bottom step, preparing to go upstairs to my kitchen for a cup of coffee to celebrate.

"I think it will be a merry Christmas after all." And in that moment, Merrilou Brown looks every bit a satisfied, jolly old elf.

The next afternoon, when Russ drives up with a Christmas tree lashed to the top of his car, he is greeted like a conquering hero.

Word about the party only just appeared in this morning's paper, but people come trickling by, peeking through the window to watch as we set the tree up in the corner. I think, at times, we should invite them inside, but then I feel like they are viewing our family the way they would look at a movie on a screen. There is Russ, so tall and handsome, laughing as the tree refuses to stand straight. I've dressed Ariel in something pretty, given over to us by a neighbor with an older girl, and Ronnie looks like such a young man, holding his own as he works with his father.

Russ has brought a few festive items, including a jug of apple cider, which I pour into clean glasses and serve with the gingerbread cookies from a tin given to him by one of the patients at the hospital. Not to be outdone by Ariel, I've donned a nice dress — nothing too fancy — and serve my family sweet treats, all while our community watches through the window. We acknowledge them with smiles and waves, and the excitement for the upcoming festivities grows. By the time we assemble in church on Sunday, there is a definite buzz, loud enough to make itself heard over the wind, and Russ faces the largest assembled congregation since the previous spring.

"The birth of our Savior is no small event," he says, standing taller than he has in quite some time. His orator's voice has returned, speaking to reach every ear. We will gather this evening, six thirty. Bring what food you can contribute and a gift, so that none will arrive or leave with empty hands. All are welcome to fellowship in the name of our Lord."

And they come.

My little girl, a Christmas delight in a green velvet dress and bouncing red curls, unlocks the door to usher in a sea of well-wishers promptly at six. Thirty minutes earlier than we intended, but even then people are lined up outside on this bitterly cold night. We've brought the radio down-stairs and set it in a large galvanized tub to amplify its sound above the crowd. The counter, most recently crowded with food-stuffs distributed on behalf of the govern-ment, is now laden with all manner of roasted meats, pickled vegetables, macaroni salads, pies, cookies, cheeses, and bread. Ronnie and his cohorts look on the spread the way some young men would ogle a girlie magazine, and we as a crowd consent to give them the first place in line.

Never in my life have I been surrounded by so much warmth. Pa was not one to entertain, and church gatherings always carried excruciating pastoral responsibility. This is a party. Nothing but jovial conversation, music, laughter, and children. The tree, festooned with tinsel and bright glass ornaments, brings out conversations of other trees in other times, and for a while the sadness that has drifted into our town melts away.

The bell above the shop door rings throughout the evening with newcomers arriving late, including those who have been scooped up out of their homes and brought on the arms of neighbors. At some point, Russ orders the radio turned off and lifts his voice above the din. Inwardly I cringe, fearing he might mistake the occasion of our gathering for an excuse to launch into a sermon. Instead, he requests that we bow our heads in a brief time of prayer, asking God to bring comfort to those who are too far away to celebrate with us, and to bring us a sense of peace about those who celebrate this day in the very presence of our Savior, Christ the Lord. Then, with an almost-imperceptible nod to someone in the crowd, a pitch pipe sounds, and he leads us in singing.

Silent night, holy night,
All is calm, all is bright.

The words and tune are so familiar, we sing at a lusty, heartfelt volume. When the last note dies away, someone launches into a new song:

On the first day of Christmas, my true love
gave to me —

With this, we threaten to drown out the raging wind outside, even when the lyrics become so fuddled with laughter we lose collective count of the days.

Though our duties as host and hostess keep us buried in the crowd, Russ's eyes rarely leave me, and I seek him above the heads and conversations of our guests. One of Ronnie's friends has rigged a fishing pole with a sprig of mistletoe and wanders through the crowd, collecting what kisses he can. At one point, Russ grabs him by the shoulder, and while the boy — and the crowd — think surely the pastor is about to eject him for such salacious behavior, Russ's true intentions are made clear as he drags the boy through the sea of people, heading straight for me. There, he takes me in his arms and brings me in for a kiss deeper than any we've ever shared this side of our bedroom door. My ears throb with rushing blood, muffling the sound of the cheers rising around us.

When we finally break away, Russ lingers, his nose a whisper away from mine, and says, "Merry Christmas, darling."

"Merry Christmas."

And around us the crowd erupts into song.

The rest of the night is buzz and blur. By ten o'clock there isn't a Christmas mouse's crumb's worth of food left on the counter, and all of the proffered gifts have been claimed. Folks linger, chatting, coats half-on and half-off. I don't mean to rush anybody, but the fatigue of the day is wearing. I send Russ upstairs with the children, as it is long past Ariel's bedtime, and they still have stockings to hang for Santa's visit. Ronnie, of course, participates in the ritual only out of consideration for his little sister, but Ariel believes with her whole sweet heart.

When the last guest is gone, I remain in the room, relishing the silence — a contented sound after so much joy. This is what I needed to feel whole, and in this moment I can forgive Russ for leaving us here for the present time. Or, perhaps, we can rebuild. Sow the seeds of fellowship we enjoyed this evening and grow a whole new community.

When I turn off the switch for the string of colored lights around the window, a flash of red catches my eye, then disappears. I lock the door, then go to the back of the room to turn off the overhead lighting. The flash of red reappears. A cigarette, of course, glowing in the darkness outside. By now it is close to midnight, and I know. I don't need to go to the window. I won't open the door, lest the ringing of the bell above it call the attention of my husband.

Heart pounding, I move the chairs I've stacked against the storeroom door, and with a shaking hand, unlock it. No need to turn on a light, as I know the dimensions of this room as well as any other in my home. We kept the door to the alley latched as long as Pa stayed here. I reach up and draw it aside, carefully, silently.

A punishing blast of cold air hits me, tearing through the fabric of the dress that grew too warm during the festivities. And yet I do not shiver, for I've turned to ice myself. I grip the railing of the loading platform and watch as he comes around the corner. He wears a thick workman's jacket and a cap pulled low over his face, and I do not need the illumination of the cigarette to know the identity of my midnight visitor.

CHAPTER 25

"You shouldn't be here." I speak softly, relying on the steam of my breath to carry the words to where he waits at the foot of the platform.

"Neither should you."

Here in the alley, we are protected from the more brutal force of the wind, but the air remains bitter cold, sharp, and dry, and there is enough of a breeze to flutter the loose edges of his coat.

"You need to go," I warn, but in response, he only moves closer, takes one last drag on his cigarette, and drops it at his feet.

"Where do you want me to go?"

"I don't care. Back to wherever you came from." I'm up against the door. One swift move on either part, and I could be on the other side, with the metal latch drawn between us. Surely he wouldn't pound on the door. Not this one, nor the shop's, nor the door to the apartment upstairs. I could flee, and he would leave, and I could crawl into the warm bed I share with my husband.

But I do none of this. I stand, still as a post, until he is once again in front of me, his hand cold against my face, his eyes warm as summer earth. His hair — grown long — escapes in wisps beneath his cap, and a soft, patchy beard accentuates the intricate contours of his face, framing the softness of his lips.

"I thought you might be . . . I mean, I really thought that my father — that he might have actually killed you." My words come out a rush of stammers, my teeth chattering against the cold, and my feelings torn between penetrating fear and exquisite relief.

To my surprise, he laughs. "Well, then, thoughts must run in the family, because I'm pretty sure your pa considered it."

"What happened?"

"I rode with him to Tulsa. We delivered the goods just like we said. Then, once we got outside of town, he stops the truck, tells me to get out, gives me a dollar, and says he'll shoot me close to dead if he ever laid eyes on me again."

"That sounds like Pa," I say, feeling nothing but pride.

"I knew he was right, and that what we

did — what happened — was wrong. But when I knew he was dead, I had to see you one more time."

"How did you know?"

"Saw the notice in the paper."

"In Tulsa?"

He shakes his head. "I've been all over. Back to the old ways, I guess. Keep thinkin' I need to leave this godforsaken country, but I keep comin' back."

I shiver, wrap my own arms around me, and find myself against him, enveloped in his coat, his scent, his voice speaking against my hair. "You should come with me."

I look straight up and say, "Jim —" before he brings his mouth down on mine, and I taste the world and tobacco all at once. I unfold my arms, intending to push him away, even making a halfhearted effort to do so, before they move around his narrow waist, climb up his shoulder blades, drawing him closer.

Hours ago I kissed my husband, he and I bound to each other in front of a cloud of witnesses. And now, with Jim, and only the pristine night sky with its thousands of twinkling eyes, I feel no less exposed. With Russ there was the response of the crowd: raucous cheers and appreciative applause. Now, the only sound is the whistle of the wind as it whips around the corners of those buildings strong enough to withstand it, and my breath — *our* breath — in a steamy night exchange.

I try to pull away, saying, "Stop."

He follows. "Didn't feel like you wanted me to stop anything."

"Well, I do. I have a life here. A life I want."

"Do you? Because seems like you were dying when I came to you."

"I'm not dying anymore."

"I can see that." He touches my face, my neck, runs his hand along the length of me. "You've fattened up a bit since I left."

I make no move against his touch, even knowing that I should, because I know in a way I didn't know before that this will be the last time I will feel it. I don't even shirk away at the flicker of pain in response to the tenderness of my flesh. I want to think that, deep down, he is a decent man, that if I tell him I want him to leave me alone forever, he will honor that request — for my sake, if not his own.

But in my own deep down, I know that isn't true. I've spent these last few months longing for him to be alive, and now, knowing that he is, I'll spend the rest of my life longing for him to return, even if only to have the chance to send him away again. And again. Every rejection a lie. Even now, I've stepped out of his embrace only far enough to draw him back. If he asks me to run away, I'll say no. If he asks me again tomorrow, I'll refuse, but only to leave him free to ask again. The next day, or week, or month.

I don't love him, but I love how he desires me. How he seeks me. How flesh and need trump practicality. He is the serpent in my garden, and I crave the burning of that sin — not the mingling of our bodies, but the knowledge of the evil amid the good, and the possibility of surprise. Jim saw that in me long before he met me. He recognized it through my wedding photograph, my tiny mounded stomach betraying my trustworthiness as a woman. He and I, in our mutual disregard for the man we held in common, are a perfect match of sorts, and like the dirt that blows through Oklahoma, he will return, because everything about me is an invitation. Alone, I could never resist him, but I'm not alone. A thin ribbon of light shines through the edges of the storeroom door, meaning someone has turned on the light, and soon we won't be alone either.

I barely have time to hiss, "It's Russ," before Jim descends the steps and the door is flung open, revealing Russ on the other side, his head cocked at a curious angle.

"Nola?"

The open door blocks his view of Jim, but I dare not flick my eyes in his direction to warn him to stay put.

"I was just on my way up." I crowd him in the threshold, but he keeps me from passing.

"What were you doing out here?"

"I needed some air. There were so many people —"

"But it's freezing."

"I know. That's why I was coming in."

Again I attempt to pass, but this time he catches my arm and holds me, his expression growing darker as he leans in close, so close I can feel Jim's touch rising up out of me to do combat with his breath. I squirm, about to protest, when Russ looks past me, onto the platform, and back.

"I thought you were done with that."

My eyes follow the track of his gaze, and land on the smoldering cigarette butt on the platform.

"I'm sorry."

He hooks a finger under my chin and raises my face to look at him. "Is there anything else you need to tell me?"

I nod, putting together the final bits that

have been bothering me with disassociated worry since Greg left. The tears that spring up at the thoughts of my children's suffering, the fatigue that overtakes me every day, leaving me powerless to maintain my home throughout the week, my willingness to give the lion's share of our food over to the mouths of my children, without the pangs of hunger that should accompany such a gesture. It's like it was after Jim left the first time, but instead of wasting away, I've been growing. Softer and, as he said tonight, fatter. The pain I felt when he brushed against me had nothing to do with the illicit nature of his touch. It is the painful tenderness every woman feels in this condition. I've experienced it before, but only now do I have the strength to speak it.

"Russ," I say, knowing Jim is on the other side, listening. Wanting him to hear. "I think I might be pregnant."

Russ responds as I knew he would, swooping me up in his arms and off my feet, spinning me in a slow circle before setting me down with chagrin, worried that he might have hurt me — or the baby — in some way. Next, he bends to kiss me, but I turn my face away. The feel of Jim's kiss still lingers — as does, I'm sure, the scent and taste of his tobacco. It is the latter I use as an excuse.

"I don't mind," Russ says, turning my face toward his, but I squirm away.

"Close the door. And latch it. We'll go upstairs and I'll freshen up for you."

He acts with comical haste, and would have carried me up to the apartment had the staircase not been so narrow.

"I've already run you a warm bath," he says, ushering me through the kitchen and down the hall as if I'm visiting royalty instead of his undeserving wife.

"That sounds perfect." *Like an escape.*

"Darling?" We stand in the darkened hallway, our sleeping children mere steps away. "Aren't you happy? I know you've had your reservations, but can't you see what a blessing this is?"

"I'm not sure there's a blessing at all," I say, already wishing I could gather my words up and swallow them whole. "I'm only two weeks late. I'll have to go in to see a doctor to know for sure."

"You can come in with me after New Year's. We'll bring the kids, make a day of it. How does that sound?"

"It sounds fine." And it does. No more, no less. "I just . . . I should have found a better time to tell you. When I wasn't so exhausted."

"What better gift?" He places his hand on

my stomach, nearly spanning it from side to side. "This is my gift. Wrapped in the most beautiful packaging I could imagine."

I cover his hand briefly with mine, then sneak away into the bathroom, where, indeed, the tub is filled with steaming-hot water, my soap and washcloth draped over the edge, waiting. Once submerged, I lather the cloth and wash myself slowly, thoroughly, saying, *"It's over . . . it's over . . . ,"* ridding myself of any memory of his touch. In a final, desperate act, I dig a fingernail along the thin edge of the soap, peeling off a long strip, which I place along the length of my tongue. Forcing myself not to gag at the taste, I press it against the roof of my mouth. As the soap dissolves against it, I run my tongue along my gums — top and bottom — forcing it against the back of my lips. I scoop up a handful of warm water, slurp it, and swish it around, filling every crevice of my mouth with cleansing foam before I spit it, straight into the tub. This I repeat five, six, seven times, until the water no longer foams as it dribbles from my chin.

Not wanting to bother with a shampoo, I run my fingers, slick with soapy residue, through the now-limp curls. A dash of perfume, and any lingering scent of Jim's cigarette will be gone.

It seems strange how my efforts to rid myself of the man only reinforce my preoccupation. Jim's return takes his blood off my hands, but so does it breathe life back into my sin. His scent dissipates, but I need only conjure his face to bring it wafting back to life. His touch disappears, but his voice lingers at what feels like the deepest, darkest corner of my ear. In a way he's kept that kind of hold on me since the moment he first walked into my kitchen, but this is more than desire. Simply knowing Jim is alive frees me from a longing to see him as such, if for no other reason than to assuage my guilt for his demise.

Before, I carried a girlish fear that he would overlook me, forget me, cease in his pursuit. Between that afternoon and now, my flesh has withered — near to the point of death — and then been restored. Now, though I only voiced it as a distraction in the moment, there seems a possibility of new life growing within. I've been cleansed and forgiven, washed clean and made whole — by God, if not by Russ. So, too, has that fear been transformed.

I get out of the tub, dry off, put on a fresh, clean flannel gown, and patter across the hall to join Russ in our bed. Only a few short steps, and my bare feet are crusted with dust. I use a washcloth brought specifically for this purpose to wipe them clean before sliding them between the sheets. Still, grains cling between my toes, and I mutter a mild curse at having forgotten my slippers.

"My goodness," Russ says, collecting me into an embrace. "Go out to smoke one cigarette and come back cursing like a sailor."

"I guess I'm not used to having anyone around who can hear me."

"God can always hear you." He says it with a cuddle, so I know it isn't a reprimand, but still I apologize again.

"Are the children asleep?" I ask as a means of turning the conversation.

"They are."

"I'm afraid it won't be as exciting a Christmas morning as we've had in the past."

"We've never had much."

"No," I say, though I think he spoke with an air of contentment while I feel more resigned. "But we've had more."

"And many have less."

I say nothing, knowing I will never have a heart more pure than this man's.

"But we have a new baby." He speaks this promise into the darkness, and I nod my head against his chest in agreement. Russ continues to talk. Before this baby arrives, we might have rain, and hope, and new life all around us, not just in this little place. I don't bother to argue that I don't want a home in this little place anymore, that I've been counting the days until he agrees to leave. It is enough in this moment to be cocooned with my husband, warm and safe, children sleeping in their rooms, in my body, or with the Lord. I close my eyes tighter against the darkness, trying to ignore the icy-cold fear at the core of me.

Somewhere, out in the wind, on the other side of the door, there is a wolf of a man who could take this all away. What a fool I've been to worry so long that he was left for dead. For the sake of my family, it is time to worry because he is alive.

CHAPTER 26

My pregnancy — if, in fact, there ever was one — does not last to meet the New Year. Two days after Christmas, I wake in the middle of the night, doubled over in pain, and by midafternoon the spots of blood have become a heavy flow.

"I shouldn't have told you," I say to Russ when he brings in a tray with a pot of weak tea and thin-sliced toast. "I knew it was too early to know for sure."

He puts on a face that I know is meant to be comforting — a flat smile, stretching his lips straight, and eyes that don't quite meet mine. "You were right to tell me. Otherwise you might be suffering this alone."

"Why alone? You're here."

"But I wouldn't have known."

"You wouldn't have known?" I shift against the remnant of the soft, dull ache that anchors my belly to my spine. He was right beside me throughout the night as I wept and bled.

"I mean, I wouldn't have known it was such a loss. I might have thought it was —"

"Nothing?"

"Normal."

I sit back against the pillows, sip my tea, ignore the toast. "I'm glad we didn't tell the children after all. They wouldn't understand."

Russ looks away. "I'm not sure I do, either, but God has his reasons."

I push the tray away, knowing I won't eat a single bite. I am too full of the knowledge of God's reason. I've done this, proving myself in one moment to be an unworthy vessel. It was my discontentment that choked the life out of me. Perhaps Ronnie was born so perfect and healthy because I was so happy to be out from under my father's roof, and Ariel — so sweet and small — born at the height of our prosperity. Those lost in between? That was a time of longing, too, as the realization slowly settled that I would never become the woman I'd once envisioned myself to be. Educated, powerful. Independent. I wasn't able to voice any of that to Russ at the time, nor can I now, as he seems determined to grieve this loss as we did the others.

Strangely enough, I don't share his sadness. Maybe because, as a woman, I am more finely attuned to the inner workings of my body, and this doesn't feel like a loss. Not like the others. More so the fact that I can't imagine the idea of bringing a new little life to take its first, startled breath in such filth-ridden air.

"It's this place," I say at last, interrupting Russ's silent prayer beside me. "Nothing can live here."

I brace myself against what I know he will say next. Something else about God's will. God's reasons. God's purpose, or plan, or time. I'm wrong, though. He lifts the tray of tea and toast up off the bed and, with a sag to his shoulders I've never seen before, sets it soundlessly on my dressing table. His back is to me, but I see his face in my mirror. Every muscle he's ever employed to keep it smiling and strong has been let go, loose and lax. Defeated, for the first time. I know it isn't this unrealized pregnancy that has dealt the final blow, but the ferocious slashing of my own sharp tongue.

"This is where we live, Nola."

"No, Russ. It's where *I* live. Alone."

Strength returns to his shoulders first, and makes its way to the squaring of his jaw, set in place before he turns around. "That's not true."

"Of course it is."

"It's temporary."

"It has to stop. It's not safe." My eyes dart toward the window, the shade pulled low, but the dull light of day hovers behind it, and I know he'll take it as a portent of the dead-thick air. I alone know the real danger hovering, somewhere. Though of course I've neither seen nor heard even a shadow of him since the first hours after Christmas, his absence does nothing to bring me comfort. Any day he could be at the door, imposing on Russ's sense of hospitality and obligation, insinuating his presence into my every waking moment. With a word he could take it all away, proving me to be the woman Russ refuses to acknowledge. Even worse — and even more possible — he could reincarnate the woman I've tried so hard to kill.

"If you could only take us with —"

I don't even have the sentence out of my mouth before Russ raises his hand to swipe it out of the space between us.

"I've told you, there's nowhere to bring you."

"Then —" I reach out, wrapping my hands around the sturdiness of his forearm, exposed by the sleeve rolled up to his elbow, and pull him to sit beside me — "come

462

home. Stay *home*. Here."

"I have to work. God has blessed us with this opportunity."

"And he's blessed you with a wife, and children. You saw all the people here for Christmas. Some, no doubt, will come to church, now that they know you. And there's food from the relief, and we own our home." All of this I've said before, so often that I can re-create the conversations verbatim, his responses as well as mine. So, for good measure, I steal his very words, the Scripture he's used against me time and time again. "Russ, you've told me that we need to wait on the Lord, that those who wait on the Lord will renew their strength."

"We are waiting."

"But I need for us to wait together. I'm not strong enough to wait on my own."

"What are you afraid of?" He edges closer. The shifting of the mattress beneath his weight dislodges me, awaking a new grip of pain. "Nola, is there something I don't know? Something you're not telling me?"

I count to eleven. When I was a little girl, Mother always taught us that a good count to eleven was the surest way to speak only what was necessary. Only what was right. A silent promise threaded itself through the numbers.

If Russ says his name, I'll tell him everything.

My confession sits on my lips, waiting for release, but Russ says nothing more. I shrug, feigning resignation, as if I've exhausted every plea.

"I need you here."

"They need me there."

"I need you more."

He smiles, touches my face, and I know I've lost again.

"If you could see the pain I see every day, how much people are hurting, you'd never ask me to leave them."

I laugh, even though it hurts to do so. "Do you think I haven't seen pain? I was at my father's side when this place took his final breath. I buried a dear friend, or at least finished the job after the storm tried to do it the first time. And I've watched every other friend I've ever had up and drive away, out of this place. You, too, now. Do you have any idea how much I hate standing at that window and watching you drive away?"

My voice stops short of shrill, the words squeezing out as my throat tightens around them. Russ lets silence hang for a moment while I look down to where our hands are listlessly entwined. The energy between us softens, becomes this vaporous cloud, as there is nothing new to say. Rather, Russ has nothing new. I, of course, sit on two unspoken truths. The first is that I have a very real reason to want to get away. The second, that I have the means to do so. The first gives little promise of resolution, but the second begs to be aired.

"Did you see the Christmas card Greg sent?"

Russ cocks his head, confused at the abrupt change in topic. "Yes?"

"He sent money, too. To buy something for the kids for Christmas, but — there's nothing here to buy. And I didn't have a chance to get to town, so . . ."

"Your brother doesn't need to buy Christmas gifts for our children." I can tell the mere suggestion wounds Russ's pride. There were, after all, a few gifts. A new paper doll book for Ariel, and a stack of *Life* magazines for Ronnie. Plus socks, and candy, and oranges.

"And he said," I continue, doling out the conversation the way we had the few trinkets on Christmas morning, "if I'd rather, I could set it aside. For whatever I want."

He draws up, sitting straight, and then inches away to see me in a better light. "When were you going to tell me about this?"

"When we had a moment alone, I guess. There was so much excitement with the party, and then this . . ." I gesture vaguely at the space between us. "And I didn't know how you'd feel about accepting money from him. From me, really. But it could change everything for us."

His brow furrows in confusion. "How much is it?"

"One hundred dollars."

Russ appears to try to understand the amount one dollar at a time. "How is that possible?"

"He's a bachelor. He works for the government. All I know is he wants what's best for us, and this money can make it happen. The children and I, we can load up in the car with you in a few days, find a little house, and just — start over."

I am clutching at him again, but he's gone so hard and cold on me that I can't grasp his flesh. His face has turned to stone, and his words crumble out of it.

"I can provide for my family."

"Of course you can," I say, trying hard not to let it sound like another lie.

"He sent the money to you, not to me. Do whatever you want with it."

Russ stands up, and I think would shove me aside if we were on equal footing, or if he were a man to shove anything at all. He strides to the door, opens it, but I call out before he can leave.

"What if I decide I want to spend it securing a little house in Boise City?"

In response, he slams it, forceful enough to capture the children's attention should they wonder if anything is amiss. Taking half the number of strides to return, he is back at my bedside and bent, his hands grasping my arms and pulling me toward him, impervious to my involuntary whimper of pain.

"I am your husband." His words come out in a storm of pain equal to my own.

"I know."

"And for as long as you've been my wife, I've never been able to put the roof over your head."

"We have a roof."

"I didn't earn it. It was given to me. Well, given to you."

"Inherited." Even as I say as much, though, I see him slipping into another place. Pent-up resentments I thought were long past. A home in a place that was never supposed to be more than a refuge. An income based on the giving of others. Now, a job grown from an act of charity. All of this in a country determined to waste itself away beneath him.

"I am tired," he says, easing his grip, but not letting me go. "Tired of letting other men do what I should do myself."

And there it is, the oldest wound of all. His choice to be a man of God kept him from going to a war where men — friends — fought on foreign soil, taking their places where he would never stand. Killed there, or brought home maimed, like Jim. Others, though, like my brother, returned strong, resilient. In this moment, I don't know which soldier Russ finds most offensive.

"Greg only meant to help," I whisper, hoping the softness of my voice will reach through and bring back my gentle, loving husband.

"I know." Now he is only touching me, but I do not move away. "Forgive me, won't you?" Then he drops his head in prayer. "And forgive me, Father, for my anger. For my pride, and most of all, for not trusting you or acknowledging the blessings you have given to our family."

He opens his eyes to find me staring, in awe at his ability to so effortlessly confess and repent. Upon his amen we are restored, as he is restored to his Savior. I've never before felt such envy.

"So what do you want us to do?"

Russ leans forward and kisses me as softly

as my question. "We'll leave that up to God. Until then, tuck it away. Someplace safe. And pray that he makes his answer plain."

I put on the bravest smile I can and manage to hold it until he walks — slowly this time, sweetly — out the door after telling me to get some rest.

There was talk about having a New Year's Eve party much like the one we'd hosted at Christmas, but even though my body has restored itself to health, my spirit isn't strong enough for a celebration. We sit around our radio and lift glasses of orange juice in a toast to the New Year before sending the children off to bed. Later, I lie in the crook of my husband's arm, listening to some of the revelry outside. It is a cold but clear night, and he asks more than once if I wouldn't like to put on my coat and muffler and join them, even for a moment.

"Now, why should I want to do that when I have so few nights with this handsome man in my bed?"

He holds me closer, which I like best, because it gives my mind a chance to wander. I haven't seen a glimpse of Jim since Christmas Eve. Not that I've ventured much out of the house other than the obligatory visit to the Browns. But I have spent a good amount of time at the window, looking out into the street, even down into the alley. I even crept downstairs once to poke my nose into the storeroom, wondering if he hadn't snuck into his old haunt as a means of escaping the cold.

The old battle seizes me — hoping that he's gone away for good, fear that he hasn't, and something darker that wishes for one more sight. A glimpse, a touch, to definitively have a door to close at my own bidding.

Despite our physical closeness in the waning hours of the year, there has been a decided distance between my husband and me since our conversation about the money Greg sent. We haven't spoken of it much; indeed, what little conversation we did have was chilly, if kind and cordial. I'd be too ashamed to admit it in the moment, but a certain relief hovers as he packs his suitcase for his return to Boise City. The feeling is short-lived, however, when he informs me that he will be staying through the next four weekends in order to make up for the time he spent celebrating the holiday at home.

"You didn't tell me that," I say, handing him a freshly ironed shirt.

"I thought it was understood."

"So I'm trading a week with you for an

entire month alone?"

"It'll pass." He stuffs in the shirt along with the rest of his things and closes the suitcase lid. "I already wrote you a letter — left it on the kitchen table. And I'll see if I can swing an extra phone call on Sunday afternoon."

"Speaking of, what about church?"

"Mr. Brown's going to fill in for me while I'm gone."

I hide my displeasure at the prospect by bending to work the latches his fingers tend to fumble. When I stand, he is there, and I kiss him, touching his face, now clean-shaven after a week's worth of scruff. "We'll miss you."

"Me, too." He kisses me back. "But I think it might be good, this time apart. For me, anyway."

"How so?"

"To think. And pray, of course. And see what the Lord would have us do."

Ariel comes barreling through the door-way, the ever-patient Barney clutched in her arms, but drops the cat in exchange for the bear hug offered by her father. He whispers what I know is a prayer over her mass of soft, red curls, and promises he will send letters written just to her, getting a promise in return that she will do the same. Ronnie

471

comes in too, and it is an odd feeling to have the entire family gathered in our bedroom. I can't remember the last time that happened. Even when I was sick in bed, Russ insisted the children come to visit one at a time, in order not to tire me.

Russ disengages himself gently from Ariel and shakes Ronnie's hand, eliciting the same promise he does every week, to take care of his mother and sister. In this moment, Ronnie needs only the slightest tilt of his head to meet his father's eye. Someday, Russ will return to find his son his equal.

It is a particularly dirt-filled day, so we say our good-byes in the kitchen, watching him go from behind the shelter of the window. I linger long after Ariel and Ronnie drop away, willing my eyes to search up and down the street, but God himself has woven a curtain to block my view, keeping him out, keeping me in. I close my eyes and press my forehead against the glass, for once giving thanks for every driven grain of dust.

CHAPTER 27

By the third Mr. Brown Sunday, the children are back in school, and Ariel is a permanent fixture in my bed. She sleeps restlessly beside me, and is usually up before the dawn, pestering me to make a double batch of Cream of Wheat for breakfast. Ronnie, on the other hand, is much less eager, and shows up to the table with his hair half-combed and his eyes half-open.

This is one of the mornings when my temperament matches that of my son. I plait Ariel's hair and tie the braids with wide, wine-colored ribbons, a Christmas gift from Merrilou Brown, but I myself am still not dressed. I convince Ronnie to walk her to school with the promise of mashed potatoes for lunch when he brings her home at noon.

"With gravy?" He presents it as a non-negotiable, but I'm forced to disappoint.

"Sorry, Son. Don't have the meat for that."

He makes a silly show of disappointment, but dutifully takes his sister's hand and secures her mask before heading out the door.

And then, total, utter quiet. This, I know, is the time Russ would expect me to pray, to listen for God's voice. His direction. Were Russ here, we would be praying together, sitting at the table, our Bibles open, our hands joined. He would read and I would listen, passive in my understanding. Other than dutifully carrying it to Sunday service, I've rarely touched my Bible since coming home from the hospital. The words, it seems, fade in and out of my understanding, like a radio station just off the dial, and I imagine my prayers do much the same. I've learned it's best to keep my head as empty as possible while busying my body with chores — cooking and cleaning — anything to keep me away from the windows. Off the street. Actively imprisoned to avoid temptation.

I pour myself a second cup of coffee, promising to be less indulgent tomorrow, now that Russ is no longer here to share the pot with me, and carry it back to my bedroom — *our* bedroom — where my Bible waits on the nightstand beside the bed. I thumb the pages listlessly. I open it, run my hand across the words, wishing I could simply absorb the truth within.

The light coming through the window is not sufficient for reading, and though it is half past nine, the room takes on the hue of some predawn hour. I move my Bible to rest on Russ's pillow and crawl back between the covers.

I awake to a room full of light, a cold cup of coffee, and a clock that reminds me the children will be home within minutes, expecting a meal I haven't yet prepared. The Bible lies forgotten on Russ's pillow as I scramble out of bed and run to the front of the house. A peek out the window reveals an empty street underneath what is turning into a clear, crisp day. The children haven't been released from school yet, so I slice a potato thin and set a pot of water to boiling, hoping to fulfill my promise. I light the second burner for a can of tomato soup. The last of the bread is a hard, dry heel, which I cut into chunks to float in and soak up the soup.

At each stage of the preparation, I go to the window, gauging my time not by the clock but by the sight of Featherling's few children released for the walk home. The potatoes are fork-tender when they first appear, a dozen or so of varying ages and sizes.

Most days, Ronnie likes to stay to have lunch with the farm kids, so I send him with a sack of butter sandwiches and an apple. Other times, when the relief food fills our pantry, I make a big meal and invite the boys into our home for slices of ham and green beans, Jell-O and molasses cookies. I've watched three days' worth of food disappear into their eager, grateful mouths, ignoring their dirt-crusted hands and allowing Ariel to eat in her room so they have one less gaze to avoid.

I see them, joined together in the midst of all the other children whose heads are bent low against the wind. Ronnie walks tall, his cap shoved so low that its bill nearly touches his nose. How he's managed to keep it all this time I'll never understand, except it is one of God's small blessings I take a minute to acknowledge. He holds his sister's hand, lending his weight to hers, and even from this distance I see that she is in animated conversation, her free hand gesticulating wildly as she grips a soon-to-be tattered school paper.

Then I realize, with familiar frustration, neither wear their masks as I — along with every other mother — insist. Still dressed in my housecoat and with bare feet, I step through the front door and lean over the railing. Wind whips my hair into my eyes, and I feel the tiny pricks of grit against my face as I cup my hand around my mouth and shout, "Ariel! Ronnie! Your masks!"

In their defense, none of the other kids seem to be wearing them either, and with the almost-clearness in the air, my admonition could be seen as a good-natured joke. In response, Ariel clamps her school paper across her mouth and nose, and Ronnie does the same with his cap, covering his face entirely, and casts his little sister's arm in the role of a blind man's cane, tapping out a pattern of steps.

I laugh and turn to go inside, catching a glimpse of something familiar as I do. I should ignore it, go straight back to the kitchen to prepare lunch for my children, but even from across the street, in broad daylight, he — Jim — compels me. The distance does nothing to lessen my feeling of vulnerability. I clutch my robe, shift my feet against the grit, and take hold of my wayward hair, forcing it behind my ear. I hear Ronnie yell something about mashed potatoes, and I holler a response, all the while praying that Jim will step back, far enough to disappear from the street's point of view. If Ronnie sees him, we'll have a fourth at lunch, for he shares his father's warm, innocent, inviting spirit.

Locking my eyes with his, I give a shake of my head. *No.* Any neighbor peering out a window might have missed the communication, but I know he sees me in a more concentrated form than does any other person, and I trust my full message to come clear. *Nowhere near my family.*

The day goes on as expected: Ariel's down for a nap after her brother returns to school for his afternoon classes. I use that hour of solitude to clean the house in a way I haven't since before Christmas, wiping away days' worth of accumulated dust, enough to turn my wash water into brownish slush.

Fruitless, endless, mindless labor. Wiping the insides of the windows with vinegar and water, knowing the other sides will retain their hardened film of dirt. Running a damp mop head over the floors, knowing the first body through the front door will not only leave tracks of soil, but particles will shake loose from their clothing, leaving a dusting like dry, tainted snow. We've all but given up on trying to protect our dishes, though Pa's lingering spirit prompts me to take extra care with our drinking glasses.

At some point, minutes before Ariel awakes, I consider sitting down, propping up my feet, maybe reading one of Ronnie's

Life magazines. But if I allow my body even a moment's respite, I know exactly what I will do. The window again, face pressed against the newly clean glass. Looking, watching, assuring myself he wasn't a vision.

That night, I wash and set my hair. I've become quite adept since Rosalie's passing, though it's something I usually reserve for later in the week. For Russ. I don't allow myself to acknowledge my motivation for doing so this evening. I twist and pin, refusing to look at myself in the process. Rising early in the morning, I coax it into shining waves and powder my face. My hand shakes as I apply a touch of lipstick, and later, too, when I add warm milk to the morning cereal, hoping to distract the children with this extra step of maternal care.

Ronnie offers to walk Ariel to school, and I shoo him out to meet his friends for a round of catch before their first class. After buttoning Ariel into her coat, I button myself into mine and tie a bright silk scarf over my hair — an item I received from the Christmas party gift exchange.

"You look beautiful, Mama," Ariel says, beckoning me to bow low so she can touch the fabric.

I give her chin a soft pinch. "So do you."

"Do I have to wear my mask?"

"Tell you what. Wear your mittens, and while we're walking outside, bring your hand up over your mouth. Like this." I demonstrate, inhaling the scent of my hand cream. Ariel follows my example, prompting a *"Good girl!"* from me, and we proceed outside.

Ariel chatters, her words muffled by her mitten, and I chime in with appropriate sounds at the slightest break in the stream. All the while, I keep my head in a constant arcing motion, looking between buildings, behind deadened trees, amid the silent parked cars.

"Mama? Are you listening?"

"Of course I am, dear. But tell me that last part again. What did Barney do?"

"She poked her head up through the hole in the blanket and it looked like she was in the ocean!"

I laugh because she does, agreeing that it must have been a silly sight indeed. By then we are at the corner where she'll have to cross the street to go to school, and Merrilou Brown dutifully waits.

"Why, Denola!" she exclaims, holding up her hand to stop the single farm truck lumbering toward the intersection. "Don't you look spiffy today?"

She says it without a hint of suspicion, and I resist the urge to be defensive.

"I was feeling a little under the weather last week. I suppose I wanted to embrace my return to health."

She gestures for Ariel to walk — *walk!* — across the street as I wave good-bye.

"Well, I'm glad you're feeling better. Feel free to pop by for coffee later this morning. I have a sour cream cake in the oven now."

"Thank you, but I have some catching up to do on my housework."

"Not enough hours in the day for that, are there?"

"There certainly aren't."

"Come on over if you find the time."

I smile my assurance and turn for home, this time going against the wind, making it impossible to keep up any kind of surveillance. Head bent, I watch my feet, glancing up only occasionally to register my progress. When I reach the shop, there he is, standing flat against the wall behind the stairs leading up to the apartment.

"Nola —"

"No." I don't even pause. I march right past, and up the stairs, and through my front door, closing it behind me and collapsing against it. My fingers shake as I unbutton my coat, and I have to slide the scarf off my head to untie its knot before draping it and the coat over the arm of the sofa. In the kitchen, I pour myself a cup of coffee, take one sip, and set it down to cool, drumming my fingers on the counter, the sound echoing in the empty apartment.

Maybe I should have accepted Merrilou's offer of coffee and cake. That would occupy an hour, at least. I picture her tiny body fighting the wind, being blown through her front door, the perfectly clean house infused with the rich smell of the cake.

I wish Russ could be here in this moment. Maybe we might have gone together to spend a moment with the Browns. Or maybe I would have been inspired to bake my own cake from what few ingredients I have on hand — something for the two of us to share at the empty table in the morning light as we spend an hour in devotion. So simple. So small.

I tell myself I've changed my mind. That I would, after all, like to sit with the Browns and chat about what changes this new year might hold. If I were being honest with myself, I would take my coat and scarf, for though the walk to their front door is a short one, the wind still blows bitter cold, and both are waiting on the arm of the sofa. But there's no honesty, even in my thoughts.

I'm telling myself a lie, as I lied to Russ, my children, and my Lord. I walk down the dark inner stairs to the empty shop, itself cavernous and nearly black, as Russ boarded up the windows the day after Christmas. I've maneuvered in this place often enough, though in total absence of light, sneaking out of bed for stolen cigarettes.

Through the storeroom and to the door, my hand finding the latch near the top and sliding it across. Cake and coffee with the neighbors — it's where I will go if I open the door to find the loading platform empty, the alley deserted, Jim nowhere in sight.

The door is open only for a fraction of a second before he is inside, giving me no time to protest even if I want to. A mere mention of daylight, and then it is dark. Pure dark, like night, and we welcome it like lovers, wordless at first, and mostly silent, save for ragged breath and staccato whispers.

"You let me in."

"I shouldn't have."

"But you did."

In response, I press myself closer to him and reach above for the latch, sliding it into place lest someone has witnessed his intrusion and would come to my rescue.

■ ■ ■ ■

Nothing that follows matches the reckless-
ness of that first morning. Every moment of
the days that follow is cool, calculated. I
walk Ariel to school, chat with Merrilou
Brown, and rush home to find him waiting
in the shop, where I've left the storeroom
door open. On the second day, I lead him
upstairs, and here we linger, too terrified to
touch, though I make a careful study of his
arm, cupping my hand over the scars at its
abrupt end. Asking him to tell me, again, of
the battle, the explosion that took it. The
details of the pain. It pleases me, somehow,
to know that he's suffered, assures me that I
don't care too much for him. He answers,
relaying the details with an air somewhere
between heroism and humility, as if it were
the course of any ordinary day.

Once, while the dust outside rages in a
nearly solid wall of wind, I ask him if he
thinks he'd be the same person if he hadn't
been so wounded.

"We are what we are, sweet Nola," he says.
"Ain't nothin' but death can change us."

At the morning's end I sweep him away,
back into the alley, and I commence cleaning, mopping every step he took, stripping

the bed, washing the coffee cup he pressed against his lips. I scrub my skin of his touch, so each day Ronnie and Ariel come home to a pink-skinned mother and a gleaming house, no matter what threatens on the other side.

Where Jim goes — where he stays, where he sleeps — once he leaves me, I don't know. I don't ask, for fear he'll take it as some veiled invitation to lurk in the shadows of our home day and night.

From the beginning I knew the time would come — Thursday night — when I would have to hear my husband's voice pressed to my ear in the Browns' telephone nook. I suffer through a meal of fried pork chops and gravy, slicing tiny, dry bites and moving my fork from the meat to the potatoes and back again.

Merrilou chatters on about how much everybody misses having Russ in the pulpit, casting sweet, apologetic glances toward her husband. "I must say, I'm sure you'll be happier than any of us to have him back of a Sunday."

I swallow a bit of gristle whole and wash it down with water. "I will."

"The way Mr. Brown and I putter around each other all day, I can't imagine what it would be like not to have him underfoot."

"Russ was rarely *underfoot*. Even before, there was always someone out there to draw him away from home." I didn't intend for my words to come across quite so bitter, but Merrilou's recoil begs an apology. "I'm sorry. Yes, of course, it's difficult having him so far away."

"Almost like you're a widow."

Now it is my turn to take offense. "No, because I know he's coming home. Week from Sunday he'll be here." I look at Mr. Brown and point my fork in mock accusation. "And *you,* sir, best be ready to step away from the pulpit."

"Gladly," he says. "It is a grave responsibility, spiritual leadership. Hard enough within the home, but for the house of God — it's why we all admire Pastor Russ so much. He bears it with grace."

"He deserves better." Merrilou's comment draws my attention.

"Better than what?"

"Better than us."

The rest of the conversation centers around Ariel and her school musical and Ronnie's aspirations to play baseball when he gets to high school, leaving me to retreat into supportive silence while Merrilou asks all the right questions and responds with appropriate enthusiasm to the answers. As we clear the plates, the phone jangles right at the designated time, and Mr. Brown suggests — as he does every week — that I answer it, "just in case it's for you."

Merrilou's words ring in my ears as I approach, and his voice — handsome itself — calls me "darling" and turns my knees to water. I fall into the slat-backed chair, throat closed, unable to utter a word in my defense.

"Nola?" Crackling silence. "Nola, sweetheart, can you hear me?"

"Yes. I'm sorry. I was lost for a moment."

"Well, don't go too far. We haven't got a lot of time together here."

"I know." But then I can't think of a single other thing to say. I catch a glimpse of Ariel out of the corner of my eye and, with my hand over the mouthpiece, summon her over. Just as Russ embarks on a story about some heroic patient or another, I exclaim, "Oh! Here's Ariel. She wants so badly to tell you about her musical at school."

Without waiting for any acknowledgment or reply, I move the telephone stick to the edge of the table and give Ariel both the earpiece and the encouragement to talk, to relate every detail about the props, and Mrs. Patty's piano playing, and what a horrible singer Bobby Fisher is, and how she will need a new white dress for the snowflake song, and new black shoes if she can, but Mrs. Patty said if everybody can't have shiny shoes, they can wear socks instead, but then they won't be able to make the *clackity-clackity* noise when they dance.

I watch the sand fall through the glass as she speaks, matching the pace of her words. Now, when I gently take the phone away after she says, "I love you too, Papa," I have some conversation to cling to.

"She seems excited," Russ says, chuckling.

"She is, indeed. Hard to believe the show is still six weeks away." I pause long enough for a new thought to come to life. "It's on a Wednesday. Will you be able to be here?"

Silence, and then a sigh. "I can't promise you that."

"This is your *daughter.*"

"Nola, please. Don't make me feel worse than I already do."

I huddle myself deeper into the alcove, bringing my lips to nearly touch the receiver. "I'm afraid, Russ."

"Darling, you know you're not alone."

"I'm afraid we might start to forget you. What if I — what if *we* — start to fill in your place?" I want him to be so afraid of the same thing that he will disappear from the other end of the line only to appear in our home by day's end and save me from the sin I might commit in the morning. Instead, he speaks so softly I have to bury the earpiece in my hair and shut out the noise from the other side.

"I am trusting you, my wife, to make sure that doesn't happen."

CHAPTER 28

The next morning, I stay in bed, giving Ronnie the responsibility of getting himself and his sister off to school.

"Headache," I claim from the shadows, and he doesn't ask any questions. Once the door is shut, I turn over in the half dark and listen to the ticking of the clock. Uncurling from my ball of warmth, I stretch a leg over to the empty side of the bed, chilled by the coolness there.

He will be here in an hour, waiting for me downstairs. Miles away, my husband trusts me not to let him in. All my life, studying Scripture, I've heard that Satan is to be seen as a thief in the night, seeking to kill and destroy. My foe, however, poses a far more insidious threat. He comes in the day, the freshest part of the morning. And he comes to love, to worship me. Even knowing his evil intent, I open myself to him.

I hate myself for the battle that rages

within. No godly woman would even consider it a choice whether or not to give her body and bed over to another man. How cruel it is for God to make me to be the wife of a man so dedicated to holy pursuits.

"You've ruined me," Russ said after our first time together. Not with condemnation, but with a mild surprise at my ability to overpower our shared virginity. Then, after a long, loving summer, and a visit to a doctor in Boise City, I told him I was pregnant. And I begged him to forgive me.

"How can I forgive?" We were in our favorite place — the backseat of his car — taking in the moonlight and wheat fields while drinking cold Coca-Colas. "You didn't sin against me. We were equal participants if I recall."

"But will God forgive? Even after all this time?"

"Have you not asked him?"

I had, of course. *We* had, hands clasped on my front porch, even huddled together in the empty church. Together we'd confessed the sin of our flesh and asked Jesus to forgive, knowing and believing the power of his blood to wash us clean. But then a new moment of weakness, and we would sin again.

"Of course, but I don't *feel* forgiven."

"Because you — we — have never given that forgiveness a chance to take hold. Not when we keep —" He shifted away, gathering his thoughts in the process. "Faith sometimes means accepting God's forgiveness as a fact. But then, to really understand, we need to repent. Turn aside." He held my gaze, touching me in no other way. "Stop."

It sounded like a line from a sermon, and probably would be someday, but in that moment it was meant just for me.

"Pa won't forgive me. Nor you, and I don't think he ever will."

"We don't need to put our faith in him, Nola. Did we sin? Yes. And there's no changing that. But we can do better from this moment."

I ran a finger along the cool green bottle. "The damage has been done."

"No." Russ grabbed my arm, giving me a new taste of his strength. "A child is not *damage.* It's a gift. Like grace — something we don't deserve, but given freely. I don't have to forgive you, Nola. Nobody does, and Jesus already has. Both of us the same, and we start fresh, and from this day I'll treat you the way I should have all along."

Which he did. We did, not touching each other again until we made our vows to each other. Now, though, my sin *is* against Russ, and I don't have his faith to guide me to mercy. I remember his words. *Did I sin? Yes. Did I confess? Yes.* And I must accept God's forgiveness as a fact. But I've never given it a chance to renew my spirit. I've been adulterous with my mind and my body, never letting Jim far from my thoughts since the night I met him, and taking advantage of every opportunity for his attention, his conversation, his touch, and all.

But I can do better. And it will start at this moment.

With my robe wrapped tight around me and my feet left bare, I brave the ice-cold of the kitchen, stairs, and shop floor, maneuvering expertly through the dark storeroom and finding the latch. I move it slowly so as not to make a sound. If he wants me, he'll have to knock. If I want him, I'll have to open, but the barrier of that small metal bolt will give me a chance to do the right thing. It will be my strength.

Back upstairs, I resist the urge to take back to my bed. Instead, I start a pot of coffee, dress, and run a comb through my hair. Unlike the other mornings, I refuse to enhance myself in any way. My skin remains dull and dry, my cheeks sallow, my lips their own natural dark. No powder, no perfume.

The woman staring back at me is not one waiting for her lover. She is a trusted wife, locked inside her house, dedicated to her home, protecting it from the lion bent on devouring her.

She needs a task for her wayward hands.

Outside, the wind blows hard, but clean. Perfect for washing, so I set about gathering linens and towels. In Ronnie's room, I pick his clothes up carefully, so as not to shake them and send clouds of dirt into the room, already in need of a good swabbing. I drop the clothing in the tub to soak and take the linens to the kitchen, where I drag the Maytag from its place in the corner and attach the hose to the sink to watch it fill as I sip my coffee.

I glance at the clock — 9:15. He should be here by now, waiting. Standing across the street, perhaps, watching for my return, wondering if I've been held up at the school, or in some conversation with Merrilou Brown at the crosswalk. More likely, he stands on our loading dock, gingerly trying to open the door, turning the knob and giving it a hesitant push, curious at the resistance.

The water rises in the white tub, and I pray for deliverance and strength. I flip the switch and watch the agitators spring to life, their sound filling the kitchen. Our bedsheet disappears beneath the water and I think, *There. I cannot take a lover on a bare mattress.* But I could, and I would, were I to open the door and find him on the other side. So I must not open the door.

Then Ariel's sheet. Then Ronnie's, and a cup of pure white soap flakes that dissolve the minute they hit the water. This is Ariel's favorite part, and I'll be sure to save some of the washing until the afternoon so she can share the excitement.

My stomach churns with the same intensity as the washer. Jim has lain within those very sheets with me. Now our mingled sin sloshes along beside the innocence of my children. How could I have brought him into our *home*? Not like Russ, with the welcoming arms of a friend and the heart of a Samaritan offering shelter to the wounded.

"God, forgive me," I say, knowing my words are swallowed up by the overwhelming rhythm of the washer. "Protect me, and send him away. Keep him away, Lord." I can make no promises on my own behalf, having no strength of my own and little evidence of God's strength working through me. But if his hand can keep Russ at a distance, surely he can do the same with Jim? Pick him up and put him down. Let him ride the winds of a storm to some other place. Let him find another woman —

My heart clenches at the thought of his sharing another woman's bed, but there is a reason I've never asked where he spends his afternoons. Or his nights. Or why he always smells of reliable Ivory soap and has clean clothes. Or why he is never hungry. All of these are the works of a woman. Not a squatter, not a hobo. A woman close by, maybe a woman I know.

"Oh, God — what a fool." The same realization I came to after that first afternoon, and here I am no wiser than before.

A tiny sound rings out above the clangor of the washer, distinguished by its high, metallic tone, something I haven't heard in weeks. The bell above the shop door downstairs. For all my confidence in the tiny metal bolt on the storeroom door, I forgot that he has a key to the shop.

No, no, no. Lord, please. No.

I measure his steps in my mind, crossing the store, up the stairs, his footfall muffled by the washer. Plunging my hands into the soapy water, I grab one of the sheets, occupying myself against his touch, feeding the fabric through the slow-turning wringer. I sense, rather than hear, the kitchen door open behind me, and my skin feels the

weight of his steps ripple across the lino-
leum. Already, weakness threatens to overtake me, and when I feel his hand cupped
against my waist, drawing me back toward
him, I can only whimper, "You shouldn't be
here."

He blows a hush against my neck, igniting
my flesh, pulls me closer, and brings his
other hand —

My heart stops. *Russ.*

And everything goes black.

"Not exactly the welcome home I was
expecting." I recognize the lightheartedness
in his voice, though his eyes hold nothing
but grave concern as he dabs at my forehead
with a cool, damp cloth.

"You startled me is all." I reach up to
catch his hand and kiss that place on his
wrist where his pulse runs warm. "I wasn't
expecting you."

"Who were you expecting?"

I can't tell if he is joking or not, so I dodge
the question entirely. "Why are you here?"

He helps me sit up against the arm of the
couch, making sure I feel strong enough to
do so, and comes to sit beside me.

"Last night, after I hung up the telephone,
I kept hearing Ariel's voice."

I chuckle. "Believe me, I *always* hear

Ariel's voice."

"Afterward, I was consumed with this longing to be home. Everything you've said to me came flooding back, and then it was your voice, not Ariel's. I could hear you as clearly as if you were right next to me."

"Oh, Russ —" I lean against him, my arms encircling his, my head on his broad, welcoming shoulder, knowing exactly what he is going to say next.

"I went to my knees and prayed," he confirms. "I asked God to forgive me for my heedlessness, and for not trusting him enough to provide for us in a way that didn't tear us apart. And then, in my spirit, I heard him tell me to go home."

"Go home," I repeat, just to hear it in my own voice. "So what did you tell the hospital?"

"That I had a family, and that I couldn't be at the hospital for all the days they required. I'm going back Monday morning —" he put his finger to my lips to quell my approaching protest — "to meet with several ministers from other churches, schedule some hours for volunteering time. The need is so great."

"But our debt is paid, isn't it? They don't need you driving in from the next town."

He pats my leg, reassuring. "We'll see, but

I hope not. I like to think I'm needed here, too."

"You are."

I pull his face close for a kiss, which he immediately deepens, pulling me across his lap like we are teenagers again. My mind reels, twisting upon itself as the relief of Russ's return collides with the fear of discovery. An unexpected deliverance. Surely Jim must see the car parked in the alley, or in front of the store. He knows — he must know — Russ is here. To stay away. More ardent embraces push Jim to the edge of my mind, and my husband seems unaware of any distraction on my part. He stands, sweeping me up in his arms, and carries me halfway to the bedroom before I pull myself away.

"We can't."

He nudges my neck. "Of course we can. The kids are at school."

"I don't have clean sheets on the bed."

"I don't mind."

I wriggle in his grasp. "I can't leave the laundry like that, undone. The soap will dry in the fabric, and then it's impossible. Besides, it's a clear day. Who knows when we'll have another one?"

He kisses the end of my nose and returns me to my feet. "I suppose I could help."

"With laundry?"

"I suppose I could watch."

"Trust me, that wouldn't help. We have a little time before the kids are home. Why don't you go over to see Mr. Brown? Tell him you'll be here to preach on Sunday. You will, won't you? Because I don't think we can take another week of him."

Russ glances at the clock. "I will."

"And I'll finish this and see what I can put together for a special lunch. They'll be so surprised to see you."

"I hope they react a little differently," he says with a wink. "Be sure to make something that you'll eat too."

"I will." I stand poised at the Maytag until Russ disappears, then immediately run downstairs to the bolted door, opening it inches, enough to see if Jim waits on the other side.

Nothing. Nobody. I open it farther, crane my head out, look in all directions, but see only our trusty sedan, coated tan with road dust, and an otherwise-empty alley. Heart racing, I run back upstairs, onto our balcony, leaning over to see as far as I can up and down the street. Russ's distinctive gait is all I recognize, and I close the door.

Minutes later, the apartment fills with the sound of the washer, and I stand in such a place as to see both doors with nothing more than the slightest turn of my head. After running the sheets through the wringer after the rinse water, I dump them in the basket and head downstairs to hang them to dry. Our clothesline consists of a single pole with four arms reaching out at the top, each connected to the next with shorter and shorter lengths of clothesline running toward the center. Considering the limited space in the alley, it is a much more convenient design than a single, long length, but it makes for an extensive drying time. I've learned over all these months not to overload it on any given wash day, as an unexpected storm could blow in at any minute, ruining several loads' wash. The rest of today's laundry will be strung about the apartment.

I've draped the last of it over the line when I see him, standing at the entrance to the alley as if he's been there all along. It is a cold, dry day, and my hands feel like they have thin sheets of ice ready to crack against my skin. I fold my arms, trapping them within the warmth of my sweater. Russ's sweater, actually. Thick and loose, swallowing my body. Other than that, I don't move.

Jim looks at our car, then at me. "He's back?"

I hold myself tighter and nod.

A slow grin spreads across his face. "I'm going to miss you, Nola."

Anything left will have to be said in these final minutes, and I hold a thousand questions on my tongue. Somehow I know if I watch him walk away, I'll follow, if only to pour them into the wind, and their answers could only make this moment more painful. I pick up my empty laundry basket and, without another glance in his direction, pull my leaden feet up the three shallow steps to the loading dock and open the storeroom door, leaving it unbarred behind me.

The special lunch I wanted to prepare turns out to be eggs and pancakes, but Ronnie and Ariel are so excited to see their father, I could have prepared sawdust and sauerkraut and it would have made little difference. At the end of the hour, when Ronnie goes back for his afternoon classes, Ariel insists that Russ read her three stories for her nap time while I continue with the wash. I rinse the clothes from the tea-brown water in the bathtub and run them through the soapy agitations until the water drains clear, and by the time I've wrung out the last tiny blouse, my back aches with the labor and my hands feel raw. Russ brings the sheets in from the line and volunteers to make up our bed — an act that eases my mind, as I've been dreading walking into that room with him. I know there is nothing amiss that would arouse any suspicions on his part, but the thought of occupying the same space with him that I've occupied with Jim fills me with dread.

If ever there was a time to confess, it is now, while he has only my own words to condemn or forgive as he sees fit. Surely, though, Jim will stay away, if for no other reason than to protect himself from my husband's wrath. He may have fought valiantly in the war, but he is no match in size or physicality for Russ. As before, each moment that passes makes my sin easier to live with and harder to tell. That night, when we are all in bed, and the wind howls around us, my body stretches the length of his within the crisp, clean sheets.

"Those nights," he speaks into the darkness, "when I was gone? I'd lie there in that narrow bunk they had for me in that little room, and I'd try to imagine what you were doing, right at the moment."

"Sleeping, most likely." I don't mention the exhaustion with which I fell into bed each night, born from the endless battle against the dirt, or the toll it took on a body being two parents for two children. That battle, God willing, will soon be over.

"Of course, sleeping. But what kind?"

I rise up on one elbow. "What kind?"

"Were you curled up, keeping warm? Or flat on your back, like this —" he demonstrates with one arm flung on the pillow above his head — "because you're too tired to move? Or, just perfect — on your side, your body like a hillside." This, as he traces my curves.

"I never knew I was a woman of such variety."

"I don't know that I did, either, until I tried to picture you, and then so much came to my head. I felt like I could remember every night we've ever spent together. From the very beginning."

"That's a lot of nights, Russ."

He gathers me up and kisses the top of my head. "It's not enough. And I want to have them all."

There, in his arms, I vow to give him all he wants — all of my life — even if it means a certain silence between us.

CHAPTER 29

It is a successful final trip to Boise City, meeting with the local clergy and extricating himself from the daily work of a hospital chaplain.

"I don't suppose I've ever thought of myself as a leader among leaders," he says that night over a late dinner. "But they seemed enthusiastic and supportive. I think it's been left in good hands."

"So no going back?" I ask, trying not to appear too eager.

"Not anytime soon. I have responsibilities here."

Indeed, hunger and hopelessness have wormed their way into the health of the people in Featherling, and a moist, incessant cough becomes a sound as constant as the wind. During his time working out of town, the church has fallen out of the habit of gathering after a storm, given that they are so commonplace now, we'd be hard-pressed to ever be anywhere else.

"Besides," he says from the pulpit, "we don't want any of our elderly members out in the dust more than is necessary."

From then on, a group of older boys — Ronnie among them — is given the task of going door to door after particularly heavy blasts to ensure that all is well within.

In a matter of days, our family restored, Russ becomes a presence in our home in a way he never has been before. He walks Ariel to school, allowing me time to clean up breakfast dishes and take the linens outside for a quick snap in the morning air before it fills with the dust of the day. Then, when he comes back home, we linger over a second or third cup of coffee. We resume our habit of reading from the Psalms together, and it is with a strong voice that I read the fifty-first.

" 'Have mercy upon me, O God, according to thy lovingkindness: according unto the multitude of thy tender mercies blot out my transgressions.' "

We clasp hands and bow our heads together, thanking God for the provision of this day. Always we have food to eat, and the roof stretches over our heads in perfect measure.

During our times of prayer, as Russ speaks

aloud the gratitude of the family, I send up my own, silent petition, that nothing again will wedge itself between me and this husband whom I love. To think of how I once spent these same hours fills me with shame enough to hold me mute, even as Russ gently urges me, through a soft squeezing of my fingers, to speak aloud. Was it only three days spent in the throes of sin? Three mornings given over to meaningless depravity?

I like to think of myself as having been dead those three days. My soul relegated to the depths of my anger as my body acted of its own accord, resurrected by God's perfect gift of intervention by sending Russ home. Every day, whenever I catch a glimpse of him — reading a book with Ariel or sorting through baseball cards with Ronnie — I never fail to ponder the disaster that might have befallen me had I not locked the door that morning. In this way, Jim continues to haunt me, and I pray for his memory to disappear, even as the man himself seems to have done.

For there hasn't been another trace of him. So complete is his erasure that I wonder if he wasn't a product of my imagination, a delusion brought on by grief and frustration and the madness of the ever-present dust. But then my husband turns to me, touches me, and my flesh immediately seizes up, wanting to push him away for its lack of worthiness. And my mind says to my skin, *Be still,* before leading myself to surrender.

Through all of this, one fear plagues me — that I might be left with very tangible evidence of my adultery. I picture a child with curly, dark hair that I can claim as my own, and some physical deformity that can only be attributed to my sin. A new calendar hangs in the kitchen, in accordance with the new year. That day in the last week of December, the late onset of my cycle, burns itself into my thoughts, and as we reach the waning of January, I double my supplications to the Lord. I pray like a woman in need of rescue, with the same fervency with which I once begged God to fill me with a healthy, beloved baby.

Please, I beg. *Not for my sake, but for Russ. He doesn't deserve such pain.*

As an act of desperation, I eat. Bread and tapioca and macaroni and pork chops and doughnuts and baked chicken and green beans and bacon — smaller portions than what I prepare for Russ and Ronnie, but more than I usually consume, hoping to keep my belly so full of food there'll be room for nothing else.

The morning when, while doing dishes, I feel the familiar onset of my time — no pain, no reason to think it anything other than my natural course — I stand at the sink and weep. In that moment, my storm ends. Calm assurance that I have survived with all that I treasure intact.

At my feet, Barney laces herself around my ankles, purring against my thick wool socks, and with joy-fueled generosity I pour her a dish of milk and stroke her tricolored coat. A thousand times, at least, I've rehearsed my confession to Russ, and it always starts with: *Do you remember the day we brought Barney home?* I'd never tell him about the other moments that made up the rising tide under his own roof. Had I not orchestrated a definitive moment in time to be alone with Jim, I might have kept myself free from the worst of my father's disdain. Now, the nearly full-grown cat is all that remains of my father's farm, and someday I hope to be able to look at her and not feel another man's kiss.

We continue to get weekly letters from Greg, and save them to read after Sunday's dinner, no matter what day they are received. The exception to this comes in

509

February, when we receive not one but three pale-pink envelopes, addressed to Ariel, Ronnie, and me separately. These, of course, are valentines, and they add a festive air to our Wednesday supper of ham steak and canned yams. Russ presented me with a box of chocolates earlier in the day, and I share them around for dessert upon distributing the cards. Ariel's depicts a sweet, pink-cheeked girl clutching a pure-white, fluffy cat, and a verse that says something about wishing much love and fuzzy feelings on Valentine's Day. Ronnie's is slightly bawdy — an adolescent boy kissing a girl whose skirt has blown up to show her bloomers and an inscription that says, *If you only get one chance, make it count!* More important, in the eyes of the children at least, three crisp dollar bills have been tucked inside each card: *To buy whatever you want. Love, Uncle Greg.*

I haven't told Greg about Russ's reaction to the Christmas money, which remains, untouched, in my top bureau drawer. I glance nervously at my husband to see if he feels the same discomfort at this gesture, but he only smiles and suggests we spend Saturday afternoon looking through the Sears and Roebuck to see if anything captures their fancy.

The third envelope is addressed to me, which is unusual because Greg always sends his letters to Mr. and Mrs. Russ Merrill, but I figure it might seem strange, one man sending a Valentine's card to another man, no matter the circumstances. I open it carefully, pull out the card, and let out a sigh at the idyllic image on the front — a quaint white house, green lawn, picket fence, and rosebush growing by the front door. On the outside of the card is written, *A home isn't a home until it is filled with love.* Inside is a crisp twenty-dollar bill and something else — a photograph, color-tinted and eerily similar to the house depicted on the card, only larger, two-storied, with Greg smiling on the porch.

Immediately, the image clouds as my eyes fill with tears, and I hear Russ ask, "Nola? Are you all right?" As I am about to hand the picture over, I see my brother's familiar handwriting on the back of the photograph.

Dear Russ and Nola,
Received a check for the sale of Pa's farm. This is our inheritance.
    Your home as well as mine, whenever you're ready to get out of the dust.
                            Love, G

I hand the photograph over to Russ, saying nothing, and close the card around the twenty-dollar bill, deciding to keep that to myself until I know how Russ will react to the photograph.

"Where is this?" he asks, passing the picture over to Ariel's delighted scrutiny.

"Washington?" I guessed. "Or near there, wherever he lives. A far cry from that little one-room apartment he's always complaining about."

"Is it for us?" Ariel bounces in her seat, too excited to be stingy when Ronnie insists on seeing the photograph for himself.

"It's not for us," Russ says, his lips thin.

"But, Daddy, he *says* —"

"We live in Oklahoma," Ronnie says, the sentence choked with resignation.

"But lots of people go away."

I place a quieting hand on Ariel's curls. "He's just showing us his house. And since we're family, he wants us to know that we're welcome there anytime."

"To visit," Russ adds.

"Yes," I say. "But if we ever decided we wanted something new, we needn't worry about not having anyplace to go."

Ariel takes the picture back and studies it so intently, I fear her eyes will cross. "Does the dust blow there, too?" She seems to direct her question to the smiling uncle in the photo.

"No, sweetie," I answer for him. "It doesn't."

"Then I really, really wish we could go."

Normally she would be chastised for pouting, but I can't bring myself to detract any more from her joy. My heart reaches out in agreement as I take the photograph and tuck it back inside the card. "We'll have to find a special page for this in the album."

I allow the children two more pieces of chocolate before sending them off to bed with promises of another piece with their lunch the next day. Russ and I stay up, sitting in the darkness, listening to love songs on the radio. At the first notes of my favorite, "Body and Soul," he stands, reaches out his hand, and pulls me to my feet and into his arms. We dance in small, aimless steps as he hums the tune into my ear while my mind fills with the lyrics.

My heart is sad and lonely,
For you I sigh, for you, dear, only.
Why haven't you seen it?
I'm all for you, body and soul.

"Russ?" I murmur against his shirt.
"Hm?"

We are in a moment of such pure contentment that I hate the idea of spoiling it in any way, but if he is so lulled . . .

"I know Greg didn't mean any offense."

He kisses the hand he clasps. "I know."

"But would you ever consider such a thing?"

He hushes me with a kiss and sings softly above my head:

I can't believe it, it's hard to conceive it,
That you'd turn away romance.
Are you pretending? It looks like the
    ending —
Unless I could have
Just one more chance to prove, dear.

Russ pulls back, smiling at the irony of the lyrics, given the closeness of this moment.

"Oh, Russ." I lift my hands to his shoulders, running my fingers through the thick waves above his collar. "Wouldn't it be wonderful, though? To have one more chance?"

"One more chance for what, dear?" He poses the question as if it were a missing lyric.

"A new, fresh, clean start. Someplace where there's life."

"There's life here." And he kisses me.

"Not beyond these walls."

"Once upon a time," he says in the silence between two numbers, "God gave me a very clear directive to come home, and I realized he hadn't given me instruction to go away in the first place. I won't make this kind of decision based on a photograph of a house, especially one that isn't mine."

"But it's —" *half mine,* I was going to say.

"We will wait. We will wait upon the word of the Lord. And I promise you, I will listen for his answer."

The onset of spring not only brings the winds howling with new fervor, it also brings the long-awaited School Spring Musicale. As an older student, and a boy to boot, Ronnie has been primarily concerned with building and painting sets for the other students' numbers — trees and castles, and large cardboard animals for the "Animal Crackers" song, in which Ariel has a solo. We have been listening to her practice nonstop for weeks, each rendition convincing us that she was chosen to sing it as a redheaded Shirley Temple rather than a girl with equal vocal ability. Still, she, along with the others, makes a valiant effort, dancing among the bouncing cardboard zoo. Merrilou helped me cut down one of her old white dresses for the snowflake song, and every student — including the big boys, who stand awkwardly, hats in hand — come onstage for the final song: "Home, Sweet Home."

We are all seated on metal folding chairs, swept up in the earnest offering of our children, wishing we had more to offer them. Most of us, at least those native to Oklahoma, grew up with lush green grasses, enough wheat to feed three countries, dew-drenched mornings, and miles of earth fed by rain. When I was little, I wore store-bought dresses to school, stockings made of silk. We gorged ourselves on ice cream and beefsteak. Now, we watch our darlings, our little girls in white dresses made of bleached flour sacks. Our boys with dirt caked in their necks and fingers. Not a single child onstage has the fat, pinchable cheeks that children should have. They sing with hungry mouths.

Be it ever so humble, there's no place like home.

They repeat the short chorus three times before Mrs. Patty motions from her piano bench, inviting all in the audience to rise and sing with the children. Russ and I stand and link arms, but I cannot bring myself to sing. Instead, I listen, because coming through the noise of the piano, and the muddled voices of the children, and the resonant tone of the audience, a single discordant sound enters.

A cough.

This alone is nothing out of the ordinary. The dust has disguised itself as the air we breathe, coating our mouths and throats, so lodged in the dryness that we have no option but to expel it by force. No conversation happens without a clearing of a throat. No silence is ever left unbroken. But this is different. Severe, and familiar.

I stand on my toes, scanning the stage, knowing in the deepest part of me which child I will see in the midst of a spasm, because I've been hearing this sound — *this cough* — for days, at least, and have made it no more than a part of the other noise in my life.

Being the littlest, a tiny kindergartner in a pond of bigger children, my Ariel is right out front, in the center, her small, pale hands cupped to her mouth, trying to stifle her cough so she can return to singing. Even from here I see her face flushed with fever. Has she been sick all day? Did I feel the heat emanating from her as I brushed each perfect curl? Perhaps I attributed her heightened color to her excitement for the program she worked so hard to prepare. From the stage, her voice rings out sweetly, but without the vigor of her home performances. Her dancing has less spring, her eyes a familiar glaze.

Stage fright, nerves, overexcitement — all buried my instinct.

I pull on Russ's sleeve. "She's sick. Go get her, now."

He gives my hand a placating pat. "This is the last song. After it's over."

"Now." I push him, and as the final notes fade uneasily away, Russ makes his way through the crowd, up the crowded aisle. The moment one of the younger boys presents Mrs. Patty with a small bouquet of roses, the children are dismissed. They file off the sides of the stage, moving as one shuffling creature, but not my Ariel. She stands, still and small, in the middle of the stage, and drops into her father's arms.

I wipe the tub three times with a Lysol-soaked rag before running a tepid bath, and then I sit beside her as she shakes, and tell her again and again how beautiful she was onstage.

"Like a real snowflake," I say, gathering her hair up off her neck. "Gave me the shivers."

"Marion Childers had the prettiest dress."

"But you had the prettiest voice. And how brave to sing and dance when you weren't feeling well."

She coughs in response, wet and familiar.

I pat her dry with a towel and drop a clean flannel gown over her head before carrying her to her room.

"Papa will come in with some water in a minute," I say, draping a blanket over her shivering body, "and for prayers. We'll all pray that you feel better tomorrow."

I kiss her burning brow and cheek and hand her a favorite doll. Barney leaps up and curls herself on the corner of the bed and begins lazily licking her paw. Soon the sound of her purring fills the room.

In the kitchen, Russ has prepared a tray with a glass of water, an aspirin, and a new card of paper dolls he's been saving as a reward for after the program.

"We have to take her to the hospital," I whisper. "Tonight."

"Not tonight. Not in the dark. We'll see if her fever is worse in the morning."

Perhaps I should be comforted by his calm, but I find myself furious instead.

"This is not a time to sit around and wait. I think she's been sick for days, but trying to hide it so we wouldn't keep her from being in the show."

"Remember, darling, I spent quite a bit of time at the hospital, and I don't know that they would do a lot for her there that we can't do here."

"But what about the tent? The oxygen? Remember, when I was there, that woman — Ladonna — she was taken for a time to get that treatment."

"Some it helps," he says, before taking my hand to finish his sentence, "and some it doesn't. Ariel's blessed with a windowless room and a mother who keeps the house as meticulously clean as possible."

"But she's still —"

"It might be just a cold. Or a mild flu, or a host of other things. The danger of taking her outside for a three-hour car ride would, I think, do more harm than good."

Now, at last, his even tone, his weighty assurance, his measured words — all work to soothe my spirit.

"I'll make some Jell-O. So it will be ready for her in the morning."

He kisses my brow. "Good girl. And then join us for prayers."

I set the kettle to boiling on the stove and

pour the powdered gelatin into a mixing bowl, praying as I never have before. As I do, Ronnie comes in, having been given permission to stay out later with his friends and stack all the chairs in the gymnasium in return for a school-free afternoon later the next week. Like any other entrance, he heads straight for the kitchen and opens the icebox, retrieving bread and butter and sugar for a late snack.

I say nothing other than the sharpest bits of conversation, handing him a knife, telling him to use a plate. "Crumbs will bring the mice out. Bad enough we have to live with all this dirt; don't need mice, too."

"How else are we going to keep Barney fat?" His cheeks are stuffed with bread and sweet butter, barely enough room to flash his father's grin at me.

"Do you let Ariel walk to school without her mask?"

"What?" Food muffles the word.

"You heard me. It is your responsibility to walk with her, and your responsibility to make sure that she wears her mask. And she doesn't, so now she's sick."

He works to swallow the enormous bite, and chases it with milk I've poured in a glass.

"She does, almost every day, I swear."

521

"Don't swear."

"I promise."

"Don't *promise* what you know is a lie."

"Ma!"

That single syllable crushes me. I am the only liar in this house, and here he stands, defending an innocence I have no right to question. Ariel isn't his responsibility; she is mine, though he good-naturedly accepts every instance where I foist her upon him.

"I'm sorry," I say, tending to the boiling water in the teapot. "I'm worried, is all."

"How sick is she?" His worry blends with mine. "Like Paw-Paw?"

"Let's hope not." The gelatin dissolves bright red in the bowl, and I look to the clock. Two minutes to stir.

"Do you want me to do that?" He comes up from the table before I can answer. "So you can go sit with her?"

I transfer the spoon to his hand, ignoring the dirt collected in his knuckles. "Another minute, and then two cups of cold water. All right?"

"Ma, I've seen you make this a hundred times."

Although I've been freed from my duty, I stay and wrap my arms around him, impeding his ability to stir. For a moment, I need his strength, the vibrancy of his youth, and a measure of affection he so rarely affords.

"I love you, Ronnie."

"I love you too, Ma."

"You're the best son a mother could ask for. You're going to be big and strong, just like your father."

"But I ain't going to be a preacher like him."

The moment is too sweet to correct his grammar. "What are you going to be?"

He shrugs against me. "I don't know yet, but anything that will get me away from here."

I release him, and he continues stirring. "You know, I said the same thing to my father, starting when I was about your age."

"Yeah? Well, don't take offense, Ma, but I think I mean it more than you ever did."

I feel his words follow me to Ariel's room, where her father kneels beside the bed. She sits up, her nightgown puddled around her waist, and leans forward as Russ applies Vicks VapoRub along the length of her back. Settling her half-upright on a pillow, he does the same to her chest, filling the room with the distinctive odor. He then lays a clean white cloth against her skin and helps her push her skinny arms through the sleeves of her nightgown, leaving it unbuttoned to the waist.

"Breathe deep," he says. "As deep as you can, even if it hurts."

She tries, and does well, both of them pleased at her shuddering determination.

"Now, drink this." He holds a glass to her lips, and she grimaces.

"It's warm."

"It has to be, so it's the same temperature as your insides." He lays a cool cloth against her brow. "Now, let's say our prayers."

She coughs in response, and I move to sit beside him. Faithful Barney doesn't move, and soon the shadow of her brother fills the room.

"We're all here," I say.

Russ takes my hand. "Gathered in agreement."

I reach back and feel Ronnie's crusty, dry grip — the hand of a man — in mine, and we join our voices in reciting the Lord's Prayer. This is not something new to our family, but it is the first time I've ever spoken these words having been delivered from evil. Or at least I thought I had. Now it seems evil has taken up residence in the tiny lungs of my daughter, punishing me for the shame I've brought into this home.

After our chorusing amen, Russ prays for a healing in little Ariel's body. A full and complete restoration of her lungs, and an end to the infection that causes the fever to rage. I join him, silently, and stay by his side long after Ronnie takes himself to his own bed.

Russ shuts off the lamp and we sit in the darkness, the only sound that of Ariel's breathing, which soon levels into sleep.

"Go to bed, Nola." He shifts himself into a more comfortable position.

"Come with me."

"One of us needs to stay with her."

"Just for a minute." I stand and take his hand, pulling it to reinforce my intention.

He follows me to where the only light comes from the lamp softly glowing in the front room. I lead him to our threadbare sofa, the very one that was cast off to us when we first moved into this apartment before Ronnie was born. Sitting, I draw him beside me, and he fidgets like a boy, ready to leave.

"Listen." I calm him with my voice. "I have lost too much to this place. We have two babies buried in the churchyard. My father and my friend died, drowning in dirt. The farm is gone, the church is dying off, my baby is sick, and our oldest is going to shake us off his shoes first chance he gets. And I —"

"You what? There's something that hasn't

been right, Nola. Not since before you got sick."

"I don't want to be here anymore. I don't feel safe."

"Darling, you know you're safe with me."

"Please, please. We can't give her much, I know. But shouldn't we at least be able to give her the best air to breathe?"

He rakes his hands through his hair. "And what would I do there, Nola?"

"What you do here. Help people. Preach. Be a father. God's call on your life doesn't have to end here. But think about the patients you saw at the hospital. The ones who got better. What did the doctors tell them to do?"

He stares at the floor. "Get away. If they could."

"We can."

Russ lifts his head and looks at me, the light glowing on his face. "Not until she's better."

Early the next morning I go to the Browns' to call in a telegram to Greg.

ARIEL VERY SICK. DUST IN LUNGS.

Within an hour, Clarence Wallis knocks on our front door with his reply.

4 FIRST CLASS TICKETS PAID FOR ON RESERVE AT B.C. STATION

I carry the slip of paper as if it is as precious as the hundreds of dollars Greg no doubt paid for the tickets, but the grim look on Russ's face calls for me to fold it carefully and drop it in my apron pocket.

"Is our girl ready for breakfast?" I keep my voice cheerful, for though Ariel can't see us, she will certainly worry if my tone matches her father's expression.

"Maybe in a bit." Russ chooses to be quiet rather than force an optimistic tone. "Take her into the bathroom, run the water as hot as it'll get. Let her breathe in the steam and encourage her to cough. The more she can cough up and out, the better."

"All right."

"And seal up the door, to trap it in. I'm afraid it won't be pleasant for you."

I lift my face in a haughty pose. "It's supposed to do wonders for the skin. I saw that in a movie once."

Worried that the precious telegram in my pocket might wilt and fade in the steam, I go to the kitchen and slip it next to Greg's photograph. Then, in the bathroom, I tell Ariel we are going on a tropical adventure, and while the water fills, I plait her hair into two tight braids. I've brought in the stool from my dressing table, and set her on it like a Polynesian queen while I stop up the doorway with wet, rolled towels, just as we've learned to do to keep out the dirt.

The room fills with moist, warm fog, and I encourage Ariel to lean over the tub so she can inhale the steam closest to the source. I rub her back the way I've seen Russ do — long, deep strokes — and give praise for her lung-clearing coughs. I can feel each little vertebra bumping beneath my palm. We didn't take such measures with Pa, not that he would have allowed such a thing, so when she asks if she has the same sickness he had, I lie.

"Of course not. You're a little girl. He was an old man. God wouldn't give two different people the same thing."

Russ would have been angry at the last bit, filling the child's head with something made of fancy rather than faith. But we are alone in a cloud too dense to even see the door, and it sounds as good as any truth I can muster.

When the hot water runs out and the steam drops to nothing but a thin film of water, I get Ariel back in her bed and bring a tray with a big bowl of bright-red Jell-O and a cup of broth from a can of soup Russ heated up during our steam.

"This is what your mama had when she was in the hospital," I say, trying to sound sunny. "And look, I got all better." Another lie, but she valiantly sips the warm broth — the price to pay for the tastier dessert. If we stay, she might grow up to be like me, her whole life played out in this barren place, her tiny body wasting away for lack of life.

Her two little hands grasp the cup, and she hands it to me, still half-full. "I don't want any more."

"You need to finish."

"But I don't like it."

I start to say what my father would have said, what Russ would have said, that sometimes in life we have to do things we don't like to do. I think about what I would do in her place, how I would sip the broth, hold it in my mouth, and let it seep into my napkin as I dabbed my lips. But here is my little girl, honest in her heart's desire, so I smile, take the cup from her, and declare she drank enough. She is only able to take a few bites of Jell-O before appearing too weak to even lift her arm, and only two more before turning her head away when I try to feed her. The fever remains, but I don't think it is my imagination that it seems lower than the night before, and after encouraging her to take a few sips of water, I leave her in a sound sleep.

In the kitchen, the smell of coffee welcomes me, even though Russ doesn't, as he sits at the table, head resting on his folded arms. Neither of us slept much or well the night before, and I hoped to encourage him to go to bed while Ariel sleeps. I touch his shoulder, and without lifting his head, his hand covers mine. I kneel beside him, ignoring the grit against my knees.

He lifts his head, his eyes red-rimmed but dry. "You have to understand," he says, as if we are already midconversation, "I've already run away from one war."

That's when I see the folded telegram, now open, lying on the table in front of him.

"Oh, Russ. You didn't run away, and this isn't a war."

"I hid."

"You weren't hiding. You were serving God. You still are."

"I could have served God in combat. I should have been one of them. I should have sacrificed —"

"Listen to me." I clutch at his shirt, the fabric the only thing keeping me from digging my nails into either his flesh or mine. "You were — you *are* — a good and noble man. You would be the same man whether or not you went to war, or here, or —" I take a deep breath — "in Baltimore." I relinquish my grip. "But I wouldn't."

"What do you mean?"

I feel everything within me go soft, like I've been holding a thick, solid breath that melts and comes pouring out in unchecked tears.

"I'm s—" but the word clogs my throat, and I swallow it in a heave that rivals anything my daughter produced in the thick of the steam.

"Nola, darling? What's wrong?" In a single, smooth motion, Russ backs the chair away from the table and sweeps me into his lap, where I bury my face in his neck, the safest place I know.

I try again. "I'm sorry."

He rocks me and makes soft noises.

"I'm sorry I want this so much. I'm sorry to be so unhappy. I don't have a right to be unhappy."

He sounds mildly amused. "Everybody has the right to be unhappy every now and then."

"I don't. Not when you love me so much."

Now he does laugh, low and rumbling, and I realize his heart is so pure, he can't fathom mine is anything less. He comforts me the way one would a child, christening me with an assumption of innocence. I know I can be brand-new again, that I can be fully restored to the woman and wife I was before my fall. But I can't do it here, not with my temptation pacing, always, to and fro, just beyond our sight.

A cry from Ariel's room brings me to my feet, Russ following suit, and we nearly trip over each other — our conversation forgotten — in a rush to her side. There she sits up in bed, crying, claiming she is melting.

"What's that, sweetheart?" I say, dropping myself to the edge of her bed.

"All that hot. It melted me."

The last word is a long, hoarse wail, and I take her into my arms, immediately understanding. She is drenched in sweat, soaked clear through her nightgown, and I press my cheek to hers. "Thank you, Lord." I reach one hand out to Russ. "Thank you, Jesus."

The fever has broken. God has delivered my child, and in that moment I allow myself the fleeting hope that God will deliver me.

■ ■ ■ ■

Part VI

■ ■ ■ ■

If thou return to the Almighty, thou shalt be
    built up,
thou shalt put away iniquity far from thy
    tabernacles.
Then shalt thou lay up gold as dust,
and the gold of Ophir as the stones of the
    brooks.
Yea, the Almighty shall be thy defence,
and thou shalt have plenty of silver.

JOB 22:23-25

CHAPTER 30

We may not be the only Okies on the train, but we are certainly the only ones in first class, and the experience is instantly humbling. Among my fellow Featherlings, my vanity was given free rein. My husband is tall and handsome, as is my son, and little Ariel unmatched in her exquisiteness. Amid the other passengers, though, we are decidedly rumpled and dirt-worn. Looking through their eyes, we are scrawny, filthy, ready to fill the car with the odor of crude ham sandwiches and government-supplied sardines. Our people are the fleas jumping off the carcass of Oklahoma, and for the first leg of our journey, nobody seems inclined to do anything other than flick us away.

To my great joy, though, it doesn't last. By the end of the first leg, Russ encounters another minister, and the two are thick as thieves comparing passages of Scripture and sermon styles. Ariel finds another little girl with a cardboard box full of paper dolls, and they are immediately fast friends. Ronnie embarks on an elaborate baseball card trade with a few uniformed soldiers on leave.

As for myself, I sit by the window, content, alone, my head against the glass, and watch creation unfold. Thirty-six hours on the train, and every one of them dominated by a single thought: *I am free.* I suffer every stop — even those that last a mere ten minutes — with impatience. Russ takes the kids out to the station to buy a snack or a magazine, or simply to have a gulp of clean, cold air. I never dare follow, though. Instead, I stay on the train, my foot tapping to re-create the *clackety-clack* that separates me from the ruination left behind.

Greg is there to meet us at Pennsylvania Station — a fact that is initially confusing to the children, that a train station in Maryland could have the name of a differ-ent state. I don't think I ever truly believed that our two lives would join together again until the moment I see him. We run to each other as if one of us were returning from war. Russ lingers, shakes his hand, as does Ronnie, and Ariel shyly offers her cheek for a kiss.

The mass of humanity milling around that train station is the largest gathering of people I've ever seen in one place, making me feel even smaller than I did in the middle of an Oklahoma dust storm. Greg leads the way, but I realize that, from the back at least, he looks like almost every other man in the station: dark coat, hat pulled low, and impossibly clean black leather shoes. I instruct Ariel to take his hand, as she has the greatest potential of becoming lost, and I simply follow her.

Though we've packed conservatively, our trunks are too numerous for Greg's vehicle, so he arranges with the porter for delivery. The first thing I notice when we step out of the station and into the semidarkness of the early evening is the icy chill in the air, like a cold slap in the face, but not necessarily unpleasant or unwelcome. I inhale, imagining a million tiny, sweet crystals coating my throat, my lungs, grabbing on to the last remnants of dust, and melting them away.

"Hey, Sis?" Greg tugs at my sleeve. "Do you want to stand here and breathe all night? Or do you want to go home?"

"That's a tough choice," I say, and look to Russ. "What do you think?"

He, too, has been looking beyond the cloisters of brick buildings and into the sparkling night sky. At my question, though, it is clear that he sees nothing but me.

"Let's go home."

Home turns out to be a neighborhood christened Arcadia, one after another of the most beautiful houses I have ever seen. Each one alone looks like the product of a dream — porches and shrubs, painted shutters and balconies, stretches of lawn that Greg assures me will be vibrant green come summer, but that now lie faded and dormant, waiting to spring to life. Windows glow with amber light; women lean in doorways calling their children home, as it is by now nearly dark.

"I've never seen so many houses this close together," Russ says with a hint of trepidation.

"Might take some getting used to," Greg says, confidently navigating the street. "But I think you'll find that we're as capable of being neighborly as the folks back home."

Ariel, Ronnie, and I sit in the backseat, with Ariel in my lap so as not to miss anything.

"Any of the kids play baseball here?" Ronnie asks.

"Usually a pickup game in the park, a couple of blocks away," Greg says. "After school and Saturdays. And of course, the high school has a team. You'll be in high school next year, won't you?"

"Yes, sir."

I notice Ronnie clenching his jaw, looking more like his ornery grandfather than ever, and I wish I could pull him to me and assure him that everything will be fine. Despite his adolescent bluster about wanting to leave Oklahoma, he is the only one of us to leave behind true friends. Russ and I had our church family, but nobody whose affections will be greatly missed, and Ariel seems to make best friends wherever she goes. Only Ronnie has been ripped away midlife, and in this he suffers the most.

"And if you're interested, I have four tickets to a Senators and Red Sox game this summer. Maybe we can look into season tickets?"

I take a mental accounting of all our resources, and even without knowing the price, know we don't have the money for such a luxury. As I hold my breath for Russ's refusal, he surprises me by turning around in his seat with a broad grin.

"Four tickets, eh? Looks like you might have to stay home on your own that day, Nola, while Greg and me and the kids eat some peanuts and Cracker Jack."

"I shall try to survive," I say.

And then, Greg stops the car.

The house, same as the photograph I've been studying for a month, but now with warmth beckoning through the windows.

"Be it ever so humble . . . ," he jokes, but I cannot bring myself to laugh.

"Oh, Mama," Ariel breathes, for the first time without the rattle in her chest that was so worrisome.

Russ gets out of the car and opens my door, first taking Ariel from my lap, then reaching in for my hand.

"Are you all right?" I say, whispering, in hopes that my brother will be left unaware of Russ's misgivings.

"I just want to see you happy."

"I am." Taking his hand, I scoot to the edge of the car seat and am about to step onto the sidewalk when I know I don't want to begin this life with a lie. With my feet planted firmly on the ground, I hold on to my husband and amend my words. "I will be."

CHAPTER 31

For the first week, Russ seems not to know
what to do with his time, or his hands, or
his mind. We go together to enroll the
children in their separate schools, and then
return to the house for the remainder of the
day. After Greg leaves to catch his train into
Washington, the two of us are left to rattle
around the unfamiliar space. My husband,
who has always filled whatever room he
entered, appears small and uneasy. He sits
on the edges of the chairs, treads lightly on
the floor, and sleeps in motionless silence
beside me each night.

I sense how hard this is for him, the toll it
takes on his idea of what it means to provide
for our family. We've walked into a home he
did not purchase, in a city he does not
know, and with no perceivable means to
support ourselves. All the money we have in
the world came from the sale of the one
thing he could claim as his own — the car

— and it is dwindling fast.

A hundred times each day, I stop myself from asking, *"Are you all right? Do you think you'll be happy here?"* because I dread what his answer might be. So I become a woman consumed with feeding my children and lavishing all the affection I can on my husband.

"We can make it like a honeymoon," I say one morning, returning from walking Ariel to school. I have a white paper sack full of pastries from a bakery I passed by on the route. "Nice, long, empty days. However shall we fill our time?"

My attempt at flirtation is rewarded, and as we lie in bed like a couple of jazz-fed hooligans in the middle of the morning, I have the chance to study him in sleep. He is as beautiful a man as he has ever been, and with his lips formed into a slight smile and his face relaxed around it, he looks much as he did on one of our first dates, dozing next to an uneaten picnic in the middle of a field ripe with wheat.

"I'm so sorry," I whisper, bringing my hand close to his face, but pulling back before our skin touches.

Almost overnight it seems, Ariel's cheeks become round, her eyes bright, and her dresses begin to strain across a healthy little-girl belly. Ronnie, given almost unlimited access to food, takes on the heft of a young man, besides growing at least half an inch taller.

It only takes one visit to my brother's church for Russ to stand and show signs of the same rebirth that has already taken root within our children. At Greg's insistence, we arrive early and spend half an hour shaking hands and verifying that, yes, we are the family from Oklahoma, and yes, things there really are as dire as the newspaper reports, and yes, we are looking forward to making a new home here. Not until I hear our voices intertwined with theirs do I realize the extremity of our accents. After years of working so hard to pronounce my *g*'s at the end of verbs and to keep my words sharp and clipped the way actresses do in the movies, I still hear traces of dust between my syllables. So I fall silent, content to let Russ's garrulous conversation speak for both of us. As always happens, he holds people enthralled with the images of what we've left behind, so much so that the crowd that eventually gathers around him has to be reminded, with nudges and tugs, when the service is about to begin.

We all get new clothes for Easter Sunday, an expense justified by my careful shopping at a secondhand shop filled with clothing of better quality than I've ever seen in anything from the Sears and Roebuck, or in any of the stores back home. Besides wanting our finest for the special Sunday service, both Ariel and Ronnie are badly in need of new things, as both barely fit into anything we brought from Oklahoma.

The most pressing need for new clothes this Easter Sunday is the fact that Russ will stand behind the pulpit of the church we've only attended twice before. It is April 1, and Reverend Sheldon, a man of wry wit, attempts to fool his congregation into thinking he was bullied out of his position by the sheer force of the Oklahoma wind, leaving a smattering of laughter still in play as Russ ascends the steps. I watch from a seat less assuming than the front and center. The children and I are near the back with Greg, and we stand briefly to be acknowledged at Russ's insistence.

Then he begins to speak, telling of the new life in Jesus Christ, celebrated with the resurrection. He tells our story, the story of our home state — the vibrant life destroyed by greed, the desolation of the empty fields, the constant battle against the endless wind and dirt. He tells of all we've left behind, including the babies in their graves, and a church once filled with people just like them.

"And we are here," he says, "seeing the new life that pushes through the snow."

Greg leans over in the pew and whispers, "He's a good preacher, isn't he?"

"The first time we saw each other was like this. He fell in love with me from behind the pulpit."

"So it's like you're starting all over?"

A woman in front of us with an impressive sprig of silk flowers on her hat turns to give us a disapproving hush, and I respond with a respectfully sober expression, glowing inwardly with a feeling I can best describe as victory.

I listen to him, and I listen to them. The scattered laughter when he tells about the massive jolts of electricity that could send a man flying across the room; the women's sounds of empathy when he describes my plight in trying to keep the house clean. They shudder at his description of darkness and clutch at their throats as if they are choking on the dust of his words. They lift their feet when he describes the sensation of walking on carpets of locusts and *tut-tut* at the thought of thousands of rabbits rounded up for slaughter. As far as they know, our little family is the reincarnation of the children of Israel, delivered from a new plague to this Promised Land, where times are hard but the air is clean. We've been brought from death to life, as are all sinners in Christ.

Already, I can tell, they are in love. After the service, they will take him over, build a wall between us with questions and compliments and offers to bake lemon cakes. If they accept me, it will be because they accept him. If they love me, it will be because they love him. Our afternoons are soon to be invaded by invitations to tea, or to speak at the ladies' Bible study, or to pray over a loved one. Other churches will want to hear, other Bible studies, other charity circles, other Christians. Russ hasn't been reborn upon our move to Baltimore, not like the children have. He has simply *resumed,* like he's been blown in and dropped down on a higher, cleaner plane.

In the midst of all my predictions coming true, Greg comes home with an invitation that far exceeds anything we could have imagined.

"A series of hearings," Greg says at supper, "as Congress debates a soil conservation bill."

"I'm not a politician," Russ says. "Nor a farmer. What could I possibly have to say?"

"Everything you said in church on Easter. People from my department will be talking about the science and the economics, neither of which are going to be embraced by the farmers. They're not going to be happy when we tell them not to plant, or that we need to sow grass where they used to grow wheat. And if the farmers aren't happy, the politicians won't be either, but we need this to pass."

"So he'd go to the Capitol?" Ronnie's voice beams with pride. "Can we go too?"

"Sorry," Greg says in consolation. "However, I do think it would be a fine idea for *you* to go with him, Sis. Make it a day. See the sights, go out to lunch."

"Oh, yes, Russ." My enthusiasm serves as a complement to Greg's exhortation. "We haven't had a chance to be tourists yet. Ronnie can see to Ariel in the afternoon, and we'll make plans for all of us to go back once school is out."

"Now wait a minute." Russ holds up his hand to halt the explosion of conversation, which includes a dissenting opinion from Ariel, who wants desperately to go too, though she doesn't know exactly where. "I'm still not clear about my purpose here."

"Quite simply," Greg says, "I'd like you to represent the spiritual toll the drought and the storms have taken on the people. You've worked with the sick, and you've buried the dead, and you've watched your whole community disappear. Tell them that. You make people believe in God, don't you? I need you to make some men believe in the power of God's destruction, not just in dollars, but in lives."

"When is it?" Russ takes a small leather-bound calendar from his breast pocket and opens it, displaying his new commitments in little square boxes.

"Coming up in a couple of weeks. I can't be sure of the exact date."

"We'll be ready," Russ says, reaching for my hand, inviting me in. Quite a change from my usual relegation as the pastor's wife. But then, at the moment, he isn't a pastor.

The opportunity comes on the second Saturday in May, meaning Ronnie and Ariel will be left to their own devices for the entirety of the afternoon. Both react to the circumstances with minimal pouting, however, as Barney became pregnant immediately following her escape from her traveling basket, and a box of tiny kittens mewl in a corner of the washroom.

"Stay close to the house," I admonish as I

give myself a final inspection in the front hall mirror. Since arriving in Baltimore, I've gained at least ten pounds, the weight manifested in the softened planes of my face. My hair has recaptured the sheen of my youth and, having escaped the brutal weathering of the dust and wind, my skin glows in gratitude.

"But, Ma, there's going to be a game at the park."

My heart nudges at my protective reserve. Since arriving, the children have taken to the fresh air — no matter the cold of these early spring days — like a dying man for water. I've been sure to dress them in their best, clean clothes, and keep them scrubbed and fresh so nobody at school would think to call them "dirty Okies." They both immediately made friends — Ronnie due to his ability to man third base, and Ariel due to her intriguing curls and fat, beautiful cat. Russ and I have made some fine acquaintances too, but I can only imagine the importance of the people we will meet this afternoon. My first instinct was to buy yet another new dress, but my Easter dress has not yet been seen in our nation's capital, so I figure it will do.

"Well then," I concede, "could you at least take her with you? Let her watch? I'll tell her to behave, and if you both do, I'll bring you back a prize from today."

Ronnie takes a moment to weigh the possibilities and declares if Ariel isn't perfect, he is going to take her prize and give it to the charity auction.

"Empty threats," I say, ruffling my fingers through his hair. He is at least as tall as me these days, and will be taller by the end of summer when he starts high school. More and more he looks like his father, shoulders broadening along with his smile.

I repeat the instructions to Ariel, making her promise to be a good girl at the park, and no, she can't take the kittens to the park because they are too little to be away from their mama, and Barney is too tired, but she can take a doll if she wants, though not a paper doll because it might blow away.

"Is it windy, Mama?" she asks, her eyes filled with fear for the first time since she got on the train in Boise City.

I glance out the window and gauge the motion in the newly budded trees.

"A bit." I kiss the top of her head. "But nothing to be alarmed about. We've certainly seen worse."

From outside, the honk of a car horn calls me to quicken my pace. Usually Greg takes the train, but today's special occasion calls for a drive, and he and Russ are waiting, not quite patiently, for me to join them. I elicit one final promise from the children to behave, then go outside, nearly trotting down the walkway to the car.

It is ten o'clock in the morning, with Russ due to speak to the committee at one. Exactly when he will be finished, however, is anyone's guess, so we've made no plans for the afternoon beyond finding someplace for a nice dinner. "On Uncle Sam's dime," Greg jokes.

The farther we get into Washington, the narrower the streets become, or so it seems with the congestion of so many automobiles threatening to pile on one another. The national grandeur of the city is lost until the moment the Capitol comes into view, with its white dome and green lawn, all seen as we drive past the glistening Potomac.

"I wanted you to get a good look at it," Greg says, as both Russ and I press our faces against the window. "The parking garage doesn't present nearly as fabulous a view. I'll circle around, drop you off, and you can give your names to the security guard. I'll meet you in the Rotunda. Or you can wait on the steps."

"Steps," Russ and I say simultaneously,

sharing our children's thirst for air. All I want to do is raise my face to the sky and thank God for his deliverance. Who would have imagined only a year ago, when I buried my friend who drowned on dry land and took in the living ghost of my father, that someday I would be here? Living in a home purchased with my inheritance. The wife of a man about to address our nation's leaders. None of it, I am sure, would have happened if not for the keeping of my secrets.

This is your mercy, Lord, I pray before adding aloud, "Show your mercy on us today."

We walk hand in hand up the endless, shallow steps.

"Are you nervous, darling?" I ask, unable to read his passive expression.

"I'll be talking about how much I love my home. I can talk about that all day long."

It gives me a pang to think that he doesn't yet consider this place to be his home, but I know that will come in time. I like to think that we are each other's home.

"Incredible, isn't it?" he asks. We've arrived, at last, surrounded by powerful white stone, making both of us seem insignificant.

"It is," I say, drawing myself closer to him. "Are you nervous *now*?"

"I have to believe God brought me here

for a reason. This might be it."

I smiled, tight-lipped, and nod. For Russ, I know, it will never be enough to consider that God may have brought us here solely for my sake. To rescue me from the temptations I was powerless to deny, or even to make a home in a place where our children can live without the constant threat of illness and death.

A gust of wind drives itself into my back, familiar in its strength, and I barely get my hand to my hat in time to save it from flying off my head. It carries with it a familiar scent that tickles at the back of my throat. Perhaps I will be forever haunted by the storms of Oklahoma, like the soldier who cannot bear the sound of a banging cupboard or a slamming door. If my husband is not willing to accept our displacement as nothing more than a means to save our family, I will do so on his behalf.

"I think," I say as Greg comes into view, "I'm not going to go in with you."

His face registers surprise rather than disappointment. "Why not?"

"Russ." I step closer to him, pulling us into an invisible space where we can ignore the hundreds of milling people. "Will I ever be enough for you?"

"What do you mean?" He touches his lips

to mine, and nobody seems to notice. "You are my life."

I know he will never ask me the same question; it isn't his way to seek such confirmation.

Greg joins us and loops my arm through his. "Are we ready, kids?"

"I'm not sure, all of a sudden," I say, "if it's my place to go."

"Of course it's your place. You're my wife."

"They won't care that she's your wife," Greg says, quietly coming to my defense. Then, to me, "You should go because you survived this too."

And so I do.

How anyone ever learned to navigate the labyrinth of passages and stairways I'll never know, but Greg proves the perfect guide, never condescending to speak directions, but keeping enough of a lead to allow us to follow both his conversation and his steps. He leads us to a room that might be smaller than I imagined, if I had the wherewithal to imagine anything at all. Two rows of long tables stretch across the front, elevated, and a row of tables face them with a bank of seats filling out the rest of the room. After giving a sheaf of papers to a young boy in a crisp blue suit, Greg instructs me to sit in the bank of chairs, three rows back, while he and Russ move toward the tables.

There are, perhaps, thirty people in the room at the time, with me the only woman, a fact that makes me all the more thankful that my dress is new, my hat in place, and my skin radiant. More than one appreciative glance comes my way, not the least from the men coming to sit at the tables at the front of the room. These, I know, are elected officials. Powerful men who decide the fate of what is quickly becoming a desert back home. I uncross and cross my legs to see if their eyes follow, and to no surprise, they do.

Greg glances back, and I send him a withering, humor-filled glare. So much for my presence being powerful because I am a survivor who matters. Greg wants me there because I am a beautiful woman, in a place where such creatures are all the more valuable for their rarity.

All around me, chairs fill, and I realize Greg's strategy in getting us into the room at the hour he did. My seat is front and center in the gallery, just as it used to be in church. Only now, my husband speaks with his back to me, while the others at their long stretch of pulpit look on. Sitting alongside Russ, one man after another speaks, extolling the need for replanting the wild grasses, rotating crops, allowing fields to lie fallow for years to come. Buying farmland and paying farmers not to work it. All of this in the name of healing the land and restoring the soil that will remain once the wind stops and the rains come.

When it is Russ's turn to speak, I hear for the first time the distinctness of his accent. Though his diction is strong, his vocabulary elevated, he comes across as a humble man, wise despite his relative youth. His is a voice of hope, someone who speaks *for* the bedraggled men and women pictured in the newspaper reports about the drought, yet not one *of* them.

The committee members lean forward as he speaks, as do I, resting my elbow on my knee. Every time I move, I distract the decision makers from their duty, so I decide on a single pose, and hold it throughout Russ's speech. When he finishes, he turns in his seat to introduce me as his wife, saying, "We brought our family here for the sake of our children, and we are so thankful for the opportunity to speak for all of those whose voices you cannot hear."

As a test, I smile, and they smile back, and I gloat a bit in my seat.

One of the congressmen is about to ask a question, perhaps directed at me, if the direction of his gaze is any hint, when the young man in the blue suit bursts through the door and makes a dignified run to the front of the room, stopping at the congressman's elbow. He leans in and whispers something that registers a look of pure disbelief on the face of every man in earshot, and the news travels down the length of the table like an oncoming cloud.

Because apparently, an oncoming cloud exactly describes what is barreling down on the city.

Amid the crowd, Greg, Russ, and I manage to find each other, and once again we follow my brother, though this time through lesser-used service hallways emptying out onto the more utilitarian side of the Capitol, where we stand among the throng, covering our mouths and shielding our eyes against the relentless, thick, grainy brown sky.

The storms have followed us home.

CHAPTER 32

My legs turn to sand, and it takes the strength of my husband and my brother to keep me on my feet.

"How . . . ?" But I cannot finish the rest of the sentence, because there are too many questions wrapped within it.

A state of near panic erupts around us, but we stand stalwart in the familiar scene. My new dress begins to collect dust within each seam; my skin absorbs the minuscule pelting of the grains of dirt. Russ hands me his handkerchief, which I immediately place over my nose and mouth, reacting out of habit. He and Greg cover their lower faces with the lapels of their jackets.

"This is unbelievable," Greg says, unable to muffle the faint amusement in his statement.

"I believe God himself has spoken," Russ says, his full eyebrows communicating a hidden smile.

Of the three, only I appear horrified at this display. But then, only I know its origin.

Greg tugs at my hand. "We need to wait inside until it blows over."

I pull back. "No! We have to get home. The kids —"

"They've lived through this before," Russ says, urging me in the direction of my brother. "They know what to do."

I plant my feet. "They were going to the park! What if it's worse there? What if they can't find their way — ?" Panic steals the rest of my thought. How easy it would be to become disoriented even in the now-familiar streets. And Ariel has grown so independent, she might refuse to take Ronnie's hand. Or he might not be able to find her at all. "Take me home!" My voice rises shrill above the wind, streaking through the crowd.

"Wait inside," Greg says, now nearly shouting just to be heard. "I'll get the car."

I give Russ a push. "Go with him."

"I'm not leaving you alone."

"I'll be right here. I'll be fine. I've been through this before, remember?"

Convinced that I'm not going to change my mind, they leave, and I back myself up against the building. True, there would be shelter inside, but I can't find anything within myself to be deserving of protection.

How stupid could I be, thinking that a mere train ride halfway across the country would shield me from God's wrath?

All around me, the din of the crowd mixes with the whistle of the wind, but certain phrases make their way out of the cloud of conversation. They curse the Okies who couldn't leave their dirt at home. They claim blindness, and breathlessness, and a weakness to stand against the onslaught of the hazy brown fog. Part of me wants to mock them, because they have no idea what it means to face such a thing on a week's empty stomach, or after months of feeling and tasting nothing but dry and dirt. The rest of me — the better part, maybe — has an illogical need to apologize. To explain that I know exactly why this is happening, and what I must do to bring it to an end. Because there is no more time, and nowhere to go where I will be out of the reach of God's judgment. They have suffered for a matter of minutes what I have endured for years. I've tried to run away, to hide within the walls of an ordinary house, to do penance by meeting the needs of my family — a home for my children, companionship for my brother, and for Russ, my heart. My love, abundant and consuming, hoping to erase any lingering bits of unfaithfulness.

Now, God has scooped up all of those bits, and he's flung them across the vastness of the country, more powerful than his own clear sky, farther reaching than any man's train.

I hear my name above the clamor and see Greg's car pulled to the side, Russ calling to me. Handkerchief in place, I wedge my way through the crowd and to the car, where Russ and Greg are changing places.

"I'll do better as navigator," Greg says as I slip into the backseat. "I'll do the seeing; Russ can do the driving. You do the praying."

I dive into the backseat, ready to fulfill my duty, though I do so silently. I hardly think at all to pray for our safe passage home, as I trust the abilities of the two men in front of me. Instead, I beg for the safety of my children, that they won't become victims of my negligence as a mother.

While Greg's decision to hand the wheel over to Russ was a logical one, driving the nearly deserted roads that spool between a dozen little towns is a far cry from maneuvering alongside a hundred other automobiles, each wanting to occupy your space, and willing to dislodge you to get it.

"Easy, easy," Greg says, determining the amount of space between each car. "Once we're out of the city, things should clear up."

They don't, and the trip that accounted for little more than an hour's travel in one direction lasts more than four going the other way. By the time we come into view of Arcadia, I am ready to jump out of the car and start walking the streets, calling for my children on the wind.

But the streets are deserted, looking more and more like home every day.

"We've seen worse," Russ keeps repeating — to reassure himself, I suppose. And he is right. We've been in dust storms that built a wall of blindness between the eyes and the end of the nose. This is more like dirty, driven snow. Thick and stinging, but adequately transparent. I keep my eyes peeled for any sign of Ariel and Ronnie, up until the time Russ stops the car in front of the now-familiar door.

All the windows are dark.

I stumble out of the car and run up the walkway, screaming, "Ariel! Ronnie!" I pound on the door and grab the knob, finding it turns easily, but when I try to push it open, it won't budge.

More pounding, more calling, more pushing, and suddenly it is yanked away from me, and I fall through, tripping over the damp, rolled towel that has been placed along the bottom.

"Just like you taught us," Ronnie says, and without giving a thought to the fact that I am filthy with dirt and his clothes and person are as clean as they were when I left this morning, I grab him into my arms, telling him over and over that he is a good, good boy.

"Where's your sister?" Surely if he is here, she will be too.

Ronnie hooks a thumb toward the back of the house. "Watching over the kittens. She doesn't want them to be scared." His young brow wrinkles with concern. "Where's Papa?"

I join him, looking to Greg for an answer.

"In the car. Waiting, he said, to know if he had to go back out to search."

"I'll tell him," I say, beating Ronnie to the offer.

Once at the car, instead of knocking on the window and beckoning him into the house, I open the door and slide inside. Russ turns to me with a worried expression. "They're gone?"

"They're fine." I should touch him, not knowing how many other opportunities I will have to do so, but I keep my hands in my lap. "They're inside."

"Then what are you doing here?"

I don't have to hold him back to keep him still. An instinct that comes with so many years of shared loss bids him to stay in his seat and look at me. He always seemed to know even before my body made its final decision to rid itself of a child. He said a final farewell the breath before my father's last. The fact that he has no perception of my adultery comes from the fact that, until this moment, it posed no threat to our marriage, because I would have lied to deny its existence. But I could not lie about my lost babies, and I could not deny the death of my father, and now my marriage dangles over the same precipice.

"I have to tell you." I look at him, drinking him in like cool water. "I did this."

"Did what?"

"This — the storm. I brought it here."

His laughter is a weapon to ward off the fear that is building itself up between us. "What can that possibly mean?"

"I thought I could get away. Run away from it. That if I confessed — repented, like the Bible says. Like God says, and be washed white as snow. And as far as the east is from the west. But the west. It's *here.* It's followed me. And I'll never be clean. I'll never —"

I've disintegrated into nothing more than a twist of tears and disjointed phrases. Any other time, Russ would have taken me into his arms, soothed me until my sentences ran straight. Now, though, he keeps a distance between us. Were I to melt, he would not cup his hands to catch me. For the first time in memory, I am utterly alone in his presence, and the storm becomes an unexpected ally. Here, in this place of safety, rocked by the wind, serenaded by the dust, I take a deep, cleansing breath, and relive it all.

"That first night, when he came into our house . . ."

"Who?"

I look at my husband through scales of shame. "Jim." After that, I spare neither of us any detail that could rise up again like some secret, treasured memory. I tell him about our afternoons, both of us reading from a single book, our sentences falling upon one another's as we whiled away the afternoons while Ariel napped upstairs. I do, however, refrain from elaboration. That first kiss in the kitchen the day we brought Barney home is relegated to "a kiss," interchangeable with a dry touch to a deacon's cheek.

Russ listens. Never interrupting, never

interpreting, not even muttering the slightest sound of understanding. He becomes something that I've never seen in him before — utterly passive. Disconnected, almost. Always, always, his face has displayed a map of his mind, sketching his thoughts before he speaks his words. Sometimes instead of his words. But I find myself talking to a death mask, Russ captured in his handsome perfection. Set for eternity, and unmoved. Until I come to the day I disappeared, and at this point I would give anything for expressionless banality. Instead, something dreadful flickers across his features. Recognition. Confirmation.

"I've always wondered," he says, more musing than accusatory.

"What do you mean you always wondered?" Even now, knee-deep in confession, I leap to my own defense.

"You were so . . . altered. And then so sick, and what with the things Mrs. Brown said —"

"You never said a word!"

"Neither did you."

"But if you had — if you'd *confronted me* . . ."

"I did. At the hospital. Don't you remember?"

"I mean, specifically. If you had asked —"

"You would have told me?"

"You would have spared me."

This takes him aback, and while he hasn't altered his posture a mite since I got in the car, he now rears back as if to escape.

"Spared you?" And then a laugh so bitter it freezes my blood. "Spared *you*? Darling, have you been listening to yourself? From what did you need to be spared?"

I can't look at him. Until this point, my gaze has traced a path from the brown window to my dirt-encrusted hands and his masklike face. But for what I have to say next, there is no place safe. Looking outside gives the illusion of being buried, my hands bear traces of Jim's touch, and I do not deserve even the image of my husband.

I close my eyes and return to the darkness that haunts me. "I needed to be spared from being alone. I needed to be spared from what happened next."

Christmas, and the New Year, and the three wretched mornings that followed.

"My God," he says, crying out to the Lord who watches me from behind the storm.

"Do you think — ? Can you ever forgive me?"

He says nothing, only presses his fingers to his eyes as if trying to gouge out the images planted there.

"I've asked God to forgive me, but that's not enough. Not for me, anyway."

He looks at me, transformed. Monstrous, all of his nobility dropped away. The landscape of his face stripped of all that ever gave it life. "Why are you telling me now?"

"Because you're my husband, and I've — I've sinned. Against God, and against you."

"I mean, why *now*?"

"Because I have to. I was wanting to protect you from all of this. I wanted to carry it all on my own. Believe me." For the first time I touch him, grabbing at the sleeve of his jacket, feeling the laycr of dirt beneath my hand. "You always told me I was strong —"

He snatches his arm away. "Do not use my words against me."

His admonition stings. "I'm sorry."

"Tell me the truth."

"I've told you everything. I promise."

"No, tell me the truth about why you've held this in up to now."

"I wanted to spare —"

"That's not it."

"I thought I was strong —"

"No."

And then, like a wellspring, truth floods me, bubbling out with my very pulse, and flows from my tongue. "I was ashamed. I hated myself, and I never, ever wanted you to see me in that light. So I hid it, buried it deep. Some days —" tears well in my eyes at the confession to come — "I'd even forget. I might go all day long and not even give a thought to what I'd done. That's how far I tried to fling it away. But then, something would happen, or there'd be a quiet moment, when I was alone, or with you, and it would come back. That's what made me think — made me wonder — if God maybe hadn't forgiven me. Because it kept coming back. And I thought, if we came here, away from where it happened — away from *him* — I could hide that part of me away. Leave it in Oklahoma. But it came back."

The sobs that racked my body have now subsided, only catching every other breath or so, irregular in how they break through the silence that has dropped between us. I can hear each individual grain of dust as it hits the car's window, and I'm sure the others must think we're some kind of crazy not to come inside. But this needs to be us — cocooned alone. Maybe not exactly alone, as the invisible presence of Jim Brace lurks between us, but we started our marriage with a conversation much like this one. Me and Russ, under the moonlight in his old jalopy of a car, parked in a wheat field. We had a third presence with us then, too. Invisible, but real — our baby, and my weeping apology. My shame, my burden, until Russ lived out his promise to carry it with me.

I've no right to expect the same now. And yet I see him, broken, but girding up before my very eyes. Filling this small space, his presence wrapping itself around me, creating a wall strong enough to withstand the storm, leaving room enough for grace.

"He has forgiven you." He says it as a fact proven thus far only to him.

"How do you know?"

"Because I have to have faith in his mercy. It's what I know to be true, that sins confessed are forgiven. And if I can't believe that he has forgiven you after your sincere confession, what hope can I have that I myself will be forgiven?"

I have no answer. I never do, so I keep silent for a few more shuddering breaths, staring at the tear in my new stockings.

"You must hate me."

"I could never hate you." Which gives me little comfort, as I know it's not his nature to hate anyone, and he takes time to gather the rest of his response. "I love you. Believe it or not, as much now as I ever have at any moment. Nothing can change that. The love

570

is still there — I just feel a little bit disconnected from it."

I look up to see the pain behind the words, and before I can stop myself, I think of Jim, what he said about his wound, the greatest pain being the strain on the connecting flesh before his arm was severed. Our marriage is that flesh, and I alone have wounded it. Only the grace of God and my husband's love can heal it.

"I know how much I've hurt you, Russ."

"You couldn't possibly know."

"If I could take it on — not even trade, but take yours on top of mine, I would."

He touches me for the first time since I entered the car. Lightly, the backs of his fingers graze my cheek, more condescension than caress. "I wouldn't let you, Nola, darling. You're not strong enough. It would kill you."

"But it won't kill you?"

"It has, a bit."

And there, right before my eyes, a part of him is irreplaceably gone. Severed. I know what it feels like to die. Not to be dead, but to be in the process. Little by little. But I've been dying for my own sin. Russ is paying a much higher price.

I clasp his hand to me, bury a kiss in his palm. "So you believe, do you? That God forgives me?"

"He does, of course."

A beat of silence before I'll let him go. "And you?"

"I will."

And since he's never failed me, my hope is in that promise.

EPILOGUE

We live through a summer, the air hot and heavy, wet with rain that seldom falls, but we do not complain. The heaviness of the air keeps it motionless, almost solid. Our skin is slick with sweat, and I embrace the feel of it, to the bemusement of our friends and neighbors. Fall delights us with its display. And winter — so much water, so much white. The air, sharp and cold, slices us, and we turn our faces to it, living pink-cheeked and red-nosed within the frost.

In the time between our first Easter and our first Christmas, Russ finds his place behind a new pulpit, and I stand proudly at his side, his lovely wife, warmly welcomed by this congregation. A photograph is taken to commemorate the occasion. Russ and I stand with the retiring pastor and his wife, matched in identical poses. Russ's hand is at the small of my waist, drawing me protectively to him.

It is the first time he's touched me since the dirt of Oklahoma dusted this place.

While Russ spoke his forgiveness with the sincerity of Scripture and treats me with the kindness of courtship, the brokenness of trust remains. There are no soft kisses upon waking, no sweet, swift embraces throughout the day. Every night I tuck in the children and go to bed, drifting and dozing while he studies downstairs. Deep into darkness, he joins me, and there we lie, parallel in our dreams. In the morning, I leave our bed as I took to it. Alone, to spend the rest of the day in careful, measured steps.

There are moments I long for a return to our cramped little apartment, where it was impossible to move without brushing up against each other. Here, in the grandness of this house, I live without the feel of his skin. Neither hands, nor lips, nor any other part of God's design. We don't speak of it; we simply agree. And the moment the smoke clears from that camera's flash, Russ takes his touch away, and I begin to burn.

It is a Sunday afternoon in April, and we spend it the way we always have, only instead of reading a letter from Greg, we listen to the latest attempt to end his reign of bachelorhood. Last night, it was the niece of a well-meaning parishioner, homely even by Greg's forgiving standards, who kept him out half the night trying to wheedle one more date.

"Aren't you ever going to get married, Uncle Greg?" Ariel asks. She rolls lazily on the thick carpet with Barney — once again fat with kittens — pawing at her ribbons.

"Besides you kids, I've yet to see the benefit."

Russ bends the corner of the *Tulsa Tribune,* to which we subscribe and have delivered weekly. "To be married is a beautiful thing," he says, catching my eye over the headlines of destruction. "Endless opportunities for sacrifice and love."

"Well, I've sacrificed enough of my time to Miss Edith Crauller," Greg says. "And until the perfect woman comes along, I'll be satisfied with loving all of you."

Just then the door opens, and Ronnie bursts in, dripping with rain, shoes covered in mud, but I don't even think to chastise him.

"Have you heard it?" He clomps to the radio and turns it on, setting his ear to find the station. "They're saying it's the worst one yet. That the whole sky turned black as night just like *that.*"

"Mama?"

Ariel, full of fear, crawls across the floor and wraps herself around my legs. Soon, our cozy back parlor, so recently full of warmth and laughter, is invaded by the cold voice of the radio newsman. Already they're calling it Black Sunday, arguably the worst of these storms yet to pester the Oklahoma panhandle. Sunlight disappeared in seconds. Darkness descended for hours. Dark still, in fact, as a nation turns its heart to the poor, the plagued, the piteous lives left in the wake of such destruction.

" 'If any man's work shall be burned,' " Russ says, quoting Scripture, " 'he shall suffer loss: but he himself shall be saved.' "

I think about Merrilou Brown, who writes occasionally, her letters filled with the same strength and resilience as her strident conversation. What would she say about such darkness, other than she felt no surprise when the sun shone bright as ever behind it?

"Is it going to come here again, Mama?"

"No, baby girl." I place my hand on her curls as substitute for a kiss I must remember to give later. Our windows are coated with thick sheets of rain, and I can hardly remember what it felt like to live with that fear. "I think we'll be spared from it ever happening again."

Later, in the latest of the afternoon, when it's time to walk to evening church, Russ suggests we leave the children at home, tended to by their uncle, who has promised warm bowls of soup and a game of Old Maid to while away the evening.

"All right," I say, thinking I might have joined them if I hadn't already donned my slicker and rubber boots. Russ does the same, and after a final good-bye to the family, we're on the other side of the door. His hand finds mine, a gesture immediately foreign and familiar, and he holds it all the way down the rain-slicked steps, down the walkway, through the gate, and onto the sidewalk, where I assume he will drop its grip.

He doesn't; neither do I; and we are both silent for the next few steps.

Looking up, I can see each drop of rain illuminated in the streetlight. I stop, lifting my face to the beauty of it — still so strange. It's cold and stinging, like tiny bits of life nipping my cheeks. I am cleansed and removed from the darkness that haunted me for so long. The rain holds every tear I dare not cry in the midst of so much blessing.

"I never thought I'd ever be so happy for

such a small thing."

I'm hoping he'll think I'm talking about the rain, and not his touch, lest he realize his transgression and take it away.

"God is faithful," he says. "Rain will return to Oklahoma, too."

"Of course it will."

"And I want to be there when it does."

He's still holding my hand, and when I try to take it away, he grips me harder. We're walking again, toward the church two blocks away. Russ seems determined in his stride, and I match him step for step at his side as raindrops patter on my hat.

I shouldn't be surprised that he wants to go back. He hasn't flourished in this place the way the children have. The way I have. The fact that he pastors a church is a matter of convenience rather than passion, on the part of both the church and Russ. He doesn't fit into the furniture. He no longer fills the room. While Featherling may have been the birthplace of my betrayal, this is the place where I confessed it, brought it to life. Here, too, for our marriage, there has been drought. The fields sown with salt. I can't blame him for wanting to get away. Return home, in the way he has always defined it. Surrounded by families who will give when they have nothing, and then bring pie.

"Nobody goes back to Oklahoma, Russ." Only my husband could see beauty in such a place, and the fact that he loves it so much gives me hope that he can still love me.

"All the more reason. There has to be somebody there by choice. I need to be where I'm needed."

"I need you."

Just then, as if orchestrated to prove my point, I begin to step off the curb and into the street, only to have Russ pull me back to a safe-enough distance to let a car go by without drowning us in the wave created when its tire hits a puddle. He's brought me close to him, his arms wrapped around me, and when I turn in his embrace, he is all I see. He is my home — not my escape, but my only shelter. Suddenly, my fear of returning to Oklahoma is eclipsed by the terrifying possibility that he might not see me as the same.

I allow the slightest dropping of my shoulder, just enough to create a space between us, and to my utter disappointment, he releases me. Drops my hand in favor of taking a pinch of my slicker's sleeve and leads me across the street, where we resume our walking.

My last words, *"I need you,"* hang between us, begging a reply. Still, there remains nothing but a constant, fluid silence until the church, its pristine stained-glass windows glowing with welcoming warmth, beckons us with shelter.

I slow my steps.

"Darling." The rain has intensified, something close to a downpour, and he reaches for me again. "We'll talk about this later. At home."

"You can't leave me again."

He looks puzzled, his face performing mini contortions with each splashing drop. "What do you mean?"

"If you were going to leave me, you should have done it last year. After I told you . . . what I told you. And I know you've forgiven me. You say so, and I believe you. But you haven't — we haven't . . ." The rain provides a valiant escort for my tears, so neither of us truly knows if I'm crying because I'm terrified, or wounded, or angry. In the end, it doesn't matter, because in the next breath I am in my husband's arms, an embrace that knocks the hat off my head, and my scalp comes alive with cool, clean washing.

"Nola, how could you think such a thing? Of course — of course we'll go back together. As a family. We'll start over, as a family. Us and the kids. We'll find a new home, or build one."

"But here —"

"*Here* is an escape. A place of refuge. But we can't stay."

"I'll go anywhere." I reach up, touch his face, thrill to the warmth of it. "I'm just so thankful that you want me with you. I didn't think you ever would again."

There's a new surge in the storm, and through its pounding I hear congregants shouting to us, teasingly, that we don't have the sense to come in out of the rain. They don't know the extent of our drought, the dryness of our hearts and skin.

"I've been a fool," he says. It's the same curse I've pronounced against myself too often.

"No, I —"

But there are no more words. No more confessions, or apologies. His lips touch mine, and in that moment, regrets wash away beneath our boots.

It has been a lifetime since he's kissed me, a passing of far too many seasons. This moment holds the familiarity of every kiss we've ever shared. Russ pulls me closer, and we search each other, working to bring to light all the darkness of this past year, bathing one another in forgiveness. When I try

581

to pull away, just for breath, he follows, trailing his lips across my cheeks, and when he kisses me again, brings traces of salt, and I wonder if his tears are intermingled with mine.

Beyond the curtain of the rain, good-natured calls continue from our flock, beckoning us to come inside, and I feel him smile against me.

"We really should go in," I say, suddenly shy at our display.

He kisses me one more time — brief, but full of promise — and takes my hand to lead me across the sodden lawn and into the cloakroom off the vestibule. It smells like wet rubber and wool, and we shake our heads, sending tiny showers into the air around us. Some complain about the damp, the aches in their bones, and the mud that will be tracked on the carpets. Russ and I smile, sharing the secret of this bounty.

The gathering of a Sunday evening is smaller than what we see in the mornings, and the rain has cut us in half again, so that the crowd assembled in the warm, dry sanctuary fits easily within half a dozen pews.

We sing:

Marvelous grace of our loving Lord,
Grace that exceeds our sin and our guilt!
Yonder on Calvary's mount outpoured,
There where the blood of the Lamb was
    spilled.

Russ himself leads the hymn, directing us
with a hand that moves without any musical
direction. None of us hold a songbook as
the chorus builds.

Grace, grace, God's grace,
Grace that will pardon and cleanse within;
Grace, grace, God's grace,
Grace that is greater than all our sin!

I sing with the knowledge of God's cleansing, feeling the gift of his rain and the
forgiveness of my husband. All of it swirling
together. Our eyes meet and my heart leaps
the way it did the first time I saw him. As
we sing about our sin, as cold as the sea,
and the cleansing blood of Christ, I feel a
part of me washing away with the tiny
rivulets of rain trickling down my flesh. The
song promises the brightness of snow, but I
am more taken by the cleansing power of
the rain. I think of how it bathed our kiss,
restoring us to each other.

When we bow for prayer, my collar sits
damp against my skin; tendrils of hair, dark

with wet and cold, graze my cheek. Through the darkness, I hear my husband's voice, thanking God for this deluge, remembering the way he once brought a flood up from the ground to cleanse the earth.

"You, O Lord, are our place of refuge," he prays. "Your mercy is the ark that brings us safely home."

I know I shouldn't, but I open my eyes, only to find he has done the same. Our gaze wraps itself around his prayer, bringing it to silence before he says, definitively, "Amen."

It is not until I open my mouth to echo that I realize how tightly I've been clenching my jaw, and in this moment my teeth begin to chatter. My body is racked with uncontrollable chills, my legs shaking against the unforgiving bench beneath me. It feels like my bones are snapping within my skin, and I clutch my arms about me, willing myself to still. With a whispered excuse, Russ is at my side, enveloping me in his embrace. He covers both of my hands with one of his, and slowly his warmth seeps through, overpowering the chill within.

"I should get you home." He speaks directly into my ear. "Into a hot bath before you take cold."

"Don't be silly." My words are loose. "I'm fine."

And I am.

More than that, I am restored. Strong enough to return to Oklahoma. So thoroughly saturated with rain, I have no fear of drought.

A NOTE FROM THE AUTHOR

Some of you may be thinking this book is a departure from my previous works. I like to think of it more as a product of growth. I've written a lot of stories about courtship and love, and most of those stories end before the wedding. Other than the Sister Wife series, I haven't had a story that centered around a marriage. (And the marriage in those books is hardly a healthy, viable one!)

Many stories use the sin of adultery as an automatic end to a marriage. I wanted to show it as a storm to survive. Marriage, in both life and literature, is multidimensional. It's a road trip, with two people stuck together, even if they aren't moving in the same direction.

At the same time Nola and Russ's journey began to evolve in my imagination, a fascination with the Dust Bowl was also spinning around in my mind, given its place in history following the rich decade of the

Roaring Twenties, which formed the backdrop for my last series. Then, as with all my books, I delved into the impact the environment had on women — how the inability to fulfill the traditional roles of homemaker, mother, and nurturer could destroy a woman's sense of self-worth.

That's when the two ideas clicked together. A woman who cannot appreciate her worth is easy prey for this particular sin. And the dust serves as a powerful metaphor for sin — inescapable, ever present. It is unbidden and unhidden. It is filth and thirst and drought. It is death, and no life can flourish in the midst of it. Sin does that to a marriage — to any relationship. The dust could only be overcome by the rain, and the rain brought a promise of new life.

I also wanted to explore the idea of what it means to be a "real" Christian. We are often quick to judge someone who behaves as Nola does, concluding that the person can't possibly be saved. But what does it mean to be a "real" Christian? It simply means believing that Jesus Christ died to save us from our sin and rose from the dead to give us new life. At the same time, our belief in Christ does not keep us from sinning — not even from engaging in fully realized, willful sin. Nola enters into the act of adultery through her own free will and through willful denial of the truth. She is drawn to it by her own desires and hides it out of a very real sense of self-preservation. (Jim isn't to blame for Nola's sin; he's just an opportunist. And one who will be held accountable for his own choices, though that was outside the scope of this story.)

And once we've sinned, knowingly and willingly, then what? Belief in Christ does not take away our ability — or our desire — to sin, nor does it provide automatic absolution for the sins we may commit. That comes only with confession and repentance, whenever the Holy Spirit convicts us.

Nola knows this. She believes it is true (though she doesn't always feel it). Her sin cannot negate her salvation, but like any sin, it separates her from a healthy relationship with Christ — just as it precludes a healthy relationship with her husband. For a time, at least. For a season. Her shame makes her feel unworthy to accept forgiveness from Christ or to expect forgiveness from her husband. But yes, she is a real Christian — a sinner saved by grace.

Writing this story in first person, present tense was something new for me, but it seemed the best choice. Nola is what's known as an unreliable narrator. To put it bluntly, she's a liar, and from page one until her confession to Russ, we can be suspicious of almost everything she says. She promises herself (and, de facto, the reader) that she will confess to Russ. She doesn't. She refuses to confront her motives, and that wall of dishonesty is what keeps her from fully embracing God's forgiveness. I wanted to write a story that lived in the intentions of the character, to show how frail and insubstantial our relationships can be without true confession and repentance. When we lie to ourselves — and God — in the moment, we believe it.

I make the point in the story that Russ loved Nola first, and that he loves her more. It's my personal philosophy that no two people can ever love each other absolutely equally. In this case, that gives me hope for them to have a happy ending — maybe not in the final pages of the book, but in the months and years to come. Russ understands forgiveness. He is spiritually healthy enough to forgive Nola, even though he's human enough to need some time before full restoration. Chances are, it will take even longer for Nola to come to the place where she fully *feels* forgiven — but not for any lack of assurance on Russ's part.

May you find the strength to believe in

the love of Christ and those people he has placed in your life, even when you feel that you've done something unforgivable. As Nola learned as a child, "If we confess our sins, he is faithful and just to forgive us our sins, and to cleanse us from all unrighteousness" (1 John 1:9).

DISCUSSION QUESTIONS

1. The Oklahoma Dust Bowl forms the backdrop and sets the tone for this novel. How much did you know about the Dust Bowl before you read the book? Has anyone in your family passed down first-hand stories of what it was like?

2. Nola's mother died when she was ten years old. In some ways, the loss of a parent at a young age is something one never gets over. What elements of Nola's current outlook can be attributed to this devastating loss? Who are some of the other women in her life who help to fill the mother role in small ways? Is there a situation in your life where the Lord has provided nontraditional sources of love and nurture or met some other need in an unusual way?

3. Nola's father is an unkind, bitter person.

What do you think made him that way? How has his behavior affected his son and daughter? How have you seen patterns like this play out in your extended family?

4. In chapter 12, Nola's father calls her by her full name: "We need to be mindful of what our sin brings back to haunt us, Denola Grace." Who do you suppose gave her the middle name Grace, her mother or her father? How is grace evident in Nola's life, even though she has a hard time seeing it herself?

5. In chapter 13, Nola remembers learning about God's forgiveness as a child, and she can even quote 1 John 1:9, "If we confess our sins, he is faithful and just to forgive us our sins, and to cleanse us from all unrighteousness." And yet her father's suspicious nature and disapproval made it hard for her to trust in God's grace. She says, "I always felt dirty, and Pa made me believe that I was." Why is it often easier to trust what people say about us than to believe what God says in the Bible? In what areas of your life have you struggled with this?

6. In chapter 17, Nola receives and accepts Christ's forgiveness for her sin of adultery, but she stops short of confessing to Russ. "I know I must also confess to my husband, but to do so now would destroy my assurance of grace." Why do you think she feels this way? Is she right, or is this just one more excuse to help her avoid confessing? Can you think of a time in your own life when you needed to confess to a loved one or do something else that was difficult, and you came up with a way to talk yourself out of doing it? What were the results?

7. In chapter 19, Nola once again tries to confess to Russ, but instead he asks her forgiveness for not realizing how difficult Jim was making things for her. Nola again backs off, reasoning that she is doing Russ a favor by not burdening him with any more regret. "This will be the price of my freedom — yet another lie to carry. But like any burden, I've grown used to the weight, and I take it on." Does her self-deception here seem logical to you? Why or why not? What are some other ways we turn things around like this, making wrong

seem right and right seem wrong? Why do we sometimes find that so easy to do?

8. In chapter 20, Russ and Nola discuss the fact that they married because Nola was pregnant. Russ says, "Sin or not — you made me feel like a man. Like I was fulfilling what God wanted me to be. Like Solomon, or David." What do you think of Russ's statement here? In what way does he feel like he is fulfilling God's plan for him? In what way is he falling short of God's plan? Do you think Russ — like many in our culture today — overemphasizes the importance of a person's sexuality? Why or why not?

9. When Nola finally confesses to Russ in chapter 32, he says he still loves her as much as ever. Does that seem realistic, or is it something that would only happen in a novel? Have you ever been in Russ's position — betrayed and deeply hurt by someone you love? How did you respond, or how do you hope you would respond if this were to happen?

10. While Russ assures Nola of his continued love, there is a distance between them that lasts for a year or more. What finally

bridges the gap? How does it make Nola feel? How realistically does this reflect real life?

11. Throughout most of her life, Nola has a hard time feeling God's love for her — or anyone's love, for that matter. Have you ever had this experience? How important is it for a Christian to feel God's love? What are some things we can do when our faith in God isn't emotionally gratifying?

12. At the end of the book, Russ announces his intentions to return to Oklahoma, and Nola — finally restored to both God and her husband — feels ready to face it. Do you think this is the right choice for their family? How do you imagine each of them will adjust to returning home? How might Ronnie and Ariel respond?

ABOUT THE AUTHOR

Award-winning author **Allison Pittman** left a seventeen-year teaching career in 2005 to follow the Lord's calling into the world of Christian fiction, and God continues to bless her step of faith. Her novels *For Time and Eternity, Forsaking All Others,* and *All for a Sister* were named as finalists for the Christy Award for excellence in Christian fiction, and her novel *Stealing Home* won the American Christian Fiction Writers' Carol Award. In 2012, she was named ACFW's Mentor of the Year. She also heads up a successful, thriving writers' group in San Antonio, where she lives with her husband, Mike, their three sons, and the canine star of the family — Stella.

The employees of Thorndike Press hope you have enjoyed this Large Print book. All our Thorndike, Wheeler, and Kennebec Large Print titles are designed for easy reading, and all our books are made to last. Other Thorndike Press Large Print books are available at your library, through selected bookstores, or directly from us.

For information about titles, please call:
(800) 223-1244

or visit our Web site at:
http://gale.cengage.com/thorndike

To share your comments, please write:
Publisher
Thorndike Press
10 Water St., Suite 310
Waterville, ME 04901